STATE MACHINE

STATE MACHINE

K.B. SPANGLER

A GIRL AND HER FED BOOKS
NORTH CAROLINA

For Fuz, Dante, and Rose

ONE

She was used to doing this sort of thing in the dark, alone, but this wasn't so bad. The man walking beside her was on the young side of thirty and smart as a whip, and he had made it plain he was happy to escort her through the labyrinthine sub-basement.

Definitely not bad at all.

"You know what's in that room?" he asked, pointing to a door halfway down the hall. "One of the largest vinyl record collections in the world."

"Really? Here?"

"Yes, here," he said with a chuckle. "Everything from Pat Boone to Jimi Hendrix. If you like classic LPs…"

"Love them." She glanced down at her watch, pretending to check the time. "Can I see them? Or are they in one of those secure areas you told me about?"

He took a passcard from his pocket as he pressed a finger to his lips.

The room was sterile. They had decided to preserve the music, not the packaging, and each record had been wrapped in a white envelope before it was filed away in black boxes. Several thousand copies of America's best albums, every single one pristine, and she might as well have been standing in a hospital's medical records room for all that was worth.

"What do you think?" he asked, his fingers brushing against her arm.

She smiled warmly at him. "Amazing."

They kissed in a corner of the room that was hidden from the sweep of the security cameras. He knew how they needed to stand and when they had to move; it was a game to him, she knew, flirting with strange women while he was at work.

When they were finished, he led her around the room, holding up an album or two as he went. They all looked the same to her, the black plastic disks in their white paper sleeves, a gold eagle affixed to each label. He asked if she wanted to listen to anything in particular; she glanced at her watch again, and led him towards the door.

He didn't want to end the tour. She dropped a word here, a hint there… It was easy to coax him into stalling their return trip, to nudge him away from the high-security areas.

Towards the storerooms.

"What's in here?" she asked, as he took her down another hallway. The air was somewhat stale, as if it were rarely stirred by anything living.

He winked. "Treasure."

The passcard came out again, but this time he followed it by tapping a code onto the nearby keypad.

"I really don't think I should—"

He shushed her, and pulled her into the room.

Her sources had told her it would be full of clutter, but it was nearly as featureless as the record room. The white sleeves had been swapped out for white boxes of varying sizes, but the same gold eagle on its seal sat above rows of neatly printed text. She leaned towards the nearest shelf and read a label aloud. "Flag standard from Battle of Torgau, 1760… What is all of this?"

"Gifts of state," he replied. "Some of them, anyway. They're mainly the ones the archivists don't think are worth the effort of moving to museums or libraries. We can't get rid of them without causing an international incident, so they're kept here."

She gave a low whistle. "In this one room?"

"No," he said, as he took down a white box barely large enough for a wedding ring. "This room is for gifts of state acquired before 1925. We didn't get all that many until World War II, and the best ones are on display. Everything acquired after that is kept in other rooms down the hall. See?" He opened the box to reveal a tiny glass bottle, an outline of running horses pressed into its surface.

"Greek?"

"Roman," he said. "Good guess."

"How do you find anything in here?" she asked, gesturing to the shelves full of ubiquitous white.

"Easy!" he said. "Each item has a serial number. They're shelved by date of acquisition, so you find the shelves with the corresponding year, and then start searching."

"So, wait," she said, shaking her head. "Say I wanted to find something from, oh, 1907? Where would I look?"

"Over here," he said. He took her down an aisle, its shelves holding layer after layer of more white boxes. She followed him, and laughed and twisted sideways as he tried to catch her in another kiss.

"Oh!" She gasped as she stumbled sideways, as if her ankle had twisted on the slick linoleum floor. She clutched at the nearest shelf as she fell, and white boxes and their contents rained down around her. "Oh no," she said, reaching towards a golden knife, its handle cut into the shape of an olive leaf. "Oh *no*. I'm so sorry!"

"Don't worry," he said with a forced smile, as he knelt carefully among the scattered objects. "Are you hurt?"

She pressed her fingers against her ankle, then shook her head. "No."

"Okay," he said. "Let me clean this up."

"I'll help—"

"No!" he said, too quickly. "There's an order to it. It'll just take a minute."

She stood and pretended to test her ankle as she moved a few feet down the aisle.

1908... 1907... 1906... 1905...

She skimmed the labels in the section for 1904. *There.*

A lower shelf. One of the smallest boxes.

She glanced behind her to make sure he was still busy sorting the mess on the floor. A brush of her skirt as she sat down to rest concealed the motion of her hand. The little white box was easy to open, the object inside small enough to be covered by her palm.

Too easy.

And it all went to hell when he looked over and saw her slip it down the front of her blouse.

She closed her eyes. He had been *so* nice...

"What did you do?" he asked, shuffling towards her on his knees.

She slipped her fingernail under the dial on her watch. It came loose from its housing with a faint click.

"I wish you hadn't seen that," she said.

TWO

Rachel Peng was sure the party planner would be fired at the end of the night. Not that the function wasn't spectacular. The entire evening had been magical, even by Washington's high standards, with a six-course meal, a jazz band flown in from New Orleans, and the heady scent of heirloom roses invading from all sides. But Senator Richard Hanlon had been seated at the table to her immediate left. The two of them were separated by sixteen feet, a couple of delicate floral centerpieces, and a baker's dozen of politicians and lobbyists, and they could not stop smiling at each other.

Those smiles were all teeth.

"He's baiting you," a woman's voice whispered in Rachel's mind, uncertainty woven into the emotion behind the words.

"I know," Rachel replied, pushing calm and composure back across their link. The lingering anxiety eased as Mary Murphy realized Rachel wasn't about to leap across two tables to reach Hanlon and crush his throat with her bare hands.

"Then stop smiling," Mary said, as she turned to speak with a passing congressman. *"People are staring."*

"I know," Rachel said again. *"That's why I'm smiling."*

Everybody who was anybody in Washington knew there was a quiet war between Hanlon and the Agents of the Office of Adaptive and Complementary Technologies. Hanlon's star was setting, and OACET's was… Well. If it wasn't exactly rising, it certainly wasn't in danger of exploding and turning everyone within a billion miles to ash, like it had been less than a year ago.

She had spent the entire evening smiling at Hanlon, a living reminder to anyone watching that OACET was closing in on him.

We know what you did, her smile said, her teeth as bright as knives. *We know what you're trying to do. And we're going to make sure you pay, and pay, and pay...*

Hanlon's smile was constant but casual, tossed off in her direction as if she were a smitten teenager intruding on his time. *That's nice,* his smile said. *Be sure to tell me how that works out.*

He finished the last of his white chocolate cake, dabbed the corner of his mouth with a napkin, and stood to work the crowd before the speakers took to the podium.

Rachel let herself relax. Across the room, the tight reds of Mary's conversational colors dissolved into blues.

A waiter came by and offered Rachel a fresh glass of champagne. She declined in favor of hot tea: she was working, and wine went straight to her head. A second waiter arrived moments later with jasmine tea steeping in a cast iron pot. He placed the pot on the table, along with a porcelain cup so thin that light burned through it, then laid a fresh-cut gardenia blossom beside the cup before disappearing in a puff of professional competence.

She ran a fingernail along the blush of the gardenia before dropping it into her water glass, where it joined six others. Each course had come with its own flower; one of the gardenias had blood-red blotches from resting on the filet mignon.

Everything was flowers. Or linen, or crystal, or silver and gold, all of it lit by candles and the muted glow of floodlights draped in nonflammable white cloth. You had to be in Congress to book the U.S. Botanic Garden for events, and there was no such thing as a politician's discount. Rachel was sure the cost of her meal would show up as a headline in tomorrow's news trawl, a stupidly large number followed by at least two zeros and an exclamation point. She was glad she hadn't been the one to buy the tickets.

A woman with a braided spill of knee-length red hair and a core the color of ripe butternut squash fell into the chair beside her. Mary Murphy—"Mare" to anyone not involved in politics—was so frail as to seem breakable, and had knotted her raw silk shawl tight around her bare shoulders to keep away the evening chill. She grabbed her own glass of champagne, and took a short but deep drink before she shoved it out of easy reach. *"Morons,"* she muttered though their link.

"Who?" Rachel asked.

"Everybody. When can you try again?"

Rachel checked her internal timer. *"Couple of minutes. I'm going to take one last walk before the speeches start,"* she replied. *"If he doesn't contact me this time, we'll ditch."*

"Hurry, please," Mare told her, as a woman in a dress worth more than Rachel's pension paused beside the Agents and pretended to notice Mare for the first time. Mare stood and greeted the other woman like a long-lost sister. *"I'm about to go on a homicidal rampage."*

Rachel broke their link before Mare could feel her laughing: the image of waiflike Mary Murphy laying waste to a roomful of politicians with nothing but a salad fork was straight out of a cartoon.

They weren't supposed to be here. That dubious privilege had been reserved for Josh Glassman, Deputy Director of the Office of Adaptive and Complementary Technologies, plus guest. Josh loved affairs like this, the slow dance-and-grind of agendas coming together in the night. If he had been the representative Agent at this function, it wouldn't have mattered if Hanlon had been placed near OACET or not: Josh would have draped an arm across the Senator's shoulders, and the two of them would have been best friends for the night.

And neither would have left their food unattended, on the off-chance of cyanide.

As of this time yesterday, Rachel hadn't even known about this party. She certainly didn't expect an early-morning call from Josh, telling her that she and Mare would be standing in for him at a black tie event and no, this wasn't optional because The Game Was Afoot. Rachel had spent the afternoon at a seamstress's shop getting the hem let out of a borrowed dress, and assuring her boss's wife that she wouldn't lose its matching necklace.

The dress fit perfectly; the matching shoes didn't. She had crammed toilet paper into the toes, but it was a half-assed attempt at a fix. Rachel hoped that whatever she had been sent here to do, it wouldn't involve running.

Tapping me for spycraft duty, she grumbled to herself. *Josh must have lost his mind.*

There were dozens of Agents who would have been better suited for this task than herself. Rachel knew she was subtle in the way of a bull setting fire to a china shop. She was more than five years gone from the Army but she was still military through and through: she knew when to keep silent and she knew when to act, and there was very little wiggle room between these. Asking her to meet an unknown contact at a formal affair was outside her usual set of skills. The sum of what Rachel knew about spycraft was that a gin martini should never be shaken, and that the Walther PPK was one of the worst guns ever made.

Which is what she kept telling herself to keep from getting cocky. She had made her target within five seconds of walking through the door.

Rachel ran another scan through her target to take in his details. He was a tall man, maybe ten years older than herself, with a core of steady denim blue. She hadn't needed to ping his badge to identify him as federal law enforcement, probably with the Secret Service: the FN Five-seven in its concealed holster did that for her. He was pretending to work security, but his conversational colors were saturated with her own core of Southwestern turquoise. He hadn't so much as tried to make eye contact with her, but she was the only thing on his mind.

Spying for fun and profit, or national security, or…or whatever I'm here to do, she thought. *Chalk one up for Team Cyborg.*

Rachel hadn't been surprised to learn her implant was applicable to intelligence work. A major reason Congress had decided to invest in the tiny quantum organic computer chip stuck deep in her brain was its usefulness in undetectable mobile communications. Put an advanced version of a smartphone and a camera in an undercover operative's head, and hello! Unbeatable geopolitical dominance!

(At least, until every country on earth got its hands on the technology, and then it'd just be roaring mice all over the damned place.)

There was one wrinkle that Congress hadn't counted on: phones piggybacked on a very small part of the electromagnetic spectrum; the implant tapped into the whole of it. After the Agents had activated their implants, they learned that chatting back and forth across the link was the least of their new abilities. The EM spectrum encompassed everything from radio waves to visible light to gamma radiation. Once activated, the Agents had spent all of five seconds poking around the universe before they threw away the useless training manuals and set out to discover what they could do on their own.

In Rachel's case, she had taught herself to use the implant as a substitute for her sense of sight. The implant's developers hadn't known that was an option.

Then again, they hadn't planned to stick the implant in the head of a blind woman.

Technically, they hadn't. Rachel's eyes had worked just fine when she had her skull cracked open and a tiny device implanted in her noggin, but shit made a career out of happening. Adapt or don't—adapt or die—and Rachel was not one to give up and let life roll on without her. After several weeks of bumping around in the dark, she had discovered the electromagnetic frequencies used in eyesight still ended up in her brain, albeit via different input channels. The result was…different.

It wasn't normal vision. It was sight entangled with touch, along with other sensations she still couldn't put a name to, and it was so superior to normal vision that if anyone ever offered to give Rachel a pair of working eyes, she would punch them in their well-intentioned nose.

Blind.

Rachel shrugged off the sudden cold shiver between her

shoulders, and reached for her tea.

Blind.

It was a word she was trying to accept. She only thought of herself as blind when she was feeling lower than low, or when the implant was off and she was lying alone in the clinging dark, or when she wasn't really thinking about it at all. And, once she had finally realized that, it was pretty much all she needed as proof that the word actually did fit her.

Blind, she thought again. As if she wasn't in a sour mood already.

The teacup was warm in her hands. Rachel sent a light scan through it to take in the details: fine bone china, its rim gilded in stripes and a subtle floral pattern. She wanted to stand and stretch her legs, but that would have meant walking, and at an event like this, walking meant talking.

An owl appeared in the middle of the table. It was as long as Rachel's forearm and looked as if a talented woodworker had sculpted it from an electric green log. The owl blinked at her and hooted once, softly, then spread its carved wings and took flight. It dipped into a low swoop, skimming the heads of the tallest members of the crowd, and then pumped its wings twice for altitude. At the edge of the pavilion, it vanished as suddenly as it had appeared.

No one noticed except for Mare, who watched the owl soar away with a smile. Mare opened a new link and said, *"Beautiful."*

"Thanks," Rachel replied, gathering up her purse as if she was headed for the restroom. *"I had to watch about a zillion nature videos to get the takeoff right."*

She scanned the room to make sure her contact had seen her, and found Senator Hanlon had positioned himself in the open door to the tent, her core still prominent within his conversational colors. The blacks and reds of extreme loathing whipped at her turquoise; the combination would have been quite pretty if she hadn't known what it meant. Rachel didn't know whether he had intended to block her or not, but there he was, and he didn't look ready to move any time soon.

Oh dear, Rachel thought to herself. *And here I am without my rocket launcher.*

There were emergency exits that could take her out of the room, but she wasn't going to slink through a side door. Rachel tipped her chin up and walked straight towards Hanlon, high heels clicking on the flagstone floor.

The sound of her shoes swelled as the white noise of the room receded, the crowd pausing in their own conversations to watch the confrontation. Hanlon's colors brightened, and a trace of brilliant yellow-white excitement appeared. He was casually chatting up some lobbyists from the telecommunications industry, and turned to look at Rachel only when she was too close to ignore.

She almost never bothered to look at a person's face—these days, faces were nothing but masks to her—but she made an exception for Richard Hanlon.

Rachel flipped frequencies until she could see him standing in front of her. Dark hair streaked with silver, kept close to his head in a classic businessman's cut. Brown eyes, West Coast bronze skin, and a smattering of freckles high on his cheeks.

Those freckles offended her. Villains should never have freckles. There should be a *law*.

He was still smiling at her, and this smile grew wider as she approached. She felt her cheeks crack as she met it with one of her own. When she was close enough, he greeted her with a smooth, "Agent Peng."

She dipped her head, ever courteous. "Senator Hanlon," she said, and swept past him.

And that was all.

Behind her, a swell of disappointment rose and fell within the crowd, bitter orange tinted with her turquoise and Hanlon's core of water-hardened wood. Rachel quickly brought a hand up to hide her smile. Did they really expect her to take a swing at Hanlon in the middle of a Congressional gala?

"Yes." Mare's mental tone left no room for doubt.

"Quiet, you."

Mare sighed, and Rachel felt her friend's presence withdraw a second time. *"Good luck,"* Mare said before she broke their link.

The function had been set up beneath a tent covering the outdoor rose garden. (Why, Rachel couldn't say: it was too early in the spring for roses, and those blooming in planters must have been trucked in from hothouses.) She headed into the building and down a long corridor that was lined with spring willows, their fronds braided together to form an arch. The lighting was dim, the everyday fluorescents turned off in favor of muted spotlights positioned at the base of each willow.

A woman appeared beside her.

Rachel jumped before she realized she had forgotten to drop the parts of the EM spectrum she used to enhance facial recognition. It had been well over a year since she had seen her own face without making the effort, and she hadn't recognized herself. She paused to look at her reflection in the mirrors tucked behind the trees.

Not bad, she thought. People sometimes asked her in that offensively inoffensive way how a Chinese woman could be so tall, and she usually told them her mother had been a product of Chairmen Mao's eugenics program. Considering how little her parents talked about her mother's past, this might actually be true, but it was much more likely she had inherited her height from her Scottish giant of a father. Her pixy cut all but styled itself, and keeping her hair short let her show off her brown eyes. The borrowed sheath dress was a rich scarlet with modest lines; congressional events were not an appropriate venue for flashing one's naughties. A gold lace necklace as simple as the dress hung low on her neck, a single sapphire teardrop in the center hinting at her well-covered cleavage.

The combination was...

She was classy.

When on earth did that happen? Rachel grinned at her reflection before she flipped off facial recognition, and resumed her walk beneath the willows.

Classy.

Well, it wasn't part of her usual mental image of herself, but there it was, and it was a hell of a lot better than learning she was the alternative. Besides, bare-knuckled brawlers didn't take down Senators—classy federal Agents did.

She had to keep herself from humming.

Her heels tapped along the tiled floors as she moved towards the bathrooms. Two women were inside, gossiping by the standing sinks. They froze as she entered, and Rachel caught the edges of her and Hanlon's names bouncing within the echoes.

"Ladies," she said to them, as she pretended to check her makeup in the old mercury mirror.

They fled.

She grinned. Classy or not, she was still OACET. Congressmen might have to pretend she was a peer, but their wives were under no such obligation.

She killed a reasonable amount of time in the bathroom, then stepped back into the willowed hallway. She peered through layer after layer of concrete and marble veneer, only to find her target still standing at attention in the tent.

Rachel sighed. It was beginning to look like tonight would be a wash. Mare would never let her forget it, and since Mare was in charge of OACET's duty roster... She groaned at a future of scrubbing stains off of the carpet after each communal dinner.

I should have come with Josh, she muttered to herself. But no, the moment Josh had given himself the night off, he had grabbed the nearest supermodel and left for a long weekend down in Key Largo.

Rachel turned down a second hallway and pushed through a set of double doors. The conservatory was peaceful compared to the ruckus under the tent. There were crickets, and the huffing grunts of a toad who had snuck in and made himself a home, but these fell silent as she wandered within the exhibit. She dragged her fingertips across the water running the course of a long, low fountain set in the center of the room, and caught herself before she could wipe the slightly oily feel of the treated water off on her dress. *Classy women don't return stained clothing to their friends*, she reminded herself. Life as a classy woman would take some getting used to, it seemed.

There was a spiral staircase in the corner. She popped the clip on the velvet rope draped across the entry, and started to climb. The catwalk at the top was wrought iron and old brass, and sturdy enough to take her weight without so much as a creak.

It was peaceful up here. She was far enough from the party that the conversational colors of the politicians blended together into a tapestry of reds and greens, held together by the mingled grays and blues of professional business attire.

In Rachel's new visual world, core colors had replaced faces. Each person had a unique static hue at the center of their body, and Rachel used these cores as an identifier, a *HELLO, MY NAME IS* sticker blazing in rainbows across the walls of her mind. Wrapped around this core color came layer after layer of surface colors, a continuously changing aura which reflected their mood. With time and practice, she had learned to pick out those elements of emotion which shaped these surface colors, and could now follow the subtext of entire conversations based on nothing but the speakers' auras.

She picked out Mare's pale creamy orange core, then bounced around the room until she found Hanlon's core of deep brown. He had pushed all thoughts of her aside: Rachel's own core of Southwestern turquoise was gone, and he wore the same reds and greens of his fellows. The reds tended towards different flavors of need; the greens, those of greed. The colors of Hanlon's companions, the telecommunications lobbyists, ebbed and flowed with the same, but she noticed that long streaks of her turquoise remained within their colors.

Well, Rachel sighed to herself, *at least I left an impression on somebody.*

Those Christmas colors were depressing. Before moving to Washington, she had assumed that anyone who struggled and fought and bought their way into politics was answering a higher calling. The idea of politicians as a different class of human being was somehow... comforting? Maybe that was the wrong way to look at it, but Rachel didn't know how else to describe the idea that there were people out there who would willingly suffer a job that was, in her opinion, slightly less appealing than working the complaints desk at an international airport. You couldn't be a politician and also be normal. Those two concepts didn't mesh in her idea of a rational world. Better if a politician was more than merely human. Maybe.

Then, after she had started spending time with politicians, she chucked her idea of a rational world straight out the window. Once she had moved from California to a run-down bungalow in Cleveland Park, she had learned that politicians were like everyone else. They enjoyed their creature comforts, their vacation time, money, fame, and the odd night on the town. As far as she could tell, the only difference between a politician and your average schmuck was motivation.

And so few of them were motivated by anything other than bright green greed.

It was sad in its way, learning that politics was just another job. Sure, the parties were nicer, and there were tax loopholes galore, but...

She didn't think she could ever forgive politicians for being ordinary people.

Screw it, Rachel thought, banging her hands down on the iron rail so hard she felt the vibrations through her toes. She decided to grab Mare and leave. They had signed on to serve their country, not to walk the thin line between political intrigue and codependent arm candy. If her target wanted to talk to her, he could visit her during office hours like everybody else.

She looped one last scan through the building, just to be sure, and saw the workaday blues of her target heading towards her.

Of course, she thought, and resigned herself to another fifteen minutes.

He skirted the twisting reds and greens. None of the politicians picked up on his core as he passed. He was an unobtrusive nobody, someone there to make sure their own lives functioned properly.

When he reached the hall, he paused. Rachel tossed a quick scan around, and located a baseball-sized rock in the crook of a nearby tree. This, she lobbed at the door with the precision of a former pitcher from Bagram Air Base's pick-up team.

The rock hit the metal door with a heavy *clang*. The man on the other side didn't jump; his colors didn't flicker. Instead, he pushed open the door and came in, casually kicking the rock off of the path as he walked.

"Up here," she called in a soft voice.

He shifted smoothly towards the iron staircase, and climbed up to join her on the walkway.

"Are we alone?" the man said by way of introduction.

"Yes."

"Sturtevant said you can make sure no one overhears us,"

Rachel nodded. Chief Sturtevant was her supervisor at the Metropolitan Police Department; that this stranger could pronounce his name was enough credentials for her to spin some cyborg trickery. She reached out and began to draw different electromagnetic frequencies into a sphere around them, weaving these into a shield which could buffer out electronic snooping devices. "Don't move around, or you'll walk out of range," she said. "And keep your voice low. I can block surveillance equipment, but anyone within earshot can still hear us."

He glanced up, towards the open windows at the highest point of the conservatory.

"We're good," she told him. "I'll warn you before anyone comes into the room."

He nodded. "Mitch Alimoren, Secret Service," he said, offering his hand.

Rachel took it. He smelled of meek aftershave, something watered-down to keep the politicians from noticing him. "Rachel Peng, OACET," she said. "But you knew that."

He nodded. "Sturtevant recommended I get in touch with you. We're already working with the MPD, but he said your team has a history of getting the hard jobs done."

"I'm assuming this is off the record?" Rachel asked.

His colors wavered slightly in mild yellow surprise. "No. We want to keep it quiet as long as we can. That's why I asked to meet here," he said, as he gestured at the gala below them. "But this is official—it *has* to be official," he corrected himself. "Once this hits the media, it'll be everywhere.

"Read this," he said, and passed Rachel his phone. "There's a file that'll explain everything."

She took the phone from him and poked the screen. "Is this a test?" she asked, as the passcode screen came up. "I'm not hacking a Secret Service agent's work phone."

The colors across Alimoren's shoulders dimpled. "No," he lied. "It's not a test. I just didn't think it through. Go ahead and unlock it."

Rachel passed the phone back to him without a word.

He peered closely at her, his conversational colors braiding blue, orange, and Southwestern turquoise into a solid strand as he weighed her personality against his preconceptions. The weaving stopped, and he nodded. He tapped out a passcode, then held the phone out to her again.

This time, Rachel ran her thumb across the screen until she saw the icon OACET's marketing team had developed for computer applications. She poked the tiny green eagle on a gold liberty's crown, and the file opened. Text, yes, but digitized text, which meant she could read it without any—

"Shit," she breathed.

THREE

"How was it?"

Raul Santino had waited up for her. He was pretending to watch basketball, but was literally glowing green with jealousy.

Rachel decided to poke him. "It was all right," she sighed, as she slipped out of her party shoes. She knocked the soles against her palms, and two wads of toilet paper hit the floor. "Nice place. Lots of flowers. Ever been there?"

Her partner glared daggers at her.

"Oh, right. You said you had a membership."

"That would be a *lifetime* membership."

She covered her mouth to hide her smile. Santino collected plants in the same way that he breathed: unrelentingly and without conscious thought, and if he ever stopped, Rachel would check for a pulse. The first thing he had done when he had moved in was turn her yard into a botanical garden; the second, to convert her house to an arboretum. She wasn't exactly happy about it, but he paid his rent on time and she was never without a ride to work.

(Not to mention how she had become an expert in plants through nothing but immersion and osmosis. She figured if this cyborg stuff didn't pan out, she could always become the world's foremost resentful horticulturist.)

"It was really beautiful," she said, scooping the sweaty wads of paper into her hand and tossing them into the nearby bin in one smooth motion. "Each table had a different flower as a theme. Mare and I were at the one with… What are those white flowers, the ones that look like roses but have a stronger scent?"

A strangled moan came from the direction of the couch. "Don't do this."

"Gardenias, right. And they left the main building open so

you could walk around and check out the exhibits. It was great. Zero tourists. I had the conservatory all to myself."

"I will destroy you."

"And the liquor! Seriously, Santino, the champagne was—" She dodged the thrown pillow, and headed to the kitchen, laughing.

He followed her, grumbling under his breath. Her partner was tall and lanky, with a core of cobalt blue, and dark hair which he kept swept back from his face. The only other feature that registered with Rachel were his glasses. The wire frames were thicker than fashionable, and the right earpiece dead-ended in what appeared to be an overlarge hearing aid. They gave him a somewhat bookish appearance, but Santino, nerd through and through, loved it.

Rachel went straight to the fridge. It was, for all practical purposes, a cooler; there was nothing in there but beer, hard cider, and a bag of baby carrots that had devolved from orange to white to a dim fuzzy gray. She opened the crisper drawer and pulled out two bottles of spring lager, cracked their tops, and passed one to her partner before he hopped up to his usual perch on the counter.

"So," he said.

"So."

"Josh said the game was afoot? Are we a-footing?"

"And then some," she sighed, as she chose a kitchen chair. "Murder." He nodded, and she waited until he was drinking before adding, "At the White House."

"What?!" Santino coughed and sputtered. "The White... *The* White House?!"

"Yup." Rachel reached into the oversized handbag dangling from her chair, and found her tablet. "Here, take a look at this."

Santino caught it on the fly, and blinked at the dead man on the tablet's screen. "Whoa," he said, his fingers tapping to resize the image. "This happened at the White House?"

Rachel nodded. "They even know who killed him," she said, and called up a still frame from an overhead camera. A fiery redhead, tall and stunning in a low-cut blazer and matching skirt, walked beside her future victim. They had their heads close together, as if they were sharing secrets.

"Uh-oh. Someone got played."

"Like the world's stupidest violin. His name was Casper Ceara, and he had a reputation for hitting on anything that moved."

"Good-looking guy," Santino acknowledged. "That, plus working in the White House…"

"Yup," Rachel said. "Nobody thought anything of it when he took our mystery woman out for a midnight tour of his penis.

"Here are the facts," Rachel continued, and counted the points off on her fingers. "One: last night, a certain Grammy-winning pop star performed a private concert for the President and several influential donors. Two: pop stars don't travel without an entourage. Three: her usual makeup artist was in a suspiciously-timed car accident, so a certain Joanna Reed was picked as a replacement. Four: Reed may have been vetted by the Secret Service, but Reed's body was found in the trunk of a locked car a few hours ago, so whoever visited the White House wasn't her."

She took a breath. "And five? Members of an entourage aren't allowed to move about the White House. They stay in a reception area in the basement, sit around until the show ends, and then pack up and leave."

Santino wasn't slow. "So if Joanna Reed was killed before… Our mystery woman needed access to the White House's basement."

"Bingo." Rachel grinned at him. "Now, guess what they keep in the White House. Beside the President and his family."

"Gifts given to the President, special collections… Mostly stuff that's been donated and needs to be stored, but not displayed."

"Aw," she said. "You spoiled the surprise." Rachel made sure to throw some sarcasm in there. Santino had an encyclopedic knowledge of pretty much everything that existed. Or had existed. Or might possibly exist in the future. Like most of her partner's traits, Rachel found this to be simultaneously marvelous and annoying.

"What did she steal?"

Rachel shook her head. "The Secret Service doesn't know. Most likely something from the same room where they found the victim's body. He was left in a locked room, of course."

"Of course. Probably one without security cameras."

"Of course. There were cameras up and down every corridor. The storerooms were kept locked except for personnel with special access, and their keycards are logged each time they're used. Plus, you know, it was in the White House, so nobody would be in the basement who hadn't received access to the building in the first place. As far as security went, they thought they were protected."

"Except when a pretty lady charms a staff member into giving her a tour."

"Yup. As always, the weakest link in the security chain is the people involved," Rachel said before she took a long pull off of her beer. The lager lacked the tingle of champagne, and felt somewhat lifeless as she swallowed. She made herself chug half of the bottle; there was no way she could afford a hundred-dollar-a-glass champagne habit, so she might as well forget the taste as quickly as she could.

"How did he die?" Santino asked, sliding the image around the tablet. "I don't see any blood."

"Poison. Strong poison. They're not sure what kind, but it shut him down within seconds. There's a copy of the preliminary autopsy findings in the file."

"Makes sense. Easier to sneak poison into the White House than a gun. How'd she get away?"

"Same way she got in," Rachel said. "She rejoined the entourage and left with them after the concert was done."

"Kill someone in the White House and then wait it out?" Her partner gave a low whistle. "Mystery Woman has ice water for blood."

"Yup."

"So," Santino said, tossing her the bottle opener. "I assume the MPD and the Secret Service are investigating the murder. Where do we come in? Um... I'm assuming this isn't just an OACET thing."

"Yup," Rachel said again, as she opened a fresh bottle. "You and me and the guys? We're good to go. Technically, we're not investigating the murder. We're tracking down the object."

"Hm," he grunted. "Seems as though that means we *are* looking into it, what with theft being the probable motive for the murder."

"Technicalities and legalities, then. Our private clue club has a great closure rate on important cases, and we fall into that blind spot between departments, so we can do more with less oversight. The Secret Service came to Sturtevant and asked him to turn us loose."

"Heh," Santino chuckled, his colors brightening. "It's nice to be noticed."

"Not so nice, maybe." Rachel pointed at the tablet, and he glanced down to find the image had changed to one of a large room full of shelves, boxes covering every inch of the space from floor to ceiling. "We have to find out what was taken before we can track it down."

Santino blinked at the tablet, his conversational colors slowing with mild shock. "Oh no," he said.

"Oh yes. And it gets better."

"Of course it does. Lemme guess: more than one of these boxes is empty?"

"Nailed it." Rachel grinned at him. "Plus, Mystery Woman moved the contents around as much as she could before she ran off. She swapped items that were in boxes of the same size, and put the boxes back in their usual places on the shelves.

"And she dumped a bunch of boxes on the floor," she added. "And they're not sure if she took more than one object, or even took anything at all."

"So..."

"So the Secret Service is doing a full inventory, and they want us to sit in," she told him. "Go upstairs and change."

Getting onto the White House grounds after midnight was surprisingly easy. A private car came to pick them up. A man who spoke a total of five words ("Let me see your IDs.") took them straight from her driveway to a side door at 1600 Pennsylvania Avenue.

The other two members of their team had beaten them to the scene, and were waiting for them just inside the security alcove. Rachel and Santino had changed into their best suits—stiff, horrid things better suited for funerals than a late-night crime scene—but Santino still burst out laughing when he saw Jacob Zockinski. Rachel flipped frequencies to find the older detective in a black three-piece tuxedo.

She blinked at him.

"Go ahead," Zockinski said in purple-gray resignation.

"I can't," she said. "My mouth's clogged. All of the jokes want to come out at the same time."

Matt Hill, the other detective from the MPD, was slumped against the wall, as if he had already laughed himself to the point of exhaustion. He nodded at Rachel, and said, "Tomorrow was supposed to be his day off."

It took Rachel a moment to wedge the context of the comment into the conversation. "Everything's at the dry cleaners?"

"Yeah," Zockinski sighed. "And you don't come to the White House in a sweatshirt and jeans."

"This," she said to Santino, "is why I always keep an emergency suit ready."

The insults had begun to flow when Mitch Alimoren pushed open the interior door to let them into the White House proper. He was carrying a nylon garment bag, which he handed to a grateful Zockinski.

"There's a bathroom you can use to change," Alimoren said to Zockinski. "And then I'll take you to the East Room. You won't be allowed to go anywhere unescorted—we're all on edge, and security's as high as we can get it."

It wasn't Rachel's first time in the White House, but the men from the MPD had the iron-jawed stiffness of people trying not to stare. She understood. When her boss had taken her to meet the President, she had set her scans as tight as she could to keep from tripping her way down the halls. An image of the White House had already existed in her imagination, a composite of rooms made up from stills and televised press conferences. In reality, it was both smaller and grander than she had expected. When it was built, the White House had been a massive structure, on par with the palaces of kings. These days, the larger McMansions had roughly the same square footage. The scope had shrunk to commonplace.

But there was something else there, some other quality that defied description. If the term "character" didn't evoke heavily scuffed floors and crooked windows, Rachel might be tempted to use it, but it was more than that. The building had its own sense of purpose. It simply *was*. Visiting the White House was like walking through a cathedral. The purpose—the meaning— of the place had sunk into the wood and stone.

Rachel wondered if that sense of purpose existed apart from the White House itself. If this building burned to the ground, if the ghost of Dolly Madison failed to carry off the art, would what came after feel the same?

She rather thought it would. It might take a couple of decades for the patina to soak in, but any building that served as such a home to power would become…*more*.

They reached the bathroom. As Zockinski changed, Alimoren briefed them on their progress. "The archivists have moved the items in the storeroom upstairs to the East Room. It's the only space we have available where everything can be laid out at once," he said. "They're still opening boxes and sorting items. It'll be a few hours before they can do a full inventory."

"You let them into the scene?" Santino said a little too sharply.

"The murder occurred last night," Alimoren said. There was defensive orange within his conversational colors. This ran from his head down to his knees, the shape vaguely reminiscent of armor. "Homicide from First MPD cleared the room this morning."

Hill crossed his arms, and Rachel kept herself from sighing. The Agents were still so new that Rachel was rarely called to a scene until after it had been processed. It drove her team crazy: she found more at cold scenes than Forensics did when the bodies were still warm.

"Can we see it?" she asked. Unlikely that she'd pick up anything, not after the scene had been trampled by the foot traffic required to move a treasure trove, but it was worth trying.

Alimoren nodded, and when Zockinski finally emerged from the bathroom in an expensive dark navy suit, he led them downstairs. Security got lighter the deeper they went: someone had had the brilliant idea that the murder might have been a ploy designed to draw the Secret Service into the basement, and had made sure they were posted in force along the ground floor. There were guards stationed at every intersection, each of them wearing the grays and oranges of stress and frustration, and too focused on proving they could do their jobs. Rachel quickly grew tired of flashing her credentials.

Alimoren noticed as her attention moved from the Secret Service on the ground to the security cameras overhead. His colors fluttered towards a deeper uncertain orange, but he said nothing.

"Habit," Rachel assured him. "I can tell where the cameras are without looking." She could tell where the Secret Service agents were stationed, too, but Santino was the only member of the team who knew her eyes no longer worked. Well, Zockinski had been dropping hints, and Hill might know because his cousin was an Agent... No. Zockinski was just guessing, and Mako Hill would never let her secret slip.

She pointed out several hidden cameras for Alimoren, just to put his mind at ease.

Odd, that. A year ago, when the Agents had first gone public, locating cameras by their frequencies would have frightened someone like Alimoren. Now, this too-simple trick helped her prove her value.

"We figure we've got maybe three more days before the story breaks," Alimoren told the group as he took them past one final checkpoint. "And then everybody in the country is going to turn into an armchair security specialist. We already know we're going to catch the worst of it," he said, a nearby Secret Service agent nodding in agreement. "It'll look good if we've made some progress on either the murder or the robbery before then."

"We'll help where we can," Zockinski said. As the oldest member of their team, and the one who met the universal expectations of what a high-ranking cop should look like, Zockinski usually ran point during interactions with those outside of the MPD. The four of them had decided it was easier that way. Not better. Just easier, especially when they were working a case.

"Appreciated." Alimoren stopped by a battered white metal door. He slid a passkey through a lock, punched a code on the keypad, and let them inside.

It was anticlimactic. There was no blood, no mess, no taped-off area to indicate where the body had been found. The room was about the size of a large kitchen and was close to empty. In the far corner, a woman with a pale pink core loaded the last few white boxes onto a pushcart. The metal shelves, some against the walls, some freestanding in rows down the middle of the room, were almost completely bare.

"Can I walk around?" Rachel asked Alimoren. When he nodded, she dropped her purse, took a few long steps away from the men, and let her mind wander.

She heard Alimoren ask her team if they wanted to join her.

"No," Santino said. "Agent Peng's working."

Her scans fell away, roaming across the floors, the walls, the ceiling, and beyond. She pushed her mind through the edges of things, deep into the thicks and thins and hollows of structures. There were no utilities other than electricity, no voids other than ventilation runs. No secret rooms, no hidden explosives attached to the gas lines… *Fool me twice,* she thought, expanding her scans to take in the rooms beyond, *shame on me.*

Nothing.

"What's she doing?" Alimoren spoke in a low whisper.

"Scanning," Rachel replied. "If I can ping it, or if it resonates on the EM spectrum, I can pick it up." She tried to ignore how the archivist in the corner was turning yellow-orange with fear and uncertainty: the woman had just realized Rachel was an Agent.

"EM spectrum?"

"Just electromagnetic fields," she answered, almost idly, "but there are a *lot* of them." She tuned her scans to search for secretions. After a visit to a hospital a few months back, she had promised herself she would learn how to detect biological agents within small spaces, and had gotten remarkably good at it in a relatively short span of time. Oily fingerprints were one thing—fingerprints were everywhere, and she had learned early on how to detect them—but she had had no idea the world was encrusted with a thick skin of… Well. Skin, for one thing. Shed skin, cells dropped from human bodies with each caress, every time a comb was moved through hair. Little flakes, little flecks, tumbling around before they came to rest, and then devoured and pooped out in turn by those miniscule things whose singular purpose it was to eat and poop, and eat and poop…

She adjusted her scans again, and the room bloomed in filth. *Blood, snot, spit, and shit,* she thought. *Life is disgusting.*

Some distance away, a tiny fleck of dead red layered over black on gold caught her attention.

"Hey…" she said, walking across the room and towards one of the empty freestanding shelves. The archivist shied away as she approached. "Somebody get me a pen and an evidence bag."

Rachel flopped down on her belly, and waited until Santino shoved a pen and a small plastic baggie into her open hand. "Thanks."

"Whatcha got?" he asked.

"This…" Rachel said, using the butt end of the pen to prod a nearly invisible piece of metal away from where it had come to rest against the leg of a shelf. She carefully jockeyed it into the evidence bag. Once it was in, she adjusted her scans for a tight visual. A gold object, much thicker than a pin but about as long, lay at the bottom of the bag.

She handed the baggie to Santino. "I think it's a really bad idea to touch that with bare skin," she warned him.

"We need an empty box," Santino said to the archivist. "Something that can be covered."

The archivist handed him a fancy white shoebox with the Presidential Seal on the lid.

"Can we come in?" Alimoren asked from the door. His voice was eager. Rachel reset her scans to normal, and saw the Secret Service agent was running yellow-white with excitement.

"Yeah," she said, brushing the floor dust from her pants. "Did you find out what type of poison killed the victim?"

"Test results are still coming in. The best guess is a concentrated batrachotoxin."

Rachel didn't bother to try to search the term. She glanced at her partner, who whispered, "A neurotoxin extracted from tree frogs."

"Any ideas on the delivery mechanism?" she asked, running a last scan through the metal object in the box. It was hollow, with a spring resting beneath a protrusion at one end.

"Injection," Alimoren said. He had closed the distance between them, and peered into the open shoebox. "The entry wound is too thick to have been caused by a syringe. Beyond that, they don't know."

"This might be it," Rachel said. "It's hollow, there's blood on one end, and whatever was inside of it is organic."

"This?" Alimoren picked up the baggie and held it up to the light. The narrow end of the metal tube was tapered to an edge along a single plane. The bulb at the other end was flat, its surface crumpled like a thick sheet of aluminum foil. There were grooves cut into the sides of the bulb, crushed and folded in on themselves by the same force that had ruined the shape of the bulb.

"I've seen something like this before," Santino said. "Can't quite place it, though."

"Looks like part of a watch," Hill said.

Zockinski's conversational colors shifted to a more confident reddish-orange and clicked into place. "He's right," Zockinski said. "It's the…ah…the part you turn to wind a watch."

"Winding crown," Santino offered, gingerly turning the end of the baggie towards him for a better view. "It's too big to be one of those. A real winding crown is just a crank to turn the cogs. This is almost the size of a penny nail."

"You're assuming the watch needed to work," Rachel said. "If it was just a storage system for the poison…"

Alimoren hissed. He let Santino reclaim the box and its contents, and started to tap on his phone.

"Check my purse," Rachel said. "There's a tablet you can use."

The Secret Service agent was too preoccupied to realize she had been watching him call up the video footage of the crime scene. He hunted around Rachel's purse until he located her tablet: the image of the suspect was waiting for him. The tablet was large enough for the team to cluster around and confirm Hill's guess.

"Yes," Alimoren said, his voice tight. "Look. She's wearing a watch."

The woman's wristwatch was large, and just barely on the fashionable side of clunky. It was meant to be seen, falling like a bangle from beneath the cuff of her suit sleeve. It was right at home on the arm of a high-end makeup artist. Rachel played with the resolution until the image squealed in blurry pixels, but she couldn't quite get a clear impression of the winding crown.

"We've sent the files to digital specialists at Quantico and the MPD," Alimoren said. "I'll put in a call and see if they can get us a good close-up on the watch."

Oh, did you now? Rachel thought to herself, and reached out to locate Jason Atran through the link. She pulled back once she found him, but he might not have noticed her even if she had pinged him directly: he was burning the midnight oil in his private lab at the MPD's Consolidated Forensic Laboratory. She lurked in his computer system just long enough to see that he was working on the footage from the White House's security cameras, and then drew her mind back into her body.

Santino was watching her. She nodded at him; her partner rolled his eyes and took on an undertone of scornful orange.

"Who's on Forensics tonight? I've got something I want tested for batrachotoxin." Alimoren spoke low and hard into his phone. Behind him, the archivist skulked away as quickly as she could, pushing the cart laden with white boxes before her.

"If this is the murder weapon, why'd she ditch it?" Zockinski asked, taking his turn examining the pin in its baggie. "She had to know we'd find it."

Hill and Santino both grinned at him, a smug pink running through their conversational colors.

"Knock it off. We could have found it without Peng," Zockinski insisted. "We got along just fine before the freaking Agents showed up. No offense," he added, nodding at Rachel.

"None taken, asshole," Rachel replied in a voice just above a whisper—they were still in the White House, after all. "Would you risk trying to stick your poison-covered weapon back into its holster? I'd chuck it as far as I could and run."

"Still." Zockinski's opinion wouldn't be moved. "We would have vacuumed the scene." He jumped as Hill elbowed him in his ribs. "We *might* have vacuumed," he amended. "But if there was even a chance in a million we could have found the murder weapon, why did she leave it behind?"

"Probably because it won't help us find her," Alimoren said as he rejoined them. His conversational colors were a bright yellow-white, with alternating threads of red, yellow, and blue hope moving through his excitement. "Our pathologists say that batrachotoxins are easy to make. All you need are the right frogs."

"Or beetles," Santino added. "Probably be smarter to extract batrachotoxin from beetles, anyhow. Melyrid beetles would be easy to smuggle into the U.S. because they look like ordinary bugs, but it's hard to miss a poison dart frog."

Alimoren blinked at Santino. "They... Forensics didn't mention beetles."

"I can get them some literature on the topic," Santino offered.

"Can we head upstairs?" Alimoren asked Rachel. "I want to get this to Forensics as fast as possible."

"Yeah—yes," Rachel said, as she cast her senses over the room once more. Nothing resonated on her scans, and that annoying too-smart voice which popped up whenever her subconscious wanted to nag her about something she had missed stayed silent. "We're good."

The news of their discovery had spread. Hope was the most complex emotion Rachel had deciphered: hope wasn't made of one color but many, each of them woven into each other for support. The primary colors that made up blue relief, yellow joy, and red passion were worn by each Secret Service agent, and they smiled and nodded their thanks to Alimoren and the small group from First MPD as they passed. Most hadn't fully shed the grays and oranges, but these had subsided somewhat beneath vivid hope.

Another flight of stairs and a long corridor, and Alimoren took them through a set of doors and into the East Room.

Again, it was both smaller and grander than it had any right to be. Rachel had never attended a formal function at the White House—she had only attended photo shoots in the Rose Garden and the Oval Office—and the East Room came as something as a surprise. It was beautiful, certainly, with its inlaid wood floors and crystal chandeliers, but it was beautiful in a way which refused to tolerate nonsense. It was a room used to hard but perfect use, like a truck stop where the bikers minded the carpets and china *or else!*

The archivists had turned the East Room into a processing zone. The white boxes laid out in row after row were tidily organized, the archivists stacking their contents neatly on the clean linens beside them. The boxes and their contents had been grouped by size, with the larger items on the far side of the room, the smaller items closest to the main doors.

"Smart," Hill said.

The rest of them agreed. It made sense to exclude items from the search based on size alone: the murderer hadn't snuck into the White House with the goal of stealing a framed oil painting. Whatever she had stolen would be small enough to conceal on her person.

A murmur went up from a group of archivists, their conversational colors flaring briefly with yellow-white excitement. A taller man broke away, carrying something carefully with both hands down one row of boxes and up another, before placing it on a folded tablecloth in front of an empty box.

"What happened?" Rachel asked.

"They found another misplaced item," Alimoren said. "Right now, they're eliminating what could have been stolen by making sure each item is in its proper place. After that, they'll make a list of what's still missing. That'll be what we use to start tracking down possible buyers."

Alimoren excused himself, and left to deliver the possible murder weapon to the FBI's Forensics team. The team from First MPD was left on the edge of the room, alone, but not unsupervised: the Secret Service agents stationed around the East Room gave Rachel the impression that she'd be shot if she tried to open any of the doors.

"What do we do now?" she whispered to her partner.

"We do what we do best," Santino whispered back.

"Wander around, try to look like we know what we're doing, and hope we trip over something useful before they learn we're frauds?"

"Exactly," he said, and moved off down a nearby row.

Rachel headed south, towards the smallest boxes. This section held the most archivists; she assumed it was because more of the smaller items had been rearranged or gone missing. She turned down a row, keeping her scans steady. Her boss would never forgive her if she accidentally stomped a path through a century's worth of accumulated history.

Her scans roamed across the hoard. There were plates and cutlery of every possible description: apparently, foreign dignitaries had once feared America's presidents lacked appropriate tableware. There was less jewelry than she had expected, and most of that came in the form of ornate broaches and pins. She saw an almost countless number of decorative containers, as well as carvings of animals, and, occasionally, containers carved from parts of animals.

She wondered if she could track America's rise to power through the quality of the gifts. There, resting near a handwritten sign noting that the items came from 1800 to 1830, was a well-worn religious icon with a decidedly Byzantine appearance, the gilt all but gone from the holy Crown. By the middle of that century, presidents were given gemstone-dotted statuettes from the Middle East, and small tapestries woven with rich colors and metallic threads. Another fifty years down the aisle, and the items became more precious still: small portraits, cameos in jade and ivory, and miniaturized depictions of nearly every walk of life, both foreign and domestic.

And that didn't even begin to cover the antiquities.

Even when she still had her eyesight, art museums had never appealed to Rachel. Paintings bored her: a certain kind of person might appreciate the effort that went into placing the head of St. John the Baptist on its party platter, but she wasn't that person. She was drawn to the antiquities instead—relics of nations long gone to dust, living on through their statues, their curios, their assorted *objets d'art*—the older the better.

Much of what was here was ancient.

Cultural artifacts, she was sure, pieces of a country's oldest memories given to help forge new ones. Gifts given to a young nation to help them remember the grandeur of the old.

(And maybe, just maybe, that all empires crumble.)

And these were just the castoffs! What did the archivists decide to keep, or display, or send out as examples of prizes won to museums and presidential libraries?

She paused by a set of boxes placed just offside the last row. These were empty, the archivists moving between them and a couple of desktop computers that had been hastily set up on a folding banquet table. Rachel recognized the pale pink core of the archivist from the crime scene, and decided to see what would happen if she started pushing buttons.

She sidled up behind the woman, and said, "You seem to be good at this."

The woman turned. Rachel ran a quick scan of her face; she was about Rachel's own age, maybe a few years older, with glasses and tight brown eyes. She gasped and ran her gaze around the room, searching for help, and barbed-wire ribbons of yellow fear and red hate mixed within her conversational colors.

"Agent Rachel Peng, OACET," Rachel said, holding out her hand. "Mind if I ask you a few questions?"

The woman took Rachel's hand with all the enthusiasm of someone handed a used plague mask. "Maddie Peguero," she said. "No, I'm… I've got to finish—"

"I'll just take a few moments of your time." Rachel was enjoying herself. Public opinion of the Agents had its ups and downs, but Peguero bore the hallmarks of a woman who had Made Up Her Mind about cyborgs, and nothing Rachel did or said would shake that. "Can you explain what you're doing?"

"Inventory," Peguero stammered.

"Well, yes," Rachel said, smiling kindly. "What's your methodology?"

Peguero must have realized the Agent wasn't about to go away. She pulled herself together, her colors wrapping tight around her body to protect her from Rachel. "Come with me," she said, her voice flat. "It's easier to show you."

Peguero took her over to the computers. "We did a full inventory in 2009," she said, pointing to the larger monitor.

Rachel plucked the image from it, and found a detailed history and description of a cut-glass wine decanter. High-resolution photos of the vessel sat in an attached file, waiting to be called up when needed. She browsed these, and saw the archivists had taken multiple shots from all angles.

"Nice," Rachel admitted. "You did this for every item here?"

The archivist nodded. "And in the other storerooms. Took us the better part of a year. It was the first full inventory that's been done on gifts of state."

"I bet you found things you didn't know you had," Rachel said.

Peguero nearly smiled. "Absolutely."

Rachel waited, but Peguero wasn't about to keep talking. "What's missing?" Rachel asked. "Anything special?"

"No…" Peguero hesitated before adding, "There are still about twenty items missing. We don't think any of them were worth the effort."

"Why not?"

Peguero shrugged. "Because we didn't keep unique items in the storerooms. If it was of historical or academic interest, we've got it either on display or on loan."

"What about items of monetary value? I see a lot of gold and gemstones."

"There's no need to break into the White House to acquire those." The archivist's colors took on the dull orange of scorn. "You can find gold and gems anywhere."

"What's your personal opinion?" Rachel asked. Peguero glanced at Rachel, her colors weaving as she weighed her options, so Rachel added, "Off the record, I promise. I just want to hear what you think happened."

"Honestly?" Peguero glanced towards the rows of small white boxes. "I think a private collector needed something we had to complete a set."

Perfect, Rachel thought. Private collectors left muddy footprints through the art community. High-level art theft required deep pockets and aggressive purpose.

"Do any of those twenty missing items belong to a set?"

"All of them could." Peguero's orange scorn flared again. "When I say 'set', I'm not talking about a matching set of jewelry. Collectors might be after a certain artist's work, or period pieces, or...anything," the archivist finished. "Anything can be part of a set."

Ouch. Tracking down a collector for a random item was harder. Not impossible. Just much, much harder.

A second muted shout went up from the archivists, as another misplaced item was discovered in the wrong box.

"I've got to go," Peguero said.

"One more question," Rachel said. "Do you have a list of items that are still missing?"

"Yes," Peguero replied. She shuffled a stack of papers around until she came up with an inventory. The list had some fifty-plus objects, but more than half of these had been crossed off by various shades of pen. "Ignore the ones that have been scratched out. We've found those. You can use the computer if you want to see what the missing ones look like. Do you know how to cross-reference a..." Peguero trailed off and her colors went pale, as she realized she had been about to give an Agent instructions on how to use a database.

"I'll figure it out," Rachel said, and gave Peguero another merry smile.

The archivist hurried away.

Rachel dropped into a folding chair and swung herself around to face the monitors. She flipped through the inventory, comparing objects on the list to those in the database. At the prompt, she saw a dozen objects. Carved ivory. Gold upon wood. Bracelets of cloisonné irises running together in a chain...

And one little lump of metal the size of the palm of her hand, worn down to blue and green and gray.

One of these things, she thought, *is not like the others.*

FOUR

The timer released her, and Rachel climbed out of a strange, old dream of the sea.

She awoke in the parking lot of the MPD's Consolidated Forensics Laboratory, feeling as though she had grabbed a three-hour nap instead of a fifteen-minute catnap. She hadn't wanted to—the induced sleep state lowered her defenses—but Santino had insisted that one of them needed to stay sharp until they got off the clock. If she had set the timer for an hour instead of those fifteen minutes, she would have felt as though she had gotten a full night's sleep, but she would have been an unwakeable lump unless she received a ping or a good old-fashioned slap.

The Consolidated Forensics Laboratory was a state-of-the-art facility, at least for a few more years. It had been commissioned to replace the chaos of individual forensics labs stationed at the major police precincts, and to keep the MPD from farming out data analysis and drug testing to the lowest bidders. The building had been designed for expansion: the MPD had learned the hard way that it was impossible to integrate new technologies into the legal process if there was no place to put them.

They had not, however, expected to give up prime real estate so quickly to OACET.

Jason Atran, fellow Agent from the Office of Adaptive and Complementary Technologies and on loan to the MPD, had staked out a private office on the third floor. The lights were on in his office, a band of gold against the slumbering blue glass of the rest of the building. His car wasn't the only one in the lot, but it had little company: scientists in the public sector tended to keep bankers' hours.

Rachel badgered the security guy to let them in, and they shuffled their way towards the elevators. She was more tired than she had been before her forced nap. Even when spun from the depths of slow-wave non-REM sleep, fifteen minutes of sleep hadn't been nearly enough. It would have been better to ride the false cleverness of a caffeine high, like Santino.

The elevator swept them up to the third floor. Around the second floor, her thoughts twitched, an awareness not of her making moved her mind as her implant gave her new information. "Phil's here," she said to Santino.

Santino's phone buzzed. He pulled it out of his pocket to check the message. "So's Bell."

He noticed Rachel's expression. "It's a proximity alert. You've got one in your head, I've got one in my phone. It lets me know when I'm within a hundred feet of a friend."

"That's a thing?"

"You haven't heard of Grindr?"

"Grind her? Not without asking!"

His conversational colors glazed over as he steadied himself for an explanation, and then saw Rachel's grin. "Please don't fuck with me," he sighed. "Not at three in the morning."

The elevator let them out, and then there were just a couple more steps to Jason's office. Santino knocked, and the electronic lock popped open.

"What?" Jason asked them through the crack. "I'm working." He was polished in the way of a male model, every inch of him long and lean and haughty. His core was the deep wooly charcoal of expensive overcoats, and this was draped with conversational colors of irritated oranges, professional blues, and cold gray exhaustion.

"Hello to you, too," Rachel said, pushing the door into him. "We know you're working. That's why we're here."

Beneath the windows on the far side of the room was a leather couch. A shock of wild blond hair was all that could be seen of Phil Netz. The rest of him was a snoring lump covered by a blanket; even his silver-light core was indistinct under the soft colors of his dreams. On top of that lump, a girl—*woman*, Rachel reprimanded herself, but she had a hard time applying that term to someone who was barely of legal drinking age—sat reading, her legs draped over the sleeping man. Her smooth gray core was surrounded by traces of silver-light and charcoal, and her conversational colors flared into bright, eager gold when she saw Rachel. The woman—*Nope, can't do it. Girl.*—leapt off of the lump of sleeping Phil and ran into Rachel's arms.

"Rachel!"

"Hey, Bell," Rachel said, returning the hug gladly. This was something of a change: whatever else might have come of her relationship with two older men, Bell's personal hygiene habits had improved dramatically. The girl still dressed like a hobo who had camped out in a yarn factory during a tornado, but at least she had begun showering daily.

Bell stepped away and adjusted her thick-rimmed glasses. These were a near match to Santino's, the result of long hours in the lab to develop a pair of casual-wear glasses capable of picking up the Agents' projections. Bell and Santino had finally gotten the battery pack to fit within the earpiece, and were stress-testing them among a small group of friends before turning the schematics over to OACET for production. Zockinski and Hill each had a pair: Hill would wear his without prompting around the Agents, but Zockinski had a tendency to forget his glasses in odd places.

"How are they coming?" Rachel asked Bell.

"Great! Well, they throw off a little heat sometimes," Bell admitted, and Rachel noticed the red rash of pain behind the girl's left ear, hidden beneath the battery pack. "A few more adjustments, and we should be ready to go!"

Phil coughed in his sleep, and Santino went over to kick his friend awake.

"Oh, Santino, don't! He's tired—he was running training seminars all day!" Bell said, hauling uselessly on Santino's arm. He picked the girl up, and dropped her, squirming, around the general vicinity of Phil's stomach. The shape beneath the blanket came awake in a multicolored surge, thrashing and swearing.

Rachel didn't have the energy to either break up a fight or find an ice pack, so she joined Jason in front of his computers.

"This couldn't have waited until morning?" he asked. In front of him were five objects, perfectly rendered and slowly rotating in three dimensions. If they hadn't been cast in shades of bright green, Rachel might have believed they were physically present and not merely floating motes of digitized light.

"Brooch, Art Nouveau period, given to Grover Cleveland upon meeting with French Prime Minister Jules Méline," Rachel said, pointing to the nearest item. It was pure luck she had recognized it from browsing Peguero's inventory list; she hoped Jason wouldn't quiz her on the others.

"Oh, fuck you," Jason said. "You could have just told me you were working the case."

"What've you got?"

He gestured towards the empty space in front of him, and another dozen objects popped into view. These were rendered in the same green color as the first batch, but lacked the details. "I'm still compiling these," he said. "I'm working from photographs. It takes me longer than when I work with video. There's usually enough data to fill in the holes when the material is in motion, but with stills…"

He shook his head. "I've been at this since the data arrived this morning. The bitch of it is when I finally get one object rendered—" he swept out an arm and another thirty objects joined the others, most of these showing the fine details of a final project "—and they call to tell me they've found it so I can stop working on it." He clenched his fist, and those thirty objects vanished. "Fucking waste of my time."

"Sorry," Rachel said, and meant it. "When are you quitting for the night?"

He waved vaguely in the direction of his computers. "It'll let me know. I give myself ten careless mistakes an hour. When I go over that, I get a fifteen-minute warning and then the system shuts down for eight hours."

Rachel inspected the gray exhaustion running through the other Agent's conversational colors. It clung to him in thick sheets, smothering him. "When do you think that'll be?"

"Who knows?" he said, smug pink cutting through the exhaustion. "I don't make mistakes."

She made an unkind noise, and turned to his system.

When the MPD had learned there was a chance they could get their hands on another Agent, this one a digital imaging specialist, they had bent over backwards to court him. Jason had told them what he wanted, and they had obliged. The private office in the new science building. The motion-sensitive computers which followed his every thought and movement. He sometimes bragged that he had more processing power than Jesus, and when he was told that made no sense, he'd grin wickedly and conjure enough green loaves and fishes to fill the entire room.

His system…*loved* him. Rachel didn't know what else to call it. It wasn't human love, more like the devotion of a well-trained dog for its master, but it was love all of the same.

And as Jason grew and adapted, so did his system.

When he had first built it, the computers had obeyed Jason, and him alone. Rachel had hated visiting his office, as his system had thrown enough distortion into her mind to make her feel physically uncomfortable. But she and Jason were trying. They didn't like each other much, but they were trying, and his system began to try to make her feel welcome, too. The distortion had eased, and she no longer felt as if they wanted to shove her out when she came to see Jason.

For Bell, though, his computers had *changed.*

Rachel had stumbled over Jason's relationship with Bell through his system. The girl was a genius with technology. Rachel had met her through a previous case, where she had learned Bell's own computer system sang like an angelic choir. That system was gone now, but it had been much like Bell herself, friendly and open, and driven to blend technology and art into a single concept. When Rachel had heard the first strands of Bell's song within Jason's system, she had very nearly murdered him. It was only after she had wrapped her hands around his throat and his humor—humor!—at the situation had jumped across to her that she realized Bell wasn't cheating on Phil, that...

Well.

Rachel didn't understand polyamory. She just *didn't*. But her friends were happy, so she had released her hold on Jason's windpipe and apologized for thinking the worst of him.

Lately, Jason's new system had begun to sound more like Bell's old one. Rachel was sure the girl snuck in after hours to tinker. New equipment that wasn't strictly in Jason's realm of digital imaging (such as the DMLS printer in the corner, busily humming and burning away) had been integrated into the system. Interactive voice-response software had been installed: Jason didn't need this, but it let Bell talk to the computer without needing an implant. And there were traces of Phil in there, his silver-light wit shaping the personality of the AI program.

Phil had even named it.

"*Hello, Lulu,*" Rachel said.

AGENT PENG, the system replied, loud and clear within her mind. It wasn't exactly a woman's voice, but there was nothing else close enough for a comparison. *GOOD MORNING.*

Technically, yes, she thought to herself, but realized Lulu could hear her, and kept going before her response created a confusion cascade. Phil had not yet gotten around to teaching Lulu sarcasm. "*What is Jason's general user history for the past 24 hours? Time usage only.*"

ONLINE SINCE 8:16. BREAKS AT 10:07, 13:28, 17:10, 21:42, 00:16, AND 02:33. HE IS WITHIN DEFINED SAFE USAGE PARAMETERS.

"*Was the duration of any of those breaks for longer than ten minutes?*" When Lulu didn't answer, Rachel prodded. "*Lulu, reply.*"

NO, AGENT PENG.

"Why did you hesitate, Lulu?"

UNSPECIFIED.

Yeah, right, Rachel thought. Jason, who was listening in, sighed. *"Lulu, do Phil and Bell have the same information you just relayed to me?"*

NO, AGENT PENG.

"Communicate that information to them," she said.

Jason, realizing he was busted, threw up a hand in a Stop! gesture. *"Lulu, hold,"* he told his system, then said aloud to Rachel, "You win."

Rachel wasn't done. *"Lulu, mark Jason's actions."*

YES, AGENT PENG.

Lulu had never given Rachel a reason to believe that it had any emotions other than an unyielding devotion to Jason. Rachel had only been able to get it to alter its programming when she made it clear to the system that Jason would benefit. *"Jason doesn't want you to communicate the information to Phil and Bell because he knows they would make him change his behaviors. This is because his behaviors were of minor risk to him. Understand?"*

YES, AGENT PENG.

"You will address this topic at a future time with Jason, Phil, and Bell to redefine safe usage parameters. Schedule this discussion for next week when all three can meet. Understand?"

Lulu didn't like taking orders from Rachel. *JASON, APPROVE?*

Rachel shook a fist at him until he grudgingly said, *"Approved."*

WHY?

The question caught Rachel by surprise. Jason fielded it for her. *"Because I don't think of my own welfare the same way my partners do. Their data gives me better input."*

UNDERSTOOD.

"Lulu, Rachel and I are talking now. Do not query or reply to us."

The computer didn't respond, and Rachel didn't feel the familiar push-or-pull of interaction through a link. "Is it still listening?" she whispered to Jason.

"Yup," Jason said proudly, and reached out to pat a server case. "But I took it out of communication mode. Lulu doesn't speak unless spoken to."

"All right," Rachel said. She was the slightest bit jealous. Not that she really wanted a super-powered computer system that bent to her whims, but... "Show me what you're working on, and then you're done."

"Here," he said, and six items in digitized green appeared with a wave of his hand.

"Where are the rest?" Rachel asked.

"I've been talking to the Secret Service," he said, that same smug pink showing through his exhausted grays. "They've located all of the items but these."

She couldn't place the source of the pink until she realized he had been talking to her at the same time as he had been on the phone with the Secret Service. "Jason, I swear, you're going to burn yourself out."

"Maybe, but it won't happen today."

Rachel scanned the couch, where Santino and Bell were doing their best to keep Phil pinned down under the blanket. She opened a link. *"Just discuss your schedule with them, okay?"*

"Is that an order?" It was a pro forma complaint, and Rachel started to hide her grin behind her hand before she remembered Jason could feel it in a link. Whatever else might come out of his relationship with Phil and Bell, Jason was much less antagonistic these days. He grinned back at her. *"I'm trying."*

"I know."

Rachel stepped away from him, and ran her scans over the six items. She never had any problem perceiving the Agents' projections. Lulu might have been responsible for processing the renders, but Jason was the source of how these green objects appeared. If he had wanted it, he could warp or twist them, give them a mouth, feet, make them dance... Her eyes had nothing to do with seeing them.

Five of the objects were what she had expected. These were

the typical bric-a-brac that she had seen cluttering the East Room—if gifts of state could be considered either typical or clutter—the small statuettes and boxes and pieces of jewelry...

The sixth was that odd chunk of metal.

The misshapen hunk of metal hung apart from the others. It was rendered in crisp greens and looked real enough to touch. Jason had spent a lot of time on it.

She reached out a finger to caress its edge. Her finger pushed through the green light, and moved through open air. *"This one is still missing?"* she asked.

"Yeah," Jason said. She felt him nod.

When she didn't reply, he looked up from putting a few additional touches on a small statuette of a horse. *"What?"*

"Nothing. I...I don't know," she amended. *"There's something special about this one."*

"Sure," he scoffed.

"Then why did you spend so much time rendering it?" Rachel said aloud as she broke their link. She was too tired to cope with a moody Jason kicking around her head. "There's more detail in this piece than any of your others."

"Test for the DMLS. I've got that one going now," he said, pointing over his shoulder at the direct metal laser sintering printer. "Should be just about done."

"Really?" Rachel threw a scan into the printer cage and found another version of the strange object, this one made of metal instead of light, and slowly growing as layer after layer of stainless steel was added.

"Yeah. I chose this one because it's the easiest to replicate. If I can get my renders to print, you'll have life-sized copies of what was stolen as props when you do your interviews."

"That's perfect," she said. "Thanks!"

"You'll still have to bring photos. I'm not going to paint them for you."

She raised an eyebrow. "I've seen you guys print in color before."

"Yeah, but that's plastic filament, and..." Jason shrugged,

almost blushing in embarrassment.

"Jesus H…" Rachel pinched the tight space between her eyes. A stress headache was starting to come on strong. "Please tell me you're not using a murder at the White House to justify your new toy."

He paused. "I'll print the other five in plastic."

"Thank you."

Several soft pulses from the computer system, like a gentle knocking on a door, caught their attention. "Lulu's done," Jason said.

There was a tremendous shout from the couch as Phil finally conquered all.

"Come take a look at this," Jason said to Rachel, lifting the shield on the printer's hopper. He fiddled with a set of clasps, and then plucked a silvery object the size of a tennis ball from a printing plate. "It's still hot," he said, waving the object back and forth to cool it. "Give it a second."

It was smaller than she had expected, with more nooks and crannies than an English muffin. The version wrought from green light must have been enlarged so Jason could refine the details. The metal printout was as thin as a dime in places, tapering out to two fingers thick in others.

"It looks fragile," Rachel said.

"It probably is. The original probably is," Jason said, correcting himself. "You could drive a car over the printed version."

She sent a light scan through it, and traced the lines of something rounded with jagged edges… *Gears?*

Her eyes snapped up to Jason's, her curiosity hitting her hard enough so he could feel it even without being in a link. "What?"

Rachel reopened their connection as she reached for the object, not willing to ask stupid questions without getting a clear reading from Jason.

"Hey, Rachel," came Phil's voice from behind her.

She turned her bare cheek into Phil's hand at the exact moment Jason placed the chunk of metal into hers, and three minds rushed into one with a decisive mental *"Fuck!"*

It was one of those dumb happenstances that had caused them so many problems during the first few months. Managing the link was hard enough: it was too easy to get lost within another Agent's mind, and through that, their sense of self. Identities were fragile things, formed from the fabric of memories and beliefs. If you found yourself plunged into a mental maelstrom made up of these bits and pieces of persons, your own identity could fragment. The best outcome was a perfectly preserved sense of self, but that was unlikely. Mostly, an identity stayed whole, but it rolled up fragments of thoughts, pieces of other selves, becoming a clumped mess that required careful carding to return to a neat and tidy *me*.

They had taught themselves to build walls. They'd never be able to keep each other out, not completely, but they could shelter their identities away behind mental conditioning. They walled themselves in—*deep* within—their own minds. Then, after those walls had been cemented in place for five long years, they started teaching themselves how to build gates. By opening a link, they cracked the gates in their private walls *just enough* to let the others in.

But not too far in, and they never went far enough away from home to lose their way back to their own mind, their own sense of self, secure behind their own walls.

Skin contact, though, could tear those walls down.

The implant was an organic computer, integrated into their very cells. Agents could choose to pass information, sensation, and even emotions via a link. When skin contact was involved, the scope and depth of that link was enhanced. Careful, cautious skin contact between Agents was immensely useful, as long as those involved were focused on a goal and were tending to their gates.

But, say, if it was late at night, and if all three Agents were exhausted, and if they hadn't meant to initiate skin contact at all, let alone touch each other at the exact same moment…

There was a rush of emotion and tangle of minds, and Rachel joined Phil joined Jason in a single mental space. Their bodies sat down where they stood, and reached out to join hands in an awkward triangle. It was a learned response: when you suddenly stopped existing as an individual, the physical side removed itself from the equation to wait for the mental side to work itself out.

The three-now-one took a deep breath, and began to look for a focusing object to bring their identities back into balance.

This, again, was a learned response: there had been many an Agent driven to the point of madness—for some, beyond— by not finding a way pull themselves back into his or her own mind. The trick was accepting that differences existed, and that these differences helped define identity.

Finding a focusing object was a matter of convenience. A focusing object was something that invoked a different emotion in each of them. If there were different perspectives attached that one object, it became a matter of aligning the emotion to the person, and using that emotion to pull the mind back into a singular sense of self.

They weren't quite sure how this worked. The scientists among them had hypothesized that belief should work better than perspective, since perspective could change and there was evidence that deep belief in concepts, such as religion or politics, was hard-coded into the brain. If three careless Agents tumbling within a single sense of self wanted to pull themselves out of a dive, it stood to reason that they should figure out which one of them attended church on Sundays, and use the definition of identity already seated within their cells.

Then again, the same thing could be said of the entire body: why couldn't two Agents who shared no genetic markers pull themselves apart through the familiarity of their own faces, their own hands...even their own genitals?

(Rachel, when she was Rachel and not an amalgam of RachelJasonPhil, thought that it was because belief was shaped by the mind, but emotions were shaped by the soul.)

The strange metal object was their way home. They felt it in their joined hands, still warm from the printer. They concentrated: concentration was key. Fragments of other thoughts, other concepts, those could introduce new emotions to the mix, and that would keep them rolling in this mental mess forever.

Important, one of them said.

Trivial, said another.

What? said the third.

Then it was just a matter of following those emotions back to their source.

The pieces of identity who felt the item was significant gathered itself together, pulling away from the Other. In that undefined space where identity existed, the one who felt the item was barely worth its time found itself, and it too pulled away. This left the one who was just utterly confused by the whole thing floating around, alone.

And then it was just a normal three-way link. This link was enhanced through skin contact, yes, but now they were just swimming in their own carelessness.

Jason broke contact first. "Fucking rookie mistake," he hissed, throwing the metal object into Rachel's lap and crawling away to put some distance between him and the others. He looked around, his conversational colors whipping in hard reds all around him, and saw Bell. The girl was staring at him, her mouth open, Santino's arms tight around her to keep her from running to him and Phil. He leapt to his feet and stormed out of the room.

"Jason!"

"Let him go," Phil said to Bell. "He's got to walk it off."

"What happened?" Santino asked.

"We got mixed up," Rachel said. "We sorted it out."

I hope. She slipped the metal object into her pocket as she searched her memories for something new. Nothing stood out. She still experienced some minor confusion separating her own experiences from those of other Agents (Christmases and birthdays, especially. For whatever reason, happy memories tended to stick. Better than the alternative; she'd much rather have the memories of opening a thousand different gifts than standing around in the dim childhood fog of funerals.), but nothing stood out as being a new addition from the Phil or Jason Memory Collections.

Rachel glanced over at Phil, who was a mix of embarrassed reds and anxious grays. "You okay?" she whispered, not quite ready to open a new link.

"Yeah," he said softly. Then, stronger: "Yeah."

He turned to Bell. The girl jumped into his arms with the enthusiasm of lovers reunited after a long tour of duty.

"Didn't mean to worry you," Phil said, brushing the girl's green-streaked hair away from her face. "It happens sometimes. We're fine."

Santino hung back, unsure if he should give his partner a hug. Rachel reached out and pulled him close, and let his cobalt blue aura and warm woody scent wrap around her. "That was hard to watch," he said.

She stepped away and nodded towards Phil and Bell. "So I heard."

"I hadn't seen that before," he said. "Zia told me that you guys sometimes...merged?"

"Good word."

"Yeah," he said. His girlfriend's violet core color was prominent in his conversational colors; he was wondering what Zia had left unsaid. "The three of you just started..." He stopped, searching for a good way to describe the wrongness of three separate bodies moving as one.

"I think Jason and Phil've gotten careless," Rachel said quietly, so as not to disturb Phil and Bell on the nearby couch. "They've been spending a lot of time together, and they've probably gotten their mental defenses tuned against each other. Casual contact isn't as big a deal to them. I jumped in the middle, and broke their balance."

"It's that bad?"

"It can be—it *used* to be," she corrected herself. "This is the first time it's happened in months."

Well, first time it's happened to me in months, she thought, and wondered how much of Jason's happier, warmer personality might be because of his new relationship with Phil, not Bell. It was possible that some of Phil had gotten stuck in Jason's head…and then she shook her head to ward off that line of thinking. She knew firsthand that Jason could be a real human being when he put his mind to it. Besides, links went both ways, and Phil didn't seem to be showing any signs of Jasoning.

She shook her head again, and moved towards where Bell and Phil were holding each other on the couch, finally ready to do damage control.

"So," Rachel said to Bell. "What have the guys told you?"

"Nothing!" Bell said, a little too quickly. The conversational colors across her shoulders dimpled with the lie.

"Good," Rachel said. "That's exactly how you should answer that question for anyone else. Now, what have the guys told you?"

Bell looked at Phil, who rubbed her back and assured her it was okay.

"They told me you were—"

"Brainwashed," said Jason from behind Rachel. She jumped: she had shut down everything but her short-range scans, and he had managed to surprise her. He grinned at her to show he knew she had been caught. It was the same grin the old Jason had used, all smooth arrogance. "We told her they lied to us before they put the chips in our heads. Then, once they had their lab rats, they walked away from us for *five fucking years* because they wanted us to lose our goddamned minds, wanted us to become…*that.*"

He pointed at the spot where the three of them had gotten lost.

"Bell knows," he said. "Everything Santino knows, we told Bell."

"Good. She should know everything," Rachel said. Then, to Bell, "Now, tell me what they told you."

"What? Why?" The girl was staring at Jason as if she had

never really seen him before.

"Because information is our first line of defense, and I need to know you have the facts right."

Jason started to complain. Rachel thought about opening a link between her and the other Agent to tell him to back off, then decided she still wasn't up for it. "Jason?" she said. "Not now."

He stepped away, furious.

Bell's attention moved from Jason to Rachel, her conversational colors dropping Jason's and Phil's cores, and replacing these with Rachel's strong Southwestern turquoise. She began to talk, slow and halting, as if telling one close friend about another's murder.

The girl knew.

She knew that five hundred young employees in the federal government had been recruited to become part of an experimental top-secret program. How they were told that this Program was critical to promote interagency cooperation.

And how that story was a lie.

That cooperation was never the goal. How the true purpose of the Program was to allow a select few businessmen and politicians to gain access to the abilities of the implant, without incurring the risks of brain surgery and criminal liability.

That to achieve this, the minds and personalities of each Agent needed to be eliminated.

That a piece of software, a personal digital assistant, had been introduced, and how this could not be controlled or turned off. How this software had been designed to hammer at the Agents' psyches for five years, day and night, until their personalities had retreated so far behind their walls they might not have ever come out again.

That Patrick Mulcahy—then, just another Agent; now, head of OACET and their champion and protector on Capitol Hill—had somehow tripped over a way to free them.

That Mulcahy had led them from behind their walls, and out of those five years of hell.

Had united them into a single Agency.

Had encouraged them to wait until the time was right to spring their existence on an unsuspecting world.

And, finally, to accept that while the world *might* tolerate cyborgs with the power to control machines with their minds, it was unlikely they would think of technologically-omniscient cyborgs recovering from serious emotional and mental abuse as anything other than a disaster waiting to happen.

And so, in a way, the Agents were still waiting.

By the time she finished, Bell was sobbing. The girl buried her face against Phil's chest and wept. Rachel waited until Bell could get a handle on herself (*a hundred and sixty-two Mississippi, a hundred and sixty-three Mississippi, a hundred and... Jesus, kid, pull it together*), and then reached out to place a hand on the girl's shoulder.

"Thank you," Rachel said.

Bell sniffed, and wiped her eyes with Phil's shirt. Phil took a deep breath, resigned.

"For what?" Bell asked.

"For keeping our secret. I know it's tough. But it shouldn't be for too much longer."

"Are you really going public with the brainwashing story?"

"Yeah," Rachel said. She knelt down, making sure that Bell was seated higher than she was: illusions of power went a long way towards maintaining relationships with those outside of the collective. Rachel didn't think she needed this extra step with Bell, but she didn't take chances. "Not us," she said, tapping her chest, and then gesturing at Phil and Jason. "And not our Administration, either. We're going to let the media do it for us."

Rachel was part of OACET's Administration herself, and knew the story would break soon. They kept a close watch on certain pieces of information in certain databases, and certain reporters were getting close to these. Once they did, it was only a matter of time before they would be able to trace that information back to its source and verify the story.

If the Agents were lucky, the story would finally give Congress the kick in the ass it needed to turn against Senator Richard Hanlon.

(Rachel wasn't optimistic. Congress didn't change, not really. Government thrived on predictability. After OACET had presented evidence that members of Congress had been directly involved in eliminating uncooperative Agents, the ranking politicians had offered a few of their less popular members up for public sacrifice. Hanlon hadn't been among them. The man had serious money, and was incredibly popular with voters. Every time OACET brought evidence against Hanlon, it was met with a *Yes, but did you consider...* They had. Everybody had—everybody knew he was rotten. And nobody seemed to care as long as the political system kept churning along.)

Bell hauled herself off of the couch, and dropped to the floor next to Rachel. *So much for body language*, Rachel thought. The girl's grays were turning on themselves, changing from the sorrow of a cloudy sky to a determined steel.

"What are you going to do about Hanlon?" the girl asked.

Rachel glanced towards Phil, who nodded.

Risky, Rachel thought to herself. Telling Bell who was responsible for developing the implant and the mental conditioning branded the girl an ally of OACET, and Hanlon didn't especially approve of those.

"We can't—we *will* not—go after Hanlon," Rachel said. "He's the living symbol of why OACET can be trusted. Once the story gets out, it'll prove that he was behind the software used in our...conditioning. By letting him live, we've shown that we obey the rule of law. Even when killing him is something we really, *really* want to do."

Phil and Jason were both nodding now, their conversational colors holding her turquoise; they agreed with her. Bell, on the other hand, was reading *Objection!* in a mix of hard reds and grays.

"Why do you let him walk around, knowing what he's capable of?!" she asked. "He's evil. He's a *murderer!* He killed over a hundred and fifty Agents before you went public!"

"We don't have proof he was directly responsible for the murders," Phil said, reaching down to touch Bell's shoulder. "We *do* have proof that he knowingly set out to brainwash us. And we can't alienate Congress by forcing them to turn on one of their own. We need Congress to think we're worth keeping around, or they'll find a way to get rid of us."

The girl shrugged him off. "That doesn't matter! He could still come after you, but…you're just…you just let him go!"

"What's the alternative?" Rachel asked her. She had a brief memory of Josh practicing the 'But Murder is Bad' speech he planned to give to the press when they started asking the same questions. "Congress has already investigated Hanlon's company, and we can't prove he entered politics to get his hands on us. To them, and to the rest of America, he's just a rich guy whose company developed a product that was turned into cyborgs. He's not legally responsible for anything."

"But *you* know." Bell was kneeling in front of her, her steely grays and red anger shading deeper.

Rachel met her eyes. Bell was able to hold her gaze for a few moments, but finally shied away.

"And there's nothing we can do," Rachel said. Bell's colors started to fade, with a sickly green coming up to replace the grays and reds; Rachel felt as if she was watching the girl grow up before her eyes. "Not legally. Which means until Congress turns against Hanlon, there is *nothing* we can do about him at all."

FIVE

"Three more, and we're headed back to First," Zockinski said in her head.

Rachel nodded, then remembered that Zockinski couldn't feel it, and was on the other side of the city besides. *"We're going to keep going,"* she replied. *"We've found a few more stores that deal in boutique collectables. We're having better luck there than in the pawn shops."*

"Right," Zockinski said. "Meet at the station for dinner?"

Her stomach grumbled in agreement. *"Maybe,"* she said, overruling it. *"Call you in an hour."*

He hung up, leaving an echo of his voice behind. She pretended to scratch her temples to rid herself of the pressure; her persistent headache was back.

We should probably quit for the day, too, she thought. She and Santino had plenty of practice questioning pawn shop owners from their early days as partners, but the fine arts dealers had not been as willing to talk to them.

Well, they weren't willing to talk to her. Santino knew enough about everything from the ancient Etruscans to modern numismatic principles to at least fake his way through a conversation. Once they realized he was making better progress without her, they had split the list of remaining stores in half, with her taking those on the cheap streets with lower rent.

She had ended up on the far west side of the Potomac Parkway, taking taxis between art galleries and asking dealers if they had recently encountered anyone with interest in *these*. If she was in a good mood, she'd carefully place each of Jason's 3D-printed objects on a convenient display case or countertop. If she wasn't in a good mood, she'd dump them out of her handbag, and if she was in an absolutely venomous mood—

say, after a cabdriver had intentionally jacked up her fare and then a gallery owner had spent a few tense minutes pretending she didn't exist—she'd make sure that the leather folio with her OACET badge landed on top.

The next store on her list was in walking distance. Rachel tugged her coat collar up and hoped that the weather forecast for tomorrow would be as promised, bright and sunny, the first real warm day of the year. Today was a dismal waste of a Saturday.

Left on P Street, came the reminder at the intersection. The thought had come up without prompting, like it used to before she had an implant, back when a name or a street sign led her to recall a barely remembered set of directions. Rachel probably wouldn't have even noticed if she still had to read a map to learn where she was going. Now, she'd look at an address and start walking, and she'd end up at the front door of her destination as if she had made that trip a hundred times before.

It'd weird her the hell out if it weren't so convenient.

The rain had started by the time she reached her destination. She glanced up and flipped settings to read the signage. An old-fashioned hanging plaque dangled from an iron hook above her head, with a badger and a fish chasing each other in a clumsy yin and yang.

Okay, then, she thought, and pulled the door open.

The smell of the place hit her like a punch to the face. Rachel had to take a few deep breaths before her nose numbed itself in self-defense.

"Raccoons," came a voice from the rear of the store.

"What?" Rachel gasped.

"My neighbors had a problem with raccoons. They poisoned them, and they came to my walls to die, the bloody things."

She tried to unearth some modicum of sense from under the man's thick Australian accent, but kept coming back to *raccoons in the walls*. "Can't you...um...?"

"Get 'em out?" A heavyset man in his late fifties rolled around a stack of newspapers and into the clearing where Rachel was standing. "I didn't know they were in there until they started to rot. Now? The lawyers are involved, and I can't touch my own building until liability gets settled. Here," he said, holding out a small tin full of cream. "Eucalyptus oil. Rub it under your nose."

She did, and her sinuses opened with a rush.

The man was ready with a box of tissues. "Happens to everyone," he said kindly.

"Thanks?"

"Don't mention it. If you're bold enough to brave the stench, the least I can offer is good customer service." He started towards the rear of the store. "Smell's thinner in the back. I think they died up here in the front room."

He gestured towards a table against the far wall. It had been pushed under an open window, and a fan and a large space heater were competing over the same electrical outlet. "Coffee?" the man asked her.

She gagged. The idea of anything in that place going into her mouth...

"Had to ask," he said. "Oscar McCrindle, Trout and Badger Antiques."

"Rachel Peng." She waved the sopping tissue at the man. "I'd offer to shake, but I'm a mess."

"Understandable."

Now that she could breathe again, Rachel was able to scan the store. It was both messy and spotless; there were piles upon piles of stuff, but not a speck of dust or trace of cobweb. McCrindle probably knew every inch of it, and could locate anything from a single baseball card to the taxidermied buffalo head staring down at her with its black glass eyes.

McCrindle matched his store. He seemed overlarge, somewhere in the middle range of three hundred pounds, but was too tidy in a white button-down shirt and pressed pants, and a core color the deep red of living garnet.

"Nice place you have here," Rachel said, and meant it. She had seen a couple dozen art galleries and antique stores that day, and the Trout and Badger seemed the only one with any love invested in it. There was an oily haze in the air, but she was pretty sure that wasn't McCrindle's fault. "Sorry about the raccoons."

The man shrugged. "Not the worst thing that's happened," he said. He wasn't quite lying, but his conversational colors took on some gray. "And I'll get a nice bit of money out of it. There're laws against poisoning large animals in cities for this reason.

"Now, what can I do for you? You're not here to browse, or you'd have turned and run as soon as you came in."

"I'm with the MPD," Rachel replied. Unless she was trying to intimidate someone, she usually avoided mentioning she was OACET's liaison to the police, not unless she was willing to answer questions like, *"You're a cyborg?"* and *"Are you really a cyborg?"*

She took one of Jason's replicas out of her purse and held it up as a prop. "We're investigating a robbery. These were taken from a secure location that required substantial planning to access, so we know they were after a specific object."

"A bank vault?" His colors lit up with the notion of a movie-style theft.

"Let's go with that," Rachel said, grinning, and began placing the rest of the replicas on the table. "I'm not at liberty to disclose the details."

"A museum heist!" McCrindle made an eager sound. "How wonderful! When do you think the story will break? I can keep quiet for a week, but I can't promise any longer than that."

Rachel laughed. "One thing at a time. I'm just here to learn if you've had any customers interested in these pieces, or ones like them."

"Yes, yes," he said. "May I touch these?"

She slid the replicas towards him. McCrindle picked up the one closest to him, a bracelet shaped from a spray of flowers. "Plastic?"

"3D-printed replicas," she replied, and then tapped that oddly-shaped sixth lump. "But this one is printed in metal."

"Are these life-sized?"

"Yes."

"Interesting technique," he said. "Loses a lot of detail of the original piece, and the colors are terrible, but good enough for Show and Tell, right? I assume you've got photographs?"

Rachel called up the archivists' records on her tablet, and McCrindle busied himself between the six objects and their dossiers. He was polite enough to not ask questions about the black lines running through certain facts, such as the donors' and recipients' names, or fish around for other clues.

She lost track of time as he worked, and allowed her scans to roam around the store. She found the raccoons—three of them, about ten days dead and ripe to the point of bursting—in the wall behind the buffalo's head. By the door, an ordered wall of colored glass bowls glowed, lit by strands of LEDs running along the shelving. There were books by the hundreds in a dozen different display cabinets, and paintings and portraits and all manner of photographs covering every inch of exposed wall space.

Aside from the stench, the store felt warm and homey. It took her a moment to realize it reminded her of OACET headquarters.

"Okay," McCrindle said. She turned her scans back to him, as he slid the metal object towards her. "This is what you're looking for."

"What?"

"To answer your question, no. I've had no customers asking after any of these items. But nobody would ask after any of these five," he said, as he pushed the plastic objects aside.

"Why not? Our specialists tell us they might be rare collectables."

"Oh, these are rare," he said. "And precious, and valuable, and all of that horseshit. You can also get ones just like them through any good antiques broker. If you're looking for something special…" he said, and slid the metal object towards Rachel, "… this is it."

He looked into her eyes. "…but you already knew that."

She glanced away as a reply.

He sighed, and rolled the object over the back of his fingers, like a magician with a misshapen coin. "It's got a history, this does. Came from a shipwreck, the file says?"

Rachel nodded.

"Lots of things out there, at the bottom of the sea," McCrindle said. He stood and made his way to a nearby floor safe, spun the dial and opened the lock, and returned with a bundle of white cotton cloth. He flipped a corner of the cloth back to show a piece of metal similar to the one already on the table.

"An orichalcum ingot," he said, his professional blues moving within pleased pinks. "I'm holding it for a buyer. You might have heard about it—Plato mentioned orichalcum when he described Atlantis."

"*The entire circuit of the wall, which went round the outermost zone, they covered with a coating of brass, and the circuit of the next wall they coated with tin, and the third, which encompassed the citadel, flashed with the red light of orichalcum,*" she said quietly. The ingot in the white cloth didn't glow in the slightest, let alone flash with a red light, but Rachel was willing to give it the benefit of the doubt.

"You know Plato's *Critias?*" McCrindle said, impressed, as he moved to return the ingot to his safe.

Shit. Rachel winced. She hadn't introduced herself as an Agent, and hadn't thought to censor herself before quoting the online text aloud.

McCrindle didn't notice. "Not too many of these out there," he said, yanking on the safe's lever to make sure the door was locked. "They discovered about forty ingots off the coast of Sicily, and the rest have turned up here and there. Turns out this mythic metal is just an alloy mostly made from copper and zinc. The only thing that makes it special is its history."

"So what's this?" Rachel said, picking up her own piece of mystery metal. "Another orichalcum ingot?"

"I doubt it. It's a part of something. Look here," he said, and pulled up an image of the fragment on her tablet. "You see these jagged edges? Your piece broke off of something much larger. And it's got writing on it."

Rachel flipped the image around in her mind, but saw nothing resembling writing. "Ah, Mr. McCrindle…"

"Oscar, please," he said. "Yes, that's writing. The original fragment needs to be cleaned to bring out the details, but it's definitely got an inscription on it. A big one, too. Covers the entire surface."

"Hm," Rachel muttered, her scans trying to penetrate beneath the surface of Jason's metal printout. There was nothing there but more metal. If there was an inscription on the original, it hadn't transferred to its clone.

"In my opinion, that's why your museum got robbed," he said. "The thief wanted this because of its history, or the inscription, or both. Although why your museum never bothered to clean it…"

"They didn't keep this item on display," Rachel answered.

"No excuse," he grumbled to himself, and his colors moved to a self-satisfied pink as he gazed proudly at his spotless (albeit odorous) store. "All right then, can I do anything else for you?"

"Thanks, but you've been extremely helpful," Rachel said. "If somebody does approach you to buy or sell, though, they're dangerous. Don't stall them. Just treat them like any other customer, get their contact information, and call me as soon as they're gone."

He nodded. "Of course. Got a card?"

This time, he saw her flinch, and his colors moved towards an uncertain orange-yellow, no doubt wondering to whom he had really been speaking (or, perhaps, what kind of murder-of-the-week scenario was about to unfold in his store). "Ah… Detective Peng?"

She passed him one of her business cards. "Agent Peng, actually."

He blinked, a thread of curious yellow winding its way into his uncertainty, and then saw her title on the card. "Office of Adaptive and… *Oh.*" Sage green comprehension moved into his conversational colors, tempered with blue relief. "That'll teach me to check a badge first. I thought you were about to…"

"I'm the OACET liaison to the MPD," she said. "I get a lot of resistance when I introduce myself with my full title." Oscar McCrindle seemed like a good person; she supposed she could run the "Yes, I really am a cyborg" gauntlet for him.

"I've always wanted to meet a—an OACET. I mean, meet an Agent…"

"It's okay," she assured him. "I get this a lot."

McCrindle laughed, a little nervously. "I should've guessed when you knew the *Critias*. Nobody's bothered to memorize that in millennia. Were you reading that aloud?"

"Yeah. But to be fair, I have read it a few times," she said. "I love poetry, and my mom's an architect. It's hard to beat Plato for stupid-long flowery descriptions of buildings."

"Huh," he grunted. He looked down at her card again, and the sage green came back in a strong surge of color. "I didn't recognize your name at first. You're the one who stole the owl."

It took her a little time to work that one through. She had performed many a questionable deed in her twenty-eight years, but she was sure she'd remember—"Oh! The wooden owl from the coffee shop?"

"Yes. When you walked off with it, you caused a bit of a fuss in the local antiques community. Do you still have it?"

Of course Rachel still had it. Madeline was the only personal item on her office desk, a memento of her and Santino's first successful case. With Jason's help, she had digitized every single carved claw and feather, and turned Madeline into her personal animal avatar. But she just nodded and said, "Yes. It's safe."

"Good," McCrindle said. "It's got an amazing story, if you'd like to hear it."

She was sorely tempted, but she already knew her owl had history. It had been beautiful, once upon a time. Most of its paint had been rubbed off through misuse, and there was a shallow scar down its left side that looked as if a chainsaw had made a pass at it and barely missed. Teeth marks on its base suggested it had been used as a chew toy for a large dog, or maybe a small lion. It had suffered water damage and erosion and all manner of abuse, but the old wood was still rock-hard and had kept itself intact. No matter what it had endured, it was still an owl.

"No," Rachel said. "It's got a new story now."

His conversational colors began weaving her Southwestern turquoise into the sage greens: McCrindle was trying to figure her out. "Interesting," he said. "Not what someone in my line of work likes to hear, though. Things without stories are just things. It's the pieces which form the wholes."

"Maybe I'll come back," Rachel told him, and as soon as she had said it, she realized she would be back. In fact, she knew she'd be back within the week with a court order, a crowbar, and the professional trauma cleaning service the MPD used after an especially morbid crime scene.

"Any time," he said, his colors a warm and friendly yellow.

SIX

Sunday was one of those bright days in early spring that brought the entire city out of hibernation. Washington D.C. was a place of parks and open spaces: on a weekend such as this, the first truly warm weekend of the year, there were farmers' markets and bicycle races and streets jammed full with food trucks and their happy customers. The cherry blossom festival was still a few weeks away, but the tourists were already beginning to arrive, smiling from their unexpected sunshine shots of Vitamin D.

If you were a murderer wanted by the Secret Service, you could do worse than to plan your getaway on such a Sunday.

They couldn't be sure their suspect hadn't left the city. Due diligence with security footage from the usual places—airports, bus stops, rental car companies, highways, traffic cameras, and the like—hadn't pinned her down. But their suspect had already proven she was good with makeup, so it was anyone's guess as to whether they were wasting their time looking for a fiery thirty-something when they should have been searching for a tottering grandmother.

Alimoren had decided to act as if the suspect was still in town. The FBI was chasing out-of-state and international leads, but unless their suspect was also counterfeiting hundred-dollar bills, Alimoren had little authority to pursue an arrest outside of the city limits. He had rallied his staff and the MPD, and had begun a localized manhunt.

(Rachel was sure the suspect had thrown on a new identity and driven straight to Manhattan as soon as she left the White House, but nobody had asked her opinion, and she was pretty sure Alimoren shared it.)

They had set up their operations office in a hotel conference room. As logistics went, a hotel in downtown D.C. was more centrally located than the Secret Service's headquarters out by the Anacostia River, or even the MPD's flagship building on Indiana Avenue. The hotel district near Embassy Row allowed easy access to museums, subways, parks, shopping, fine dining…all the usual places a savvy criminal might decide to use as her smokescreen.

Plus, convenient on-site parking. Even the White House didn't offer that.

Rachel had her feet up on a table, and was enjoying a good cup of coffee and her third cinnamon bun. Hill was sprawled in the chair beside hers, a baseball cap pulled low as he pretended to catnap. The two of them had agreed hours ago that a catered stakeout was by far the best kind of stakeout. Sit back and let the computers do all the work? Yes, please!

A couple of feet away was a bank of monitors that had been set up on folding tables. Jason Atran, sitting in his own office across the city, was coaching a digital imaging specialist from the MPD in how to use his own proprietary blend of facial recognition software.

"—knew how to use it, we'd be done by now."

Rachel moved her attention from the cinnamon bun to the MPD's specialist, who was slowly turning red with suppressed rage. "Yes, but—" the specialist began.

"Listen," Jason said, his voice as crisp within the room as if he had been standing there (which he was, but only Rachel could see his avatar as it stomped around and fumed in bright green). "You're used to *shit* software any monkey can program. Mine requires a brain to use."

"Gonna do something?" Hill rumbled softly.

"Nope," Rachel said, much more loudly. "I'm not his mom. If he wants to be an asshole and alienate his coworkers, then he can deal with the fallout."

Jason's avatar scowled at her, but he took a breath and nodded. The Jason on the monitor then said, "Sorry. Okay. Let's try this again. Normal facial recognition systems uses established facial features and comparing them to an existing database. You're using older methods. Statistical algorithms, mostly. Your program examines features, such as the space between the eyes, the contours of the face...mostly single-vector items. You can trick the system if you're smart and good with makeup, which we know your suspect is. So, you need to use my software, which doesn't rely on those older algorithms."

"We *can't* use better software," the specialist said. Her reds were fading, but orange was moving up to replace them: she wasn't as angry at Jason as she was at the resources provided to her by the MPD. "The software's not the problem—the problem is the cameras. Some of our traffic cameras haven't been replaced in a decade. Why should we invest in 3D or imaging software when the cameras have poor resolution?"

"That's why you need my software," Jason said. "There are more cameras now than there were when your programs were written. Mine bundles two or more perspectives into the same image."

The MPD's digital specialist leaned towards the screen so quickly her folding chair nearly shot out from under her. "So you've got multiple cameras working simultaneously—"

"Yes," Jason said, his old grin peeking around the edges. "I can trick old cameras into generating 3D images. But it requires an insane amount of processing power, so if you can help me pick out no more than ten likely sites..."

Rachel, reassured that Jason wasn't about to do any new damage to OACET's reputation, went back to ignoring him. She let her scans sweep through the walls, and into the hotel lobby. She watched as excitable travelers and bored employees shifted into distinctive pops of color. Not for the first time, she wished core and conversational colors showed up on camera: it'd be relatively easy to pick out a suspect based on a core color, and much harder to conceal a core by changing a wardrobe or a face.

Maybe in a couple of years, she thought to herself. *Get Mako to figure out exactly how I perceive colors, and get him to replicate that frequency...*

But if she did that, then she'd have to disclose that she also perceived emotions, and if she did *that*, then there'd be a mad rush on assessing the extent of her abilities, and how these applied to the Fourth Amendment, and whether she violated personal privacy, and...and...

Maybe in a couple of centuries.

"Mako says he wants you to drop by his office," Hill said.

"How do you do that?" she asked him. "I was just thinking about him."

"Psychic."

"Come on."

He smiled. "You're easy to read."

That she believed. "What does he want?"

Hill shrugged.

"Right." Mako Hill couldn't be more different than his cousin. For one thing, Mako actually enjoyed talking. She nearly reached out through the link to ping the other Agent and ask him what he wanted, but stopped herself in time: she wasn't quite ready to turn her day over to incomprehensible mathematical formulae.

She was, however, ready to do something—*anything!*—other than spy on the Secret Service.

Over pizza the night before, Zockinski had made an excellent point. Yes, it might be common knowledge that gifts of state were kept in the White House basement, and yes, a collector might have spotted an object that he wanted in a database, but how would that collector know the best way to get access to the basement would be through slipping a ringer into a superstar's entourage? Or that the poonhound with a reputation for sneaking off into the storerooms with the ladies would be working late that night?

The four of them had poked at that question until a single answer popped up: someone at the White House had told the collector how to break in.

Then, they played process of elimination. It hadn't been

an archivist, as they could have removed the object from the storeroom themselves. They didn't think had been a politician because... Well, the four of them didn't have a good reason to explain that, other than observing the inner operational workings of small organizations didn't seem to be in the wheelhouse of most politicians, and politicians had bigger crimes to commit, besides.

Which left the staff and security, and since they were playing a rousing game of *Most Likely Suspects*, they decided to start with the Secret Service. A staffer, like an archivist, could scoot in and out of a storeroom without raising any questions—hell, they had video footage of the murderer and her victim doing that very thing!—but it'd be harder for a member of the Secret Service to explain their presence in an unused corner of the basement.

And maybe, as Santino had pointed out, this wasn't the first time that the storerooms had been robbed. There were multiple items still unaccounted from the stacks. Maybe these thefts had been going on for years, beginning after the archivists had completed the inventory, and this was just the first time there was evidence of a crime. After all, if the staffer hadn't been murdered...

They decided to start with the Secret Service. They had no real evidence, just half-formed suspicions, so Rachel and Hill were crowd-watching while Santino and Zockinski went to talk to Alimoren about how well he knew his own people.

So far, the morning had been a waste of time. She was watching for telltale bursts of color, such as those yellow-white blooms of intense energy that marked excitement, or the reds of something gone wrong. If there was a change in the case, the mood spectrum of the entire room would shift, and she'd be searching for the odd man out. Or, if news came in which meant nothing except to those deeply involved, their colors would give them away. She had seen the normal pops and color changes which marked all social interactions, but for the most part the Secret Service wore the professional blues of work that needed doing.

She didn't know what Hill was looking for, but she trusted him to tell her if he saw it.

In the meantime, they watched and waited, and ate cinnamon buns.

Her scans...*pulsed*. She wished there was another word for it, that distinct sensation of movement when her implant wanted her attention and she hadn't preprogrammed a signal. The closest description she had was when the dental hygienist found a thin spot on the enamel, and not-quite-cold pressure pushed against her mind.

She followed its prompt, and cast her scans back into the lobby. Through the walls, autumn orange and cobalt blue walked side by side, a step behind worn-out blues: Zockinski and Santino, following Mitch Alimoren. The Secret Service agent was bright red. Apparently, the conversation had gone as expected.

Rachel dragged her feet off of the table, and gave Jason's avatar a nod as she headed towards the door. Hill stood and pretended to stretch before following her.

"One of these days, you're going to follow me into the bathroom."

He grinned at her. "Not likely."

They met up with the three men in the lobby. Alimoren was furious; if his conversational colors hadn't given it away, she could have read his anger in the set of his shoulders.

"In here," he said, pointing at the hotel's courtesy business center. They moved into the empty room. Smartphones and hotel-wide Wi-Fi had rendered the room obsolete; Rachel guessed the last time someone had used the fax machine puttering idly on its dusty table was weeks ago.

Alimoren turned on them, his anger lashing out like red-tipped whips. "I wanted to say this once we were all together," he said quietly. "I'm grateful for your help. I appreciate your attention to detail. But if you think I haven't already considered that my own teammates might be responsible, you are seriously mistaken. I've got people I trust conducting an internal review. Don't make a bad situation worse by throwing accusations around without proof."

Alimoren's brief speech left her properly chastised. The others, too: shame was a thin, watery red, and it began to seep into their conversational colors.

Zockinski took point. "Would you like us to leave?"

"No." Alimoren ran a hand over his face. Exhaustion seeped from him like a wet gray cloud. "Of course not. You're doing your jobs, and it's a question I'm going to have to get used to. Just…"

"…let you pursue this part of the investigation?" Santino asked, when Alimoren seemed unable to find the right words.

The Secret Service agent nodded. His anger hadn't vanished, but it was pulling back as he worked his way through it. "Yes."

Poor guy, Rachel thought. Someone at the Secret Service was going to lose their job after the story finally broke. Alimoren was too close to this, and he must have known he'd be considered a good candidate for public sacrifice. Deep beneath his angry reds was a sickly nervous yellow.

They were turning to leave when Jason pinged her.

"Rachel?"

"One sec," she said to the group. Then, she joined Jason in the link. *"What's up?"*

"I've got a hit with a sixty percent positive." He felt her confusion, so he added more words. *"Facial recognition? Remember?"*

"Oh!" She waved at Alimoren, then grabbed the nearest computer screen. "Mitch Alimoren, the lead from the Secret Service, is here," she said aloud for Alimoren's benefit. "I'm touching a monitor. Access it and talk to him directly."

The screen hummed into an image of Jason's face. "Jason Atran, OACET," Jason said. The image of his face jumped, and Rachel goosed the connection to keep the signal steady. "The MPD and I are monitoring eight locations with high foot traffic throughout downtown D.C. We just got our first possible positive."

"Possible or probable?" Alimoren asked. His conversational colors had paused, as if he was holding his breath, the professional blues pushing against an eager yellow-white.

"Possible," Jason said. "Sixty percent."

Alimoren nodded, his colors unsticking themselves as the blues washed his excitement away. "That's pretty low."

"It's the highest we've gotten so far," Jason replied. "Here."

Rachel felt Jason take the signal from her as he moved data around. A new face appeared on the screen, a woman with short brown hair. "This is a composite we created from images taken from three different camera angles," he said. "I wouldn't mention this information to a lawyer. Composites are easy to pick apart in court."

Alimoren studied the image, bright strands of blue and a thin thread of yellow-white weaving into each other as he tried to decide the right course of action. The blue swallowed the yellow-white into itself a second time, and Rachel guessed that the composite didn't look enough like the suspect to get his hopes up. "Okay," Alimoren said. "I'll send a team to check it out. When and where was this taken?"

"Two minutes ago, at the Dupont Circle Metro Station."

Alimoren's yellow-white flashed, a mirror of everyone else's conversational colors. Dupont Circle was less than three blocks away. "What?"

"I work fast," Jason said with a smirk.

"Still got her on camera?" Rachel asked him.

"No. I'm searching for her now. I'll keep you posted."

Jason's signal vanished, and the group rushed back to the conference room. Once there, she watched Alimoren pick and choose from among his own men. Santino nudged her, and she sighed and stepped forward to make sure they weren't overlooked.

Most Sundays, Dupont Circle was transformed from a city park to a busy farmers' market. Men and women walked by in shirts with too little fabric, pretending the early spring sun was enough to keep them warm. Some of the nearby roads were closed to thru traffic, allowing food trucks and produce stands to spring up like organic mushrooms and fill the air with the heavenly smells of ripe vegetables and Korean BBQ. The stores along the streets leading to Dupont Circle were open for business, with sidewalk sales and smiling bakers offering fresh-baked pastries. The backdrop to this cheerful chaos was modern office buildings competing for space with embassies, with bankers and hairdressers sharing counter space with ambassadors at their local coffee houses.

Sometimes Rachel loved living in D.C.

Alimoren had managed to secure a handicapped spot on the east corner of Dupont Circle for the surveillance van. Rachel and Santino had ridden along with him and his team, Secret Service agents dressed for undercover work. Alimoren's team was fiddling with micro-fitted earpieces, tiny two-way devices that picked up not only Alimoren's radio commands, but also the vibrations from speech so the team members could talk to one another. Their communications expert offered one to Santino, who declined in favor of his phone and Bluetooth headset, and then Rachel, who had to quickly hide her grin behind her hand.

"I'm good," she assured him. "Just let me observe your frequencies."

The man blinked in curious yellows before leaning towards the van's microphone. "Testing?"

"Received," Rachel replied. The Secret Service agent's colors lit up, and she grinned back at him. "You never see my lips move or nuthin'!" she said aloud.

"We should always be so lucky," Santino said. Her partner was coated in the sallow green that he often wore when the cyborgs showed off their abilities. It was part jealousy, part misery, and part knowing that he was, by OACET's standards, less capable.

"All right," Alimoren said, and the chatter in the van broke off. "I'm going to allow some leeway today. If you see anyone matching the description on the warrant, bring her in for questioning. If you find anyone who *almost* matches the description on the warrant, bring her in for questioning. We're here to do due diligence, so be duly diligent."

His team nodded, and they began to file out the passenger's side door. Surveillance tactics and common sense dictated that an entire van full of people not leap out from the back all at once, but Rachel considered it just as suspicious to have a dozen men and women step out of the car in ones and twos, like the van was chock-full of clowns in their street clothes.

Rachel let them leave before turning to Alimoren. "What does the warrant cover?"

He turned from the console, his colors a blend of annoyed and confused oranges. "What?"

"You know Agents can scan for concealed firearms, right?" she said, and some of the annoyed orange fell away. "So, if I locate someone who might qualify as a suspect, will the warrant cover me if I search them at a distance?"

Alimoren's uncertainty grew. "I don't know. It's not something I've thought about."

That was a half-truth: he had thought about it, but not to the extent where he had decided it impacted him.

"It's better if I obey the letter of the law at all times, rather than risk your case getting tossed in court. If I can't do that, I'll stay in the truck and help Jason with the cameras," Rachel said.

"No, go ahead and join my team," Alimoren said. "A dead body in the White House gets you a really friendly judge. The warrant permits full-person searches, and doesn't get too specific about the details."

"All right," she said. "I won't be on the radio line unless something happens. Having a bunch of voices in my head isn't good for me during surveillance duty."

And with that, she hopped out the passenger door of the van to join her partner on the sidewalk.

Rachel had realized early on in working with the detectives that there was a high possibility she'd be turned into the team's portable intercom system, so she had squashed that notion as quickly as Zockinski had brought it up. Yes, she *could* run a four-way phone call, but so could the phone company, and *they* didn't have to worry about accidentally shooting a bystander because they were distracted by the chatter in their heads. She insisted on limiting her conversations to one other person, and that was usually Santino. If the four of them absolutely had to talk to each other? Well, that's why the MPD had a contract with Motorola. It was easy for her to pass this same message to Alimoren, and let him know that it was her duty as a responsible Agent to stay off of the party line until such time as she was needed.

(In respect to Zockinski and Hill, it helped that they had been partners long before she had come to the MPD. She located them through their cell phone signals, and then watched their conversational colors as they moved through the crowd, pacing each other like wolves selecting a deer for dinner. There was a good twenty feet between them; they appeared to ignore each other, but their colors shifted in unison as they examined one suspicious-seeming person, then another, and so on as they walked back and forth across the square. The two men were already so deep in each other's heads that they had no need for Rachel.)

She and Santino strolled down Massachusetts Avenue. Santino stopped for a corndog, claiming that he needed a prop to help them blend in with the tourists and the local foodies. When Rachel said he looked nothing like a tourist and no self-respecting foodie would touch a corndog, he added a side of chili.

"Why didn't you take an earpiece?" she asked him. The button-sized devices seemed like the type of technology Santino would love to add to his roster.

He tapped his glasses. "Bell and I've already played around with them. We thought we could integrate them into the design so we can hear OACET's projections, too. There's a feedback problem we can't figure out. I'll stick with Bluetooth until we fix it."

"But you look like a dork. Authentic Vincent Vega in a Banana Slug tee-shirt dork."

He shrugged, purple humor running across the simple red pleasure of his chili corndog.

They were walking through a cluster of Japanese tourists when Jason stepped into her mind without so much as a courtesy ping. *"Rachel?"*

"Jesus, Jason! Knock first!"

He ignored her, and pushed an image into her head. *"This is live from the traffic camera on Q Street."*

Rachel staggered out of the foot traffic, and found a convenient niche against a building. Jason's link was so strong it made it hard for her to think, and she couldn't see anything other than the live feed of a brunette crossing a busy road he had dumped straight into her head.

She pushed, hard, until he backed off and she could inspect the feed. *"This is the same woman from your composite?"*

"Yeah," he replied.

Rachel watched her move, and thought: *Nope. No way it's her.* The woman at the White House had been confident, measured. This woman was dressed like a well-kept soccer mom, and moved as if her mind was somewhere else.

Jason heard her. *"She's a block away and heading towards the farmers' market. Go check her out."*

"My eyes don't work, Jason. I don't see faces. I see the people under them. It's not her."

He paused. *"And you think I'm arrogant."*

"Fine." She snapped the word and their link at the same moment so he wouldn't realize he had struck home.

Santino was pretending to check his phone as he used his body to shelter hers from the sidewalk traffic. "Everything okay?"

"Yup," she replied. "Jason says the suspect is one block north." She turned and started walking back the way they came, towards the bustle of the farmers' market. "I figure we can get to the market ahead of her, then wait and watch as she makes the rounds."

"Sounds good," Santino said. He placed a quick call to Alimoren to update him. By the time he was done, they had crossed back into the marketplace. "Separate or stick together?"

"Separate," she said. The average person tended to notice mixed-race couples more quickly than they would notice either her or Santino if they were alone. She scanned the market, and saw that Zockinski's autumn orange and Hill's forest green were still working the crowd. "I'll go west."

Her partner nodded, and touched his Bluetooth headset. *"Test."*

"Loud and clear," he told her, and then turned to lose himself in the marketplace.

Rachel meandered towards the food trucks. They hadn't had them in California, not during those five lost years, and they were something of a novelty to her. She nodded towards an older Middle Eastern man selling cheese and dumplings out of a brand-new truck, and wondered if she could scratch up enough spare change from the bottom of her purse to get herself a couple of potato knishes for dinner.

Then, her scans caught on a core of bluish gray, and she nearly gave herself whiplash in her mad rush to track it to its source.

No, she though. *It can't be him! The color's off. More of a poppy-seed gray than a cartoonish seal gray... Besides, that's a woman. That's...*

...oh hell no!

The woman still looked and moved like a stylish soccer mom, but it was likely as carefully constructed a persona as the one she had worn to the White House. Rachel's scans met a thick layer of makeup that changed her complexion and the finer contours of her face. Professional blues dominated her conversational colors, and these lashed out and pried apart each person she passed as she searched for someone within the crowd.

She reached out to Santino's phone. *"Positive ID,"* she told him. *"How do I spin this for Alimoren?"*

She heard him fumble with the headset. "You made her by

her...y'knows?" he whispered.

Rachel dropped back behind the food trucks to keep out of the suspect's line of sight. *"Her colors, yeah."*

"How sure you are that you've got the right person?"

"Sure enough to ping Jason and thank him."

Rachel followed the woman from the other side of the food carts. The suspect's face was thinner, her eyebrows altered to look further apart. Her hair was a different color and cut after she had lost the red wig, and she now sported a longish brown bob. She was wearing a trendy but loose jacket, and a pair of Armani jeans that looked painted to her body but moved easily when she walked. A stylish pair of sneakers finished the outfit: she was ready to run if she needed to.

"She knows she could be caught," Rachel mused through the phone line. *"She's definitely here for a reason."*

"Maybe a handoff?" Santino asked. "Is she carrying the object?"

Rachel started to protest. She always tried to avoid prodding around clothing and what lay beneath. Larger devices, like guns and most knives, she could pick out no problem, but they were chasing a piece of metal the size of her palm and that involved a slower, more...*thorough* set of scans.

"Just do it," Santino muttered. They'd had this discussion many times before. "You heard Alimoren. We've got a warrant for her so it's legal, and if you asked someone if they'd rather have you stare at their naked bodies or pry into their minds, I bet nine times out of ten they'd rather be naked."

"Reading emotions is not the same as reading minds," she said, as she fine-tuned her scans to go through pockets and purses and all manner of private places. *"And who's part of a hivemind here anyway, you or me? I'd much rather have someone in my head than staring at my body."*

"Yeah, right. Ask Zockinski which he'd rather... Y'know, this might be a gendered issue."

"Jesus, Santino. Go write a paper on it."

"Good idea!"

"*Shut up,*" she muttered. The connection with her partner fell silent as he placed a call to Alimoren to bring the Secret Service up to speed.

Rachel reached the end of the chain of food trucks. Rather than loop back and overlap with the Secret Service agents coming towards her, she opted to park her butt against a convenient lamppost. An awning had come loose and hung from its metal frame; Rachel figured that if she kept her face behind the printed vinyl, she'd be as well-concealed as if she was still hiding behind the trucks. She took her tablet out of her purse for an excuse to stand against the post, while a hundred feet and a row of farm stands away, Miss Armani pretended to shop for tomatoes.

"Well? Anything?" Santino was back on the phone line.

"*Give me a minute. I'm being as careful as I can. I don't think the warrant covers learning if she's got an IUD.*"

The mystery object wasn't in the suspect's purse or pockets. Rachel took a breath, and went deeper.

"*Cleavage,*" she reported to Santino.

"I'm a big fan."

"*No, asshole, there's a travel wallet stuck between—*"

Her partner was laughing at her. "I know. I'll tell Alimoren." Their connection fell silent again.

Rachel forced herself to relax, and shifted her butt around to try and get comfortable. It was a pleasant morning; there were worse ways to spend her time than waiting for the bust to happen. She flipped around in the contents of her tablet. Josh had archived an entire file of baby animal pictures for her, a fallback for those days when she needed an Emergency Kitten, stat.

She had her face firmly planted in her tablet: anybody watching her would have seen just another nobody at the farmers' market, killing time online as she waited for her friends to finish shopping.

Except for Miss Armani, who had made the turn around the farm stands just as a chill spring breeze tossed the awning around, and whose conversational colors suddenly changed from professional blues to an unmistakable Southwestern turquoise.

SEVEN

"Santino!"

"What?"

Rachel kept her head down and her scans fixed to Miss Armani. *"She recognized me!"*

"She made you?"

"No! She knows my core color! She recognized me!"

The suspect knelt to pet a passing puppy, laughing. There was no orange within her colors, but the professional blue had hardened around the turquoise.

"I'm joining the Secret Service's party line. She's not nervous. She's got something planned."

She heard Santino talking in a low voice, and then Alimoren asked: "Peng?"

"Here. Suspect recognized me. She's unarmed but confident, and carrying the object."

"Are you sure?"

"Yes. It's a thing I can—" Rachel caught herself before she went on the defensive, and redirected the conversation to take herself out of it. *"I scanned her to locate the object. She's got it strapped under her bra, but she's not carrying a gun."*

"What about poison?"

Shit, Rachel swore to herself, and heard Santino chuckle nervously as her private thoughts were broadcast to the Secret Service. *"She's wearing another huge watch, but I can't check her for poison. Not unless you buy me more time to run frequencies."*

"We don't have it," Alimoren said to Rachel. Then, to the others: "She's not carrying a gun, but proceed as if suspect is armed and dangerous. Somebody find a set of gloves. Work gloves, heavy-duty ones."

Miss Armani had left the dog and its owner, and was walking

back towards the food carts.

"Agent Peng?" Alimoren's voice came on the line. "Does she know you spotted her?"

"She's not acting spooked, but..." Rachel mulled it over. *"Yeah, probably. If she knows about me, she knows I can see through walls. She'll figure you put me here to keep an eye on her."*

"I should've kept you back at the van," Alimoren said. "Okay, we're coming in. Peng, don't move."

"Gotcha." Rachel said, resolved to scroll through an entire gigabyte of cuddly animal pictures before getting involved.

At the end of the row of farmers' carts, two men in casual clothing and hard professional blues turned towards Miss Armani. Rachel watched as the suspect made them, her colors weaving as she weighed her options. Then, her colors reclaimed Rachel's turquoise core, and she turned back towards the Agent.

"Shit. Alimoren, she made your guys. She's coming back towards me."

"Hang on, Peng." Hill's voice was calm and steady. She pinged his signal and found him flanking the suspect.

Miss Armani noticed him, too. She was close enough to wink at Rachel as she tapped the face of her watch with two fingers.

"Hill, back off!"

The big man did, passing Miss Armani at a safe distance. She watched him leave, then nodded to Rachel.

"There are too many people here, Peng," Alimoren said. "Pull out. We'll get her when she tries to leave."

"What if she takes a hostage?"

"Then we'll deal with it, but I don't want to force her hand."

"Right," Rachel said, and pretended to finish up her business before dropping her tablet into her purse. Miss Armani was closing fast, her conversational colors rich with Southwestern turquoise. *"Alimoren, she's coming up on me."*

"You're covered." Alimoren was all business. "She draws anything on you, we'll put her on the ground."

Rachel wondered if maybe that's what Miss Armani had planned: the Secret Service and the MPD were trained for chest shots. That metal fragment would be reduced to so much dust by the time they were through with her. Then again, nothing about the suspect suggested she was suicidal—not her colors, not her posture, and definitely not her confident smile.

"Don't," Rachel said. *"She's not armed, and I won't let her touch me. Connecting to Santino's phone and all lines within one meter of his in 3...2...1..."*

She heard Santino telling those around him to gather around him and take out their phones, and she looped her perspective through his device and those nearest to him.

(She hoped all of those signals were associated with the MPD or the Secret Service. She didn't have time to be selective, and there was a decent chance some family type couldn't figure out why his phone was suddenly showing an attractive brunette bearing down on him. Not to mention that if she got caught hijacking a protected phone line, she'd find herself in crazy-hot water with the FCC, the FBI, the NSA, and every other acronym with a vested interest in secure communications.)

"Agent Peng." Miss Armani's voice was strong, an accent placing her as French. Rachel would have bet a large sum of money on it being fake.

"Didn't catch your name," Rachel said.

Miss Armani waved a hand, as if her name wasn't of concern. "How many guns are on me now?"

"Enough. They're worried about poison. They'll shoot you if you try to touch me."

"Of course," the woman said, keeping herself a clean five feet away from Rachel. "Please tell them I know I'm caught. I'll come quietly."

The lie was so smooth that Rachel didn't see the distinctive dimples in the other woman's colors. Pain rang through her like a bell before she realized what had happened: the suspect had kept her talking until she was on the other side of the lamppost and could take advantage of her arm's-length head start. Rachel had instinctively charged after her, turning so quickly that she had slammed the entire right side of her body against the metal post.

Rachel snarled and dove forward. The brunette had a lot of muscle and was dressed to run; Rachel was in a business suit, weighed down with an extra five pounds of gear, and today (of course) had been the day she went to work in that one pair of boots that had too much heel.

Miss Armani sprinted towards the door of a nearby coffee shop.

"Alimoren!" Rachel shouted in her mind, as she threw her purse to the ground and charged the door. *"Tell me you have somebody covering the rear exits!"*

"I pulled them off to cover you!"

Damn it! Miss Armani was too clever by far. Her confrontation with Rachel had been a feint used to draw Alimoren's backup into the marketplace.

Miss Armani raced through the open door of the coffee shop and yanked the handle as she passed. The door began to close, and it bought her a few more seconds as Rachel had to stop to haul it open. The store was a straight shot from front to back, and Miss Armani won another few precious seconds from Rachel by tipping a table and chairs to the ground behind her.

Alimoren shouted in Rachel's head until she yelled at him to shut him up, and then took herself off of the party line. She began sending her location to the map of D.C. on Santino's phone. Her partner could track their progress more efficiently than she could deliver a running commentary of street names.

And running it was—Miss Armani could *move.*

She was across the street before Rachel could clear the alley. Rachel jumped out of the way of an oncoming sedan, and found herself on the far sidewalk in the middle of the lunchtime mob.

The two of them raced through the crowd, Rachel hollering at anyone in earshot to trip the fleeing suspect. No good. They were over another street and within a public park before she could convince someone to stick a leg out. A uniformed MPD officer Rachel didn't recognize tried to intercept by boxing the suspect within one of D.C.'s ubiquitous memorials, but Miss

Armani was quicker. She was up and over the eight-foot fence like a monkey.

Right, Rachel thought, darting around the memorial and onto the straightaway of the road behind it. *Someday I need to hunt down the person who invented Parkour and break his knees.*

Miss Armani had put a couple of hundred feet between them and was trying to push the distance. She wasn't wearing anything digital. Shocking, really: these days, everyone beeped. If Rachel had been any other Agent, she might have lost her in the maze of D.C.'s parks and alleyways due to the lack of any signal to track. But she had a fix on Miss Armani's core of poppy-seed gray, and Miss Armani couldn't shake her short of dropping into a bucket of paint.

Miss Armani was starting to flag. She might have been able to get a head start through trickery and keep it through sheer speed, but Rachel relaxed with fifteen-mile jogs. Miss Armani didn't have the endurance to outlast her.

(Between now and then, Rachel was sure the blister on her ankle would swell up to the size of a small melon. She wished she could just shoot this woman and be done with it.)

The opening notes to N.W.A.'s "Fuck tha Police" chimed in her mind. Only God and Hill knew why Hill had told Rachel to use that as his ring tone.

"Busy," she told him.

"Where is she?"

"Check your map," Rachel replied, and then sent her location to Hill's phone. *"Corner of 18th and Riggs. Looks like she's trying to throw me off before she doubles back to the Dupont Circle Metro Station."*

Hill laughed. "Idiot," he said. "I'll call the Metro cops and have them waiting."

"I owe you a beer."

"Yup." He broke the connection without saying goodbye.

Rachel settled her stride into a decent rhythm and ignored the tugging at her ankle. Blisters she could live with; she was just thankful she hadn't bought those boots with the four-inch heels.

Miss Armani took two turns, back to back; the second turn took her across a busy street. She threw another hasty glance over her shoulder at Rachel, and saw the Agent closing the distance as she weaved through the moving hazards of the four-lane road.

Rachel waved to her.

Miss Armani put on as much speed as she could, but she was nearly spent. Threads of gray exhaustion were starting to wind their way out of her lungs to drag the blues down.

Rachel reached out to Hill's phone. *"I was wrong. She's not headed for the subway,"* she said when Hill answered. *"Can you keep tracking my signal? She's getting punchy and I don't know what she's going to try next."*

"Yeah." Hill hung up on her a second time.

Miss Armani was starting to panic. She kept checking on Rachel as she ran, quick peeks which happened more and more frequently as her colors shifted towards a frantic reddish-orange. A group of teenagers, heads buried in their smartphones and oblivious to the world, blocked a goodly part of the sidewalk; rather than push through them, Miss Armani made a hard right and tried to cut back across the four-lane road.

This time, the two of them weren't as lucky. Miss Armani narrowly missed being run down by a city taxi. The cab braked hard, its rear end bucking slightly to the side, as the driver leaned on the horn and swore out of his window. A curiosity slowdown on Rachel's side of the road followed, the drivers focused on Miss Armani as she staggered towards the sidewalk. They didn't notice Rachel, and she was left trying to avoid death and injury and their front bumpers. There was a tense moment when she realized it was either jump or lose her shins, and her feet landed on the hood of an old Mercedes before she was off and running again.

Thanks, she whispered to that little piece of Other living in her head. *I'm going to assume that was you,* she thought, as she dodged a flatbed truck (no acrobatics were needed this time, just a quick twist of her hips to skirt the chrome). *I know I could never jump on top of a moving car before you started messing around with my reflexes. I promise I'm getting us cookies when this is over.*

She hit the sidewalk, and noticed that Miss Armani was at the edge of her endurance and had begun to stumble. Rachel put on a fresh burst of speed and then, finally, was within shouting range.

"Hey! Braintrust!" she called out. "Want to stop? I can do this all day!"

Miss Armani tripped and fell, but caught herself before she hit the ground.

"Is that a yes?" Rachel jogged up to grab Miss Armani's arm before she realized it was another trick. The other woman was tired, yes, but she had taken those few moments to recover. She swung around to face Rachel, a quick fist leading. Rachel ducked and slipped under the woman's arm, then came up fast with a right hook. The woman took it across her jaw while swinging wide with her other fist. Rachel avoided this easily, throwing her weight to the side and smashing her opponent with a left cross in a perfect Dempsey roll.

It was a hard fact of Rachel's life that she was rarely able to cold-cock a man twice her size. She simply lacked the mass. The same went for when her opponent was another woman; less mass didn't necessarily mean less resilient, and the woman in Armani jeans knew how to take a punch. There was also the issue of poison: Rachel wasn't willing to risk anything other than rabbit punches, in and out before Miss Armani could tag her back.

The other woman stared at her, stunned but still fully conscious, and her colors crisped into firm blue resolution as she realized Rachel outclassed her in a drawn-out fight. Her eyes slid around Rachel towards the busy street.

"Don't even think about it," Rachel warned her, and moved across her path. No way was she running across that miniature highway again, not three times in the same day.

The competing reds of anger and panic flashed over and within themselves as Miss Armani tried to decide what to do. These snapped tight in a weave as she made a tight turn on the sidewalk. She cut left, sprinted down a utility alley, and tried to run across the gardens behind a row of high-end townhouses.

Rachel threw her scans down the street to get her bearings, and started chuckling to herself. This close to the center of Washington, almost every townhouse was either an embassy or the private residence of someone important enough to employ bodyguards. She counted to sixty as she smoothed down her suit coat. When the minute was up, she rang the bell of the third townhouse, a bright yellow mess covered in ivy and a flag she didn't recognize on the pole beside the door.

A man with the core color of a granite quarry appeared in the door's beveled window.

"MPD for pickup," she said.

He disappeared without a word. A few moments later, the door opened and two more large men hustled Miss Armani into Rachel's waiting handcuffs.

"Need me to fill out any paperwork—" Rachel started before the men slammed the door in her face. "Guess not.

"Well, come on," she said to Miss Armani. "Off to jail you go."

Rachel moved the woman to the curb and forced her to sit, legs crossed, on the pavement. Rachel leaned against the bumper of a nearby SUV, out of arm's reach but close enough to kick the suspect in the face if necessary.

The woman glared up at her. There was a mouse swelling over one eye, and she seemed to have developed a serious limp.

"Just in case you're thinking of blaming those on me," Rachel told her, "think again. I've been recording this whole lovely chase scene. I expect it to be a huge hit at the OACET holiday party. Which reminds me…you recognized me. Now, how did you do that?"

The woman in the Armani jeans shrugged. The gesture was somewhat muted by her pose and the handcuffs, but the message got through.

"Aw, c'mon," Rachel said. "The Secret Service agents are a couple of blocks away. This is your one chance to talk off of the record."

This time, the suspect replied. Her French accent had relocated somewhat closer to Quebec. "You just told me you were recording everything I say."

"Yeah, but I'm a consummate optimist. It's my single biggest failing."

"What?"

"Sunshine and kittens, everywhere I look."

"What?"

"Who told you how to break into the White House?"

Nothing.

"Okay, then," Rachel said, and resigned herself to silence.

Miss Armani glanced down the sidewalk, her colors turning over and under themselves as she judged her chances.

"Don't be an idiot," Rachel told her. "I'm not running you down more than once in the same day."

The woman didn't answer.

"Fine," Rachel said, and settled back for some impromptu sunbathing.

Hill arrived before the Secret Service, his long legs better equipped to navigate city streets and back alleys than any surveillance van. He took in Rachel leaning against the SUV, the motionless woman sitting on the ground.

"You didn't bring any coffee?" Rachel asked him.

He ignored her and knelt beside Miss Armani, and bent low to look her in the face. The suspect's colors wrapped tightly around herself, but Rachel didn't see any signs of Hill's forest green core within them.

"Is she talking?" Hill asked.

"Nope."

Hill's colors shifted towards a professional blue, with flecks of purple scattered across them. The purple grew stronger and pulled itself into a line pointing down towards Miss Armani. "What embassy is this?" he asked.

"Not sure. One of the Eastern European ones, I think," she said, playing along. It was always fun to watch Hill work. He was First MPD's best interrogator—he was the best interrogator she had ever seen, really. Rachel imagined some sort of crossroads deal had gone down, where the Devil traded Hill a silver tongue, but Hill could only use it a limited number of times before screeching demons came to drag him away.

"I ever tell you about the time I got jumped by those guys from Topanastan?"

"No?" She ran a quick search for the term and found that not only was the place a figment of his imagination, but the majority of results were for nude Jennifer Aniston photos. This was going to be good. "You did not."

"So my unit and I are just outside of Kabul," he said. "We're supposed to be running reconnaissance, but our lieutenant is a God-awful joke, and we all know he's sent us out because he doesn't know what else to do with us."

"And you get jumped."

"Of course we get jumped," Hill said. "We're lucky, things have started to calm down because winter is right around the corner. Nobody wants to be caught in an altercation, which could turn into a situation, which could turn into a firefight, which could turn into another battle."

"Right."

"These guys, they turn out to be from Topanastan. Nobody in my unit speaks whatever the hell version of Afghani they speak in Topanastan. They have two guys who speak maybe ten words of English each, and most of those are words are for fruit. Cherry, pomegranate, apple…"

"Got it." Rachel was keeping a close watch on Miss Armani's colors. The woman was staring off into space and feigning boredom, but her conversational colors were wrapped within Hill's core of forest green as she listened to his story.

"They took us back to camp and interrogated us for three days. You remember what they did over there."

"Hell yes," Rachel said, loosening the laces on her boots.

Blood flowed, and her sore ankle started to pound in time with her pulse. "Very effective interrogators. Lousy communicators, but great interrogators."

"Torture's not always physical, you know. Some of the guys in my unit had the skin stripped off of the soles of their feet, but me? They just…talked to me."

Rachel suppressed a shudder when she realized Hill wasn't lying. "I bet you learned a lot from them," she said. "About how to…talk."

"It's amazing how much talking you can do when you only share a couple of words. I still can't eat fruit," Hill said. He grinned at Miss Armani. "The Secret Service gets you first. You better talk to them, or you and I are going to have one long, involved conversation."

Neither Rachel nor Hill expected the woman to smile back. She did, traces of blue confidence returning. She was more comfortable talking than fleeing. "I *love* when it's long and involved," she said, rolling the words within her accent.

The van arrived, and Alimoren, pleased in pinks, decided to take her to Indiana Avenue. It was the closest MPD station, and as good a place as any to slam a suspect in a locked room until they figured out who had jurisdiction over the arrest. Rachel and Hill assumed they were done, but Alimoren tapped Rachel on the shoulder and sent her back in.

Problems with the chain of custody tended to summon defense attorneys, so Rachel watched from the sidelines as three female officers and a female Secret Service agent made sure that Miss Armani stripped to her skivvies. The wristwatch was removed by the Secret Service agent, who had taken the precaution of slipping a pair of heavy-duty construction gloves over a pair of skin-tight nitrile surgical ones.

They found the nylon travel wallet taped to her torso. Two of the officers carefully removed this, while the third made sure Miss Armani wasn't about to make another escape attempt.

Rachel held out a small Tupperware container, and an officer placed the nylon wallet in the bottom of the bin. Rachel ran a long, careful scan through it and came up clean: no small ticking bombs, and nothing that resembled poison, lurked inside the Velcroed folds.

The object itself, however, was fragile, held together by pockets of stone embedded within old, old bronze. It reminded her of scraps of coral, so thoroughly worn by the sea that shells and sand had fused into its structure.

She nodded to the officers, and walked out of the women's holding cells to rejoin the men.

"We got it," she confirmed, holding up the plastic bin in triumph.

Mitch Alimoren and the other members of the Secret Service team went blue in relief.

"How do you want to handle custody?" Zockinski asked Alimoren. He not-too-subtly nudged Rachel's foot with his own as he spoke.

She knew what he wanted. If Rachel wanted to, she could sweep in and yank Miss Armani away from Alimoren, and there wasn't a thing he could do about it. She had been the one who had slapped the cuffs on the suspect, and she was an Agent besides: as a member of OACET, she outranked most other federal officers. Her rank was legal doggerel left over from when OACET had been a Congressional wet dream, with the Agents' charter written so they had the authority to intrude wherever and however they deemed necessary in federal matters. They never invoked that clause of their charter if they could possibly avoid it. The longer they refrained from abusing that power, the more likely Congress would forget about it and the risks it posed.

So she smiled at Alimoren and said nothing, and when the Secret Service agent looked away, she kicked Zockinski in the shin.

The detective pulled her aside. "Come on, Peng," he whispered. "This'll look good for us."

"And what else do we get out of it?" she snapped. "The Secret Service is going to burn for this in the media. Letting them claim they found the item and the murderer is the best possible option for them."

"But they didn't," he growled. "*We* did."

Rachel almost never put herself in a showdown with Zockinski. She considered him a friend, for one thing, and she was pretty sure he knew—or at least had strong suspicions—she was blind. Staring him down was risky. She could mimic the kinesthetics of a person with working eyes easily enough, but prolonged eye contact practically shouted that something about her was broken.

She turned her cyborg stare on him, and he took a step back. "The Secret Service knows what we did," she whispered. "Everybody in the MPD'll know it, too. *Those're* the people I want to impress, not Oprah or Ellen or whoever's got the popular couch these days."

Rachel stomped off to put the door of a women's bathroom between her and Zockinski.

Sometimes she hated her job. Her *real* job, not the enjoyable crime-solving chores that came with working for the MPD. Mulcahy had put her at First District Station to make alliances within law enforcement, and to prove that OACET was worth keeping around. She had already done this with the MPD and several federal organizations. Today, she was working on the Secret Service, and Zockinski's professional ambitions weren't her concern.

By the time she left the bathroom, Miss Armani had been processed and sent down to Holding. Rachel followed the signal from Santino's phone, and joined the men from First MPD in front of Miss Armani's cell.

"Where'd Alimoren go?" she asked.

Zockinski didn't look at her. His core of autumn orange appeared redder than usual, his anger coloring the rest of his emotions, but there was enough of Alimoren's workaday blues to make her think that they hadn't ended up in Holding by accident.

"He's making calls," Santino answered.

And left the four of us alone with the suspect? Rachel thought. *Okie-dokie.*

It wasn't the oldest trick in the book, but it was up there. Miss Armani was looking at an eternity of formal interviews with the Secret Service. Before those began, she might say something unguarded to the local yokels who had brought her in.

Rachel wondered if she should go hide in the bathroom again so Hill could work.

"Fingerprints came back," Zockinski said, speaking a little too loudly. "Jenna Noura. She's a professional art thief." He pronounced it with a short *O*, and chopped up the *R*.

"That's Noo-rah," the woman said, settling back on her bunk as if getting ready for bed. "It's Lebanese."

"Pretty name," Santino said.

The woman rolled her eyes at him before turning away to face the wall.

"The Secret Service says you're wanted by Interpol."

No answer.

Santino tried again. "That wristwatch you were wearing when we brought you in? It's just a watch. If you give us the one you wore to the White House, it might help us track the pieces back to its maker."

No answer.

"Gonna talk to us?" Hill asked.

"Not now," replied Noura. "Let me know when you've got something worth my time."

The four of them glared at the woman on the cell's bed as they realized they weren't going to make any progress. They had Noura's name, her arrest record, and enough evidence to put her away for life, and none of that was enough to get her to talk to them without a lawyer present. Noura wasn't new at this. She knew motive was her only bargaining chip, and she'd hold onto it until she could turn a deal to her advantage. They needed more to work with before she'd disclose anything worthwhile.

"C'mon," she said to her partner. "Let's see what we can learn from that chunk of mystery metal she stole."

There was a chuckle from the bunk.

"Something funny?" Rachel asked Noura.

"You people. If the White House archivists didn't know what they had, you don't have a chance."

They waited to see if Noura would say anything else, but the woman fell silent again. Rachel watched as Noura's conversational colors slowed and hazed over into cloudy dreams.

Unbelievable, Rachel thought. A three-mile sprint through city traffic, a beating from an Eastern European goon squad, and an arrest, and the woman was still able to catnap.

The four of them left the room, and waited until the fire door had shut before they began to talk in low voices.

"She might be right," Rachel said. "We spoke with a lot of antique dealers, and nobody knew what that metal object was."

"It's from an old Greek shipwreck," Zockinski said. "So maybe we can narrow down where it came from. How many of those were there?"

"Thousands." Santino said. "Wish we could get our hands on it. If I could see it, maybe I could... I don't know. Photographs aren't enough."

"Where's it now?" Rachel asked. "If it's still here, I can probably scan it for you. It'd be the next best thing to handling it in person."

Santino went an eager yellow-white, and led them on a fast hunt through the building for the small Tupperware box and the nylon wallet preserved within. They found it on a supervisor's desk in the evidence lockup, guarded by an officer who had been ordered to not let it out of his sight.

"Fine," Rachel said to the guard after five minutes of futile arguing. "Just don't move it while I scan it." She had hoped that Santino could examine the object for himself, and save her the effort of running frequencies. Her mood had gone dark: Zockinski kept snapping at her, and she had realized she had lost her tablet when she had dropped her purse to run down Jenna Noura.

She leaned against the cinderblock wall of the hallway, and let her scans move into the room on the other side. They passed through plastic and nylon, and ran through the metal object. It had survived the theft and footrace intact. Oscar McCrindle was right: there was scratches within the metal, all but eroded unless she burrowed deep.

"Got it," she said. Deep, careful scans were difficult. She moved slowly, turning the object over in her mind as she worked. She could feel every single nook and cranny as she scanned them, as real and as solid as if she were examining the metal with her fingertips.

"That antiques dealer I told you about? The one with the dead raccoons? He said there was writing on it." Rachel narrowed her scope until there was nothing in her scans except the fragment. "I see...something. I don't know if I'd call it writing."

"Here." Santino held up his phone. She flipped her perspective across to its screen. Santino winced in oranges. "Whoa," he said. "That's...uh... You think that's writing?"

"Maybe?"

"I can't...I can't make it out."

"I could be wrong," she said.

Santino moved the phone closer to his face. "This is like staring into a mud puddle,"

"Oh hell," she muttered. "It's a perception clash. Let me run the spectrum."

Rachel could usually move her perspective from her mind to another Agent, or to a screen, without issue, but there were times when what she perceived didn't have a direct equivalent within the visual spectrum. She swept her scans across and through the corroded metal, keeping them slow, and shifting frequencies every ten seconds.

Not every frequency could penetrate metal, and those that did tended to leave a garbled image on the screen. Santino shook his head each time she changed frequencies. "No," he said. "Bad. Bad. Worse. Bad... Wait, go back and try that one... No..."

They had done this before, but never using such an old and damaged item as the metal fragment. Rachel was beginning to think the source material was the problem when Santino shouted, "Wait. *Wait.* Go back!"

She flipped back along the spectra until Santino turned yellow-white with excitement. He held up the phone, his eyes wide and his colors vivid. "Do you see this?"

Rachel tracked his finger along a series of rough edges. She let his finger leave a line where it traveled, and as he moved, the unmistakable silhouette of a mechanical cog emerged on the screen.

He handed his phone to her, and slowly slid down the wall to sit on the floor.

"Santino?"

Happy purples were starting to crowd out the bright excitement as he laughed quietly to himself. "Call Alimoren," he said, smiling up at his team. "I know what this is."

EIGHT

"The Antikythera Mechanism."

Santino spun the monitor to face the others. The screen showed crusty chunks of metal, fused into a single piece by time and sea water. She could make out a large circle containing a set of crossbars, and that was about the end of what was recognizable.

"Yay?" she ventured.

Zockinski and Hill both chuckled.

They were standing in Jason's lab, the metal printout of the fragment sitting on a worktable. For reasons she didn't quite understand herself, Rachel had been keeping this one in her pocket. The Secret Service still had the original fragment, and Alimoren had promised to drop it by the Consolidated Forensics Laboratory for further analysis.

Rachel assumed she and the others at the MPD would never see it again.

"One question," she said.

"Yes, it's worth killing for," her partner said. "It's an out-of-place artifact."

"A…a what? An out-of-place…" Zockinski started.

"Artifact," Santino repeated. "Something that doesn't align with the evolution of similar machines. The Antikythera Mechanism is one of the best examples. They found the first pieces in what was left of an ancient Greek shipwreck in 1901, and have been recovering fragments off and on since then."

Rachel dragged the now-familiar metal printout towards her. This version of the scrap of metal hadn't changed. It was still a shapeless blob, the faint chicken scratches that she had found on the original lost during the printing process. "And this is worth killing for, why?"

"It's part of a computer. Part of the *first* computer."

"Bullshit," Zockinski said. "That piece of metal's got to be thousands of years old."

Rachel sighed, and accessed Google. "Spell…Oh! Never mind."

As soon as she had entered the first five letters of *Antikythera*, page after page of information had leapt into her. Hill watched her face as she skimmed some of the lighter articles, his colors changing from orange scorn to yellow curiosity as she processed what she read.

"An analog computer?" she asked Santino. "This is a real thing?"

His colors glazed over. "Yes," he said. "Star charts. Astrolabes. Sectors. Slide rules. You could even make an argument for an abacus. Analog computers have been around for millennia."

"Fascinating," she muttered. It would have been, too, if some asshole hadn't stolen her purse after she had ditched it to chase down Jenna Noura. They had taken her wallet, smashed the screens on her backup phone and tablet when they couldn't break her password, and dumped a papaya smoothie over the rest before abandoning it at the corner of the farmers' market. Her purse, notorious within the MPD, had somehow made its way back to her, and she was now poking through the contents to see if anything was worth salvaging.

(Santino hadn't let her bully him into chauffeuring her around the city to track the RFID signals on her credit cards, and she was in the process of cancelling everything in her name. At least she had been wearing her badge when she went after Noura: OACET already had enough problems with technologically-savvy trolls pretending to be Agents. She hoped losing her business cards wouldn't come back to bite her.)

"Render's done," Jason said.

A series of green dials appeared in midair. Hill and Santino, both wearing their glasses, began to circle them in a careful clockwise inspection, while Zockinski dug around in his pockets for his pair.

Rachel left the table, holding her sticky hands away from her body. "Lose 'em again?" she whispered to Zockinski.

"No," he whispered back, his colors staying well out of the reds. Apparently, she had been forgiven in the excitement. "Not after the last time. Santino said he'd start charging me."

She snickered. The glasses were an investment of several thousand dollars in parts and labor. Santino must have laid down the law when he had needed to build Zockinski a third pair.

They turned back to the space in the center of the room, where Jason was reconstructing a long-lost machine out of light.

Jason was a showman and a showoff, both. The Mechanism came together in pieces, floating towards each other in a slow, careful ballet. Each gear was so precisely crafted that they shone like glass mirrors instead of polished metal (a detail only slightly less impressive, in Rachel's opinion, considering that they were neither). There were dozens of them, each rotating slowly as they joined, sliding into each other to become a whole.

Once the individual gears had aligned, Jason added the exterior details. A case of semi-transparent green emerged to surround the gears, encasing most of these but allowing two dials on the front and one on the back to remain exposed. On one side, a small handle spun. Inside the case, the gears turned, and the hands on the dials turned accordingly.

Rachel thought it was beautiful.

"Which model did you use?" Santino asked Jason.

"Michael Wright's. It's the one with the most material available for download. Saved me a lot of time."

"Yeah, but that one's out of date," Santino said. "There's been a few new discoveries since he put that one together."

Jason glared at him. "Do any of those discoveries change how my render looks?"

"Well, no, not really, but—"

"So," Jason said, "this is how the Mechanism would have appeared when it was new. And this…"

As he spoke, the case vanished. The gears began to erode, crumbling and falling apart until they resembled flattened stones more than metal. The circle and crossbars she had spotted earlier emerged, and Rachel realized that this piece of the Mechanism was significant mainly because it was the largest chunk to have survived.

"… is how it looks today."

"Sad," Zockinski said. "It was pretty."

"That's what you get when you lie at the bottom of the ocean for two thousand years," Jason said.

"Some scholars think it also had gemstones," Santino said. "The Mechanism was a celestial computer. The ancient Greeks used it to plot planetary movement, so it might have had gems to correspond to each planet."

"Right." Jason swept a hand through the render. The pieces flew through the air and came back together, but remained in their decayed state. He spun the render and it split in two. The smaller half was made from tiny fragments; the larger, from the circle and crossbars, as well as several other goodly-sized chunks of metal.

The larger half of the Mechanism faded away as the smaller doubled in size. "If the pieces of the Mechanism are a puzzle, *this*…" Jason said, as a now-familiar fragment appeared and moved to join the others, "…is where our own mystery metal would fit."

The piece of metal that they had recovered from Noura slid into place. There were gaps from erosion all around it, but a shiver ran down Rachel's spine as she realized they had located the biggest single fragment from this section of the Mechanism.

Santino was smiling like a maniac. "They've got about eighty percent of this thing figured out," he said. "They know how it works, and what it does. But they still don't know who made it, or how, or whether there are other ways to use it. If Rachel's right, and there's writing on our fragment—"

"I'm right," Rachel said. She felt detached, as if she had gone out-of-body and her mind was traveling while her soul remained at home. She reached out and took control of the render from Jason, and moved it backwards through time until the Mechanism stood fresh and new again. Their fragment fit snugly within a section covered in careful writing. "I'm right," she said again, quietly.

"We found a national treasure," Zockinski said. "The Greeks are going to flip out about this."

"So are the mathematicians," Santino said. "The Mechanism used a unique planar differential, so the coding processes are..." He trailed off as he realized the others were staring. "We might have discovered a new way of *thinking*, people," he said. "It took fifteen hundred years before any civilization evolved to the point where they could build devices even half this complex! It's a big fucking deal."

"Think we can get a vacation out of this?" Hill asked. "Be nice to go to Greece."

They returned to their earlier chores while they fell into good-natured squabbling over whether traveling to Greece to return the fragment fell within the MPD's purview. Then, Rachel looked up from the mess of her handbag and glanced towards the door.

"Who?" Zockinski asked.

"Alimoren," Rachel replied.

There was a fast knock, and the Secret Service agent let himself into Jason's office. He cradled a small black box against his side. Rachel sent a scan through it, and her heart leapt.

"Is Noura talking yet?" asked Zockinski.

"No." Alimoren joined Rachel at the table, keeping some distance between himself and what was left of her purse. He pulled the 3D printout of the fragment towards himself, and carefully placed the little box next to it.

So strange, how she could see the original piece of the Mechanism before Alimoren opened the box, but once he lifted the lid, once she was exposed to that odd piece of metal...

She shoved her hands into the ruined mess of her purse to keep herself from touching it.

"Santino asked me to bring this by," Alimoren said.

Yeah," Santino said. "Rachel and Jason can scan and process it more quickly than the archivists."

"If it's part of the Mechanism," Alimoren added, "it's going back to Greece, so work fast."

"How long do we have to work with it?" Jason asked.

"Not long," Alimoren said. "We've got a meeting scheduled with the Greek embassy tomorrow morning at nine. We're going to turn it over to them regardless of what you find, so make sure you get what you need before then."

"Aren't you going to catch hell from our own people? Seems as though they'd want to get their hands on this, too," Rachel said, thinking of Maddie Peguero and the other archivists.

"One of the conditions for turning it over will be that the Smithsonian Institution has the right to do testing and analysis. And if it *is* really part of the Mechanism," Alimoren added, his colors flickering over themselves in a cornflower blue wink, "then they'll get access to the rest of the device, too."

Santino whistled. "Everyone wins."

"Yeah," Alimoren nodded. "Speaking of which…" He reached inside his suitcoat and emerged with a handful of somewhat rumpled envelopes. "There's a cocktail party at the White House tomorrow night. It's to thank everyone who helped close this case before it hit the media."

"Um…" Zockinski began.

Alimoren shook his head. "The President won't be there."

Of course not, Rachel thought. The President wouldn't be caught dead (so to speak) at any event connected to the murder, even if it was to celebrate its resolution. There'd probably be a bunch of high-ranking political folk in attendance, mainly those who had interests in law enforcement, but the President and most of his cabinet wouldn't touch it with a two-state pole. The closest they'd get to that cocktail party would be Pennsylvania, bare minimum.

"Still, we wouldn't have caught Noura without you," Alimoren said as he passed out the envclopes. He looked straight at Rachel as he said, "Please come."

Rachel noticed his colors were holding quite a lot of her Southwestern turquoise, and she nodded.

She slid a fingernail through the heavy paper, and banged the envelope around on her palm until the invitation slid out. The writing was embossed, which made it easy for her to read; flat ink didn't register on her scans like the plastic polymers used to print raised text.

"How did you plan this so quickly?" she asked. "We bagged Noura just a couple of hours ago."

Alimoren chuckled. "The White House specializes in social events. This is our version of inviting friends over for a backyard cookout."

"Plus one?" Zockinski's colors went from an excited yellow-white to a dull red in the time it took for him to remember that his wife would need to buy a new outfit.

"Yes. Please keep in mind your guests will be vetted, so... I hate to say this, but be considerate about who you ask, okay? We've had to turn some guests away in the past."

"*Rachel...?*"

"*I'll bring Phil,*" she assured Jason. Her girlfriend was out of town until Tuesday, and bringing Phil meant nobody would feel excluded.

"*Thanks,*" he said, and then he turned a sickly shade of orange as he realized that Bell would most likely meet the Secret Service's criteria for an undesirable guest.

"*She's about my size. I've probably got a dress she can wear.*" Rachel was glad it was a cocktail party and not another black-tie gala. She'd have hated to beg a dress from Hope Blackwell's closet twice in the same week. Her boss's wife was always generous with her clothes, but Rachel still had the borrowed outfit from the fundraiser at the Botanic Gardens lying in a heap on her bedroom floor.

"*Okay...um... Rachel? Would you—*"

"*Nope,*" Rachel cut him off as his apprehension reached her. "*I am not telling Bell to dye her hair.*"

"I just thought that as long as you were helping her choose an outfit, you could—"

She severed their link while pushing a sensation of disgust towards him.

Men! she snarled to herself, and then quickly amended that to *Humanity!*

She was as bad as Jason, really. It'd be nice to think that if people could see core colors, they'd be less likely to make judgment calls based on appearance. Deep down, she knew that was pure delusion, and she didn't let herself buy into it. Human beings were born to fight: differences just gave them an excuse. If Mako ever did manage to replicate how she perceived the world, she'd probably be responsible for the Indigo-Khaki War of 2062.

There was paperwork—there was always paperwork—and Rachel signed her life away to become the official temporary custodian of a national treasure, with the promise that she would deliver it to the Greek embassy at precisely nine-fifteen in the morning. Alimoren left, taking Zockinski and Hill with him, and then Rachel, Jason, and Santino got to work.

They did their best to keep themselves from touching the fragment. Santino gave a very brief lecture about oils from skin, contamination, degradation, and so on, and made them promise to inspect it with their scans only. And she and Jason still rushed to grab it when Santino stepped out for a fast bathroom break.

"Oh, God," she breathed when Jason tipped it out of the box into her eager hands. The fragment was heavy and light, all at once, and she turned off visuals to let the moment sink into her.

"You were right," Jason said. "It was special."

"Still is," she said. The piece of metal in her palms lost its chill as it took on the heat from her hands.

"How did you know?" he asked.

She remembered Oscar McCrindle, intent on matters of history, and couldn't quite find the right words.

"Can I?" he asked, and there was a brief moment of shared

reverence as his skin brushed against hers. It wasn't deep enough of a link for either of them to find the answer, and neither of them wanted to go deeper, not after the other night…and then she felt slightly empty as he took the fragment from her.

They had it back in its black plastic cradle by the time Santino returned, the two of them pretending to have been studying the fragment *in situ* the entire time. He did them the courtesy of pretending to be fooled, and then put the two Agents through hours of aggressive data collection.

Lulu forced them to take a break sometime after midnight. Santino, aware that this was his one shot at the fragment, hadn't wasted a moment. He and Jason had worked as a team, recording and profiling the fragment from every possible angle. They had identified the resonant frequencies of its metallic properties, and Santino wanted to keep going until they were classifying nanoparticles.

Sadly, their primary scanner had developed a roaring headache and had made enough mistakes to trip Lulu's safeguards.

"Ow ow ow ow ow." Rachel's headache had set its teeth firmly in her skull. "Guys, please. Even the computer wants to go to bed."

Lulu had been set to silent mode, but Rachel still felt as if the machine was waiting for the opportunity to tell Jason that it, unlike *some people*, could go all night.

"Rachel's face is red," Phil said. He had arrived with pizza between the raster and reflection tests, and was playing solitaire while waiting for them to finish. "At least take a break until she goes down to Code Orange or something."

"That's not how it works, but…yeah. Red. That." Rachel realized she was barely coherent, and went to sprawl out on the cool of the linoleum floor. She wished—not for the first time—that someone would find a spare implant for Santino so he could stop using hers as his surrogate.

The men joined her, settling down in a messy circle around her. She had turned off visuals, so she jumped a little as she felt

Phil's hand close over hers.

"*Let me try something,*" he said. He pulled her head into his lap, and spread his fingers across her temples.

Agents made a great alternative to aspirin. They had learned they could share physical sensations across a link, and a link enhanced via skin contact could reduce one Agent's pain by spreading some of it to another. Rachel thought Phil was going to pull half of her headache from her; they had helped each other in this way many times before. She wasn't expecting the feeling of his hands across her head to fall away, a sensation of drifting peace rising to replace it…

"*Damn, Phil, what is this?*" Rachel heard herself giggle aloud, and couldn't be bothered to care. "*I feel high.*"

"*You are high,*" he replied. She could feel him grinning at her. "*Jody made an autoscript the last time she smoked up.*"

"What?!" She gave a reflexive mental push, and the peaceful mood slipped off of her like a silk dress falling to the ground. Suddenly sober with a merciless headache, she flipped on visuals to glare up at Phil. "*If this shows up in my pee…*"

"*It's fake, Penguin,*" he said. "*It's a synthetic experience. It's the same thing as when I trick your mind into thinking I'm sharing heat with you when you're cold.*"

Rachel tested that logic, and decided there was nothing illegal about getting high off of a stored memory. "*Well, then,*" she said, as she settled back into Phil's lap. "*Let's hope Jody buys the good stuff.*"

His hands came to rest against her temples again, and she let herself float away.

"Why does she keep laughing?" Santino asked Phil.

"Stress!" she shouted. Then, more quietly, "So much stress."

"You showing her Jody's new autoscript?" Jason asked Phil.

"A new script? What does it do?" Santino asked him, ever curious about the discoveries made by the collective.

Jason explained.

There was a long, *long* pause before Santino said, "That's just not fair."

"Want a copy of this script?" Phil asked her.

"Oh God no, I'd never get off of the couch."

It had been a long day. She might not have wanted to go into a deeper link with Jason, but she trusted Phil not to go poking around in the darker regions of her psyche. There was a quick warning between them, and then she took down the barbed wire lining the tops of her mental walls. He stumbled a bit before he found the right balance, and then, as her mood transferred to him, he started to giggle, too.

He let her move into him so she could use his eyes as her own. Seeing through Phil's eyes was a novel experience. The closest she came to normal vision was when she was walking about in her digital avatar, and that provided a rather flattened three-dimensional perspective on the world. She had forgotten how limited normal vision was until the room and its occupants showed up as mere shapes made up of curves, planes, and angles.

"What?" Phil asked, as he picked up on a thread of sadness moving into her mood.

"Nothing!" she said quickly.

Not quickly enough: Phil had spotted it, the comparison between old-time silent films versus IMAX theaters with stadium seating.

"It's not that bad!" Phil said defensively.

"What isn't?" Santino asked.

"She's…" Phil gestured with a hand before Rachel grabbed it and clapped it back down on her forehead. "She pities us poor unevolved lesser beings."

"Hey!" Jason threw a pizza crust at her. She tracked it from Phil's perspective, which meant she missed it by a mile as she tried to knock it out of the air. "Santino's the only one here who's unevolved."

"Jason!" Rachel and Phil spoke as one, appalled.

"It's fine," Santino said. Rachel was thankful that she wasn't running emotions: that tone of voice wasn't used for any purpose other than polite social camouflage.

"We'll get you a chip," she said, reaching over to pat Santino on his knee. "As soon as we get this mess sorted out, you'll be the first one we put under the knife."

"They use a stereotactic craniotomy," he said. "Not a lot of knives."

Normally, Rachel would have jumped on him for the nerd comment, but she just patted his knee again. "See?" she said. "You'll make a better cyborg than any of us."

"It's fine!" he insisted. "Hanlon will never let anyone make new cyborgs. Not OACET-class cyborgs, at least. I'm just glad I get to work with you guys."

"Hanlon gave th' technology to Congress. The U.S. government owns it. As soon as they realize we're invaluable, they'll make more of us. And we'll insist on *you*," Rachel said, pointing at her partner. "We need new blood to stay alive. Oth'rwise, you know, that thing will happen where we all turn into dumb-ass Disney executives… Groupthink! Can't have groupthing...groupthink. Not if we want to do something *real*. If we stay...uh...flexible, OACET might actually be able to make things change. F'r once. Break up this shitty gridlock of a political system."

The sober part of Rachel's brain warned her to keep quiet. When certain topics came up, she had a policy of sealing her mouth shut. Religion, politics, taxes (*oh Lord, don't let them get me started on the Army*), she was a firm believer that anyone willing to discuss these topics had already made up their mind on them, and there was nothing she could say to change their opinion.

She usually wasn't remembering someone else's stoner high in real time.

"'kay, listen," she said. "Nothing *changes*. Politicians, they get into office and stay there. It doesn't matter what they do—they'll be there forever. Look at Hanlon. Everybody knows what he did, an' nobody cares. He smiles an' looks pretty for the cameras, an' they'll let him go on *forever*."

"Everybody doesn't know," Phil said. "Not yet. The news will break any day now." Anxiety ran across his fingertips, but her buzz was too strong, and she instinctively pushed her sense of peace straight back into him. He sighed, and submitted to the sensation. "Damn, that's good," he said, his voice slowing almost immediately. "But it's another week, maybe three at most, an' then everybody *will* know. If we're lucky, we'll finally get enough public pressure to force Congress to move on him."

"Won't happen," she muttered. "Never happen. Tell 'em, Santino. Microwave memory. *Ding!* and the story's done."

"Microwave memory?"

"That's what I call the general public's attention span," Santino replied to Jason, eager to direct the conversation away from what he was sure he would never have. "Rachel liked the sound of it. It's when stories heat up really quickly, but are over and forgotten within days. Once the first news story done, the media and the public move on to the next one."

"Yeah," Rachel said. "News doesn't stick. An' politicians are startin' to use that. It's political theater…they can get away with the *worst* shit, as long as they know something juicier will come along tomorrow."

"I don't know. I think Phil might be right," Santino said. "Yes, it's only the really crazy stories that have any sticking power with the public these days—it's got to be flat-out drama to capture the public's attention—but OACET's always been one of those stories. When the news of what Hanlon did to you comes out, it might be enough to permanently sway public sympathy."

"Or," Rachel muttered, "remind them they're fuckin' terrified of us."

"That's what I'm worried about," Jason said. "They already think we're ticking bombs waiting to explode. Learning what Hanlon did might backfire on us."

That got her attention. It was sincere, and Jason usually didn't do sincere. Honest, yes, the man was brutally honest, but his honesty was his armor. Sincerity cost him; she flipped on visuals for a brief peek at his mood, and found he was deeply gray with sharp jagged points of yellow, misery and fright all the way down to his charcoal core.

"It'll be okay," she said, pushing good feelings—*comfort, security*—at him. Their casual connection wasn't deep enough, and he waved them aside. "No," she insisted, struggling to face at him while still keeping her head in the cradle of Phil's lap. "It'll be okay! We've done everything right. We've built alliances, we've proven we can function within society. We've done everything *right!*"

"All it takes is one," Jason said. "One big fuck-up, and all of that goodwill is gone. We're relying on the public's perception of us to keep us safe, but they can't remember what happened yesterday when there's new bullshit being screamed at them all the damned time."

"That's a risk," she admitted. "Big risk. It's okay, though. We try."

"Trying isn't enough," he muttered. "We're still human. We try, but we still fuckin' *fail!* Hanlon just has to wait until one of us gets caught."

"Same applies to Hanlon," Santino said. "He's made too many mistakes with OACET. You've spent the last year showing the public that he's a monster and you're not. The brainwashing story might be the last straw."

"Hope so," Rachel muttered, and turned off visuals again to relax in the soft dark. "We've got nothing left in our anti-Hanlon arsenal after that."

"Nothing?" Curiosity moved from Phil into Rachel, nudging her forward.

"Well, no. There's some stuff left," she admitted, riding Phil's emotions as much as the memory of the perfect high. "Hanlon's rich an' powerful. There's always something shady goin' on with people like him. You can bet Mulcahy's looking for proof that he's… I dunno. Funding the Contras with information stolen from the Democratic National Committee or somethin'."

"We're with you," Santino said.

"I don't need to turn on emotions," she threatened. "You're patronizing me, I can tell."

"Yeah, but we're also interested," Phil said as he poked her in the middle of her forehead. "You never talk about this stuff."

"Where was I?"

"Hanlon. Government conspiracies. The contemptible state of today's media and the public's attention span."

"Eh," Rachel grunted. "Whatever. Doesn't matter anyhow. Thirty years from now, we'll probably be braggin' to our grandkids about the good old days when news cycles lasted for whole days instead of measly minutes. Same ol' song, forever."

"Except now there's us," Jason said.

"Yeah," Rachel said, smiling. "Now there's us. We're different."

"Well," Phil said. "Today, we're different. Maybe those grandkids will think we're *soooo* boring with our cute first-gen brainchips."

"Yeah, but today, we *are* different," Rachel said. "There's never been anything like us before, not in Washington. Not in politics. We're a sea change. An' America *needs* a sea change."

"Mr. Smith the Talking Atomic Bomb goes to Washington?" Santino asked.

"Exactly!" Rachel said, nodding so hard that she broke skin contact with Phil. The buzz vanished and her headache returned, albeit much subdued. "Oh! Phil, you're a miracle worker," she said, and flipped on visuals. The men appeared around her, bemused in blues and purples.

"You're fun when you're stoned," her partner told her, grinning.

"I've seen each and every one of you drunk," she retorted. "Don't laugh at me unless you want me to queue up the video of last year's Christmas party."

She dusted herself off and moved to the couch, grabbing what was left of her soda on the way.

"No, it's interesting," Phil said. "You never talk about politics."

"Because it's pointless. We don't have a political system. We have a holding pattern," Rachel said. "It's all about creating new and exciting methods to game that holding pattern so a handful of people make progress while the rest of us stay stuck in the same place. It's pretty depressing.

"I think..." Rachel took a moment to run through her next words, looking for bumps in the road. "I think I'm glad we're taking the fight home. We might be able to shake up the system. There's nothing that's not completely fucked-up about how OACET was created, and it was all done legally. It could *still* happen, if Hanlon comes up with a different technology and gets his hands on another group of dumb kids! It's time somebody does something about that, and..."

She trailed off. This had all sounded so much better when she was stoned.

"Well," she finished weakly. "The way things are going, that somebody is probably OACET."

"It'd be nice," Phil said. "Not the legal fucked-up part. The part about how we might be able to keep this from happening to anybody else."

"Yeah," Rachel said. "I don't know if it'd make all of this worth it, but it definitely would help me sleep at night."

"All right," Santino said. "Rachel? Ready for another round of scans?"

She groaned, and tried to sink into the sofa before Santino dragged her back to the fragment.

Another hour, and after Lulu's safeguards tripped a second time, Rachel declared she was done. The fragment was stored in its black box, and the box transferred to the pocket of Rachel's suitcoat.

The four of them cleaned up the trash and closed down the lab, and made their way towards the parking lot in a small, sleepy group.

It was by chance that the blister on Rachel's heel chose that moment to pop.

Thanks, Noura, she grumbled to herself, as she grabbed a light pole to steady herself and nudge her feet as far down into the toes of her boots as they could go.

Jason was walking beside her, and was paying enough attention to feel her mood shift. "You okay?"

Jenna Noura…

And then Rachel remembered what she had wanted to ask Jason.

"You need to teach me how to erase something from a computer," she told him.

His colors turned orange. "You haven't figured that out yet?"

"And not leave any marks."

Most of the yellow turned to white: apparently, this was not as easy as it sounded. "Rachel—"

"It's important," she said quietly. "The woman who broke into the White House recognized me."

"So? You've been in the news a bunch of times."

"Put me and six other Chinese women together, Jason. Could you pick me out of that lineup?"

"Yeah," he said, yellow surprise pushing out the shock and scorn. "Of course."

"Well…" She hadn't expected his fast and honest answer. "Aren't you special? I'm going to assume there's a file out there somewhere with my picture in it. Maybe there's other information that we shouldn't leave floating around."

"Damn," he muttered. "Fine. Call me. Not tomorrow—I'm jammed until the party at the White House. Maybe the day after tomorrow. You should know how to do this by now."

"Yeah, yeah, I'm a truly shitty cyborg," she muttered, "Just teach me this."

"All right," he agreed, as Santino shouted at them to hurry up.

NINE

This would be their last year in the OACET mansion. The lowest bidders had been scrambling to transform the husk of an old post office into a new headquarters for the cyborgs. It was shaping up to be spectacular, government contractors notwithstanding. Mare Murphy had argued to Congress that if OACET was to serve as the public face of American technology, they should receive a building to match their status. The underlying theme of *And you owe us!* had sealed the deal, and an abandoned postal hub near Judiciary Square was being retrofitted to the Agents' specifications. The design would incorporate the best of both worlds, with the original neoclassical architecture preserved, and the crumbling plasterwork rebuilt over a complex web of structured wiring and point-to-point cabling. From a cyborg's perspective, the building would sing.

Rachel was sure she'd loathe it.

OACET's temporary headquarters were located outside of the city proper, in an old mansion on a hill overlooking the Potomac River. The mansion had been seized in a drug raid in the 1980s, and had remained unsold and uninhabited until it had been turned over to OACET the year before. During its decades of vacancy, the government used the mansion as a property overflow warehouse. Security was tight, but it had been used much in the way of a family storage unit: rarely, and largely ignored unless something went wrong.

The mansion was a comfort in the way of an old pair of jeans, a favorite song on the radio. It was crammed to the rafters with the accumulated clutter of three decades of asset forfeiture, with everything from oil paintings to catering equipment to the occasional speedboat shoved into every square inch of available space. OACET had cleaned the mansion as best they could, and had reminded the many federal agencies who used the place as a dumping ground to auction off some of the valuables that had been gathering dust. Unfortunately, as soon as space was cleared, new items flooded in to fill it. The federal government abhorred a vacuum, especially one located within easy driving distance.

Rachel picked a cautious path up a rear staircase. A tumble of antique rugs had been left there, courtesy of the FBI's Art Crime Team. She scaled three flights like a mountain goat, then paused at the top to take in the chaos below. In the early days of occupation, the Agents would have had the rugs sorted and stacked in the solarium within hours. Lately, it had become harder to find Agents with enough spare time to handle the routine housekeeping needed to control the mess. Almost everyone in the collective had assignments which kept them out of the mansion during the workday. Their fledgling hivemind no longer needed a hive to survive. She knew this was progress, but she still felt the loss.

Time to buy my sapphire, she reminded herself. Down in the medical lab, a small pink sapphire was waiting on four final payments to the Department of the Treasury. She had picked out the stone when they had first moved into the mansion, its electron resonance a peaceful note within her mind. It had been more expensive than she had expected, and she wasn't sure what she'd do with it (either a necklace or a ring, that was a given; she couldn't afford a second sapphire to make a matched set of earrings), but she'd be glad to have it once the mansion was no longer home.

She passed through two sets of mahogany doors and the upper floor of the atrium to end in the west wing. Back in the mansion's prime, this area had been set aside for guests, and the top floor was made up of massive bedrooms and overdone *en suites*. The doors down the length of the hallway stood open, the clatter of keyboards and muffled media blending with her footsteps into white noise.

Correction: one door was closed.

Rachel knocked on this door, a politeness they maintained for the toddler usually found playing in the confines of a deep marble soaker tub converted to a crib. Avery was the child of two Agents, and this had placed her parents in the unique position of two telepaths raising a non-telepathic daughter. Mako and Carlota had realized early on that their daughter wouldn't be exposed to language unless the Agents made the effort to talk when around her, and this had been a rule since the day Avery was born.

It took her parents a little extra time to realize that they needed to impose more rules. The Agents hadn't fully recognized how many social norms they had phased out of their repertoire. Agents didn't bother with doorbells or phones. They spoke and laughed and shouted at things no one else could see. They manipulated and twisted technology as their needs demanded, usually without physically touching the machines. When they were interacting with non-Agents, they tried to keep these behaviors in check, but Avery had three hundred and fifty convenient babysitters who allowed themselves to *be* themselves within the safety of the mansion. Hence, the closed door and its printed sign:

THE OUTSIDE WORLD BEGINS HERE

"Who is it?" The voice came, loud and booming, from within the cavernous bedroom on the other side of the thick mahogany door.

"It's Aunt Rachel," she said, smiling. Mako had known she was coming from the moment she was within a mile of the mansion.

The door opened, and a giant black man with a familiar core of forest green greeted her. "Rachel! Good to see you! Please come in!"

She stepped into the room, and Mako Hill grabbed her in a bear hug. He was open in a way his cousin could never be: Matt

Hill had been to hard places, but Mako was still soft. At least, as soft as a seven-foot-tall, three-hundred-pound mountain of weightlifter's muscle could ever be.

"Air…" she gasped into Mako's chest.

"Right, right. Sorry, tiny one!" Mako released her, and headed off to the workstation where Santino was fussing over a stack of stray papers.

Rachel waved to her partner on her way to the makeshift nursery. She wasn't surprised to find Avery strapped into several full-body onesies. With a multitude of surrogate aunts and uncles, Avery was guaranteed constant adult supervision, but she was a brilliant child and had entered the phase where she had started testing limits. Lately, Avery had found that she could get an immediate reaction when she hurled her diaper at her babysitters, and that this reaction was all the more intense when the diaper was full. Mako and Carlota had begun strapping Avery into jumpsuits. She could still wiggle out of them, but it took her a minute or so to fumble with the buttons, and that was enough time to intervene (or, if Avery was especially quick about it, to scramble for the paper towels and the Lysol).

The toddler was playing with her stuffed dinosaurs, and she held one up when Rachel knelt down beside the sunken tub.

"Hello, Avery!"

"Ankle 'osaurus," Avery said, and threw the plush toy at Rachel's head.

"Sweet pea?" Mako's voice was even louder on this side of the door, and Avery instantly started to pout. "We don't throw things, and we never throw things at other people."

" 'orry," the little girl mumbled.

"Thank you for apologizing, Avery," Rachel said, as she scooped up the bright purple dinosaur. "Do you want me to play with you?"

"Yes!"

Rachel climbed down into the sunken tub. It was big enough for four adults to share a comfortable soak, and made a paradise of a playground for a toddler. Mako had lined the bottom and sides with slabs cut from gym mats until every square inch of marble was thickly padded, and filled the tub with toys and board books. Avery waddled over to Rachel and dumped one of these books into her quasi-aunt's lap, then curled up in her arms, stuffed dinosaurs forgotten.

Rachel read aloud to Avery, something sweet about a bear in love with the moon, until the little girl's head grew heavy. She gently slid Avery across the mats to the warm spot within the sunbeam, and tucked the purple ankylosaur beside her.

"She's asleep," she told Mako, as she quietly stepped out of the tub and closed the bathroom door behind her.

"Oh, thank God," Mako said aloud, blue relief washing over him. "Poor kid's due for another growth spurt. She'll sleep like a champ when that happens, but right now you can't get her to nap. You just have to try to run down her batteries until she crashes on her own."

A television mounted on the wall just outside of the bathroom turned itself on, and a camera moved itself around the bathroom until it focused on Avery, still slumbering in the tub. The monitoring system was programmed to pick up physical cues from the toddler, and to notify the nearest Agents within a minute of when she was likely to wake. Rachel had decided that she'd invest in whatever innovations Mako and Carlota decided to take to market. They might force themselves to behave as normally as possible around their daughter, but they had also elevated cyborg-centered childcare to an art.

Rachel pulled the nearest chair out from the table, and rocked it to make sure its legs were still attached. None of the furniture in Mako's office matched, and all of it was in terrible shape. The man's size alone made him murder on housewares, and when he was deep in a project he became the stereotypical absent-minded scientist to boot. As he tended to crush a chair to kindling every other week, and as everything in the mansion was technically intended for auction someday, Mako insisted on filling his office with the junk nobody would miss if it happened to end up in the trash.

He had also filled his office with computers. Unlike Jason's system, Mako's wasn't comprised of a series of new, polished machines networked together to form a whole. These computers were ancient, and clunked along like cars with broken axles roped together in a caravan: they got to where they were needed, eventually, but the ride was terrible.

Mako loved them. He said he spent his day around grumpy old men who made bad jokes and didn't care if anybody laughed.

The back wall was covered in whiteboards. Rachel approved: dry erase ink fluoresced at a unique rate, and it was easy for her to read Mako's notes.

Read? Yes. Understand? No. But that was expected, as Mako's purpose as their resident computational physicist was to determine precisely how the implant functioned, and he wasn't making any progress. Nearly a year ago, he had set up the wall of whiteboards and had grouped the facts under the *KNOWN* and *UNKNOWN* headings, claiming he'd start with the basics and develop a working body of knowledge from there.

He had stalled out within hours.

Patrick Mulcahy had a not-so-secret trove of documents. These were earmarked as blackmail material, and thus far had never been distributed outside of the collective. Receipts and bills of lading, mostly, with the occasional email printout between certain members of Congress on the topic of Problematic Cyborgs, Management Thereof.

Mako hadn't cared about that, claiming the Agents already knew they had been manipulated and abandoned. What they didn't know was how their implants worked. Mulcahy could chase after blood, but Mako would pursue knowledge. He had pored through this trove looking for data, and had found too little for comfort. He insisted that a device as advanced as a miniaturized quantum organic computer would have been developed through small incremental changes, each one building upon the successes of previous trials. There was no evidence of this. Oh, there was *some* data, scraps of information here and there, on the previous test subjects. There was none on the techniques used to develop the technology. As far as the record showed, the methods and materials needed to construct the implant had emerged from thin air within Hanlon Technologies nearly ten years ago, and had been used to put the first version of the implant into production soon after.

Rachel walked towards the nearest whiteboard. Items listed under the *KNOWN* heading took up a single board, while the *UNKNOWN* heading had been written across each of the rest. She paused to read the new notes added to the section on their avatars, and tried not to laugh. Mako might not swear aloud around his daughter, but he had no problem writing out descriptive profanities.

The other Agent came up beside her, and laid one huge hand against the board. "I'm about ready to give up. There's a piece missing," he growled. "A *huge* piece. I can't find it. I've looked everywhere! I can't explain how we can do what we do, not with the information I have now."

She grinned. "Maybe I can get Senator Hanlon to talk to you. Think you can shake it out of him?"

"Please!" Mako stared at the board. "That's probably the only way I'll get answers. Nothing we do makes sense."

"Well, *yeah.*"

"No," Mako said. His colors took on a professional blue, and Rachel realized he meant what he said. "I'm not trying to be funny. The range of abilities we have doesn't correspond to what we know about the electromagnetic spectrum.

"Here," he said, and a puppy appeared. Like all of their projections, it was bright green. Mako waved, and the puppy wagged its tail at him and barked before gamboling off around the room, three feet off of the ground. "Just look at that thing. It's an autoscript I wrote for Avery, so it's essentially a computer program. Once I get it running, I don't need to micromanage it. As long as I have peripheral awareness of what it's doing, it'll function. *That*, I understand!

"But I wrote this script for Avery, because she can see it. Now, how did *that* work, I ask you? She doesn't have an ISO, and it's—"

"Wait." Rachel cut him off. "What's an ISO?"

At the table behind them, Santino turned purple and squeaked.

Mako stared down at her. His colors had stopped moving altogether. Even the bright green puppy had stopped galumphing about on its too-big feet. "That would be the Implanted Spectrum Operator," he said. "The…uh…"

"The chip in our heads," she sighed. "Got it."

"Did you honestly think it didn't have a name? Technically, it's the ISO-157, which suggests there were over a hundred and fifty iterations before they made a successful prototype, but I can't find—"

"I got it!"

Mako paused, and she saw the same purples appear within his conversational colors. These warred with her Southwestern turquoise as he tried not to poke fun of her.

"Mako? Honey? I shoot people for a living. Choose your next words carefully."

"Yup." He stared at the ceiling for a few moments. The green puppy wandered back over to the table and sat at his feet. When the purples finally dissolved, Mako patted the nearby tabletop. The puppy leapt up in a movement more feline than canine. "I made this little guy for Avery because she can see our projections. I can take a stab at how that happened: she's the daughter of two Agents. There's a persistent myth that brains stop changing after we turn thirty, but we got the implants when we were all in our early twenties. Also? That myth is bullshit. Our brains continuously rewire themselves based on our tasks and our environment. We've gradually rewired ourselves to be more attuned to frequencies within the electromagnetic spectrum. It's possible that Carlota and me, we might have passed part of this rewiring down to Avery. That's not usually how trait inheritance works, but it's the best explanation I've got until she's old enough to consent to testing.

"Now, our ears and eyes? We didn't change those. Physiologically speaking, human beings have a limited capacity for what we can perceive. There are entire bands of the EMF that we can't detect without the right tools. This little guy," he said, pointing at the puppy, "exists on a frequency we're already biologically predisposed to perceive. It's like discovering you can suddenly see a whole bunch of brand new colors that were already there."

"Don't forget people like Hope," Santino added. "How do you explain her?"

Hope Blackwell was Patrick Mulcahy's wife. She had no problem seeing or hearing the Agents' projections. They appeared as clearly to her as they would to any Agent.

(In Rachel's opinion, nothing explained Mulcahy's wife. The woman was just plain weird.)

"Santino's got his glasses, so he can see what we project—"

"—I'm making progress on the auditory hookup, too. When I get that to work, I'll be able to hear them—"

"—so these things we create? If it were just Agents who could perceive them, I'd say they were a shared illusion. But they *exist*, even if they are made of electromagnetic radiation. Which begs the question: how can we shape *light?*"

"And why different shades of green?" Santino said, as he passed his hand through the puppy's head. "If you can control the EMF to the point where you can generate constructs, you should be able to render in every single color in the spectrum.

"Really, the only explanation is that we don't have an important chunk of data," Santino added. "I think the implant gives you access to a part of the EMF nobody knew about."

Mako's colors glazed over in irritation.

"You two have this argument a lot?" Rachel asked him.

"All the fuckin' time," Mako muttered. His colors shifted towards Santino's cobalt core, and Rachel caught the hints of the sharp-edged blues and yellows of intent within them. "Actually, this is relevant to your case."

"Motive or device?" she asked, and when a confused orange

appeared, she clarified her question. "Would this be relevant to why the item was stolen, or how the Mechanism works?"

"Maybe both," Santino said. "This is what we were talking about before you got here."

"Great, she said, and claimed a chair at the table beside her partner. She pulled Jason's metal copy of the fragment out of her suitcoat pocket, and dropped it on top of a stack of papers. "I'm dying to know why a chunk of an old clock was worth robbing the White House."

"The inscription," Mako said.

"We're not done translating it," Santino said. "The fragment is conclusively from the Mechanism. The forms for the text match—"

"The size and shape of the letters," Mako explained.

"—but there's so much erosion that we have to fill in the blanks." Santino pointed to Mako's computers, chugging and whirring along as they crunched the data.

"It might take weeks!" Mako, delighted by the scope of the problem, banished the puppy to the aether with a wave of his hand.

"How much could they write on a small chunk of metal?" Rachel muttered.

Santino was glowing. "Definitely enough to fill in some of the gaps in its history," he said. "If we're lucky, enough to fill in the gaps in the math it uses."

Rachel closed her eyes. Anything that came out of her mouth was sure to backfire on her, she just *knew* it.

"Penguin?"

"Fine," she muttered. "I'll bite. Why are there gaps? Isn't math just…*math?*"

Both men's colors took on a semi-opaque glaze, a phenomenon that Rachel associated with persons trying to manage a sudden confluence of stupid questions and civility. "Humor me," she told them.

"Right," Santino said, his colors weaving blues and greens and oranges together as he tried to think of the best way to explain the problem. "What's your opinion about math?" he asked. "Gut response."

"Study your math, kids. Key to the universe," she said in her best Christopher Walken.

"Good. So, why does that quote come to mind?"

Rachel went with the safe answer. "It's the only universal language that exists. It's fixed, constant. The rules never change. If we ever bump into an alien race, we'd be able to communicate with them using math."

"That's right," Mako said. "Now, what if we told you that's wrong?"

"Wait," Rachel said, holding up her hand. "Am I right or wrong?"

"Yes," Santino said.

"Holy Jesus," she sighed. She got up and raided an old mini fridge that held Avery's snacks, looking for something harder than a soda. Nothing. She returned to the table and passed out three juice packs in silvery pouches.

"Perfect," Santino said, holding out his pouch. He took a Sharpie from a cup on the table, and sketched out a triangle on the side of the pouch. "So, say your alien race shows up. Which one of these 'rules' of math will you use when you want to talk to them?"

"The…uh. The right ones?"

"Okay. How do you decide which ones are right?" he said, showing her the triangle. "Seventh-grade geometry… In triangles, all the angles add up to 180 degrees, right?"

"Sure."

"That's basic Euclidian geometry—"

"—or normed vector space—" Mako added, trying to be helpful.

"—but if you move a triangle onto a curved space, the angles don't add up to 180 degrees anymore," Santino said, squeezing his juice pouch to bend the triangle out of its flat plane. "So is that basic rule of math right or wrong?"

"Depends on the situation?" Rachel hazarded.

"That's the easiest way to say it. It's also incomplete," Mako said. "It's a rule that can be simultaneously proven both wholly accurate and inaccurate."

"Here's where Mako and I disagree," Santino said, his colors turning orange and yellow with annoyance and confusion. It had the hallmarks of an ongoing battle between the two men. "I say all rules of mathematics are conditional. They can either be proven right, or proven wrong, depending upon strict conditions of application. Like my trick with the triangle, and changing the conditions in which it exists. You *have* to have these conditions, or there's no reason to have these rules at all because they're of no practical use. But Mako? He believes all rules of mathematics exist in some philosophical state in which they're both right and wrong."

"Not true," Mako said. "I believe that mathematics is an evolving set of constructs, and the rules which can be used to explain them—*not* define them!—evolve along with them. Like the dinosaurs."

Rachel put her head in her hands.

"It's not as confusing as it sounds," Mako said.

"Santino is orange," she said without bothering to pick her head up. "And if Santino thinks this is confusing bullshit, I'm pretty sure you won't be able to explain it to me."

"Don't be such a defeatist," Mako said. "Did you know we're closer in time to the Tyrannosaur than the Tyrannosaur was to the Stegosaur?"

"What?" Rachel sat up, and threw her scans towards the bathtub. Avery was still sleeping soundly, one arm draped comfortably over her plush Ankylosaur.

"We hear the word *dinosaur,* and we think of a single period in time," Mako said, as he picked up Santino's marker and sketched a thick black line across the old wooden tabletop. "As if all of the dinosaurs that ever lived were a single lump sum of animals. But that's not the case at all. The timeframe during which they occupied the planet stretched over millions and millions of years. The Stegosaur lived 150 million years ago," he said, marking one end of the line with an X. "We live here," he said, as he marked the other end. "And the Tyrannosaur lived 66 million years ago. That's 84 million years between the Tyrannosaur and the Stegosaur, and only 66 million years between the Tyrannosaur and us."

Mako's third X was slightly closer to humanity's end of the line. It was big enough so Rachel could see it without adjusting her vision. He tapped on it with the marker's tip, dotting the table with permanent confetti. "In evolutionary science, we have rules which explain the Stegosaur, the Tyrannosaur, and us. Since we generally think of both the Stegosaur and the Tyrannosaur as dinosaurs, we assume the same set of rules can be applied to explain both of them. But they lived millions of years apart. The planet had changed substantially during that time.

"See what I'm getting at? If this is an analogy for math, we can use one set of rules to explain a Stegosaur. Some of those rules can also be used to explain a Tyrannosaur, but we have to add some rules and take away others to clarify that explanation. And then we get to our end of the timeline, and we have to change the rules *again* if we want to explain human beings. See?"

"I see it's all conditional," Santino grumbled.

"I see it's all *evolutionary*," Mako said, pointing the marker at his friend. "Math is the universal language of explanations, not absolutes. Saying math is situational imposes limits on how and when terms can be used."

"That's exactly what I'm saying!" Santino shouted. Mako jabbed the marker at the closed bathroom door, and Santino lowered his voice. "You're arguing philosophy, not math! If math is to have practical value, it needs restrictions. You can't put a space shuttle on the moon using dinosaurs."

"Said the man who forgets where rocket fuel comes from," Rachel grumbled.

"Precisely!" Mako said, his colors lighting up with praise for Rachel.

"Come on, Mako, that was a joke!"

"Doesn't mean you aren't right. Math is conceptual, not conditional. Pieces of rules can be moved around, but within the set parameters of a specific set of circumstances, the rules can only be used to explain themselves.

"*That's* why they're useful," he continued, looking straight at Santino with blue intent. "They explain concepts, not situations. You can't use math to explain anything general."

"Guys, please." Rachel started stabbing at the weak spot on the juice carton with the plastic straw. "Mechanism. Murder. Motive."

"All related," Mako said.

"What Mako and I both agree on," Santino said, "is the Mechanism predated what was known about applied advanced mathematics by fifteen hundred *years*. Any new information in that inscription could be invaluable."

"Like...*urh!*" Her straw bent sideways and split down the center. She threw it in the general direction of the trash can, and pushed the silver pouch away from her. "Like the name of the person who made it?"

"That, or new mathematical formulae," Santino said.

"There is no such thing as new—"

"Some of us think that there are better ways to verify old mathematical problems." Santino's words ran over Mako's. "And the inscription on the Mechanism could provide insight into these methods."

"That, we also agree on," Mako said. "There are huge gaping holes in our knowledge. The Mechanism uses Babylonian math, not Greek, and—"

"—there are nearly as many different types of math as there are languages, because math is *not* universal—"

"This is like watching your parents argue when you're too young to understand it," Rachel said. "I'm not getting anything out of this."

"Right." Mako resigned himself in a purple-gray sigh. "Okay... What we're talking about is missing knowledge.

Information changes everything. When we were first activated, how did you know you could talk to machines?"

"It was obvious," Rachel replied. "The damn things never shut up."

Mako nodded. "And how did you know you could control them?"

"I…" Rachel paused and thought back to the chaos of those first few weeks. She had lost her eyesight just days before full activation, and juggling two life-changing events at the same time had left her memories in a muddle. "Someone told me? I don't remember."

"What if you hadn't been told?" he asked her. "Would you have figured it out on your own?"

"Yeah, no doubt. Machines are noisy as hell. At some point, I would have snapped and told one of them to be quiet."

"Okay," Mako said. "Now, what if machines weren't noisy? What if they didn't impact your daily life at all? Would you have still discovered you could control them?"

"Hm." Rachel leaned against the table. She ran her finger along the rough chronology of the line Mako had drawn on its surface. *Millions and millions of years…* "Good question. I really don't know."

"We probably would have," Mako said. "Someone would have tripped over it, given enough time. But you're right—machines are everywhere, and they never shut up. Learning we could control them was…" he snapped his fingers. "Bang. Easy. Done.

"There's no way we've reached the limits of what we can do," he said. "The EMF is part of every single experience we have as sentient beings. As we acquire new information, we expand our abilities."

"Actually, Rachel, you might be the best example of this. You know, when you figured out your eyes didn't have…to…" Santino's voice trailed off. Her Southwestern turquoise was wrapped within grays, with voids where nothing could be seen, his emotions tiptoeing around the topic of her blindness.

She nodded, quick and hard, to shut him up. "I get it."

"We're still learning," Mako said. "There are holes in our knowledge. The potential applications for what we can do are remarkable, but until we get the information we need to patch those holes, we're just a bunch of kids with neat party tricks."

"Take me, for example. I can block the EMF, and…" He looked down towards Rachel. "May I? It'll help prove my point."

She nodded again, and braced herself against what was coming.

When she wanted to block the EMF, she pulled frequencies together into a tight weave. She usually imagined the EMF as strands of thread as she worked, selecting and drawing the best of these threads into themselves to form a light, flexible barrier. Practice had made perfect: at first, she had been unable to see clearly within the shelter of her shield, but now she could use most of her usual visual frequencies while also keeping out the busy chatter of machines. And she could always feel the collective, no matter which frequencies she used, or how tightly she drew them together.

Mako's abilities were one of a kind. The Agents were limitless, uncontrollable… Except when Mako stepped in. He could wrap an Agent in his mind and set them down beside him. He was OACET's ultimate designated driver; on more than one occasion, Mako had been the one to break up a bar fight and keep an Agent from making a huge mistake involving someone's credit score.

His shield slammed around her like a steel prison. The steady presence of the collective that she could always feel in the back of her mind ceased to exist, and the dark came crashing down.

"Can you break it?" Mako's voice rumbled across her body.

She pushed, hard, her mind pressing against every part of his barrier. Then, when she had made no progress, she started to test for weaknesses. She found there were no seams to Mako's shield, no points where separate frequencies had been joined. He had forged them into a whole. Where she wove frequencies together, he created a single impenetrable, impermeable alloy.

"No," she said. "And I'm trying."

He let his shield drop, and Rachel's world came back in a wave of color and shared minds.

"See? Every time we discover a new party trick, we expand our understanding of what we can do. But why am I the only one who can do this particular trick?" Mako asked. "I can't teach the others how to block our access—I haven't even been able to develop methods to test how I do it."

"It *is* a good trick," Rachel admitted. Even Patrick Mulcahy with his iron will couldn't force his way past Mako. Together, the two of them had finally answered that age-old question of what happens when an irresistible force meets an immovable object, which was black out, regain consciousness, laugh, vomit, laugh again, and then head off in search of beer to kill the headaches.

"This is a hole in our knowledge we need to patch, the sooner the better," Mako said. "There's nothing else out there that can block our access to the EMF. Just me. The telecommunications industry has been working on blocking us since we went public, but they're making no progress. If Santino and I can figure out how I do it, our problems would be over."

Rachel started laughing. The very idea that their problems could ever be over…

"Think about it," Mako said. "People are scared of us because we can control machines. But if there are OACET-specific security protocols, then we won't be able to access them."

"Update the firewalls to keep Agents out," Santino said, "And people will have lost most of their ammunition against you."

"Except I'll still be able to see through walls, or be accused of mind reading, or go out-of-body into a secure area…"

"*Most* ammunition," Santino repeated. "There'll always be those folks unhappy with OACET, but somebody's always going to be unhappy about something."

Not able to talk to machines? Interesting…

It wouldn't be the end of the world for Rachel. She thought back over the last couple of weeks and, with the exception of Lulu, couldn't remember the last time she had interacted directly with a machine. Some of the others might miss the constant chatter of the digital ecosystem in their heads, but her?

She realized she was smiling.

Mako grinned back at her. "Right? Okay, I'll admit it might not fix everything, but it'd be a good start. All we need to do is find out what's unique about me, and then we can start to develop what I can do as a security protocol."

"This all ties back into what we're saying about the Mechanism, too," Santino said. "A little bit of information can change everything. It might reframe our entire perspective."

"Or," hedged Mako, "help us to better understand something we already think we know."

And there's our motive, Rachel realized.

Any private collector who wanted the information on the fragment could have simply sent an anonymous email to the Greek embassy and attached a copy of the photograph. That would have gotten the procedural wheels turning. Months later, the information on the fragment would have been released, joining the rest of the data on the Antikythera Mechanism within the public domain.

Time-consuming, maybe, but cheap and easy. And zero chance that your hired cat burglar would be caught in the process. It was certainly the best option.

Unless you wanted to keep that information a secret.

TEN

"I shouldn't be here."

Rachel slipped her arm around Bell's waist. The girl was shaking like a leaf, and sickly yellow through and through. "Yes, you should. You wear that dress better than I do. I'll cry if you don't show it off."

Rachel wasn't kidding. Bell was wearing a little gold number that Rachel had found at the back of her closet. Rachel didn't remember buying it. Based on the dates on the price tags, she had been deep in her third year of life as a brainwashed cyborg at the time of purchase. Why she had splurged on an expensive Flapper-style dress was anybody's guess, but she was glad of it. She had coaxed Bell into trying it on, and the dress had turned from clumsy beads and folds into something straight off of a catwalk. Bell's hair with its bright green highlights had been tucked up under a matching headband, and the curls that had slipped loose helped call attention to the polished gold of her lipstick and eyeshadow.

It wasn't a conventional type of beauty, but on Bell, it was stunning. Phil had nearly driven off the road trying to sneak peeks at her in the rearview mirror.

Bell had seemed happy enough with her appearance while getting dressed, but now, as the South Portico of the White House loomed in front of them, she had started to balk.

"Come on," Rachel said, prodding her towards the sidewalk. Jason and Phil, deep in conversation in a private link, hadn't noticed that the women had fallen behind. "Besides, Zia will be here. Nobody's going to notice you anyhow."

Sad but true: Santino's girlfriend was the Platonic ideal of the blond bombshell. She had curves upon curves, extraordinary blue eyes, and degrees in astrophysics and engineering technology from MIT. Before she had been recruited to OACET, Zia had planned to be one of the first humans on Mars, and that was quite possibly because leaving planet Earth would be the only way she would ever get any peace.

Rachel steered Bell towards the doors to the Diplomatic Reception Room. Once they had caught up to the men, she unfastened the girl from her arm and transferred her to Jason's, trying not to laugh at the mental image of passing him a nervous hummingbird. Then, Phil took Rachel's arm, and together they crossed into the White House.

"Think she'll be okay?" Phil asked her.

"Honestly? I'm not sure if she's ready for a night like this," Rachel replied.

"Who is?" Phil glanced around, his colors swimming in raw yellow-white energy as he took in the splendor of the reception parlor. *"I never thought I'd be here. Ever!"*

A small cough at her elbow brought her down to earth, and she went through the rituals of security and coat checks with a Secret Service agent. She hoped he'd be rotated off duty soon; nobody wanted to work through their own party.

And then they were inside.

The Diplomatic Reception Room was lit by crystal sconces and firelight, with several small tables strategically located for partygoers who wanted to drop into quiet conversation over *hors d'oeuvres.* The oval room was decorated with painted wallpaper, scenes of early American life playing out above the wainscoting. Much of the antique Colonial furniture which lived in the room had been removed to make space, with fancy but practical reproduction loveseats brought in to line the walls.

The four of them were fashionably late. The other guests already milled about in their finery. Bell's colors slowly slid from a terrified yellow to an uneasy orange as she shot quick glances about the room; Rachel flipped frequencies to see another young woman about Bell's age, dressed in vivid blues with long braided hair to match. A scan of the adjacent China Room showed a buffet, the silver chafing dishes overflowing with a dozen delicacies. The smells of fresh bread and bacon floated through the open door.

Yup, she thought, as her scans hit on Santino, Zockinski, and Hill, looming over the prime rib carving station like lions at a kill.

She brought her scans back to her normal range. Phil was still radiating eager energy beside her. His hand on her arm burned, and he was taking up more space in her head than usual.

"Calm down," she told him. She scanned the structure until she found the nearest concrete, and ran her mind through her favorite grounding medium before she passed a sense of serene composure back across their link. *"It's just a party."*

"It's a party at the White House!"

"The President isn't here. It's a party with a few politicians who had nothing better to do on a Monday night. You've been to dozens of these."

She felt him run his own scans across the building. His scope and range weren't as developed as her own, but she had a professional interest in watching how he worked. Phil focused on the structure instead of the people within, taking in the splendor of the place as he moved from room to room.

"Scanning the White House is totally illegal," she said with a mental grin.

"Like you haven't done it," Phil replied.

"Damn straight. My first time here, I was tripping over myself."

They began to mingle. Phil was the perfect gentleman, willing to meet and greet whoever crossed their paths. Between the two of them, they knew a goodly number of the other guests, and were happy to talk shop with those from the MPD or the Secret Service. Phil worked with the MPD's bomb unit, and was always happy to spin a tale about the city's latest close call. Tonight, it was pipe bombs: Phil had the crowd in stitches over the problems of downloading plans and building bombs without knowing precisely what to do with them after you made them.

"...he decided the best place to store them was in the trunk of his car! That way, they're out of the house, right? So, there's this huge box of pipe bombs sitting over the gas tank, and I'm on the phone with this traffic cop who really wishes he had called in sick…"

"Rachel!"

It was a joyful voice, close to sunlight. Rachel stepped away from the group from the MPD to find two women, one with a core color of violet, the other a classic polished bronze, moving towards her.

Rachel reached out and seized the feeling of concrete, hard, as Zia came in for a hug and a quick kiss on the cheek. She had grabbed the concrete in time: Santino's girlfriend felt nothing but Rachel's clear sense of self, peppered with happiness at seeing her friend. She was even able to tell Zia, quite truthfully, *"You look fantastic!"*

Like Rachel, the other woman was wearing the traditional little black dress, but that's where the comparisons ended. Where Rachel's dress was a layer of lace over a silk shell, Zia's was thick brushed cotton, with sleeves so long they draped down to her fingers. It was simple and modest, and she wore it without jewelry. On anyone else, it'd be downright frumpy; on Zia, it did nothing but call attention to her natural beauty.

"Thank you," Zia said aloud. Then, in the link, *"You've met Kristen?"*

"Zockinski's wife?" Rachel said. "Yes, last summer."

The third woman turned an uncertain orange, and Rachel and Zia flushed in shared embarrassment at their minor social flub. The two Agents immediately dropped into the conversational safety net offered by the thrill of being at the White House— can you believe we're really *here?*—and helped steer Kristen Zockinski's colors back to a safe, stable blue before she insisted that the two Agents come with her to help pry her husband off of the buffet.

Rachel declined in favor of keeping all of her fingers, and wandered towards the open door to the Map Room. The ladies' restroom was concealed towards the back, and the

Secret Service had left the room itself open for party overflow. Twin to the China Room located on the other side of the oval Diplomatic Room, the Map Room held additional chairs and couches, and—

Oh! There's Maddie Peguero.

The archivists were keeping to themselves in a corner of the Map Room, a tight cluster of scholars whose jobs had no overlap with those in law enforcement. Peguero glanced up from her plate full of crêpes and spotted Rachel, and her colors began to twine around themselves in yellow and red barbed wire.

Rachel gave her a jolly smile and a wave on her way to the restroom.

When she popped back into the party, the first thing she spotted were two thick ropes of her Southwestern turquoise, the first wrapped around a core of citrus orange, the second around a core of purple velvet that had faded in the sun. She had seen both colors recently, but didn't know who they belonged to until she flipped frequencies to take in the owners' faces. The citrus belonged to a balding, jovial man with a thick sandy beard: she recognized Randy Summerville, one of D.C.'s more formidable telecommunications lobbyists, from his photograph in OACET's dossier. The purple belonged to a younger man whom Rachel didn't know, but the color was *so* familiar...

She wracked her brain trying to place them—*Where have I seen those two hues before?*—before she remembered that she had spotted them at the Botanic Gardens gala.

Summerville had been one of the lobbyists talking to Senator Hanlon.

Once, Rachel sighed to herself. *Just once I'd like to go to a nice party and not have to swim with the sharks.*

She started a timer. Based on her past experiences with lobbyists, those who had a specific bone to pick with her would take a half hour or more to casually circle the room before cornering her for a long, long chat. She assumed the delay had something to do the ratio of alcohol consumption to pliability, and resolved to keep herself to a single glass of champagne.

Hmm...

She opened a link with the other Agents in the room.

"Guys? Best behavior tonight," she told them. *"There are some big-name lobbyists here, and they're thinking about OACET."*

It was a very slight exaggeration, and Rachel held on to the feel of concrete as hard as she could so they wouldn't catch it. Straight-up lying couldn't be done through a link, but she needed them on their toes. Better to think that everyone they spoke with could be a threat, than take one drink too many and say something that could turn around and bite them.

"Shit." Phil and Zia both started peeking around the room before Jason yelled at them to keep their heads down. The other three Agents dropped back into their conversations, their party colors weighed down by professional blues.

Sorry, guys, Rachel thought to herself after she broke the link. This should have been an enjoyable night for everyone. They weren't ever fully free to be themselves, not around outsiders, but there were enough friends here to make it comfortable.

She returned to Phil's side, and laughed at the appropriate moments until the timer went off in her head. Then, she excused herself, gathered her coat from the Secret Service agents by the door, and slipped out to wait on the South Portico porch.

It took Summerville a few minutes to find her. When he turned the corner to find her nestled in the darkest corner of the Portico, she was smiling at him, two fresh glasses of champagne waiting on the stone railing beside her, a third held lightly in her hand.

"Hope you don't mind, but I've exhausted my spycraft quota for this week," she told him.

The man started laughing. "You're getting a well-deserved reputation, Agent Peng."

"Who, me?" she said, gesturing towards the extra glasses of champagne with her own. "Surely not."

"Randy Summerville," he said, as he picked up the glass and parked himself against the shadowed wall.

"The telecommunications lobbyist," she said. "I'm aware.

Where's your friend?"

A flicker of surprise ran over him. "Who? My assistant?"

Ah. That cleared things up; she had thought the second man was awfully young to be active in politics. She threw her scans back towards the party, and found the core of purple velvet waiting by the buffet table. The young man's face was red from pain, as if someone had punched him in the mouth. Now that his boss had left him alone, his conversational colors had changed: he was still wearing her Southwestern turquoise, but also the barbed reds and yellows of hate and fear.

That man, Rachel thought, *does not like me at all.*

"Would he like to join us?" Rachel asked. As long as her evening was ruined anyhow, she might as well start collecting data for OACET's ever-growing collection of dossiers.

Summerville shook his head. "Thank you, but he'd get in the way."

"Just for the record, I'm not the Agent you want to speak to about alliances or strategy."

"I'm aware," he said with a slight grin. "But you are the one I want to talk to if someone needs to be put in prison."

Oho? She ran his conversational colors. He was enjoying this, with purple humor and the same yellow-white energy that dominated the personalities of those who loved a good verbal sparring match, but there was also a serious and strong professional blue beneath these.

There was some worn denim in that blue, too much of it to be a coincidence… "You told Mitch Alimoren to get me to come to this party," she guessed, remembering how earnest Alimoren had been when he pressed the invitation into her hands.

"Alimoren's an old acquaintance," Summerville said, his surface colors retreating slightly from her Southwestern turquoise. "I'm at the White House about once a week, and he handles my scheduling."

"That wasn't exactly an answer," Rachel said, but the way his colors had flinched away from her question had given him away.

"Let's see how this conversation goes before I drag others into it."

"Fair enough," she allowed. "Who needs to go to jail?"

"Senator Richard Hanlon."

She had choked on her champagne when Hanlon's core of water-darkened brown swelled within Summerville's thoughts, so she was coughing, hard, before he got the words out. "Sorry," she said. "Wrong pipe. What were you saying?"

The purple humor dropped away from him. "Agent Peng? We're both busy people."

Realization struck. "You know what he did to us."

"The brainwashing? Yes." Summerville nodded. He tugged his suitcoat closed as the evening air reached him. "Nearly everybody in Washington knows. What he did to OACET was beyond criminal. If Congress had any balls, they'd hang him out to dry. I've been pushing my employers to move ahead and sever ties with him on principle."

She was stunned, and kept checking his colors to see if he was lying. She had assumed the telecommunications industry had accepted Hanlon wholesale, warts and all, but Summerville meant what he said.

"Surprised?" He grinned at her. "Not everyone in Washington is out to destroy you. A few of us are still decent human beings."

"Maybe a few of you," she admitted. "But what about your employers?"

Summerville's colors fell towards gray, and she read volumes in that shade of storm-churned sky.

"Right," she said.

"My employers have a vested interest in Hanlon," he said. "He's promised them he can find a way to block you."

A brief memory of her visit to Mako's office flickered in her head. "Your employers have been working on a way to keep us out of machines since we went public."

"Can you blame them?"

No, she couldn't. The Agents didn't require a subscription service or peripheral equipment to maintain their links. If the technology ever worked its way into the general population, every telecommunications carrier from digital satellites to old-fashioned land lines would go bankrupt. Preventing the Agents from accessing machines was a solid step towards regulation.

"My employers weren't making any progress on their own," Summerville said. "They decided to change their strategy. Since Hanlon's company invented the implant, they decided to throw their support behind him, and see what he might come up with."

She turned those ideas around, and found that no matter which way she looked at them, they made sense.

That might be a major reason Congress won't touch Hanlon. If he's promised Big Communications that he'll find a way to keep us out of their phone lines, they'll buy him some time…

There's also the money angle. He ceded the rights for the implant over to the government, but if he gives the patent rights for blocking the implant over to the telecommunications industry, they'll make a crazy return on their investment…

But Mako's the only thing out there that can block us. If Hanlon fails…

Hanlon would be a scapegoat twice over, for causing the problem in the first place, and then for failing to fix it.

He's got to be scared shitless.

"Did I say something funny?"

"No," Rachel said, pulling on the feeling of concrete until she could wipe the smile from her face. She set her mostly full glass of champagne down with a sharp, *Focus, woman!* "Is he making any progress? We've been working on the same problem, and thus far we've hit a wall."

"Really?" Summerville blinked at her in surprised orange. "I thought you'd want to keep your abilities."

She shrugged. "We don't like being society's monsters. It'd be easier for us if people didn't automatically assume we're screwing around with machines."

"Ah," he said, sage green beginning to show.

"We've been working on security protocols that'll keep us

out of closed systems," she said, and then took something of a risk. "Maybe your employers would like to collaborate with us instead of Hanlon. They might make more progress if they have test subjects."

The sage green dropped a shade deeper, and snapped tight across the lobbyist's torso. "I think we might not be on the same page," he said. "I don't think I fully explained what Hanlon's trying to do."

She suddenly felt the cold. "Oh?" she asked, her head tilted as if he had said something almost, but not quite, of interest.

"Hanlon's not working to develop firewalls to keep you out of machines," Summerville said. "He's working on a way to block your access to the entire EM spectrum."

She knew it was coming, but it still hit her like a punch, and in her head, the room went dark around her. She had her hands locked at the small of her back before realizing that cocktail dresses clashed horribly with parade rest. "Interesting approach," she said, as she pretended she had been reaching for her glass of champagne.

"It would solve everything," Summerville said. "My employers can't permit OACET's abilities to be made available to the public, and you'd…"

He trailed off, unable to find a polite way to end that particular thought. Rachel did it for him. "We'd go back to being normal people."

"They can't take the implant out," he said. "Not without causing irreparable damage to you. The best solution is for Hanlon to find a way to block your access to the EMF."

Rachel made a noncommittal sigh, convinced that Summerville could hear her pulse hammering in her head. She was suddenly very aware of Phil and Jason and Zia, all shouting at her via the link as they pushed their way through the partygoers to reach her. She mentally waved the other Agents off, promising to tell them the cause of her distress after she was done with the lobbyist.

Rachel reconnected with the concrete foundation, and

grounded herself, hard. *I'm tired of Hanlon,* she realized. *I'm tired of him throwing a new threat at me every fucking time I turn around.*

It was a credible threat, too. Hanlon's company developed the implant, so it stood to reason that they could find a way to turn it off. One day, maybe not too far in the future, there might come a knock at her door and men in white coats to take her away. It wasn't too hard to imagine a second round of surgery in which a new implant was wrapped around the old, shielding it from the EMF.

Killing it.

Killing her, and the rest of OACET.

"Tell me," she said, as she met Summerville's eyes. "If you could stop Hanlon while protecting your employers' interests, would you?"

"Yes," he said. Yellow surprise moved into his conversational colors at the question, but she didn't spot any signs of lying.

"Do you have children?"

"What?"

"Do you?" He did, four of them, but strangers seemed to take offense when she recounted the details of their dossiers without prompting.

"Yes, but—"

She very nearly followed that up with her story. Her mouth was open, she was drawing breath, and then the sum of her intelligence rose up to remind her that she was talking to a man who manipulated powerful people for a living.

Hey! she roared at herself. *Get the fuck away from Summerville—right now!—before you say something that'll pull us all under the ground, you stupid, stupid woman!*

"Good. I find I trust parents more than other people," she lied, as she turned from him. It took a moment to move her thoughts from one path to another. "Let your employers know that if they choose to work with us, we can develop the security protocols they need. Hanlon has started something he can't finish."

She downed the last of her champagne in a quick, hard sip. "Even if he does develop some method to block our access to the EM spectrum—which is unlikely—we'll never let Hanlon touch us. Never again. His version of a solution would be worse than the problem.

"Don't let your employers trap themselves," she finished. "If you're serious about helping us put Hanlon in prison, you need to cut him out of the equation. He's all talk. Working with him is just a time sink for your employers. OACET's here, and if we *are* going away, it'll be because we worked with someone other than Hanlon to find the exit. It'll benefit everybody if Hanlon's out of the picture entirely."

Summerville's colors rolled in and out of themselves. It was a unique motion: she saw none of the ins-and-outs of weaving that accompanied a man trying to make a hard decision. Instead, there were the greens of what he wanted, and there were the reds of what he felt others wanted, and these couldn't blend together. She felt as if she was watching oil and water try to mix.

"I'll do my best to convince them," he finally said. "That's all I can promise."

They shook hands, and Summerville walked back into the White House. His assistant was at the door, waiting. The young man shot Rachel a red-hot glare before he took Summerville back into the party.

Rachel took a deep breath. Then another, and another, drawing on the feeling of concrete beneath her. When her usual meditation strategies failed to calm her, she walked down the stairs of the South Portico, turned the corner, and followed the path to the Rose Garden.

The garden's title was a misnomer. It was more of a manicured lawn than a garden, with the flowers and shrubbery relegated to beds lining its edges. At this time of year, there were no roses to be seen. It was a space intended for the day; the early spring bulbs had closed for the night, and the new leaves on the trees were nothing but black streaks against the sky. Rachel slipped out of her heels and walked into the center of the grassy lawn, and reached out to Patrick Mulcahy.

The head of OACET appeared almost instantly.

His avatar was tall and broad, and wearing sunglasses and an impeccably tailored suit. Neither glasses nor suit were necessary, but Mulcahy would never choose to appear at the White House as anything less than his best self. If his green avatar were made flesh, his hair would be a sandy blond, his skin a dark Irish tan, but his features wouldn't change one whit.

"Rachel," he said.

She nodded at her boss. *"Sorry to get you out of bed."*

His avatar didn't smile, but she felt a chuckle roll across their link, and realized he was probably still tucked under the covers some five miles away in his home out in Kent. "Don't worry about it," he said. "What's happened?"

"Randy Summerville approached me. He let me know that Hanlon is actively trying to find a way to block our access to the EM spectrum."

He didn't reply. It took her a moment to realize this wasn't news to him.

"Did I sleep through a meeting or something?" she asked, annoyed.

"No," he said. "I put the Hippos on Hanlon. They report back to Josh, and he reports to me. Nobody else knows."

"What do the Hippos think?" The Cuddly Hippos were former members of the armed forces. Like Rachel, they had been recruited into OACET under the assumption that their skillsets would contribute to the overall value of the organization.

Unlike Rachel, they had been professional killers.

There were only three of them—two assassins and one traps expert—and Mulcahy didn't let them apply their skills to their fullest extent. The Hippos resented this; Mulcahy kept them from putting a bullet through Hanlon's skull through sheer dominance of will.

My God, what was he thinking, to put them right on Hanlon's tail...

He heard her. "It keeps them busy," he said. "And I trust them to follow orders. They're professionals, not sociopaths."

Rachel took a breath and steadied her walls. Her conversation with Summerville had shaken her. Mulcahy shouldn't have been able to pick up on her stray thoughts. Fucking rookie mistake, as Jason would say.

"To answer your question, they now think Hanlon is better left alive than dead," he told her. "They've been watching him long enough to realize that he's so far in over his head that he'll never recover. It's turned into a game for them. They have a pool going on how long he'll be able to fool Congress and the telecommunications companies."

She swung her mind back towards the White House, where Jason, Phil, and Zia were waiting by the door. One word from her, and the three of them would be down the stairs and running through the garden to learn how Summerville had spooked her to the point of panic...

"Hanlon might be able to hold on long enough to do us damage," she said, trying to keep the image of men in white coats from her thoughts.

Mulcahy's avatar stared at her impassively. She had the sensation that he was studying her emotions in the link, looking for cracks in her composure. "What did Summerville want?" he finally asked.

"To form an alliance with OACET, I think," Rachel said. She wasn't sure what he had found, but the feeling of being dissected and analyzed had disappeared. *"He said he wanted to put Hanlon in prison, but he was clear that he won't go against the interests of his employers."*

"How did he read?"

"He wasn't lying. Wait!" she added quickly. *"Jenna Noura? The woman who stole the artifact? She lied to me yesterday and I didn't catch it."* The right side of her body was still sore from when Noura had tricked her into slamming herself against the lamp post. *"It's official: I can be tricked. They're both professional con artists. I wouldn't trust what Summerville told me."*

"Show me," he said, and Rachel queued up the recording of her conversation with Summerville.

Rachel's perception of the emotional spectrum could only be captured when she was the source of the recording, and Mulcahy frequently used her to snoop on the mental status of Washington's various figures when he met with them in public places. She'd follow her boss as a member of his personal security team, close enough to watch but not close enough to hear him speak. After the meeting, he'd review her feed and compare the emotional changes in his opponent to the changes within their conversation. If the topic was especially time-sensitive, he'd have her send her perspective directly to him via a live link. He said knitting her perspective into his own gave him a hell of a headache, but it was often worth it. He was many, many months behind her in terms of reading emotions on the fly, but he had picked up the fundamentals and was able to recognize a basic lie.

He watched the exchange without comment, then ran it again to catch anything he might have missed. It took a goodly amount of time: Rachel wondered what the Secret Service thought of her, standing around on the lawn of the Rose Garden, doing a suspicious amount of nothing… She was glad she had been the one to have caught Jenna Noura, as that was probably the only reason that a polite man with a gun hadn't arrived to escort her back to the party.

"All right," Mulcahy finally said. "I know Summerville by reputation. He's said to be a decent person. I don't think he lied to you."

She didn't need the link to hear his unspoken *but…*

"He could have easily brought this to Josh," he added. "I think he's trying to recruit you."

She slapped a hand over her mouth before she started laughing. No reason to stress out the four nice Secret Service agents lurking in the bushes. *"Recruit me?"*

Mulcahy grinned at her. "Spycraft 101. Feed someone a scrap of valuable information, and they'll begin to trust you. Think of it as investment capital in a relationship."

"I thought we were pretending to be politicians, not spies."

He sighed. "You'd be surprised at how often those two overlap."

"Probably not."

"No," he agreed. "Probably not. So, my take on your conversation is that in the short term, his employers' interests and Hanlon's are the same. Over the long term, their interests don't mesh with Hanlon's, and he knows this. He's caught between doing what's politically advantageous today, while positioning himself and his employers for the future."

She gave a small, careful nod. That much she had figured out on her own. *"He knows Hanlon is going to fail."*

"Or he's not going to let his employers commit themselves to a short-lived strategy. In either case, I want you to consider him a potential ally. Wait a few weeks. If he doesn't contact you by then, approach him and introduce him to Mako."

"Right," she said, and set a timer for two weeks and six hours.

"Now," he said, in that quiet voice he used when he was particularly focused on a problem. She felt the hairs on the back of her neck rise. "Why did you ask him if he was a parent?"

"It's—" she began aloud, but caught herself. *"It's not an issue. I was about to take the conversation in one direction, and decided it might cause problems, so I redirected."*

"Why would it cause problems?" he asked.

Rachel paused. He was OACET, and he was... Well, he was Patrick Mulcahy. He'd know if she tried to lie. She reclaimed her connection to the concrete and said, *"There's an analogy I use when I try to explain what it's like to be in the collective. He didn't need to hear it. It wasn't appropriate to the conversation."*

There. One hundred percent truth.

And he still caught the sense she was hiding something within her words. "You're getting better at that," he said.

Rachel glanced over her shoulder, pretending to look towards the South Portico. *"I need to get back to the party."*

There was a flicker of amusement across their link. "Good

night, Penguin. Thank you for contacting me."

She nodded, and he vanished.

She stared at the empty air and moved the newly vacant space in her mind around, testing its qualities. Then, when she accepted anew that she'd never figure out what her boss really wanted from her, she picked up her shoes and walked back towards the light and music.

ELEVEN

"Don't come here hungover. It throws off my results."

Rachel glared at the small bald man in front of her. "I'm not hung over," she said. "I haven't been sleeping well."

Her dreams were about shipwrecks. Even the autoscript designed to put her in a sedated sleep state didn't help; it kept her in a deep sleep where she was lost, not quite dreaming but still tumbling around the bottom of the ocean like a broken bag of bones…

"Then don't come here when you're sleep-deprived," the man muttered, as he typed another series of commands into the computer. "Now, turn it off, and look straight at the light."

"Pick one or the other," she said. "I can turn off my implant, or I can look at the light. I can't do both."

Dr. Gillion was usually deep within the angry reds, but today he was especially furious with her. "What?"

"Obviously you have problems understanding what it means to be blind," she said. "Which is strange, considering your line of work."

There was a not-subtle cough from a nearby chair. Bradley, a large man who worked as Gillion's secretary except when Rachel was in the office, was accustomed to reminding the two of them that they had a witness.

The world's foremost neuro-ophthalmologist gritted his teeth. "Look at the light, focus on it, and then turn off your implant," Gillion growled. "Your muscle memory can hold your left eye steady long enough for me to get a reading."

"Fine," she said. She fixed her scans on the red light in front of her left eye, and then flipped off her implant. The light and the examination room vanished.

She had contacted Dr. Gillion and his organization, Visual

Cybernetics Incorporated, after an especially difficult case in which a bombing victim had lost the use of his eyes. Rachel had decided that since the world at large was hell-bent on careening wildly out of her control, she'd do what she could to fix it. If that meant outing herself as blind to a scientist who specialized in studying the connections between eyesight and the human brain, she could live with that decision.

If she had known that Gillion was a cut of prime Grade-A asshole, she wouldn't have bothered.

Gillion styled himself as a living, breathing Albert Einstein, and his colleagues let him get away with it. He was an unparalleled genius in his field, yes, but he was also conceited and more than a little misogynistic.

That attitude hadn't gotten much traction with Rachel.

After their initial meeting, Gillion had called Bradley into the exam room and had told him to assume sentry duty. Both Rachel and Gillion had agreed to this arrangement: Gillion didn't want to get sued for punching a patient, and Rachel didn't want to go to jail for murder.

(And she had made sure Bradley was properly terrified of her. Not that she had wanted to traumatize the poor bug-eyed man, but it was either that or risk seeing her name in the tabloids under a headline using some version of the words *Reputable Source, OACET Agent,* and *Blind!* Thanks, but no thanks.)

"Now," the odious little doctor said, "turn it back on."

She did: the red light was where she had left it.

"Again."

They repeated the process several times, both of them silent except for Gillion barking the occasional order. Then, once he had his readings, they repeated the process with the other eye, and then moved on to a different battery of tests.

For all of his faults, Gillion was thorough. It took several hours to complete the testing regime, and by the end, Rachel felt as hungry and as mentally exhausted as if she had spent the entire time out-of-body.

"I'll call you the next time I need you," Gillion said, and left the room.

"Two days' notice!" she shouted after him. "Give me at least two days' notice before you expect me to show up!"

Gillion didn't answer her. She rounded on Bradley. "How can you work for him?"

Gillion's assistant blinked his overlarge eyes at her before fleeing.

She ripped the electrodes from her scalp, and stormed out of the office.

She was standing on the sidewalk, staring straight up at the sun, when Santino pulled up to the curb in his tiny hybrid. They were three blocks from Visual Cybernetics Incorporated when she was finally calm enough to turn thoughts into coherent words.

"Tell me why I suffer through that... that..."

"You called him a 'prick of mountainous proportions' last time."

"That prick of mountainous proportions and his *ego!*"

He sighed as he turned into the parking lot of a convenient fast food restaurant. "Because Gillion will use this data to develop a version of your implant that can help process various EM frequencies, and turn those frequencies into stimuli for the optic nerves," he said. "It'll be analogous to how the cochlear implant functions for the deaf. It'll transform the lives of hundreds of thousands of people. You can suffer through a couple of hours of Gillion and his ego for that."

"Right," she snarled. "Right."

"And when he wins the Nobel Prize for Medicine—"

"Oh, I'll be damned if that fuckin' jackass wins the Nobel thanks to me—" she started, and lapsed into a nasty sulk when she realized Santino was laughing at her in purples.

She was most of the way through her cheeseburger when Zockinski's ringtone (Los del Rio's "Macarena"—when he made that request, she had realized that he and Hill were just messing with her) sang out in her head. "One sec," she said to her partner. Then, to Zockinski, *"What's up?"*

"How's your day off?" the detective asked her.

"Over, I assume?"

Zockinski laughed. "Yup. Come to Indiana Avenue. Jenna Noura wants to talk to you."

"'You' as in me and Santino, or 'you' as in me, myself, and I?"

"Just you," he said. "She says you know why."

Zockinski disconnected, and Rachel was left wondering what the hell Noura had meant by that.

They drove up and down the streets near Indiana Avenue until they finally found a parking spot, and then headed towards Zockinski's cell phone. The detective was waiting for them in the prisoner holding area, Hill standing silently beside him. Off to the side were several uniformed officers, and a man in a shabby tee-shirt fiddling with the monitoring equipment.

"He's already talked to Noura," Zockinski said, pointing at Hill.

"How'd it go?" Santino asked.

"I think he's in love," Zockinski said. "She made him smile."

Rachel pressed the back of her hand to her forehead and fell into Santino's arms in a full Southern Belle swoon.

"Funny," Hill said.

"So what does she want?" Santino asked, as he propped Rachel on her feet.

"She wants to talk to Peng," Hill said, pointing at Rachel. "Didn't say why."

"Maybe she likes you," Zockinski said with a wink.

"Her timing's bad," Rachel said with a dry laugh. "Becca gets home tonight."

"What's the setup here?" Santino was looking around the prisoner holding area. The MPD's station on Indiana Ave was more of an administrative showpiece than their own station, its location in the center of the city placing it decidedly in the "law" side of the "law and order" equation. It was adjacent to the city's courthouses, and allowed a certain amount of comfort for those persons working with the police.

"Like ours," said Zockinski. "Normal one-way mirror that

lets us see into the interview room. Everything is recorded."

The guy in the tee-shirt waved.

"Nifty," Rachel said. She borrowed Noura's dossier from Hill, and went to talk to a master thief.

Jenna Noura was sitting quietly, a paper cup of coffee beside her. The officers must have decided she was enough of a risk to leave her handcuffed to the table, and the cuffs looked overlarge on her wrists. She brightened as Rachel entered the room, strands of hope held up by Rachel's Southwestern turquoise: whatever it was she wanted, she was sure Rachel could deliver.

"Bored?" Rachel asked her.

"A little," Noura replied. "I'm highly susceptible to cabin fever."

"Prison's going to be rough for you, then." Rachel opened the manila folder and flipped frequencies to examine Noura's file. "You're thirty-one. That's awfully young to be looking at a life sentence."

"Maybe there's something I can do for you," Noura said. She spoke slowly, the words something of a caress.

Oh, please. Rachel was used to innuendo in interviews, but she hadn't expected it from Noura. "There is something you can do," she said. "We need to know who hired you. Would you like me to get you a lawyer?"

"No," Noura said. "Just you and me."

"Okay." Rachel waited. When Noura didn't offer any new information, Rachel started writing out her shopping list on the folder. *Beer, hard cider... Becca's coming back, so buy that bread she likes... Throw out those old carrots before she notices...*

"I don't know who hired me," Noura finally said.

"Sorry, then," Rachel said, as she added a few more items to her list. "You're useless. Enjoy prison."

"I've got other things to offer," Noura said in that same sensual voice.

Rachel kept writing. *Flowers... I should buy some flowers, but Santino gets so pissed when I buy hothouse roses...*

"I'm one of the world's best art thieves," Noura said. She

leaned towards Rachel, like a cat settling in for a long stretch. If the jumpsuit had a low neckline, and if Rachel had been limited by a set of working eyeballs, the view would have been deep and smooth.

As it was, Rachel rolled those eyes as hard as she could. "Knock knock," she said, as she pushed her grocery list aside.

"What?"

"No, who. As in, 'Who's there?'"

Noura's conversational colors changed to an annoyed orange. "Don't waste my time with jokes."

"Damn!" Rachel slammed her palm on the table. It was a swift, unexpected motion, and Noura leapt backwards at the loud *pop!* "You already knew the punchline."

Noura wrapped her colors around her, and they settled into professional blues.

"Does that ever work?" Rachel asked.

"More often than it should," Noura replied. She scooted her chair back and sat up primly, handcuffs and all, changing from seductress to schoolmarm as easily as slipping off a sweater.

"You were saying? World's best art thief?"

"One of them," Noura said. "Do you know how we work?"

"A broker, I assume."

The woman nodded. "The client approaches the broker, and I get my jobs through the broker's intermediaries. There's never any fewer than two degrees of separation between me and a client."

Rachel pretended to make a tick in Noura's folder. "Good news for the client when you get caught."

"Right. And if I were a stupid woman…" Smug pink started to show within Noura's professional blues.

Rachel took that pink and ran with it. *That first day, back in her holding cell… She knew what the fragment was before we did.* "You might not have information about your client, but you did get information about the item."

"Of course," Noura said. "I've got an excellent reputation. My clients know to treat me with respect. They'll tell me exactly what it is I'm stealing, so I can make sure they're paying me a fair price commensurate with the item and the risk involved."

"And breaking into the White House…"

"Huge risk," Noura said, raising one hand. The other came up to meet it. "Huge payout."

"Tell me this also came with a huge stack of information to help you plan your getaway."

"That, and…" Noura looked at Rachel, her conversational colors sharpening to a point as she waited.

On the other side of the mirrored glass, Santino turned yellow-white with excitement, but neither of the detectives seemed to pull anything significant from Noura's last statement.

Something science-y then… Rachel leaned forward. "Tell me they weren't stupid enough to give you a backup wristwatch."

Noura inspected her fingernails. "I'm not about to kill my own frogs."

"Mhmm," Rachel said. "Just White House staffers trying to get lucky."

"I was careless," Noura said. Mournful gray and sickly green guilt pushed aside the professional blues. "He paid the price."

"Technically, you'll still be the one who pays the price," Rachel told her. She wished Noura didn't feel guilty about killing Casper Ceara; it was easier to deal with the bad guys when they were simply bad. "That's what our justice system is for.

"If you cooperate, the justice system can be lenient. That's why they invented plea bargains. As you murdered someone in the White House," Rachel said, fingers tapping on her notepad for emphasis, "you're completely screwed unless you can give us something good. *Extremely* good. Names. Account information. That wristwatch. Hard data we can use to track down your client, and patch some of the holes in our security."

Noura nodded. "What time is it?"

"Two-thirty-eight," Rachel said automatically, before realizing she hadn't actively consulted her implant.

Fabulous. I'm a living, breathing Timex, too.

"Good," Noura said. "You're going to need to take me out of

here."

Rachel laughed.

"Let me tell you how this will happen," Noura said. "You drive me to where I've stashed my information, and I give it to you. I need to sign for it in person before they release it."

The woman wasn't lying, but her conversational colors were somehow...*off*. Rachel couldn't figure out why Noura's colors struck her as strange until she realized that there were small voids, empty places where colors and movement should be.

So that's what a lie of omission looks like, she realized.

"Or," Rachel said, "You tell us where it is, and we get a warrant."

"No," Noura said with a smile. "I go with you, or this doesn't happen."

"Talk me into it," Rachel said. "You haven't given me a good reason."

Noura pointed towards the manila file. "May I?"

Rachel found a blank sheet of paper, and tossed it towards Noura. It glided over the steel table, Rachel's pen rolling beside it. "Be my guest."

Noura tore off the smallest corner of the top sheet, scribbled a few quick words on the paper, and then pushed the paper towards Rachel with one hand while holding the notepad in the other as a shield against the men and the cameras. Before Rachel could take either scrap or notepad from her, Noura dragged them both out of reach.

"Uh-uh," Noura said. "Eyes only."

And with that, she ate the scrap of paper.

"Oh Lord," Rachel muttered, loud enough for the men to hear. If she hadn't already had her frequencies set to reading mode, she would have missed Noura's message altogether. "Talk about melodrama."

Her bluster was purely automatic. Inside, she had gone shock-white and cold at what Noura had written.

Glazer says hello

"Got it?" Noura said.

"I don't think I understand," Rachel lied.

"It's simple. You drive me to a specific location, and I give you the goods," Noura said with a smile. "The rest is all up to you."

"Drive?" The icy pit in Rachel's stomach grew. She trusted her augmented senses above normal vision except when it came to piloting a massive metal device through one of the world's busiest cities. With practice, she'd probably be an excellent driver, but the learning curve would be steep and paved with tombstones.

Noura took her silence as confusion, so the thief tried to dumb it down. "I've hidden the data. I'm the only one who can get it back. You'll need to *get me out of here* if you want it."

The emphasis on those five words was slight, and Rachel might have missed it if Noura's conversational colors hadn't been pointing straight at Rachel's Southwestern turquoise as she said them.

"Let me see what I can do," Rachel said.

She stepped out of the interview room and shut the door behind her, her mental wheels spinning to come up with a reason to give Noura what she wanted. It had to be a good one, good enough to get Noura out of lockup and alone in a car with Rachel—*oh shit I can't drive what the fuck am I going to do*—without tipping anyone to the real reason she was about to break every protocol in the book—*oh God oh God this is going to be a disaster*—

Mitch Alimoren was there, glaring through the glass at Noura. "She'll talk to you," he said to Rachel by way of greeting. "She'll talk to Hill. But she won't talk to the Secret Service."

"Probably because she thinks we're easier to play," Rachel said, faking a chuckle. "Thanks," she said, as Santino handed her a hot cup of coffee.

Catching Alimoren up to speed took a little extra time. So did the jokes: the men couldn't get over the part where Noura had eaten the scrap of paper. Rachel fed their laughter, declaring she would *not* be the one who went after it, and when they had finally pulled themselves together, she had a plausible story lined up.

"What did she write?" Alimoren asked, his colors moving slowly towards curious yellows.

"A bunch of numbers," Rachel replied. "I think it was a combination, or coordinates, or part of a phone number or a bank account…"

"What were they?" Santino asked, and she rattled a series of digits off the top of her head. Her partner jotted them down and got to work decoding them. "Not latitude or longitude," he said. "Maybe it's part of an IP address…"

"Hell if I know," Rachel replied, and then made sure to put her left foot exactly under Hill's as he turned back towards the mirror. She gasped as she jumped, and hissed as the coffee burned her hand, and excused herself from Hill's apologies to go run her hand under cold water in the nearest bathroom.

The bathroom was empty. She leaned against the door and took a deep breath, then another, and grabbed onto the feeling of the cinderblock walls around her. *Glazer says hello…*

And as the cool of the bathroom soaked into her, she realized she had panicked for no good reason.

Nobody at First MPD—not even Santino—knew she had helped Jonathan Glazer escape from police custody. It had been the lesser evil: Glazer was combat-capable and had extensive military training, and she was sure he would have escaped without her assistance. Tossing him a MacGyver lockpick was her way of saying, *Go on, get out of here, and don't hurt any of my people while you're doing it.*

In exchange, Glazer had bought OACET time and credibility.

Rachel still considered it more than a fair trade.

She laughed quietly to herself, the sound of it bouncing around the empty room. So what if word had gotten around the darker side of society that she was willing to aid and abet? Noura had nothing to offer OACET. Pretending to cooperate with Noura would only ensure the thief would willingly turn over all information to buy Rachel's goodwill.

It's not as though Noura had any proof. Glazer had escaped in the middle of a firestorm. Nobody was sure of anything, and the only security footage that did exist showed Rachel permanently crippling his partner.

She's not leaving this station, but I can still convince her she'll get something for nothing, Rachel thought. *And maybe this'll tell the underground gossip mill that I can't be bought.*

Well, she corrected herself, *not unless it's for the right price.*

Rachel ran her hands under the tap, sprinkled some water on her dress shirt, and left the bathroom. She was beginning to feel pretty good about the situation when she realized that Noura's message had a second meaning: Noura had admitted she was in contact with Glazer.

Oh! She had to shove her fists deep in her suitcoat pockets to keep from dancing around like a happy child. After breaking out of First MPD, Glazer and his partner had disappeared. Despite the MPD's best efforts, the manhunt had turned up empty. This was the first solid lead since they had vanished. If she could somehow coax Noura into telling her the details, maybe she could track down Glazer and his partner, and finally check that item off of her To-Do list.

This, Rachel told herself, *is turning into a very good day.*

She swung around the corner, and stopped dead in her tracks. The colors within the interview room were Southwestern turquoise and poppy-seed gray, through and through.

Good mood gone, Rachel sighed, tipped her chin up, and walked into the room wearing her best poker face.

"What?" she asked as the men turned towards her.

"Alimoren wants to play along," Santino said.

"If she keeps stonewalling us, we'll never find out who hired her," the Secret Service agent said. "There's a bigger security risk out there than chauffeuring Noura to her drop site."

Beneath her poker face, Rachel winced. Alimoren had a point: learning how Noura got into the White House took priority. But...

Santino saved her. "Rachel doesn't have a valid driver's

license," he offered.

Zockinski and Hill went a dark sage green. "*That's* why you make us drive everywhere," Zockinski said.

She shrugged. "We live in the city," she said. "Driving didn't seem important. I haven't had a valid license since I enlisted, and I did that when I was eighteen. Trust me, you don't want me on the road."

"No problem," Alimoren said. "Detective Hill, Noura seems to like you. Can you drive? That'll let Agent Peng focus on Noura."

Hill nodded.

"If we do this," Rachel said, as she felt the weight of inevitability settle on her shoulders, "the Secret Service takes custody of her. Not me and Hill, or OACET and the MPD in general. I want to go on record that I think this is a bad idea. She asked about the time—maybe she's got friends out there who are ready to help her escape."

"Agreed," Alimoren said. "I don't like this, either, but I'll make sure the Secret Service bears the responsibility. You'll have backup the entire way."

It was done except for the details, and Rachel allowed herself to grin like the wickedest of witches as she returned to the interview room.

"First," Rachel began, as she returned to the chair across the table from Noura. "I don't have a driver's license, so I'm not driving you anywhere alone. Hill will be our driver."

Noura began to protest, and subsided only after Rachel shot her a private wink. "Fine," the cat burglar said, hope rising in a multicolored surge.

"You should know that if you're trying to play us, it won't go well for you," Rachel continued. "We're not your average cops— we're used to dealing with criminal masterminds." She put an oh-so-slight emphasis on *"dealing"*, and watched the threads of Noura's hope twine around each other and strengthen.

"As long as you're fair with me, you'll get what I've promised you," Noura said.

"You really need a lawyer here," Rachel told her. "Otherwise, you've got no guarantees that we'll keep our deals."

"I'm not concerned." Noura smiled. "Rumor has it that you keep your side of the bargain."

There was a slight flurry of curious yellow on the other side of the mirror, and Rachel decided to wrap things up before her too-smart partner began to revisit old mysteries. "Well," she said. "For cops, we do okay. Now, you're also going to need to wear a remote transmitter…"

It took another hour to get Noura released into their custody, and another few minutes of pretending that the police cruiser they were using for transport had been issued to them at random. It wasn't: the MPD kept a couple of cruisers fitted out with hidden recording equipment. Anything Noura said during transport would be seen and heard by Santino, Zockinski, and Alimoren and his team as they followed in a surveillance van.

Rachel approved. She was still burned out from overuse as a camera during the past couple of days. Anything that took some of the strain off of her brain was fine by her.

Noura didn't. When Hill opened the rear door of the cruiser for Noura, she peered inside in disdain. "You must be kidding," she said. "It smells like vomit."

"It's a police car," Rachel said, as Hill put Noura in the cruiser. "They all smell like vomit."

"Even the new ones," Hill added.

The door slammed shut on Noura, and they were underway.

Noura wasn't chatty. Her colors moved in searching patterns as she evaluated the road around them, offering directions as they went. She took them a roundabout way: it was only after Noura took them past Dupont Circle that Rachel realized Noura was retracing her steps.

"Tell us the address," Rachel said. "It'll be easier."

Noura gave her one of those knowing smiles, and told them to take the next right.

Finally, after another fifteen minutes of navigating traffic, she said, "Here."

Hill glanced up at the building. "Yup."

It was a commercial mail drop in a good part of town. Foot traffic would be regular, peaceful, and predictable; the clerks would be attentive and helpful. "You mailed the package to yourself?" Rachel asked.

"Yes," Noura said. "But not under my name, and I wasn't the one who bought the drop box."

Smart, Rachel admitted to herself. There was no way they'd get a warrant to search through each customer's mail. If Noura decided to back out now, it might be months before they got their hands on the package.

If there even is a package, and if Noura didn't just create this wild goose chase out of thin air to give you the opportunity to let her go...

Hmm.

Hill slid the car into a conveniently empty space (everyone declined to mention the fire hydrant), and left to scout the store. After some cautious poking around, he gestured for the women to join him.

Rachel helped Noura out of the back seat, and leaned in close. "Tonight," she whispered. "They're expecting you to try to escape while we're here."

Noura didn't reply, but her bright hope tempered itself within an uncertain orange.

"Don't worry," Rachel assured her, loud enough for Hill to overhear. "We keep our promises."

"They told me you could do that," Noura said. "I didn't believe them."

Rachel and Hill exchanged a glance. "Do what?" Rachel asked.

"You know what a person is thinking," Noura replied.

Hill chuckled.

"Is this another rumor that's going around?" Rachel asked him, and he nodded. "Aw, fuck me," she said. "Don't people have better things to do than make shit up?"

"You swear when you get defensive," Hill said, his colors

richly purple.

Rachel put a hand at the small of Noura's back, and all but shoved the woman towards the clerk while she went to cover the rear exit.

She almost didn't believe it when Noura returned with a package. It was plain white, with hunter's orange duct tape securing the edges. Rachel scanned it and found nothing but printouts and an overlarge wristwatch.

"I'll be damned," she said to Hill. "Nutty thief came through."

Hill nearly smiled. "Bombs?"

"No, it's clean. I'm not opening it, though," Rachel said, dropping the package in a large evidence bag. "I usually know a bomb when I see it. Poison is trickier."

"It *is* clean," Noura said, slightly yellow from the implied insult. "I packed them myself."

"Forgive me if I don't believe you," Rachel said. "You lied to me."

"I'm a con artist," Noura replied. "Don't take it personally."

"No." Rachel shook her head. "I don't know what people are thinking, but I *am* one of those freaks who can read microexpressions." It was an excuse she had used a couple of times before, and she decided to put it out into the MPD gossip pool to get ahead of the mindreader rumor. "You're the first person I've met in years who's able to lie without me catching it."

"Oh," Noura said. "That. Don't you know that a con artist never really lies?"

"What?"

Noura smiled at her. "We *always* believe what we say. It's the best way to sell the con."

There were more implications in that statement than Rachel could process. "That's..." She groped around for the right description. "...sociopathic."

The woman shrugged. "You asked," she said. "That's how it works."

Interesting. Rachel mulled over Noura's words. *How does that work? If I read emotions instead of minds, she's not just telling the truth, she's feeling the emotions that go along with it...*

Her grandmother's favorite saying had been that you can tell the truth without telling everything you know; even lies of omission seemed to register as voids within conversational colors. But if you were emotionally disconnected from the truth, maybe a lie could exist on the same fundamental level as truth.

It put her recent conversation with Mulcahy in a new light, maybe. Nobody could lie within a link, but if she was getting better at hiding her emotions...

Wait. **Is** *it possible to lie within a link?*

Rachel thought she might be able to make out the edges of an answer, but it slipped through her mental fingers as she saw the gunman bearing down on them.

TWELVE

Rachel didn't know what tipped Hill off. For her, it was the man wearing professional blues, marching towards them with a newspaper wrapped around his right hand. Those blues were... *wrong*. The hue was closer to gunmetal than suits or uniforms, and Rachel threw a scan through the newspaper. She was already shouting and moving when the man pulled out the subcompact handgun.

Hill was moving, too. He hit Noura high, Rachel hit her low. Between them, they knocked Noura out of the gunman's path as he fired four times, *bangbangbangbang*, fast as lightning.

They almost made it. Three shots went wide. The fourth caught Hill in his right shoulder and moved through skin and fat and muscle, and then smashed into Noura's jaw.

The woman's colors were utterly white as her hands came up to find a void. An unearthly howl started from where her mouth used to be.

Rachel didn't have time to assess the damage. "Hill?!" she shouted.

"Good..." he grunted.

Back in Afghanistan, her service weapon had been a military Sig Sauer P229 Combat pistol. She had fallen in love with the gun, and had stolen it when she had gone stateside to join OACET. It wasn't standard police issue; neither was the custom fast-draw shoulder holster she had started wearing as a compromise to herself for ditching her bulletproof vest. The gunman might have been expecting her to be armed, but he wasn't ready for her to lunge for cover behind the nearest car, her weapon already out and drawn on his chest as she rolled.

She didn't take the shot. He was staring at her, Southwestern turquoise woven tight within the gunmetal blues, and she realized as she was about to pull the trigger that he wouldn't shoot her. He was there for Noura's poppy-seed gray, and there was something else in there, something white wrapped up in orange…

"He's after the package!" she yelled to Hill.

"It's in the car! So's Noura!"

Hill's voice was muffled. She snuck a quick scan behind her, and found him in the back seat of the police cruiser, holding his suit coat against the hole in Noura's face. *Good*, she thought. *That'll keep them safe—*

Two shots rang out, and the headlights of the car beside her shattered.

"Don't!" the first gunman shouted in an unfamiliar accent, his conversational colors white in sudden dismay. "It's the Agent!"

Okay, Rachel thought. *I've definitely got some immunity here. Let's buy our backup some time.*

"I'm coming out!" she shouted, holding up her gun in a loose one-handed surrender.

The first gunman drew down on her again, and sent a few shots into the pavement.

"Or not," she muttered, and reached out through the police car's hidden receiver to the Secret Service. *"Alimoren? Where—"*

"Here!" Alimoren's voice came from behind her, and he joined her at the car. "Where's the package?"

"In the car. Hill's shot; looks like an easy through-and-through. But the bullet hit Noura in the face on its way out."

"Dead?"

"No," she told him, and she added her diagnostic autoscript to her scans before she ran them over Noura. *Severe damage to mandible…moderate damage to sternocleidomastoideus… severed external jugular vein…* She didn't understand most of the anatomical terms the script threw back at her, but "severed" and "jugular" never belonged in the same description. "She's seriously injured."

Alimoren's blue relief faded. "Shit."

"They don't want to hurt me," she said. "But they'll keep me pinned down."

"Go behind the cars," he said. "I'll cover you."

She nodded, and started running.

"Get Noura to a hospital!" Alimoren shouted, as he took three quick shots towards the alcove where one of the shooters had found light cover.

"Nearest hospital!" she agreed. "Meet us there!"

Take us there, she told that small piece of Other in her head. *I don't have time to find the directions. Get us there in one piece, and I will give you so many cookies...*

She ran in a low crouch to the police cruiser, head down and gun ready. Alimoren was drawing the fire of the two gunmen she knew about, but where there were two gunmen there were usually more...

She popped the electronic lock on the cruiser's front door and was safely inside before her imaginary third gunman could shoot her. Hill was banging on the Plexiglas shield with the car keys: there was an anxious moment when she couldn't get the safety window unlocked, but between the two of them they managed to get the keys in her hand.

Rachel peeled out, the gunmen firing at the back of the cruiser. There was a loud pop as a side view mirror shattered, and another as the rear bumper was hit.

"Stay down!" she shouted to Hill. "They're trying to take out the tires!"

"Go! *Go! Go!*" he shouted back.

Rachel put a couple of blocks between them and the gunmen before she eased off the accelerator. "Holy God," she said. "That was too close."

"Why didn't he shoot you?" Hill asked.

"I'm OACET," she guessed. "They knew who Noura was, they knew who'd be transporting her, and they knew if they shot me they'd bring every Agent in the country down on them and *fuck me why am I driving?!?*"

The calm, emotionless void that let her act and react in a

gunfight vanished. Rachel found herself gripping a steering wheel—a *steering wheel!*—and driving down a road.

A real road with real cars and live human beings on it.

"Oh Jesus…oh Lord…" She heard herself praying, and her brain went on a tangent to wonder if God would forgive her for being a lapsed Catholic if she accidentally ran down a bunch of politicians. "Where's the clutch?"

"Clutch? It's an automatic."

"What? *What?* I can't drive an automatic!"

"You're…" Hill was baffled. "You've *been* driving one!"

"Are you kidding? I'm from Texas! We don't do automatics in Texas! I think it's illegal to *own* an automatic in Texas!"

She was babbling. Babbling was fine. Babbling let her focus on her embarrassment, and not on the metal projectiles hurtling around them.

Rubber squealed on pavement, loud enough to break through her chatter and redirect her attention to the road. There were shapes—huge *moving* shapes—with spots of color within. These flared with various hues of yellow and red as she shot around them, drivers and passengers feeling everything from the heady flush of a near-miss to full-on road rage.

"Turn on the siren!" Hill had finally recognized the more immediate threat didn't come from Noura bleeding out, and was trying to force the thief into a seatbelt. The woman keened, the sound of it full of raw pain.

Siren… That, Rachel could do; she had played with the layout of the MPD's cruisers on previous trips, and she could trigger the siren without hunting for the command. The dome lights sparked on, and she gasped and tried to quell the sudden nausea that hit her as some of the frequencies she used to see began to resonate to the sound of the siren.

"Peng?"

"I'm fine!" She dropped a few of her favorite frequencies, deciding that she could either be sick and unable to see, or just unable to see, and the metal shapes lost their edges. Chryslers and Hondas turned into coupes and minivans, and their polarized glass vanished altogether.

I'm fine, she told herself. The details didn't matter. The space between the vehicles mattered, the speed at which the vehicles were moving mattered… *Remember Frogger? This is exactly like Frogger. I was always good at Frogger.*

The siren cleared them a path, and she was starting to feel a little calmer when Hill said her name a second time.

"Did she die?" It was a fair question. Rachel couldn't hear Noura's pitched whine over the sound of the siren.

"No. Check our six."

"Fuck you," she muttered. "Hard enough to do this without— aw *shit.*"

Three vehicles, two SUVs and a sedan, were closing on them. The occupants were gunmetal blue.

"Thought so," Hill said. "They ours?"

She threw another fast scan towards them to pick out any of the RFID tags that the MPD and federal agencies used to track their vehicles and equipment. Nothing.

"Nope. They really want that package," she said, and (*God help us!*) she goosed the accelerator.

"Or Noura dead. Think they want her dead more than they want you alive?"

"We're not going to find out!" she said, and shouted over the siren: "Alimoren! If you can hear us, we've picked up a tail. Three vehicles. We need backup!"

Nobody answered. Somewhere, off in the corner of her mind, pings were flooding her in waves as the collective picked up on her fear and anxiety.

"No!" Rachel hollered through the broadest link she could find. *"You can't help me, and I need to focus! Out!"*

A car whose driver was somehow blissfully oblivious of the drama speeding towards him pulled out from a parking space. Rachel threw the wheel to the left to avoid him, and careened off of a city dump truck.

"Fuck!"

"Truck is fine—keep going!" Hill yelled.

"Fuck *fuck fuck!* What do these people think a siren *means?!*"

She tried to seize on the feeling of concrete to ground herself, but that made things worse. Each time she found a new focusing object, she was already moving past it at mind-wrenching speed.

A mass of moving yellow metal came out in front of them. "School's out," she muttered. "Shitshitshit*shit*…"

"Kids!" Hill gasped.

"I'm *aware!*" she snapped.

Three vehicles came around the dump truck: she made out the shapes of two SUVs and a late-model sedan, all of them occupied by men in that gunmetal blue. She didn't have the time to scan them for weapons, but the woman who was now missing the lower part of her face was enough reason for her to assume they were armed.

She tuned her scans forward and away, mimicking the cone of normal vision as well as she could. She fought against adding new or different frequencies, keeping her visuals as clean as possible… And everything was still a mess of speeding vehicles and jaywalkers and traffic cops and… *Why did Noura have to do this after school let out?!?* Rachel thought, yanking the wheel to the side to avoid what might have been a child, or a very small man, or maybe a dog walking on its hind legs—

"Talk to Alimoren?" Hill asked, holding his phone up.

"Now?!" Rachel shouted. "Are the two of you *insane?!*"

The rear windshield exploded into flying glass. Hill was out of the line of fire, but Noura's colors fluttered, soft and weak, as the glass peppered her body. The plastic barrier between the seats kept the safety glass from hitting Rachel, but she stomped on the gas anyhow: that windshield hadn't broken by accident.

"They really want her dead," she said. *Focus on the road focus on the road focus on the road oh God oh God…* She whipped the wheel to the left. Tires shrieked as she crossed two lanes, and she pointed the car towards an empty street.

"Wrong way!" Hill shouted, pointing at something. She was dimly aware of the white arrow within the black rectangle.

"Where are you going?"

"That's a *great* question!" Rachel shouted back. They were lucky: the narrow road stayed clear until they were back in the main streets.

"Shit!" Hill was pointing again, this time at the second SUV, now driving straight towards them. "Peng! It's them!"

"Aww!" Rachel hauled on the steering wheel again. The old plastic was slick beneath her hands, and the wheel kicked back on her as she tried to get them out of the path of the second SUV. The car skidded sideways, the momentum yanking it closer to the SUV before Rachel could hit the accelerator again. Luck was still with them; somehow she pointed them between a flock of taxis, and they were back in the slow lane before the other two cars managed to pin them in.

She took another right—*If I keep taking rights, we'll end up back where we started*—and this time, their luck ran out. A minivan tried to get out of her way by crossing two lanes of traffic, its driver a bright spot of sickly yellow terror. Rachel swerved to avoid it, driving over the curb and onto the sidewalk. She heard metal tear apart as the rear bumper was ripped from the cruiser.

"Peng!" Hill shouted.

"Yelling is not helping!" she shouted back at him.

Her scans brought back the peripheral image of Hill with his phone pressed to his ear. "Next left! *Next left!*"

Left was a blur of energy. It was another main road, at least six lanes across, its drivers too committed to making the light to yield the right-of-way to a police car. She drove the heel of her hand into the horn again and again, trying to clear them a path before they reached the intersection.

Between that and the siren, it must have worked—*Did the lights just turn red on the other three streets?*—as the intersection was suddenly clear in a cacophony of blaring horns and squealing tires.

She slowed as she took the left, hoping to catch her bearings. *Howard University Hospital.* The name came to her as if she had planned to drive to that particular hospital all along, and suddenly knew she needed to backtrack the way they had come.

"We're headed in the wrong direction," she said. "Tell Alimoren we're going to Howard. Put backup between us and the hospital."

Her subconscious twitched, and she knew the sedan had navigated the intersection. Rachel realized she was no longer paying attention to the cars, just their occupants; she could tell a bus from a pickup truck by the number of people and where they were sitting in their featureless hunks of plastic and chrome. Every time that gunmetal blue appeared, she jumped and tried to take evasive action.

Traffic grew tight, bottlenecked by a couple of cars whose drivers had tried to pull to the side to make way for her, but had somehow managed to merge into a cluster of fenders instead. The sedan closed the distance as Rachel leaned on the horn, trying to blast the congestion out of her way.

"Can't do it!" she shouted.

"Bike lane!" Hill shouted back.

She couldn't help but turn and gape at him, horrorstruck at the idea of putting the cruiser among unprotected blotches of color that moved too fast to predict. "Absolutely *not!*"

"Go go *go!*"

"No!" She slammed on the brakes and spun the cruiser around, and then drove the cruiser straight towards the sedan. The gunmetal blue shape in the driver's seat went white and yanked the sedan out of her path.

"Chicken, motherfucker! *Chicken!*" she howled with glee, and put the cruiser on a straight shot towards the hospital.

"You're crazy!" Hill yelled.

"Yeah, probably!"

One of the SUVs reappeared, and Rachel gasped aloud as she realized the gunmetal blue in the passenger's seat was carrying a large rectangular object that shone with literal gunmetal. She skipped the cruiser back across the road before they could get a shot off, but Hill was close enough to make out the weapon.

"Assault rifle!" he called, leaning over Noura's bloody form to shield her.

"Seatbelt! Get in your *seatbelt!*" she shouted.

A series of jolts, fast and strong, ran through the steering wheel and into her hands, and she realized they had taken fire.

"They're too close!" Hill was still curled protectively over Noura, a hand on her head to keep her steady. "Shake 'em!"

"Aw *hell!*" Rachel shouted.

The same intersection that had saved their lives once before came up in front of them, the cars just starting to untangle themselves from the chaos she had created. Traffic was moving slowly, but it was moving, with enough space for a police cruiser to navigate if it had an excellent driver…

We are fucked, Rachel thought to herself.

She couldn't see Hill at all; he was a foggy shade of white panic.

She put her life in the hands of the collective, and drove straight at the intersection.

The lights changed without warning, and Rachel wiggled the cruiser through the traffic as confused and angry drivers stopped dead in their tracks.

Hill whooped.

She couldn't explain. Not without confessing to Alimoren and anyone listening that Agents were hacking into the traffic system to protect one of their own. Hopefully, the changes to the system would be lost in the confusion of the chase.

The SUV couldn't make it through the intersection in time, but the sedan was smaller. It leapt through the traffic like a wolf after a rabbit, and Rachel caught another glimpse of metal in the arms of the man riding shotgun—

Three streaks of white shot down from the sky, so intense they burned across the inside of her mind. They drove themselves into the sedan's engine block in a perfect *WHUMP,* the three sounds coming so close together that they blurred into a single booming noise.

"Wha—" Hill hauled himself upright. "Was that—"

"Yup!" Rachel realized she was grinning like a wild woman. She let her scans slip behind her to watch the sedan slow down, its motor turned to so much slag by the anti-materiel rifle. "The cavalry is here!"

Two down, one to go...

"Who's shooting?" Hill asked.

Good question. Rachel wished she could spare a moment to process the environment, but she and her implant were tag-teaming survival skills. Instead, she shouted, both aloud and through the link: *"Who's out there?!"*

"Me and Ken," a woman's voice replied in her mind.

Relief washed over Rachel. "Hippos," she said to Hill. "It's the Hippos!"

"You hit?" he asked, and she had to check his colors to see concern and confusion warring to understand what he meant.

"Was I shot?" she replied. "No! Use more words!"

"What?"

"Talk more! The Hippos can hear us!" A large shape loomed out of a side street. She spun the wheel, hard. Metal ground against metal as she raked the police cruiser against a car. Beside her, Hill's pain-red surged as his bad shoulder cracked against the divider. "Hold on!" she shouted at him, and took another right turn into traffic.

Horns blared, and Hill hollered something fierce as she realized she had gone the wrong way down another one-way street.

This wasn't an underused side street. Four lanes of traffic were trying to pull off of the road for her, but they had all been moving at a goodly clip and she hadn't given them enough warning. *You're gonna kill people if you keep this up!* she swore at herself, and spun the wheel again. The police cruiser slid across two lanes before she got it under control, with Hill shouting at her from the back seat that she had gone the wrong way.

"I *know!*" she roared, as she fought to bring the cruiser's nose around. "That is *not useful information!*"

Rachel stomped on the gas, and the car leaped forward. She

felt a sudden, almost overpowering need to head back the way she came, so she took the next couple of rights as fast as she could.

"We shook one!" Hill called.

She threw a scan behind her, and found a single SUV trying gamely to keep pace.

"What's this 'we' shit?!" she shouted back at him, and Hill started to laugh.

The lights were in Rachel's favor, and the intersection in front of them was a wide open space. She wasn't ready for the second SUV to come rocketing out of the side street and slam into the rear of the cruiser.

The car spun again. This time, Rachel had no hope of bringing it under control; the cruiser was a rear-wheel drive, and the collision had broken something important. She turned into the skid and waited until the spinning had stopped.

She couldn't hear anything but the siren and the pounding in her head. When she was able to throw her scans around, she checked on the SUVs; men were emptying out of the two cars and marching towards the cruiser.

"Fuck," Rachel groaned, turning her scans towards the back seat. "Come on, guys, we need to—"

Noura.

Running wasn't an option. The thief was moaning and red through and through with pain, her colors starting to fade around the edges.

And Hill was—

Rachel jumped, unable to align the strong professional blues of Hill's conversational colors with his posture. He was lying as if his neck had snapped in the crash, his head and good arm sprawled in plain view from the rear window.

He muttered something,

"What?" She couldn't make out what he was trying to say.

"Play dead!"

Hill, you're a goddamned genius.

Rachel let herself slump forward, her head coming to rest

against the greasy steering wheel. Behind the cruiser, the goon squad was advancing slowly, handguns ready but hidden from plain view in pockets and sleeves.

Closer...closer...

The gunmen were distracted; most of them kept checking over their shoulders. Rachel couldn't hear over the sound of her own siren, but she was sure that backup was finally close. She could have scanned the city, stretching out in all directions until she pinged on their backup, but there was an easier way. She reached out to the Agent on the rooftops instead. *"Ami, ETA?"*

"Sixty seconds."

Too long, Rachel thought. The men would be at the car within moments; Ami and Ken were racing to get in position, but they were still a block away, and Washington's rooftops were of all different heights and made for a shitty transportation system.

The other option was to try to hold them off. A fast scan for her trusty service weapon put it on the floor of the passenger's side, where it had fallen during the chase. *And Hill's shoulder slows him down...*

They might let me live, but I am not in the mood to turn today into Hill's last stand.

She let them get within five feet of the car before she stomped on the gas.

The cruiser was broken but not beaten. Its engine responded with a thunderous roar, and they were half a block away before the men started shooting. More jolts carried from the back of the car into Rachel's hands, and she and Hill both yelled as the front windshield turned into a spiderweb of glass, with craters punched straight through it.

Hill shouted again, but this time there was a joyous yellow streak within him. Rachel checked behind them to see the welcome shapes of squad cars and the furious reds and excited yellow-whites of the officers.

"We got them!" His voice was hoarse. "We got both drivers!"

Rachel laughed with relief as two squad cars came up to flank them. "Finally!"

She turned off their siren, and the world came back to her. Details leapt up to greet her, and she laughed again as she scanned the environment and found herself in what barely remained of a car.

And then she heard Hill say, "Shit."

"What?"

"Noura," he said.

She checked the road ahead, found it clear, and took the time to do a thorough scan of the backseat. It was soaked in blood, and Noura's colors were taking on an unforgettable blend of vivid blues and deep blacks. The woman slumped in her seat, held in place only by her seatbelt and Hill's hands.

"Alimoren!" Rachel shouted, as she turned the siren back on and pushed the details of the world out of her head again. "This isn't over! Noura's barely hanging on!"

She pushed the cruiser to its limits. The rear tires had been shot out, and the car shuddered as it threw the last scraps of rubber.

"Hospital!" Hill yelled.

"We're close!"

"I know! Left! *Left!*"

Sparks poured from the rims as Rachel leaned into the turn.

Another corner, and a building loomed before them. Rachel ignored the security towers; Hill shouted something obscene as she clipped a concrete bollard.

"Alimoren!" The rear of the car was all but gone, and she had to shout to make herself heard over the sound of metal grinding across the pavement. "Call Howard University Hospital! Tell them to be ready to receive three patients in critical condition!"

"Three?" Hill shouted back. "*Three?!?*"

"We don't have brakes!" she told him. "Find me a place to put this beast!"

She thought she heard him swear, but there was no way she could be sure, not with the noise in the cab. She did see him point, and she steered in that rough direction, realizing as they jerked over the curb that he had put them over a sidewalk, a lawn…

"Aw *shit!*" she yelled, as the tall, thin shape in front of them resolved into a flagpole.

"Do it!" Hill told her.

"Alimoren! Front entrance! The flagpole! Tell them—"

THIRTEEN

The dream was worse this time. She was in pieces: in pain. Parts of herself spun off and got lost across the ocean floor, and she could see and feel every bit of it, every portion carried away by the crabs, the fish that tore out her eyes—*hah! suckers!*— the cold, emotionless eternity of the drifting currents…

She woke shouting.

"Agent Peng!" It was a stranger's voice, and she felt a man's hands press her shoulders down against a bed. "You're safe— you're in the hospital. Your doctor's already seen you. The airbag knocked you out. We don't think you have a concussion, but you should still try to stay quiet."

She closed her eyes. *Hospital…* "Detective Hill?"

"Here." Hill's voice came from a couple of feet away. Rachel activated her implant and flipped on visuals. Hill was lying in the room's second bed, his shirt and undershirt gone. A nurse was doing a final cleaning on his arm, a neat line of surgical staples holding together the small entry wound. The exit wound on the other side of his arm was slightly larger, and had already been treated and taped.

"Noura?" she asked, but she already knew. Beneath the haze of a mild morphine high, Hill's conversational colors held equal parts of green guilt and Noura's poppy-seed gray.

"Didn't make it," Hill said.

Rachel sank back against the bed. "We tried," she said. "We tried."

At least she hadn't watched Noura die. That twist of vivid blue when a life was extinguished… Terrible. Beautiful. The last time Rachel had seen it, it had taken her months to drink the memory out of her head.

"She had lost too much blood," the man who had first spoken

said to her. He was wearing a nurse's scrubs.

"And crashing a car on her didn't help," Rachel muttered.

"Oh, you guys barely tapped that flagpole," a woman said as she entered the room. Rachel slammed a hand over her mouth to keep herself from smiling. "You had shed most of your momentum on the grass. Noura was already a goner by then."

The nurses paled slightly at hearing this. Their surprise was understandable: the brunette was dressed in scrubs and a white lab coat, and the nurses weren't used to doctors being quite so callous in front of their patients.

Rachel, who saw the assassin's dark gray clothing beneath the stolen hospital outfit, thought that Ami was actually playing the role quite well.

"Doctor Jenny Davies, OACET physician," the woman said to Hill. Then, to Rachel: "I made them dilate your eyes to check the stability of your connections."

It was such a bullshit phrase that Rachel couldn't help but giggle. "Thank you."

"That's why it's *so bright in here*," the other woman told her.

"I had wondered," Rachel said, and pulled her pillow over her head to try to hide how she was about to die from laughter.

"Good," the false doctor said. "Stay like that until I can find you some sunglasses."

"Okay!" Rachel squeaked.

She pulled the pillow tight across her face and started to giggle uncontrollably. It was her normal reaction to stress: once the danger was over, she laughed herself silly. Hill, who had seen it before, assured the nurses that she wasn't having a seizure, and made them leave her alone so she could burn off the last hour.

When she could think again, she reached out to locate Ami. The former assassin had already ditched her borrowed scrubs and doctor's whites, and was halfway across a nearby parking lot. She had found a pair of jeans that didn't quite fit her, but otherwise she looked like any other civilian trying to remember where she had parked her car.

Rachel opened a link with the other Agent. *"Please don't steal one."*

"Penguin, you are just no fun anymore," Ami replied, but shifted her path towards the exit.

Rachel felt Ami's laughter, and realized the other woman had set her up. Ami knew better than to pop the lock on the nearest Toyota and tootle off down the road. She sighed, and asked, *"Why isn't the real Jenny here?"*

"You hit the flagpole ten minutes ago. I was the only one who was close enough to cover for her before they tested your eyes for a concussion and decided you needed immediate surgery."

A quick wave of horror crashed over Rachel. *"Thanks. And thanks for taking out that sedan."*

"No problem. We were in the area anyhow. Mulcahy has me tracking some of Hanlon's employees, and they had an office a block away from that mailbox store. He had me check in on you when you left Indiana Avenue."

"We gonna get in trouble with Forensics?"

"Nope," Ami replied. *"There's not a lot left of a bullet once it goes through an engine block, and Ken's already gathered up the pieces. Now, if you'll excuse me, I need to yell at him. He can't find the rooftop where I left my rifle."*

That comment sounded offhand, but there was an undertone of sadness and worry. Rachel sympathized: she knew she would mourn if her own service weapon went missing. *"Good luck. I owe you a huge favor."*

"Introduce me to your delicious detective friend, and we'll call it even."

"Deal."

Rachel came out from under the pillow and made noises about how bright the room was until someone found her a sleeping mask. Hill waited until the nurses had finished cleaning his arm and left the room before he said, "That wasn't Jenny."

Rachel nodded. Hill had gone partying with Rachel on many a Friday and Saturday night, and Jenny Davies sometimes came along. "Ami is OACET," Rachel said. "You can trust her."

"I got that," he said, and waited.

Rachel sighed. "She's the reason we're still alive."

It took Hill a moment, and then three bright white streaks moved across his conversational colors like gunshots. "She's the one…?"

"Her, or one of the other Cuddly Hippos." His conversation colors moved into curious yellows, so she explained: "Hippos aren't much to look at, but they can kill you without even trying."

He thought about this, his colors weaving the yellow uncertainty into reds. "You guys have assassins?"

"Former assassins," she corrected him, very quickly. "Mulcahy doesn't let them kill anyone, so these days, they work our security."

His colors went pale.

"Oh, come on. You and I used to kill people for a living, too. The whole world is full of reformed murderers who were just following orders."

A mournful red came and went around his hands. Rachel had never seen that particular pattern before, but she a pretty good idea of what it meant.

"Sorry," she said, too tired to offer anything more than a half-assed apology. The adrenaline rush was over, and she was crashing. She tossed the mask aside, pulled the pillow back over her face, deactivated her implant, and went to sleep.

There were no dreams this time, just the normal background noises of a busy hospital serving an urban community. She woke to heavy breathing, and activated her implant to find Santino peering under the pillow.

"She's alive," her partner announced to the room at large. "She just swore at me."

"Yay," Zockinski said, sarcasm dripping from him in pools of green and orange to hide his blue relief.

Rachel hurled the pillow at him.

"Alimoren?" she asked as she sat up. The nap had done her good: she could think clearly again. *Head, still attached to neck?*

Check. Oh, I'm going to be sore tomorrow.

"Outside at the crash site, sorting shit out," Zockinski told her. "You and Hill have so much paperwork to do."

"Was anyone hurt in the chase?" Rachel held her breath. *Please please please...*

"No," Santino said. "Absolute miracle if you ask me."

She glanced at her partner. Santino was still wearing the thick grays of stress. A streak of orange had appeared as he came to terms with the situation; now that he knew she wasn't hurt, worry was being replaced by annoyance as he could not believe she was so stupid as to have gotten behind the wheel of a car.

"I didn't have a choice," she told him.

"She reading your mind again, Santino?" Zockinski asked.

"Shut up," she told him. *God, it's good to be alive.*

There was a knock against the frame of the open doorway, and Alimoren entered. The Secret Service agent's colors moved between frustration and relief. "That was some driving, Agent Peng."

"There's a reason I didn't renew my license," she said. "Was anyone hurt?" Santino bristled slightly as she asked the question a second time, but she needed confirmation.

"The downtown area's pretty shaken up," he said. "But no serious injuries."

"The package?" Hill asked.

Alimoren shrugged. "Just papers and that second watch," he said. "Most of it looks to be documentation on White House protocols and on the Mechanism, but Joanna Reed's profile was in there."

Reed... Reed... Rachel couldn't place the name until she remembered the alias Noura had used to break into the White House. The alias taken from a makeup artist who was found dead in the trunk of her car... "That's one more mystery solved."

"Reed's murder? Maybe. We didn't find any fingerprints or DNA at the scene, but from the other forensics, it looks like Reed was killed by a man. He left a lot of trace—shoe impressions, glove prints, and so on."

"You think she's got a partner?" An uncomfortable orange-red winced across Zockinski as he realized he had referred to Noura in the present tense.

"We know someone hired her," Alimoren said. "We also know someone wanted her dead, and they wanted the information she hid in the packet retrieved. At this point, everything else is guesswork."

"Sounds like the person who killed Reed is inexperienced," Santino said. "Noura was careful. She wouldn't work with a partner who would put her at risk."

A flash of orange anxiety ran across Alimoren as Santino spoke. Rachel kept her face blank and went on nodding in the right places. The guys were beginning to use her as their barometer, and any changes in her body language might have repercussions.

Anxiety can mean a whole lot of things, she reminded that little nagging voice in the back of her head, *and Alimoren's anything but inexperienced.* She decided to file Alimoren's reaction away for later, but another memory came up, this one of blue relief when she told him Noura had been shot…

Damn, Rachel thought.

She tried to remember exactly how he had reacted, how the timing of the situation had played out. She hadn't exactly been paying attention to Alimoren. *He showed blue when I told him Noura was shot,* she thought, as she pretended to pick at her fingernails. *Was he relieved because Noura survived, or because there was a moment when he thought she had been killed?*

She shelved the whole mess. When she got right down to it, she didn't read emotions as much as she tried to interpret a color wheel. Might as well set her and Santino up in business as a team of feng shui landscapers. Plant red begonias in the southern part of your garden for good luck in spring, or some such… And she abandoned that train of thought, too, before her mental image of her maternal grandmother could yell at her.

Rachel's scans pulled her attention to her hands. The nurse

had likely wiped her down while she was unconscious, but there was blood caked around her nails, and had soaked into her shirt cuffs. She didn't remember touching Noura, but it had been a hell of a five minutes.

She stood and stretched. Everything seemed to be in working order.

"Be right back," she told her team, and left in search of a bathroom.

Once the door was locked behind her and she was elbow-deep in antibacterial soap, she reached out to the collective. There was a general round of hellos, but the greetings were more subdued than she had expected.

"We're used to your near-death adventures by now," Phil told her. *"Get over yourself."*

She laughed aloud. *"Ami already reported in?"*

"Yup," he replied. *"A fake doctor is still good enough to let us know you're alive."*

"But you will be getting a full checkup from me this afternoon." The woman's voice was strong and sweet, like the best cup of coffee, and Rachel agreed to join Jenny Davies at the mansion as soon as she was released from the hospital.

She left the link and returned to her bed.

Alimoren was gone. The nurses had returned, and were forcing Hill to move his arm in gentle circles to test the give and play of the bandages. Hill was told he'd need to stay a few more hours for observation, but Agent Peng? They couldn't seem to find her doctor, but if she felt comfortable walking...

She couldn't get out of there fast enough.

They snuck out the back to avoid the media, and circled to the rear of the hospital where Santino had tucked his hybrid in a quiet parking lot. Rachel nearly dragged her partner the entire way: hospitals played havoc with her emotional scans.

"Want to drive?" Santino asked her.

Rachel shouted at him so loudly that a woman in nurse's scrubs two rows over jumped and ran for the safety of her car.

She scooched down in her seat, praying nobody with press

credentials would recognize Santino or his tiny hybrid, and didn't come up for air until they were on the Potomac Parkway.

Santino was telling her about how he and Zockinski had followed Alimoren to the postal depot when Mako's voice knocked on her mind

"Ping Peng. Peng, ping? Mako!"

"Polo," she replied as she opened a direct link.

"Hey!" The other Agent stepped into her head, his presence larger than life. *"Heard you almost killed my cousin."*

"Almost. As gunshots go, it could have been worse. He'll be okay."

Relief came through the link. She concurred: there was just something comforting about second opinions. *"All right,"* Mako said. *"You're on your way to the mansion?"*

"Yeah. Jenny said she wants to murder me in a sterile environment."

"Good for her. Send Santino to me before you croak. I need to talk to him."

"Roger."

"No, no, Mako. May-ko. Roger is working with the NSA this week."

"Shut up," she told him, and stepped out of their link.

Santino was watching her in bemused purples. "Was I boring you, or did you get a call?"

"It was Mako," she confirmed. "He says as long as we're stopping by the mansion, he wants us to check in with him."

Santino brightened. "He's made progress on the Mechanism?"

"I guess so," Rachel said.

He turned towards her, his attention sharpening to a bright point. "Something wrong?"

Rachel pointed to her shirt sleeves, now rolled up as many times as possible to keep the drying blood from touching her skin. "Noura's *dead*, Santino. Hill got shot," she said. "How does a Sasquatch machine fit into all of this?"

"Sasquatch machine?"

"Y'know, Bigfoot? Something that shouldn't exist but does?"

His bemusement changed to vivid purple humor. "You think Bigfoot exists?"

"No! I—*ugh*." Rachel slumped against the passenger's side window. "The Mechanism. You and Mako keep trying to sell me on the idea that something two thousand years old is still relevant today, but I don't see it. And people are dead because of it… I don't know. It makes no sense to me."

"Of Peleus' son, Achilles, sing, O Muse, the vengeance, deep and deadly; whence to Greece unnumbered ills arose…" Santino could have kept going—unlike her, he had actually memorized the classics—but he knew his partner lived and breathed poetry and she had recognized the source as soon as he had started speaking. Instead, he grinned at her, smug in pinks.

"Unfair," she muttered. "Unbelievably unfair. You can't just drop the I-bomb around me."

"*The Iliad* is timeless," he said. "Love and loss, striving for fame and immortality… These themes are as relevant today as they were when it was written. If they discovered an unknown fragment of *The Iliad*, would you dismiss it as irrelevant crap?"

"You can't compare a machine to the human experience."

"I'm not," he said. "I'm comparing it to the fundamentals of how the Mechanism operates. To the right people, mathematics can be as timeless as poetry."

She glared at her partner. Santino gave her a dainty pink smile.

"Stop making me understand things," she grumbled under her breath.

"Never."

The OACET mansion was quiet. The usual gardeners were there; OACET had recruited heavily from wildlife management, and many of those Agents with outdoors specialties couldn't be placed as liaisons. In the meantime, they were bringing the landscape back to life. The riot of early spring flowers was on, yellow trillium and purple crocuses spreading out in tidy clumps throughout their new beds. The gardeners cornered Santino and rushed him away, asking for his advice on a suffering cluster of *Puschkinia scilloides.*

Rachel meandered towards the basement, stopping to chat with various Agents as she made her way to the medical lab where Jenny was waiting. Her physical was quick: Jenny ran a diagnostic scan through Rachel's body, applied an ophthalmoscope to her eyes, and reminded her that she was a moron with a death wish.

(Rachel agreed she was an idiot but she quibbled over the part about the death wish. If angels feared to tread somewhere, she felt they probably had a damn good reason to do so, and she respected their decision. She just wished the others who shared this mortal coil with her felt the same.)

The pile of rugs that had covered the stairs had been moved. It was a smooth climb to the west wing. Mako opened his door before she could knock. "Avery's sleeping," he said, gesturing towards the bathroom. "She's finally hit that growth spurt. C'mon in."

Two of the old chalkboards had been repurposed. Rachel recognized the fragment from the Mechanism, sketched out in Mako's messy hand. Santino was sitting in his customary place beside the computer array, reading over the data spindling off of an ancient dot matrix printer.

"How's it coming?" Rachel asked them, settling into one of Mako's rickety old kitchen chairs.

"A friend at the Smithsonian has been helping with the translation," Mako said. "She *loves* the level of detail in your scans. She wants to see if you can go to Greece with their team when they examine the rest of the device. You've created more accurate images of the inscriptions than any—"

"No," Rachel insisted. She still wasn't fully free of her headaches, and the prolonged scans from the other night set her skull to pounding if she thought about them. "Sorry."

"Had to ask," Mako said. "She'll say it's a huge loss, you know. Much of the original inscription still can't be read. You might be their best bet for deciphering more of the text."

"Ask me again when my head's stopped pounding from the

first round of scans," Rachel said.

"Fair enough," Mako said. "Thus far, nothing that's been translated is too dramatic. We've known the inscriptions on the back were an instruction manual for the Mechanism. The writing on the piece you've found is more of the same."

"Anything of interest?" Santino asked.

"The Mechanism applies a deterministic system—" Mako began.

"No. I'm not doing this again." Rachel cut him off as quickly as she could. "Not after the day I've had. What have you found? Simple, small words, please."

"Sure," Mako said, not at all bothered by her request. "We've known for years that the Mechanism doesn't allow for random variables. It plots the movement of the sun, the moon, and the five planets the Greeks knew about at the time of its construction. Normal, predictable events," he said, and added, "It's got a function to predict eclipses, another for the Olympics, and it can be adjusted to account for leap years."

He paused. "The section you recovered? The inscriptions suggest the Mechanism was also used in horoscopic astronomy."

"Nice!" Santino said.

Rachel glared at her partner. There was some gray within his conversational colors, at odds with his show of excitement.

He noticed, and shrugged. "It's what I expected, but I had hoped it was something more... I don't know. Dramatic? A solution to an ancient mathematical proof, I guess."

"This is still incredibly significant," Mako said. "No one's ever been able to nail down exactly when the Mechanism was created. Greek astrology was in a transitional phase around the same time, so anthropologists will be able to date when, and maybe where, it was built. It's a good step towards learning who created it, too."

"Still, I'd hoped it was something more esoteric," Santino said.

"Yeah, me too. But it's definitely not nothing. This is a cultural—"

"Wait," Rachel said. "Astrology, as in lions and tigers and bears in the sky?"

"No tigers, and Leo is a part of the Ursa Major family," Santino said. "But yeah."

Rachel pulled her arms over her face. Her sense of loss was so sad and sudden that Mako dropped into the chair beside her and wrapped her in his overlarge arms. "Penguin?"

"Astrology," Rachel said, incredulous. "I know people are killed for the dumbest reasons, but… *Astrology!*"

"It's not nothing," Santino said, as he folded up the computer printouts for later reading. "This can help shed light on an important aspect of Greek culture. Many ancient Greeks believed in astrology. They felt it let their gods communicate with them."

"Right!" Mako said brightly. "People've always died for religion. This is nothing new."

"People die because of stupid shit all the time," she said. "And it's always pointless."

The two men couldn't think of a good reply to that.

"Are you sure you wouldn't want to go to Greece with the Smithsonian team?" Santino asked, trying to break her mood. "It'll be months before the details are finalized. Your headache will be long gone by then."

Rachel shook her head. "Can't do it. We're still banned from traveling outside the country. Besides, I'm too busy here. Have them make a few more OACET Agents who specialize in law enforcement, and then maybe I'll get a vacation."

There was a quick blaze of color between Mako and Santino. "What?" she asked, unable to place the streak of excited yellow-white lightning.

"Nothing," Mako said, too quickly.

She sighed, and sent a light scan over him. Beneath his shirt, his arm was wrapped in cotton gauze, a light haze of pain red hovering near his skin. Rachel sent a deeper scan through the gauze, and found a number of tidy dime-sized excisions in his soft tissue.

"What happened?!" she demanded, reaching out to grab his hand. His embarrassment jumped across at the contact. She needed to mull over his mood before she hit on the answer. "You did this to *yourself*?"

"Rachel—" Santino began, but by then she had trained her scans on him. She found the same cotton gauze and small injuries on her partner's arm, but where Mako's were already beginning to heal, Santino's were fresh.

She looked around the room and, yup, there they were, hidden in a cardboard box. A couple of test tubes, with pieces of Santino floating in an unknown liquid inside them.

Rachel held up her hands in surrender, and walked over to the window to get some air before she decided to murder the both of them to keep them from inventing new problems.

"Penguin—" Mako said, as he glanced towards the bathroom door.

"You're two of the most rational, intelligent people I know," Rachel said, keeping her voice as calm as she could manage. "At least, when you're not drinking. Since you're both sober, I'm sure there's an excellent explanation for the self-mutilation."

"We're trying to figure out why Mako can block your access to the EM spectrum."

"Right. Of course you are," Rachel said, as her fingernails sank into the wood of the windowsill. "So, what? You've moved straight to blaming our DNA?"

"Well, we didn't move *straight* to DNA sequencing," Mako said. "If we had, I would've just collected mouth swabs. We're also running conductivity tests, which is why we needed larger samples."

"DNA is part of it, though," Santino added. "We're playing process-of-elimination at this point, and since OACET doesn't have the tools for sequencing here, we'll need to send the swabs out to a private lab—"

"Oh lord," Rachel muttered. "Please tell me Jenny knows about this."

Flickers of yellow-orange trepidation ran through the men's

conversational colors. "Well—" Mako began.

"Of course she doesn't. Why would you consult a doctor before you decided to cut yourselves up?" Rachel sighed. "I suppose you want a sample from me?"

"No, no," Mako said, but Santino had already started nodding. "That's not necessary. We're paying for these out-of-pocket, and we've got samples from a few other Agents. Santino is the control."

"Control for… Wait. *Wait*. They did full genetic screenings on us before the surgery, so why would…" Rachel let herself trail off as she realized what Mako was implying. "Don't tell me you think the implant is *changing* our DNA?!"

Santino went purple and began to laugh.

"Yes and no," Mako said. "First, you have to understand that DNA isn't a single *thing*. It's made up of—"

The look she gave him would have frozen whole chickens.

"Probably, yeah," Mako sighed. "It's integrated into our very cells, Penguin. It's definitely changed *us*. So… yeah, Santino and I think it's made some minor epigenetic changes. I mean, look at what Avery can do."

Rachel hadn't felt the urge to claw out the tiny object in her head for months, but it returned anew, that same sickening terror she had experienced when she had first realized her implant wasn't just along for the ride. She returned to her chair before the sudden surge of nausea could knock her down.

The men didn't notice. "Mako and I will compare the other Agents' current genetic profiles to what they were before the surgery," Santino said. "And then against Mako's past and current profiles. Maybe something will show up that marks him as an outlier."

"This sounds really…" Rachel stopped herself before she said *insane*. "Involved."

"Mako's genetic makeup is just one possibility," Santino said. "We'll test it while we search for others."

"Besides, this is something we've needed to do anyhow," Mako said. "We don't know what the long-term effects of the implant will be. Five, ten years from now? I might have the most splendid of brain cancers." He rapped a superstitious knuckle on the wooden desk. "Routine screening might help us catch any changes before they cause serious cellular degradation or mutation."

"Right," Rachel agreed. Her nausea surged again. "Why aren't we doing that anyhow?"

"Because OACET's spending is tightly watched. Congress is trying to control us through controlling our operations budget. Several hundred thousand dollars for preventative genetic screening isn't in the budget."

"But it *should* be." Santino picked up the conversation. "Congress should be looking at OACET as a major financial investment."

Rachel picked her head up off of the table.

Santino rolled on, oblivious to her sudden shift into predator mode. "Say Mako and I find a way to control what data an Agent can access, and there are no medical side effects whatsoever. Why wouldn't everyone want one?"

Rachel moved her attention towards Mako. He sat there, smiling at her, blissfully unaware that what he and Santino had been discussing was already built into OACET's long-term plans.

"Want what?" she asked cautiously.

"The implant!" Santino said, grinning like a maniac. "Everyone would grab it. It's the next generation of smartphones. More utility, more capacity—"

"Minecraft in your head," Mako added. "Major selling feature, right there."

"—and don't forget the collective."

"No." Rachel shuddered. "*God*, no! It's bad enough with just us. There's no way I'm going to add every single Verizon customer to my psyche."

"Exactly," Mako said. "So, we've got a lot of bugs to work out. Removing the communal elements of the collective is almost as important as making sure the average schmuck can't take control of a nuke. It's not going to happen any time soon."

"It *will* happen, though," Santino said. "Eventually. Then the really big problems will start to show up."

"Don't." Rachel held up a hand. She already knew where this was headed. "Just don't."

The men ignored her. "The implant isn't cheap," Santino continued. "What was it, about ten million per item?"

"If you figure in research and development costs, yeah," Mako said. "But production costs are still incredibly high. It's a quantum organic computer, so you've got to grow each device so it'll be compatible with its user. Not everybody will be able to afford that."

"Barely anybody, really. Just the upper class."

"And then you've got a society where the wealthy are blended into their tech."

"Not to mention each other—we might be able to downplay the connection to the link, but there'll always be some element of collective consciousness involved. So it wouldn't be the usual issue of the Haves and the Have-nots... This'll be one where there's a small group of people who are intrinsically connected to each other, and to the tech which runs the world."

"And those outside of the new collective will be a fuck-all ginormous group of people who won't be allowed to sit at the cool kids' table."

"*Ever*. It'll be a whole new dimension to the usual stratified societies."

Rachel watched the two men, amazed. What they were discussing fell outside of the usual scope of OACET's Administrative meetings. Their colors were brilliantly yellow-white as they painted the future of the human race in broad sloppy strokes. "This is what the two of you do in your spare time?" she asked them. "Sit around and discuss how we're going to destroy civilization?"

"Pretty much," Mako said, shrugging. "Or maybe save it, really, if we can implement strategies to kill these problems before they get traction."

"Wait, what?" Rachel blinked. "OACET didn't invent the implant. Who decided we were the gatekeepers for a global societal clusterfuck?"

"OACET did." Santino was an unpleasant combination of smug pink and jealous green. "Going public put a face on it."

"But this is all *years* in the future," Mako said. "Decades, probably. There're so many problems to solve, and so few of us."

"It'll take time to do properly," Santino agreed. "This isn't something we can rush. We'll just have to keep working on it," he said. The pink faded from his colors, the purple-gray of resignation replacing it.

"Of course you will," she muttered. This wasn't just another technological puzzle for Santino. There would be no new implants, no new cyborgs, not until the security holes were plugged. Until that happened, her partner would forever be outside the collective. A friend, true, and the best of allies, but nothing more.

She knew it killed him.

"Fine," she said to Mako, as she stood and started to unbutton her pants. "I volunteer, but you're cutting up my butt. I'm not scarring up anything that'll show in a bathing suit for this lunacy."

Her partner, ever the gentleman, went into the hall to wait.

FOURTEEN

The old front door of their house worked about eight months of the year. Rachel and Santino would ride that sweet spot until mid-May, and then they'd have to wrestle with knobs and shims until early September. Nothing seemed to bring it to square. They had changed out the hinges and planed down the sticky bits, and it still got hung up on the corners.

Rachel opened the door to the season's first squeak of wood grinding over wood. She glared at the bulky monster; she had no energy to deal with anything else, be it human or humidity.

"I'm going to take a bath," she said. "And then I'm going to burn my clothes." The cuffs of her dress shirt had gone stiff as the blood had dried. Whether it was Hill's or Noura's was anyone's guess, and Rachel didn't much care. She just wanted it off of her body.

"Good. You smell awful," her partner said, and then surprised her by pulling her into a hug.

Warm relieved blues and the rich reds of belonging swept over her; Rachel returned the hug gladly. They had discussed the car chase on the way back from OACET headquarters, and the reality of what should have happened had finally sunk in. "I could have killed someone," she said. "It's a miracle I didn't."

"Yeah," he said. "But…"

He struggled to put a positive spin on it before giving up.

She nodded against his chest. "It'd have been one thing if Noura survived, but… Yeah. That whole mess was a waste."

"You're alive. Hill's alive. Nobody else got hurt, and the Secret Service has eight new people to interrogate. That's not a waste."

He didn't quite believe it—Noura's poppy-seed gray lingered within storm clouds at the edges of his conversational colors—but Rachel appreciated the sentiment and told him so.

Santino let her go, and she made her way upstairs, a bottle of red wine in one hand and a bell-shaped glass hanging by its stem from the other.

Her bathtub was one of the reasons she had bought the house. The master bath had been renovated by the previous owner, and a freestanding soaker tub took up a third of its footprint. The porcelain tub was shaped like a lady's slipper, one end higher than the other for safety during those long baths when you couldn't quite stay awake.

Rachel nudged the lever for the freestanding tub faucet all the way to the right, and dug around under the sink until she found an old bottle of cinnamon-scented bubble bath. She usually avoided bubbles. She didn't respect them. Bubbles were too scatterbrained to deserve respect.

Today, she needed something to be different.

Her service weapon went into its usual spot in her nightstand, her bloody shirt into a garbage bag. Then she knelt by the edge of the tub and watched the water pour down, down…

She let her mind go within the movement of the water.

Noura.

The thief's death had hit her harder than she expected. It wasn't the loss of Noura herself, and God knew that Rachel's own hands were redder than Hill's, but…

Killing people on purpose was one thing; not being able to protect someone from getting killed was something entirely different.

"Sorry," she whispered, and decided she might drop by the local church next Sunday. Maybe. If she had the time.

She turned off the water, and stepped into the tub. The water was almost hot enough to scorch her skin, but she pushed through until the bubbles sat at her neck. One deep breath, followed by another, and then the water felt merely toasty-warm and welcoming. Even the new incision on her left buttock felt better, the waterproof bandage blocking the sting of the water while letting the heat soothe the wound.

Wine, bath, and book, she thought. *Let's do this.*

The Braille e-reader was slightly thicker than a tablet, its back and edges sealed in some sort of silicone to make it waterproof. Calling it a first-generation device would have been generous: the thing was so far removed from the production line that it might as well have come from the technological equivalent of a farmer's table. The silicone was lumpy, the metal shell beneath covered in deep scratches where a Dremel tool had kicked sideways, but the reader's face was as smooth as glass. Santino and Mako had made it for her, and it had quickly become one of her favorite things in the world.

Rachel poked the upper right corner, and the device hummed to life. Its face started to churn, and she flipped off visuals as she began to read.

It was smut. She had told the Agents who converted books for her that she needed to master Braille before she plunged herself back into high literature. Romance novels and paperback mysteries, with their familiar lexicon and predictable rises and falls in plot, were good practice. She said she was honing her fingertips on Brontë and Evanovich, Austen and Steel...

And she knew she wasn't fooling anyone.

She wasn't sure how the e-reader worked. Santino said it was like an Etch A Sketch, but with iron instead of aluminum, and magnets to push and pull the raised bumps into place. There were no buttons save for the power switch; a nudge from her implant and the text refreshed, as easy as turning a page.

Her skin was ten minutes from wrinkly, which was good; she tended to misinterpret letters when she had sat in the bath too long. The words flew beneath her fingertips, a world of ripping bodices and sassy heroines...

When it came down to it, she had regretted nothing about going blind except her inability to lose herself in a book. Once she no longer had her eyesight, reading had become a chore. Books were her first real love, but there was a severe disconnect between her and the words when she had to concentrate to see them.

Braille had bridged that gap. She had picked up a children's book in Dr. Gillion's office, one with text and Braille both, and idle curiosity got her flipping through the pages. Braille had been one of those things that she hadn't felt played a role in her new life—*I'm not really blind. I can read if I have to*—and it had never struck her as an option.

Gillion had kept her waiting long enough for her to realize there might be another way for her to get lost in a book. Rachel had almost thanked him for that.

She was picking up Braille faster than she had thought possible. Jenny Davies had told her Braille wasn't technically a second language, that it was just a different way of internalizing English, and that she shouldn't be so insufferably smug about her progress. Rachel had stuck her tongue out at her friend, and had gone home to read.

The implications for language acquisition via the implant hadn't escaped OACET's resident scientists. Imagine an Agent receiving the same kind of language instruction as a student in a classroom. Where the student would remember a word here or there, feedback from the implant might assist in everything from interlanguage processing to improved comprehension of variation between the first and second languages. There was no good way to test this hypothesis, as nobody in OACET had a specialization in languages. There were a few dabblers—Rachel was one of them, with her hack-and-slash fluency in Mandarin Chinese—but a calling to study multiple languages and a job in federal service rarely aligned, and OACET hadn't gotten lucky enough to pull such a specialist into their roster. There was some floundering about with what *might* happen and what would *probably* occur when an Agent sought to acquire a new language, or what outcomes *could* result if a non-native English speaker developed autoscripts in their native tongue, but it was all guesswork. Nobody had the spare time needed to test these theories by mastering a second language from scratch.

For herself, Rachel was just happy she could read again. There were dozens of ways she could perceive text, but none of those came close to having nothing between her and a good book. In that respect, her eyes and her fingers were nearly the same, and she had finally bridged the physical gap between herself and plain, unadorned text.

Today was Sabrina Jeffries, with her dukes and their desires. Rachel didn't much care about lavishly embroidered cummerbunds (and what might be found beneath), but Jeffries wrote the most delicious ladies…

There was a knock on the bathroom door, and she flipped on visuals to see Santino, anxious oranges moving through professional blues.

"If you make me get out of this tub, I'll shoot you," she warned.

"Idle threat. I know where your gun is. Listen," he said from the other side of the door, "the White House murder story just hit the news feeds."

Rachel groaned and started to bang her head against the back of the tub.

"Yup," he said. "Ten minutes."

"Thirty!" she shouted.

"Fifteen."

"Twenty," she said, staring wistfully at the mostly-empty bottle of wine. "I'm slightly drunk."

She moved the Braille reader to its private shelf, and went to take a shower to rinse off the bubbles. By the time she was dressed, her buzz was mostly gone. *Hummingbird metabolism,* she thought to herself as she dithered around with her makeup. *Still can't decide whether it's a blessing or a curse.*

Her stomach grumbled, and she made her way to the kitchen to cram herself full of energy bars.

Santino wasn't there, which was odd: he usually paced the lower level of the house while waiting for her. She searched for his cell phone, and found her partner reading a book in his garden, a bottle of hard cider beside him.

She kicked open the storm door. "Santino, what the hell?"

He flushed an embarrassed red. "Oh, shit," he said. "You were in the shower when Alimoren called. He said that you and Hill should…uh…"

"Hide?"

"Yup. He promised he'd take the blame for the car chase, but unless you want to do interviews for the rest of the week, you guys should lay low."

"Nice," Rachel said, as she went back inside to reclaim her bottle of wine. "Mandatory state-sponsored vacation time. Can't beat it."

On her way down the stairs, her implant twitched, requesting her attention at the motion sensor that Santino had set up over their driveway. She cast her scans through the front of the house to find the sunny citrus core of Randy Summerville as he walked towards the front door.

"Today?" Rachel muttered to herself. "Why on earth did he decide today was a good day to drop by?"

She reached out through the link and pinged Mulcahy, who told her that Summerville's visit was most likely a good thing, but no, he could not sit in on the conversation as he was currently doing damage control after one of his Agents had torn up a goodly portion of the landscaping in front of Howard University Hospital, and perhaps she could handle this on her own?

Fine, she thought, as her boss snapped their link. *First I'm a spy, now I'm a politician. What a week this has been.*

The doorbell chimed.

"Coming!" Rachel called. She ditched the wine glass and its companion bottle behind a lush cluster of red-edged dracaenas, and ate a handful of lemon thyme from a window garden to kill the smell of alcohol.

Then, smiling politely, she gave the doorknob a firm yank.

The door had come unstuck again, and flew open with a crash.

"Mr. Summerville? What a nice surprise. Please come in," she said, as if threatening prominent lobbyists with her front door were an everyday occurrence.

Over Summerville's shoulder, a flurry of reds and blacks had popped out of the car: Summerville's assistant, now acting as his chauffeur, was marching up the driveway, asking in a neighbor-rousing tone of voice if his boss needed any help. Summerville quickly waved the young man back to the car with assurances that he was fine, but it was too late. Mrs. Wagner, Rachel's elderly next-door neighbor, had appeared on her front porch with a golf club in her hands.

"In the house," Rachel muttered. "Hurry up, hurry up…"

Rachel maneuvered Summerville into the foyer and slammed the door behind them. Mrs. Wagner had all the time in the world at her disposal, and expected all persons within earshot to share her fondness for idle conversation. She had also adopted Rachel as a surrogate…something. Not a daughter. *Definitely* not a daughter. It was more like she thought of Rachel and Santino as feral cats who had moved into the abandoned house next door, and she was trying to domesticate them through proximity and the occasional gift of food.

Through the door, Rachel watched as Mrs. Wagner cornered the young man on the way back to his car. His colors took a quick leap towards orange, but didn't shed her Southwestern turquoise.

"Your assistant doesn't like me much, does he?" Rachel asked.

"He doesn't like anybody much," Summerville answered. "He's my nephew. Bright, but my brother didn't hug him enough as a child."

There was the mournful red of family secrets in there; Rachel decided to go easy on Summerville's assistant.

"Would he like to join us, or maybe sit in the garden while he waits?" she asked. "Gardening's a hobby for my partner, and he's always happy to give a tour."

"Jordan would appreciate the offer, but he needs to get some work done," Summerville replied. Dimpling appeared across his shoulders with the white lie.

Good, Rachel thought. She hadn't been looking forward to throwing oddball topics at him to see if she could catch him lying. Her experience with Jenna Noura had shaken her in more ways than one.

"Well, what brings you by?" Rachel asked, inviting him into her private study. "Were you in the neighborhood?"

Summerville raised an eyebrow. "Please. It took a lot of work to get your home address. This is definitely not a social call."

"I appreciate the honestly," Rachel said, as she helped herself to the chair closest to the window. "It's a timesaver. I assume you've heard I can read microexpressions?"

"Actually, they told me you're a mind reader. Among other things…" Summerville trailed off as he took in her study. Since Santino had moved in, every room on the main floor of their house was always spotless. Sunlight played off of glass on the built-in cabinets, Rachel's collection of poetry and paperback romance novels behind it. Hundreds of books, all of them well-loved, their spines broken and covers torn to hell. The leather armchairs were overstuffed and comfortable, with standing lamps peeking over their backs like curious birds, and even more books stacked in neat piles across the nearby coffee table.

It was a room made for reading. Definitely not the kind of room one expected to find in the home of a blind woman.

"Oh?" she asked, all innocence, and glad her Braille reader was safely upstairs.

"Never mind," he said. "People are idiots."

"I agree. What brings you by?"

Summerville sighed and settled back in his chair. "The news just broke that a man was murdered at the White House."

Rachel said nothing, her chin propped on one hand. She began to weave her frequency shield, to make sure anyone (*cough, young nephew Jordan, cough*) trying to snoop with a surveillance device would get an earful of static.

"Rumor has it," he continued, "that the woman who murdered him was killed on your watch."

She caught herself before she could react. *Interesting*, she thought. *Is that what Mulcahy meant when he said he was doing damage control? Making sure that Alimoren wasn't able to dump the blame on me? Alimoren promised to take the heat, but pushing it onto OACET would be so convenient...*

"Nothing?" he asked her.

"You know I can't comment on any ongoing investigations, whether real or figments of imagination."

Summerville watched her, his colors weighing her Southwestern turquoise against three different hues of gray stress. One of those grays hung heavy across his shoulders, and was weighed down at the bottom by a streak of Hanlon's woody brown core.

Rachel pretended she had discovered something of particular interest under a fingernail, and didn't meet his eyes.

"A year ago," Summerville said, "I thought OACET was the worst thing that could possibly happen to this country."

"Me, too," she said.

"I bet you weren't working to pull OACET down," he said. "Like I was."

That got her full attention. Her head came up, and Summerville's colors fluttered and paled as her eyes caught his. "Oh?" she asked, as mildly as she could.

"Please don't pretend that's news to you," he said. "OACET keeps its secrets, but everybody knows you have one of the best information networks around."

Rachel dropped her gaze and nodded. "To be honest," she said, "I was surprised when you approached me at the White House."

It was true: OACET had initially identified Summerville as a possible threat, but that had been reassessed after Rachel had begun a working friendship with a local city judge. Rachel had been tipped off to Summerville's involvement in a possible anti-OACET movement during the Glazer case. Summerville had been courting the judge, who had his sights set on attaining political office. One thing led to another, certain people got shot, and the judge and Rachel had developed a solid professional relationship. It seemed as though the judge had passed that message on to Summerville.

Summerville confirmed this: "My employers and I were..."

angry…when you turned Judge Edwards. We had plans for him."

Rachel grinned. "I didn't turn him. I showed him that OACET was made of people."

"You did," he said. "And he convinced me."

She chuckled. "I hope OACET had something to do with that. We work hard to show we're just everyday civil servants who got stuck in a bad situation."

Summerville's colors rolled towards purple amusement as she fell into the patter of the OACET party line, and she shrugged, caught. *I actually like this guy,* she thought. *God help me.*

"Yes. You do go above and beyond to show that you're worth keeping around," he said. "Not just when you're working, but after hours, too… Your people donate your time, your abilities… Must be stressful."

"It's easier than you think," Rachel said. "We're still rebuilding our lives, so we might as well define ourselves as people whose value offsets their risk."

"Exactly so," he said. "That brings me to today. The car chase through the city. How often are serious public relations disasters going to happen with you and your people?"

Rachel didn't reply. Instead, she pretended to look over her shoulder at where Mrs. Wagner, wearing nothing but angry reds, had forced Jordan to take refuge in the front seat of his car.

"Agent Peng," Summerville said. "I will try to convince my employers to back OACET *only* if I'm sure that their endorsement won't backfire on them."

Holy. Freakin'. Crap.

Rachel stood. "Would you like something to drink?"

Frustrated orange started to crawl out of Summerville's fingertips; he was itching to make progress. Still, he said, politely, "Some water would be lovely."

Rachel left the study and closed the French doors behind her, sealing Summerville away.

If the telecommunication companies backed OACET…

This was an entirely different conversation than the one she had had with Summerville at the White House. There, they had been playing with the idea that Big Telecommunications might sever ties with Hanlon. Now, this…

This could be *everything*.

She found the two nicest glasses they owned, and let the water from the tap run over her hands until they stopped shaking. A few deep breaths, and that cold, calm Rachel who could shoot someone in the head and not think about it until later had taken over.

If Mulcahy wants me to be a spy, then I'll be a spy, she thought. *So. Spycraft 101 it is… Feed him a little bit of information to seal the deal.*

Back to the study, and to her favorite chair, where she told Summerville: "*If* I was involved in that incident, it wasn't by choice, and would have been only while trying to save a life."

"Admirable, I'm sure, but irrelevant. Not when the media can turn the facts against you."

"Has that happened?"

"Not yet," he admitted. "Mitch Alimoren and the Secret Service are taking responsibility."

"Well," she said, as she felt a rush of relief at hearing that Alimoren was keeping his promise to OACET and the MPD. "If the Secret Service is responsible, then isn't this discussion irrelevant?"

"Not if we decide to build a long-term alliance with you. How often will things like this happen?" Summerville asked. "To you, or to other members of OACET?"

"We're well aware the media enjoys spinning facts into straw," she told him. "Generally speaking, we go out of our way to never do anything that could be perceived as a violation of the social contract. Since we can hide our tracks better than anyone else, it's assumed that we're always doing terrible things and covering them up—I think this says more about the rest of society than OACET, by the way—but we *always* try to abide by the law. We know if we're ever caught breaking it, that's when you'll all come down on us and rip us apart.

"We're not perfect," Rachel continued, thinking of magically changing traffic lights and a stolen pair of hospital scrubs. "We still make mistakes. But it's better to try to be the kind of people we want to be, than risk being ruined because of a stupid decision."

"I suppose that's the best I can ask," he said.

"If you can find a better way to live, please tell us, and we'll do it. Now…" she said. "What did you mean by 'backing' OACET? Be specific. I'd like to avoid the confusion from our last conversation."

"We'll remove our support from Hanlon and dedicate our resources to OACET instead," Summerville said.

"Does that include backing us in Congress?"

"It depends," he hedged. "Stunts like that car chase today—"

"In routine matters only," she clarified. "And if Congress decides to come after us like they did when we first went public. We don't want to go through anything like that again, not alone, not without strong support."

"I think Mulcahy and some of my employers would need to define limits on when and how we would help OACET, but I don't see a problem with that arrangement."

"That's fair," she said, after carefully checking his colors for signs of lying. "What do you want from us in exchange?"

"Nothing more than what you suggested at the White House," he replied. "We want volunteers from OACET to work with our technicians to develop security methods."

"To keep us out of secure areas, or to block us completely?

"To fix—to *block*—you." Summerville was perplexed. "Wouldn't OACET benefit if you could pretend the last five years hadn't happened and go back to your normal lives?"

Fine. Spycraft 101 it is.

"We'll comply with anything you want if you're pursuing security protocols. But if your goal is to block us, we…" Rachel began, before staring off into space, as if searching for the right words. She wasn't: she had mapped out her game plan in the kitchen. *All or nothing, and we might win everything.*

"Agent Peng?"

She sighed, and hunched over the slightest bit. "Call me Rachel, please."

His colors took on a wine red hue. With her legs tucked beneath her, her body curled in on itself, he couldn't help but be reminded that she was a rather small woman who was just a few years older than his nephew.

Summerville was a lobbyist. He read people—powerful people—for a living. She was not about to try to manipulate him with anything more than small doses of honest body language. The backlash would rip her head clean off.

She didn't like to be cornered into telling the truth, but the truth was sharp and could cut deep. If used properly, it was one hell of a weapon.

"If I'm ever asked, I'll deny having this conversation," she told him, glancing out the window as if to make sure no one was snooping in the bushes. "Do you remember when OACET first came out? How there was a very vocal minority who suggested that there was one easy way to solve all of the problems we posed?"

She slid a hand across her throat. Anybody watching would see a woman adjusting the collar of her shirt. Summerville saw something quite different, and nodded.

"Say somebody does find some way to block our access to the EM spectrum," she said. "That'd be no different than murdering all of us."

A pop of orange scorn mixed within green disbelief moved into his surface colors. "Agent—Rachel…"

"I know you think that turning us back to normal would be helping us," she said. "It's natural to think that the problem is the implant. Get rid of that, problem solved. Right?"

Summerville nodded.

"Remember when I asked if you were a parent?" Rachel said. "I was going to tell you a story that explains what it's like to be a member of OACET, but I decided better of it. It's an offensive comparison, and parents think less of me when I use it, but I use it because it's true. Can I tell you that story now?"

She paused, and watched Summerville's colors roll in and out of themselves as he tried to work out her train of thought. "All right," he agreed. "Tell me."

Rachel closed her eyes, and took in the room. She checked the weaves of her shield again, tugging and twisting frequencies until she was sure they were wrapped as tight as she could make them.

She hated resorting to these awkward descriptions. Only those within the collective could understand what it meant to be a part of it; analogies were fumbling, inadequate words that did nothing but clutter up the empty space between an Agent and an outsider.

"Everybody wants to know what it's like to be a cyborg," she began. "We've all tried to explain what it's like, and we can't. There's no comparison close enough to explain what it's like to be yourself..." she said, holding up one hand, "...while also being part of another." She netted her fingers together. "Once they're together, you think it'd be an easy thing to pull them apart, but its not.

"Parents..." she began, and paused as if she was trying to gain courage.

"Go on," Summerville said, earnest blue working its way out from his core.

"Parents *know* that each child you have changes your entire family. If, God forbid, something happens to that child, your family won't go back to how it was before. There's a new normal.

"We can't go back," she said in a rush. "If Hanlon finds a way to block our access to the EM spectrum, he shuts down our community. Our family. Our very *selves!* Imagine that sense of loss, to have the new normal gone forever."

She let herself turn towards the sun-bright windows of her study again. "Blocking our connection to each other would probably kill us," she said. "Or we'd spend the rest of our lives in misery, trying to find a way back to what we had lost."

Summerville watched her for a few long moments, until

Rachel pretended to shrug off her malaise and gave him the bravest of big-girl smiles. "Anyway," she said. "We can't help you if you're looking for a way to fix us. We've already been broken. The way we put ourselves back together might not have been the best or the prettiest solution, but it's where we are now, and we aren't looking to change it."

Rachel thought Summerville might keep her waiting while he decided what to do with what she had told him, but he broke into a wide grin.

"You're good," he said, his conversational colors mostly purple but with pops of laser-like professional blue scattered throughout. "You're *very* good. Another ten years on you, and even an old warhorse like me won't be able to tell when you're playing him."

She nodded to acknowledge the hit. "Still," she said, "that doesn't make what I said any less true."

"Yes," Summerville said. "I can tell that, too. But I don't think my employers will like what you're proposing. OACET is a threat to their business model. They'd be happier if you were blocked altogether."

"Happier?" Rachel seized on that word as a green the color of greed came up within Summerville's colors. She remembered him at the Botanic Gardens gala, festive in his reds and greens, same as every other lobbyist or politician.

"There's always room to negotiate," Summerville said. "If the price is right."

"Your employers are willing to back us instead of Hanlon, and support us in Congress? And no further discussion of blocking our access to the EM spectrum as the best course of action?"

"If the price is right," Summerville repeated.

Rachel threw her scans to the backyard. Santino was lying on his back in the middle of the patio, arms and legs spread wide as he soaked in the spring sunlight. She smiled at the idea of her partner making a gravel angel in the loose stones of their patio.

"Then let me propose an alternative," she said.

FIFTEEN

"You did what?"

Becca's tone was beautifully, peacefully bland. Rachel didn't need the emotional spectrum to know that white shock had settled over her girlfriend like a collapsing snowdrift.

"I offered to let OACET work with the telecommunication companies to develop a universal implant for the general public."

"Yes. Okay," Becca said in that same snow-white voice. "That's what I thought you said. Why… Now, why would you do that?"

"Because I'm a *genius!*" Rachel shouted the last word as she collapsed backwards on the grass.

Rachel's bungalow was an easy walk to the edge of Rock Creek Park, a woody stretch of land that started at the Smithsonian National Zoological Park, meandered through large patches of the city, and then turned north towards Maryland. This section of the park was mostly trees, but there were grassy spots if you knew where to look for them. Spring was well and truly here, and they had decided an afternoon picnic would be a good way to celebrate Becca's return. The texts had gone out, and it had turned into an unofficial group outing with a side order of a food fight. After Rachel and Santino had picked up Becca from the airport, they joined Phil, Jason, and Bell at the park, and the six of them had immediately begun hurling potato salad. Hill had arrived after the ruckus was over, but he had brought a jumbo bag of chips, so it had all started up again with crunchy bits.

After the fun had ended, Rachel and Becca had moved themselves out of harm's way to catch up on the past week. They had tucked themselves away on a scrap of lawn that had managed to survive the winter, Becca talking about this and that, pieces of trivia and gossip she had learned at her bankers' convention in Bermuda.

(Becca was a banker in much the same way that astronauts were pilots: there was some overlap of tasks but these were performed in entirely different environments. Becca, beautiful Becca with her long, dark hair and her core of smooth jade green, understood how money *worked*. That, in Rachel's opinion, made her an honest-to-God wizard. In this modern world where money was abundant but unattainable, and those who did get their hands on it tended to squander it or worse, someone who knew how to bend it to her will might as well be doing magic.)

After Becca had finished her last story about five-star dining with A-list celebrities flown in for the event, Rachel had told her what she could about the break-in and its repercussions.

She was lucky the story had already hit the news cycle, as it freed her to go into some detail about the investigation. Hill's wounded shoulder, with his arm stuck in a sling, gave her account of the car chase some extra credibility. Rachel was told in no uncertain terms that she should never go to a party at the White House without her girlfriend again ("I don't care if I was in the Islands! It's the *White House!* You call me so I can get on the next plane home!"), and then ended with her conversation with Randy Summerville.

That was the part where Becca had gone white with shock.

Understandable, really. Their relationship was still somewhat new, and while Rachel had trusted Becca enough to have an honest conversation about Senator Hanlon and those lost five years, she was still cautious about introducing her to OACET's deeper secrets. She certainly hadn't told Becca how OACET believed that the implant, or something similar, was the inevitable future of information technology.

Well, it *was*. Since they couldn't get the genie back in the bottle, they might as well try to cram it into some sort of packing material and stick a label on it.

For OACET, the major issue was the collective. They

absolutely had to remove the hivemind from the equation: nobody in OACET wanted to be networked to a bunch of early adopters with disposable income. The minor issues were the implant's ability to override security measures, and the cost of the device and its corresponding surgery. If those three concerns could be met in a less comprehensive, less expensive version of the implant?

Goodbye, smartphones.

Then, decades from now? Hello, new iteration of a technology-centric society.

And then, if OACET survived to see that day, they'd no longer be freaks.

This was a long-term plan, designed to play out over their lifetime. OACET's Administration had assumed that it would take a couple of years before OACET was considered a credible organization by both the public and private sectors. OACET would spend those years building good karma, and then, once they had shown that their implants made them useful, valuable members of society, they'd see who wanted to work with them to develop the next generation of personal communications technology.

Santino's OACET-compatible glasses were a test case. Her partner didn't know that Mulcahy was using the prototypes to establish OACET's presence within the technology supply chain. After the final version of Santino's glasses were distributed to those who worked with cyborgs, OACET would move on to developing medical devices, or tools to improve remote access...maybe even get patents on some of Mako's baby-monitoring equipment.

There was money to be made from the implant and its myriad applications. They just had to survive until their potential trade partners calmed down enough to realize that OACET wasn't a liability but a fantastic investment opportunity.

Rachel had offered Summerville an alternative that was already part of OACET's strategy, which could be summed up in an easy three-step process:

Step 1: Work with us, not against us.
Step 2: Help us change the technology so future generations
    won't include a hivemind, and address the security
    and cost barriers of the implant.
Step 3: Profit.

She had expected Summerville to need some time to wrap his mind around what she had proposed. No. As soon as she had started her pitch, his conversational colors had frozen, stunned by her suggestion. This, she had expected. She *hadn't* expected how quickly the greens of financial possibilities would appear, along with pleased pinks entwined around her Southwest turquoise and the eye-searing OACET green. Summerville (or his employers) had already imagined the implant as a marketable device, one subject to service plans and rate changes and bandwidth surcharges…

Rachel had spent the rest of her pitch feeling rather like an especially dim student who was telling the teacher what he already expected to hear, but she could live with that. As long as the telecommunications industry believed that OACET would work with them towards achieving mutual goals, she didn't care who got the credit. She had shown the recording of their meeting to OACET's Administration, and even Mulcahy had laughed at how well the whole thing had played out.

Ahead of schedule, and doing fine, Rachel thought to herself. *Not a bad place to be.*

"Promise me you won't tell Santino, okay?" she said to Becca. "I don't want him to know about this until it's a sure thing." To have that opportunity dangled, and then wrenched away… No. She refused to do that to him.

Instead of replying, Becca's colors twisted once, twice, and then a third time, turning into frightened yellows surrounding a strand of OACET green. These twined into themselves, like climbing plants who used their own vines for support. Finally, Becca asked in a small voice, "Are you sure Summerville's not going to hold what you told him against you?"

Rachel jumped as quickly as if Becca had pressed a branding iron against her ribs. Her girlfriend usually had about as much interest in the implant and the collective as Rachel had in different species of earthworms. Becca considered Rachel's involvement in OACET to be a high-stress job that required her to be on-call at all hours of the day and night, but she also considered the implant to be nothing more than a glorified cell phone. That she'd react to Rachel's decision to sell it to Summerville as such…

"What do you mean?" Rachel asked cautiously.

"OACET's security comes first—OACET's security *always* comes first! You've told me enough so I know to watch what I say to anyone asking after you, and here you are—"

"Oh. That," Rachel said, as calmly as she could. Becca's temper could catch fire like a torch put to dry grass. "Becca, it's always been part of the—"

"No. You said yourself you don't know if you can trust this man," Becca said. "You don't even know if you can get an honest read off of his emotions! Why would you offer him a proposal this…this…this *huge?!*"

She sat back and waited.

"Because he'd already thought of it," Rachel said. "His employers already hoped that the implant could be retooled for profit. I just repackaged the idea for him."

Rachel wasn't sure how that explanation went over with Becca, because that was the moment when Ami hit the ground beside them in a perfect three-point landing.

Becca screamed and crab-walked backwards before she recognized Ami.

"There are no trees around," Rachel said, pretending that her heart wasn't trying to pound its way out through her ears. She hadn't seen the other Agent coming. "How did you get above us?"

"A magician never tells her secrets," Ami said.

"What's wrong with you?!" Becca had found her voice. "You

scared the—"

"Never show weakness in front of an assassin, babe," Rachel told Becca. "It's just chumming the waters."

"Former assassin," Ami said in a purple-gray sigh, as she settled herself on the grass. "Is that potato salad in your hair?"

"No," Rachel said, combing through the mess with her fingers until she found something sticky.

"Anyway, back to the Summervilles," Ami said, as if she had been part of the conversation from the beginning. "Randy Summerville hasn't been considered an active threat for several months. He used to be, but he's been significantly downgraded. And at Rachel's recommendation, we've just opened a dossier on Jordan Summerville, his current assistant. Jordan was pretty active in the online OACET hate communities before he went to work for his uncle. He must have gotten *The Talk*—" Ami used airquotes to set off those two words— "from Summerville about private lives and professional personas, as he deleted every rant he'd ever posted about OACET."

"Then he *is* a risk?" Becca asked. She had snuck back towards Rachel, but was keeping her girlfriend between herself and the former assassin. Rachel decided that Becca didn't have to know that Ami could take out two people as easily as one, especially when they were conveniently aligned.

"Not really," Ami said with a shrug. "It was all typical young adult hate screeds. He also went through and deleted his posts on the sports boards. Kid does not like the Yankees one bit."

"A *lot* of people hate us," Rachel assured Becca, before remembering a normal person wouldn't find that a comforting thought. "We've gotten good at recognizing those who're just venting versus those who'll follow through on their threats."

"Yup," Ami agreed, before turning her attention to Hill, who was resting on his good arm near the food. "But I'm not here for business. Let's talk shop later."

"There are a couple of clean plates left," Rachel said, pointing towards the leftovers. As Ami moved towards the detective under the guise of fixing herself a snack, Rachel opened a link.

"How did you sneak up on me? I've got a proximity alert and scans running."

"Easy. I told my GPS to put my location at the mansion, and you use your scans like eyes. You might run your scans at a full 360 degrees, but they're dependent on your field of focus. Becca's a good distraction." Ami must have felt her shiver through the link, as she followed that thought with a comforting, *"Don't worry. Nobody can maintain a constant state of surveillance without training."*

Rachel nearly groused about how she *was* trained; Ami caught the feeling behind the complaint before Rachel could put it into words. *"Aw!"* Ami said. *"You're adorable."*

"Rachel?"

She flicked her scans forward. Becca had scooted around her and was watching her face, thin trails of yellow curiosity and red aggression twining around each other as she searched for a target.

On impulse, Rachel leaned forward and kissed her on the tip of her nose. "You're cute when you don't know why you're angry," she told Becca.

Becca grabbed the back of Rachel's neck, and Rachel grinned at finding herself scruffed like an ornery kitten. "I know why I'm angry," Becca growled against her lips. "You've spent months explaining why you *have to* do things a certain way, that you *have to* protect yourself, and now you're stepping out of your tight little logic box—"

Santino, walking towards them, went bright crimson with embarrassment as he choked on his soda.

"Santino, explain it to her," Rachel said, putting a safe arm's length between her and her furious girlfriend. "I don't know if she'll believe me."

"Uh—"

"Shut up."

Her partner folded his long legs and dropped onto the grass beside them. "OACET's all about risk management," he told Becca. "They play short and long games at the same time. The long game's the end goal—that doesn't change. The short game can be adapted as long as the risk is acceptable and any changes made will advance the goal."

"Listen to the smart person," Rachel said, with a polite golf clap for Santino. "Him make good talky-words."

"Rachel's in Administration, so she's got more flexibility in making command decisions than Zia, or any of those guys," Santino said, pointing towards the Agents playing on the grassy field. "They have to get any serious changes approved. Rachel can just go ahead and run with it."

"I'm responsible," Rachel said, nodding sagely.

"God!" Becca sighed. "You have the *weirdest* job! Is this how they run the NSA… Never mind. I'm better off not knowing."

Santino opened his mouth, and Rachel shook her head at him, ever so slightly. If the easiest way for her girlfriend to understand OACET was to put it in the context of a high-security government job, then Rachel wasn't about to dispel that notion.

"No, wait… I thought there was one long-term goal? Getting rid of…" Becca glanced around. "You know? *Him?*"

"Hang on," Rachel said. "Let me put up a shield."

She sent out her scans to sweep the grounds, scouting about for anything wayward or untrustworthy. Nothing pinged as atypical: they were on camera, but every living soul in Washington was on camera in one way or another, and nothing seemed especially interested in their presence. Still, better safe than sorry: Rachel gathered up a few of the conventional frequencies into a rough shield and stuck these up around the park, a chainlink fence to deter the neighborhood's digital dogs from snooping on their conversation.

Ami noticed. *"What's up?"* the former assassin asked, a hand moving oh-so-casually to the ankle where she kept her smallest gun.

"Girl talk," Rachel replied.

"'kay," Ami said, and returned her attention to Hill.

(Rachel was beginning to worry about Hill's chance of

surviving the night. Like most Agents, Ami valued living in the moment. She wasn't alone: Hill seemed to have gotten over his aversion to assassins, as red lust was sneaking into his conversational colors. Rachel had hoped that Ami would give Hill's bullet wound a minimum of twelve hours to heal before she took him to bed, but that was starting to look extremely unlikely.)

"All right," Rachel said, as she gave a final twist to tie off her shield. "We're good."

"The Senator," Becca said, almost whispering. "Isn't holding him accountable OACET's long-term goal?"

"Sort of," Rachel said with a shrug. "It's a priority, but it's also more of a mid-term goal. Our long-term goals are focused on how we can best survive in normal society."

"Right," Santino said. "It's not like everything will be perfect once Hanlon's removed."

"*If* he's removed," Rachel said. "I don't know—I go back and forth on whether we'll ever be able to put him in prison. He's wealthy, famous, and politically connected. It's hard to hold that combination accountable for anything short of cold-blooded murder."

"That's what worries me," Becca said, settling down to rest her head in Rachel's lap. Sunlight caught her hair, turning it into a living tangle of dark golds and browns, and Rachel wondered anew at how she had managed to convince this amazing woman to put up with her crazy life.

"What does?" Rachel asked, tucking a strand of Becca's hair behind her ear.

"Hanlon is a self-made man," Becca said. "He's managed to become one of the richest men in the country, he's more popular than Steve Jobs ever was, and OACET *insists* on playing games with him."

"Becca—"

"I know there's a lot you can't tell me, but what you have told me scares me," Becca said. The reds and yellows were back, and Rachel noticed these were beginning to wrap around her Southwestern turquoise in a protective embrace. "He's a dangerous animal, and you've backed him into a corner."

"What's the alternative?" Santino asked. "If the world was fair, he'd already be in prison."

"God, guys, I know you're not this dense! You've gone to war with him, so, maybe… Listen, you *know* there are casualties in war. And you've got…" Becca couldn't finish, and just pointed at Ami.

"If he dies, the entire world comes after us," Rachel said. "There're enough people out there who'd move on us if anything happens to Hanlon. *Anything*. We're scared he might get killed in a four-car pileup, since they'd find a way to blame it on us."

"I know, but… What you're doing isn't *smart*," Becca insisted. "Every day he's running loose is another chance for him to come after you. You say you're all about risk minimization—you have to realize that!"

Rachel looked at Santino. He returned it, slightly sick in yellows. "We do," Rachel admitted. "And he knows we're about to drop a huge bombshell on him, soon. He's not going to go down without a fight."

Becca was starting to burn again, her reds so strong that Rachel almost forgot why she couldn't feel the anger where Becca's bare skin lay against her own. "If you *know* he's not going to go down—"

"Honey?" Rachel said gently. "We're getting into things I can't talk about. Can you please accept that we're aware of the risks, and that killing him isn't an option? That's about as much as I can say."

Becca blinked, and then started laughing. "Oh my God," she said. "Forget everything I just said. I'm telling you to go out and kill another human being… No. This is insane—this is *not* good for me."

Rachel leaned over to rest her forehead on Becca's. "I try to keep things interesting," she said.

Becca cracked up, hard, before shoving Rachel aside and leaving to find a soda.

"What set off the Hanlon discussion?" Santino asked.

"Oh," Rachel said, a little smile playing around her lips. "This and that."

"Uh-huh," Santino said, as he gathered his legs beneath him. "Sure. I came over here to tell you I checked the office messages. Kowalski called. She wants you to get back to her. She'd got the results on Joanna Reed."

"Who?" Rachel asked. Erin Kowalski was one of the Medical Examiners with the MPD's Forensic Pathology Unit. Since the only woman's body Rachel knew of was Jenna Noura's, she didn't immediately recognize the victim's name. She got there eventually: Joanna Reed was the makeup artist found dead in the trunk of her car. "Oh. Reed. Right."

Kowalski's request wasn't a new one. When Kowalski called their office, she often refused to speak to anyone other than Rachel: Kowalski didn't especially like Santino, but she hated Zockinski and Hill with the intensity of someone who had been set on fire and left alone to burn. Rachel was sure the two men hadn't been (quite) that hard on Kowalski, but she was the kind of person who carried a grudge.

Rachel took up her new tablet, and disappeared into the nearby woods for privacy.

Kowalski answered almost immediately, her face surrounded by the sterile whites of a pathologist's office. "Peng?"

The woman looked exhausted. If Rachel could see her in person, she was sure Kowalski's colors would be shades of gray, with spots of reds run so far down that there would barely be any anger left in them.

"Hey, Kowalski. Is everything okay?"

"No," snapped the other woman. Apparently, there was still some punch left in her anger. "The FBI got our bodies first. They let us play with them after they were done."

Rachel needed a moment for that one. "Oh," she said, once she put the words in their proper places. "You just got access to Joanna Reed today?"

"Yesterday. Results came back today. Peng, they missed some

trace."

"The FBI?" Rachel didn't quite believe it. The FBI's forensic pathologists were among the best in the world. "What did they miss?"

"Saliva. Protocol is to collect evidence from the hands, which they did. But Reed was dumped fully clothed and in a winter jacket. They assumed she had been wearing that outfit when she was killed."

"She wasn't?"

"They dressed her in the jacket after she had been killed. Since she'd been dropped and dumped a couple of times, it didn't raise any flags until we found carpet fibers on her shirt."

"Her sleeveless shirt?" Rachel guessed.

Kowalski chuckled. "Dead right."

"That's a scary phrase coming from a pathologist, Kowalski. Where was the saliva?"

"Her elbow. Looks like she tried to fight him off. The skin had a very minor abrasion, so she didn't hit him too hard, but she did pick up enough saliva to run DNA."

"You're running DNA right now? How long?"

"Give us a day or two. Can I call you direct?"

"Please do," Rachel said, and gave Kowalski her private phone number. "It'll forward directly to me, so I'll pick up no matter when you call."

After Kowalski had signed off, Rachel decided that DNA evidence would be nice, especially if a suspect ever turned up.

We've got nothing but two dead women, she reminded herself. *And one of them had nothing on her but a piece of metal from a two-thousand-year-old Greek shipwreck.*

She wished she had gotten a good look inside the package before the Secret Service had spirited it away. Alimoren would probably call them once the bad publicity of a car chase through downtown D.C. blew over, but until then, she and her team had been sidelined. No leads. No nothing…

Glazer says hello.

Maybe not quite nothing.

She reached out to Jason, who was lying in an odd pile of legs and arms, only a third of which belonged to him. He wasn't too happy to pull himself out from under Phil and Bell, and he came storming into the woods.

All Agents were photophobic, the implants on their optic nerves increasing their sensitivity to light, but Jason had an extreme case. He wore dark glasses no matter what; on particularly sunny days, he tucked his dark hair under a wide-brimmed ivy cap and kept it low over his eyes. The shade of the wooded glade eased his headache almost as soon as he stepped under the trees: Rachel felt his relief as the pain he had accepted as his constant companion vanished.

"What?" he asked her, his sharp tone missing a few of its usual teeth.

Rachel tossed a scan back towards the picnic, where the others gamboled about in the afternoon sun. Then, she checked her walls to make sure they were good and tight. "Glazer," she whispered aloud.

She felt his own walls harden at Glazer's name. Jason knew. Except for Glazer and his accomplice, Jason was the only other person on the planet who *knew*. "Okay," he whispered back. "What's going on?"

Rachel told him the quick and dirty version of what had led up to the car chase. "Noura had information about what happened with Glazer that nobody could know," she said, her scans firmly fixed on Ami to make sure the assassin wouldn't drop out of the trees a second time. "Nobody except those involved. So unless you've been talking—"

Thick red anger bubbled up within Jason, and she waved away her implied insult.

"—which I know you *haven't*, there's something else going on here. Something that I want to get ahead of. I need you to teach me how to look at data."

She had never seen colors fall so quickly before: one moment, his usual red-hued conversational colors were floating around his head and chest; the next, they had gone gray and puddled at his feet. "How…" he said, as he fumbled for a reason. "If you find data, how about you just call me, and I'll handle it for you?"

The look she gave him must have screamed pure murder, as he said, very quietly, "Or I can teach you."

"Thanks. What do we need?"

She felt him reach out and wander around the innards of her new tablet. "This," he said. "It's perfect. Brand-new, factory-fresh settings. It's training wheels for data diving."

"Data diving?"

"If you're serious about this, you've got to start coming to the meetings…" he muttered, and then opened a deep link. He ran into her walls, hard. *"Hey!"*

"I didn't know! Tell me what you need from me before you assume I know what's going on," she said.

"If you want me to teach you something, you have to let me teach you," he said.

"Can't you just—"

"No. Help me out, okay?"

Jason sat, cross-legged, and gestured for her to join him on the ground. She did, facing him, her new tablet splitting the space between them. It reminded her of their unintended merging of the other night, where they had found themselves seizing the 3D-printed replica of the fragment as their lifeline.

"Here," he said, holding her new tablet out with both hands, like a heavy plate he needed her help to carry. *"Put your hands on mine. We're going in together."*

She stared at it as if it were a flat shiny snake. "Um…"

"Come on," Jason said aloud. "You have to feel your way through this. It's more of an art than a science."

"Who taught you this?"

"Nobody," he said. "I *like* computers."

She muttered something nasty, and placed her hands over his.

Nothing passed between them, or between her and her tablet.

"Walls," he said.

"Right, right," Rachel sighed, and let him in. Resignation,

slow and grumpy, passed from Jason's mind into her own. "Oh, come on! I'm trying!"

"Do you want to learn this or not?" he snapped.

A memory of Glazer's cold, viperlike stare bubbled up from where it had been lurking in her subconscious. *"Yes,"* she said, and took down the rest of her walls.

Jason's mind joined hers, their identities a safe, courteous distance from each other. Together, they entered the tablet.

When Rachel interacted with a machine, she did so at the most basic level, using her mind like an extension of her fingers. She'd poke and prod, and make the occasional connection like she was flipping a switch, but for the most part she kept herself to those commands that didn't require her to have anything but the most superficial knowledge of how the machine functioned. She could find files on a phone, or turn on the siren of a police car, only because she already knew how to do these things.

Jason carefully bundled her mind within his, and took her into the code.

She had visited these depths before, but briefly. It made no sense to her at all. She had expected the code to flow past her in ruler-straight green streams, or bounce around in pictures, something her mind could grab as *This! This is something that exists. This is something real. This is something you can change.*

No. The closest comparison she could think of was wandering through pockets of air with different qualities. *Here* was a cluster of warmth, *there* felt thin and empty…

Rachel had always stepped out of the code as quickly as she had entered. What could she do with *air?*

(Other than run around in it, of course, waving her arms and generally making a mess of the place, and she dreaded the fancy lying she would have to do when she took her tablet back to the store for a refund.)

"It's not air," Jason, somewhere both beside and inside her, all at once, said. *"But it is elemental. Not the air-fire-water kind of elements,"* he added quickly, *"but like carbon, gold, aluminum… The code makes up this world. Here, it's the atomic components*

of what exists.

"We can't do much with atoms," he said. *"They're so small, their size puts them out of our reach. But when code comes together in packets, it gets bigger, like a chunk of Italian marble made up of... whatever marble's made from. Silicon and calcium?"*

"Sure," Rachel said, as clueless as he was when it came to rocks.

"Don't just 'sure' me—I'm going somewhere with this. How can you tell if a wrecking crew's taken down a building?"

"The...uh...the big pile of rubble?"

"Yeah. Now, how can you tell if a plumber's fixed a broken pipe?"

"The footprints on the kitchen floor."

"Don't be a smartass. Say he's good and cleans up after himself. How can you tell he was there?"

"Is this a trick question? If he knew what he was doing and everything works, I don't think you can."

"Right!" Pride, fast and sudden, came from Jason. *"So, you can either go into the code like a wrecking crew and leave a huge trail behind you, or like a craftsman who can change the code so it doesn't seem as if anything's happened."*

"Lemme guess—you're the craftsman?"

"No," he said, and this time the pride was for himself. *"I'm the symphony's conductor."*

"What?" It was such an odd comparison that she heard herself say it aloud.

"Don't lose focus. Code's not what you think it is. There's a gap between what code is, and what it does. Code has meaning, but when you use a computer, you're looking at the program...the execution of code."

"Because..." She saw the rough shape of Jason manipulating code in his thoughts, and pulled his half-spoken comparison straight out of his mind. *"Because the code is the sheet music, and the program is the song?"*

"Exactly!" he said, pleased.

Rachel remembered Bell's old computers, the ones that sang

like a choir, and wondered if she had helped Jason come up with this analogy.

"*This is how I've always looked at code,*" he said, picking up on her thoughts as if they were his own. "*Since joining OACET, at least. I haven't told Bell about it. I think it might hurt.*"

"Yeah," she agreed. The girl's passion was exploring the boundaries between art, technology, and humanity. Dangling this ability in front of her would be cruel. "*But... I don't see anything to shape! Am I missing something?*"

She felt him nod. "*You need to stop thinking of code as a thing. It doesn't make sense to a human mind. There's too much of it, and unless you're a programmer, there's no way to look at it and know what it's supposed to do. Even a good programmer can't make sense out of all of the code—you can pick out pieces here and there, but it's hard to get a feeling for the big picture. That's why you need to bring a computer into it.*"

"*The implant.*"

"*Yup,*" he said. "*It crunches the data for us, turns it into something we can understand. It'll let you be the craftsman, not the wrecking crew. What do you want to try?*"

"*Huh?*"

A new wave of exasperation, well-muffled but still there, moved between them. "*Pick an app that's on your tablet,*" he said. "*Fix it in your mind.*"

"*Uh... Weather Channel?*" It had come preinstalled on the tablet.

"*Good. Got it?*"

"*Yeah?*"

"*Let go,*" he said.

"*What?*"

"*Let go,*" he said again, and he pushed her.

Strange, this feeling of falling without a body. For her, it wasn't anything like flying (it was more of a controlled plunge in which she tried her hardest not to scream), but she knew that somewhere nearby, Jason kept pace as he read the currents within the code like a falcon.

And then she was there. It looked no different than the rest of the airy nothingness around them, but somehow, she knew she was where she needed to be.

"*Okay,*" Jason said. "*I put a puppy in the code. Find it.*"

"*What?*"

"*A picture. Of. A. Puppy,*" he said. "*It doesn't belong. Find it.*"

She peered around her. "*I don't see a puppy.*"

"*It's code. You're not looking for a real… Forget it. Let your implant do the work. Give it the puppy, and let it go through the data for you.*"

Give it the… How do you give a computer a puppy? A brief giggle came and went as she imagined herself presenting Lulu with a wiggly beagle. She fixed an image of a puppy in her mind's eye, and then another, and another, just in case Jason had stuck a Rottweiler in the same file where her implant was searching for a Chihuahua. *This, or something like this,* she said to that piece of Other. *Find it.*

She found herself moving, and reached out to grasp… nothing. Whatever it was slipped through her idea of her fingertips.

"Good!"

Rachel found herself blinking at her hands. Her real hands, her flesh and blood ones still resting on her new tablet, with Jason sitting across from her in self-satisfied pinks.

"What happened?"

"You found it!" he said, pleased. "We'll do that a few more times until you get the hang of location, and then we'll start working on manipulation."

"Hey, good," she said, as she flipped visuals off and on to orient herself in her own body. "Why did you pull us out?"

"Five minute break," he said. "For as much time as you spend in the code, you have to spend that much time out of it. You can get lost in it if you lose your focus."

"Lost?" she said, panicking. "Like, *lost*-lost?"

They were still joined tightly enough for Jason to feel her terror at losing her sense of self within a computer. "No," he said, pushing a sense of calm towards her. "That can't happen. Machines don't have identities. You can get some bad vertigo, though. Once, I had to disconnect completely to take myself out of Lulu. Gave myself a fucker of a headache."

Rachel slumped in relief. She hadn't even considered the possibility that she might disappear within the code—

She jumped up and ran to the edge of the underbrush before she dropped to her knees, retching.

"Maybe this isn't for you," Jason said.

"Oh, God." She wiped her mouth with the back of her hand. "No shit."

"How about a compromise?" he said, as he moved a safe distance upwind. "I teach you how to find and erase the puppies, and you call me if you need to handle something more complex?"

"Deal," she said. It'd be nice to master data diving, or whatever the cool cyborgs were calling it, but that was just her ego talking. She'd start small, and see where she could go from there. Puppies were friendly and safe and...

Glazer says hello.

Jason moved a little closer. "Why do you always think of this—" he said in a low voice, as he showed her a warm sandalwood hue. "—when you think of him?"

"Oh." Rachel hadn't realized she was moving colors through their link. "That's *how* I think of him. That's how he appears to me."

"Really? You think he's...uh..." Jason wasn't used to thinking in colors. "...brown?"

"No, it's just how I see him. There're no correlations between personality and core colors," she said, and quickly added, "that I've noticed. I might be wrong."

"I would have thought that he'd be blood red."

"I wish," she sighed. "Wouldn't life be easier if the psychopaths didn't blend in?"

SIXTEEN

She was back in the dream of the sea when her owl woke her.

Rachel came awake at the loud *pop!* as the owl appeared in empty air, its green wings flapping to get her attention. "Damn," she grumbled. Nobody pinged you when you had a privacy alert up, not unless it was an emergency. She wasn't too worried: she was OACET administration, and she worked with the police. For her, nighttime emergencies were routine occurrences.

She flipped her implant from passive to active, and visuals emerged. The owl had landed on the headboard, and seemed to be watching her with its wide wooden eyes. On the other side of the king-sized bed, Becca snorted in her sleep and rolled over. The owl shied at this, a quick flutter moving across its wings, as if surprised to find someone other than Rachel in the room.

"Knock it off," Rachel muttered as she slid out of bed. "I didn't program you to do that."

The owl gave her a slow blink, and vanished.

Rachel found her robe, a ratty terrycloth mess of a thing, and shuffled into it as she made her way down the stairs. Halfway down, her owl popped in again, hooting softly.

"I'm coming, I'm coming," she said. "Let me put on some coffee."

She had barely made it to the kitchen when her owl appeared for a third time. It stayed airborne, wings flapping furiously as if it were trying to slap her.

"All right, all right, *all right!*" she hissed, waving both hands to shoo it away. It refused to leave, disappearing only when she took her privacy message down.

The collective flooded in.

Holy Jesus! was her own singular thought. It was an honest prayer. She had never felt this much raw anxiety from the collective, and fewer than half of them were awake. The anxiety grew as more Agents came online, each newcomer adding their emotions to the link.

Then, a strong sense of control from a single source: the chatter and anxiety subsided as Mulcahy began to talk.

"I apologize for waking you," he said. *"We've gotten word that this is the day when the full story breaks."*

Rachel felt a sharp twinge from her knees, and realized she had dropped to the kitchen floor.

"In six hours, the Washington Metro *will run a front-page story,"* Mulcahy said, and then waited three long heartbeats before he added, *"It was written by Jonathan Dunstan."*

The cloying panic that was already within the link thickened: Dunstan was Hanlon's pet reporter.

"Stop," Mulcahy said. Calm flowed from him into the collective. When they had pulled themselves back from the edge, he continued. *"I've read the copy. It's fair to us. Not kind, but fair. It's not what any of us would have expected from Dunstan. We're assuming that Kathleen Patterson at the* Post *is due to go live with her story in the next few days, and Hanlon and Dunstan decided to move first. Since Patterson has been fact-checking this story for the last few months, a propaganda piece would backfire on Hanlon. Dunstan's version might not be the version we wanted, but it is strong and credible.*

"Fortunately for Dunstan," Mulcahy added, putting a little humor into his words, *"he's close to a good primary source."*

Mulcahy took a mental breath. During his moment of quiet, Rachel felt the tension began to drain out of the collective. Safe behind her mental walls, the private part of Rachel began laughing like a lunatic. *He says red is blue, and we all say, right, okay, that must be blue if you say so, and suddenly it is blue—*

The head of OACET waited until the collective digested this last bit of information, and then pushed on. *"The major issue we'll have to address in interviews is that we claim to be in favor of transparency, but we chose to hide how we had received five years of emotional and mental conditioning."*

That private part of Rachel couldn't stop laughing. *Conditioning! Received!* Mulcahy was using the nicest words.

"Remember: we're victims. We were never under any obligation to disclose how we were affected by the conditioning, not unless we were a danger to ourselves or to others. Over the past year, our actions have shown that whatever trauma occurred, we are able to manage it. As we pose no threat, we chose not to parade around our past in the public eye.

"Nobody has the right to tell us otherwise. Please be sure to remind them of that at every opportunity."

Rachel found that the manic hyena hiding in her brain had finally gone silent. She pulled herself off of the floor and moved towards the nearest chair, bare feet padding on the cold tile.

When Mulcahy resumed speaking, the steel edge in his tone had softened. *"Today will be hard. There's no escaping that. But most of our close friends and family members have been told, and we've done our professional due diligence when needed."*

Rachel knew he was talking about her. Not just her—all of those Agents who, like her, played their roles in the public eye. Over the past six months, Agents employed in law enforcement or politically sensitive positions had disclosed the details of what had been done to them to their supervisors, and requested an assessment by an independent mental health professional. Rachel had personally sat through eleven different screenings conducted by three different psychiatrists and one social worker. The social worker was the only one who had guessed she was skirting around certain truths, his conversational colors flickering in and out of suspicion and pity, but Rachel had yet to meet an assessment test she couldn't beat.

"This isn't the first time our lives have been turned upside down. We're too familiar with how this will play out. Be sure to maintain your normal schedules. You can give interviews when you see the need, but Josh will be responsible for the official statement, and you can decline requests for media content in lieu of that.

"Also, consider enhancing your personal security, and be alert for possible threats. The general public has gotten used to us. This

will remind them that we're still here."

"Rachel?" Becca's voice was muzzy from sleep. She stopped in the doorway as Rachel held up a hand, asking for silence.

Mulcahy was nearly done. *"I've left a copy of the article in the OACET community server. I suggest reading it..."* He paused. *"They don't know about the missing fifty. Everything else, we can survive."*

Rachel exhaled, relieved, and pulled the larger part of her consciousness out of the link. "Sorry," she told her girlfriend. "Office politics."

Becca hit the kitchen lights, flinching before her eyes adjusted and she could take in Rachel's mood. "Uh-huh," she said.

"Really!"

"Liar," Becca said, as she moved towards the coffee machine. "Is it serious?"

"Yes." The link was all chatter. From a distance, Rachel heard Mulcahy field questions. "Give me a minute?"

"Sure," Becca said. She stared at the coffee machine, a contraption of siphons and glass of Santino's making. "Um..."

"Just heat up some water in a pan," Rachel said. "I hid some filters in the flour canister."

"Oh, thank God," Becca muttered, and fished around in a cupboard for a couple of mugs.

Agents were beginning to drop out of the link, leaving to warn their friends and family. Rachel called up the copy of Dunstan's article and skimmed through it. She hated reading in her mind: the words seemed too close to the backs of her eyes, and her motion sickness usually kicked in.

In spite of Mulcahy's assurances, she was astonished by the level of detail in Dunstan's article. Yes, it focused mainly on the Agents'...*conditioning*...and tended to gloss over Hanlon's role as its architect, but there were facts within the article that were new to Rachel. One quote from a former U.S. Air Force General, taken from his written recommendation to Congress before the final vote on whether to pursue the OACET program, stood out:

"...the questionable mental state of the three ISO-152 test subjects we interviewed is cause for serious concern. These three subjects appeared unwilling, perhaps unable, to participate in routine social interactions. While able to complete all required intelligence testing and cognitive task analyses, they displayed neither humor nor frustration, or emotion of any kind. We have observed nothing other than a steadfast competence in these men, which is deeply disturbing: while we encourage the younger members of our community to follow orders and work as a group, intelligence operatives working alone must be able to apply creative thinking to difficult problems. I have deep reservations of whether the proposed large-scale trial of the ISO implant can deliver on its creators' promises. The ability to communicate without using a telephone or homing pigeon is not indicative of proficiency in undercover fieldwork."

It was a good quote, strong and true, but it struck Rachel for personal reasons. She had met with its author a bare handful of hours before she had passed the final OACET qualification exam. General Keith Condon had been reserved but concerned, and had asked her several times if she was sure that she wanted to follow through with her candidacy. At the time, Rachel had thought he was being thorough. She hadn't imagined that he might have been trying to warn her.

People have known that OACET shouldn't be allowed to exist since Day One, she thought. *It's a bloody miracle that Hanlon's been able to get away with this charade for as long as he has.*

She returned to Dunstan's article, skimming the bulk of it, and pausing here and there to digest new information. By the time she reached the end, her head was throbbing, but she knew Mulcahy was right.

We can survive this, too.

After she was done reading, she stayed deep within the

collective, bumping into the others when she could and talking in hushed mental voices about the upcoming week. There was less anxiety than she had expected; most of them were relieved that the waiting was finally over.

When she dropped out of the link, she found Becca sitting beside her at the kitchen table. Becca pushed a heavy mug towards her. Fresh hot coffee came up to the lip, dark and just a little sweet. Rachel wrapped her hands around the cup and soaked in its warmth.

"So?"

Rachel flipped on emotions to find Becca a mild gray. This was progress: a few months ago, a mental midnight meeting would have sent her into worrisome reds, but she was getting used to life with an Agent.

"Tomorrow," she told Becca.

The woman's gray thickened and knotted like a lump around her heart. "Oh." Becca said. "Oh, honey."

"We knew it was coming," Rachel said, but the much-used phrase sounded hollow.

"That doesn't make it any better," Becca said.

"And it's by Jonathan Dunstan, not the reporter we had hoped would break the story." She saw confusion move across Becca's colors, and explained. "Most politicians have a reporter they use when they want to put a specific slant on a story. Dunstan belongs to Hanlon, so…"

Becca winced in reds. "Oh no."

"I just read the copy. It could be worse," Rachel admitted. "It could be a *lot* worse. Dunstan acknowledged that Hanlon was involved in the…" She couldn't say it, but Becca still reached out to cover Rachel's hands with her own. "Anyhow. Dunstan paints Hanlon as the owner and CEO of a multinational corporation, and implies that Hanlon had so many projects going at any given moment that he couldn't have possibly known all of the details. So, yes, Hanlon may have approved the…*conditioning*, but he didn't know exactly what would be done, or why."

"Will that argument stand up?"

"Maybe. Patterson—the reporter we'd hoped would break the story—will release her own version in a couple of days. We'll see what happens then."

There was nothing more to say, and Rachel let her girlfriend take her back to bed.

An hour, maybe two, and Rachel gave up trying to sleep. Even with the implant off, there was too much going on in her head. She slid out of bed, found her jogging gear, and kissed Becca goodbye.

Her usual jogging paths were closer to home. On nights like this, when *home* was a confusing word and the hivemind buzzed in her head to the point of madness, she ran south, away from her comfortable suburban neighborhood, across the confusion of city streets, down to where the woods and the wide grassy spaces cradled the presidential monuments. Down to where the tourists were thick in the day, and, at night, after they had scurried back to their hotels and motels and timeshare condos, the land was open and free.

Rachel ran until her lungs ached, thinking of nothing. Her implant warned her when a camera buzzed or a cellphone came near; sometimes she changed her path to avoid getting tagged by a cop or a camera, but mostly she just forced herself to keep moving.

She was not expecting a half-naked Patrick Mulcahy to walk out in front of her.

Momentum carried her forward even after she told herself to stop. Her palms slapped against his shirtless chest, and she nearly tipped straight into his mind. But she had recognized him in time, and her walls were up, so all that came back to her was a feeling of sweet, impossible peace.

Peace? From Mulcahy?

He was smiling, with restful colors she had never seen within him playing across his body. "Hey, Penguin," he said.

Granite… Granite… There's no concrete? Where am I? Rachel thought, scanning the region as quickly as she could. The waterfalls at the Franklin Delano Roosevelt Memorial came back to her, greens and golds turning within themselves in liquid light. She assumed they had the place to themselves until she caught a lump of softly-colored dreams sprawled across one of the granite slabs at the base of a waterfall, a woman, deep in sleep and nesting within a pile of discarded clothing...

Rachel's jaw dropped as she recognized a very naked Hope Blackwell. "Jesus, Mulcahy!" she hissed at her boss. *"Here?!"*

He chuckled.

Okay, then, she thought to herself. *I've learned the secret to ultimate stress relief. Now, all I have to do is convince Becca.*

"You'd set me on fire if I did anything like this," she said.

"I'd set you on fire if you *got caught* doing anything like this," he told her. "Nobody's around. I've got an arrangement with the local security. You out for a run?"

When she nodded, his grin turned wicked, and they were off.

It wasn't anything like jogging: jogging was sensible. They *ran.*

Even her mad chase after Jenna Noura had been nothing compared to this. She felt like a kid again. Up and down, over rocks and tree roots, sometimes shouting out loud from the joy of it. She was fast, but Mulcahy was nothing but legs and muscle. If he wasn't in bare feet, and hadn't just finished a hard workout (so to speak), Rachel wouldn't have had a chance in hell at catching him. The two of them kept pace as they raced through the woods surrounding the memorial, looping over and across their paths in wide circles to keep Mulcahy's snoring wife within easy reach.

She lost track of time, burning thought to ash under the pounding of her sneakers on the earth. When she checked Mulcahy's colors, he was wrapped within relaxed blues and the steady, strong red of belonging, and she let herself join the rhythm of her feet to his until the tension of the last few days fell from her.

They returned to the waterfalls. Mulcahy dove straight into the shallow basin, racing style, and Rachel caught a wave of emotion from him as he moved through the rapids—*free!*

She opened a link. *"How did you go from being an adrenaline junkie to a politician?"*

"I told you," he replied. *"Spycraft and politics are very similar. I do miss the explosions, though,"* he added, almost wistfully.

"Bet you could get rid of some Congressional gridlock with some well-placed dynamite," she said.

"Oh, don't tempt me," he said. *"That might be the only way I'll ever get those idiots to start moving."*

She nodded through the link as she dunked her arms in the water to cool down. That was as far as she'd go: she didn't know how Mulcahy could swim in this water. Things peed in it.

(Apparently, things also had sex in it, which she should have assumed, but the threat of a hideous staph infection was slightly more real when otherwise sensible people—people she knew!—were splashing around in the water as if it were their own private bathtub.)

"It's chlorinated," her boss replied. He did another couple of laps, and then hauled himself out of the water onto the rocks beside her.

The two of them panted like beached whales on the granite slabs, far enough apart so they wouldn't accidentally dive into each other's psyches.

"I'm not looking forward to tomorrow," she admitted aloud.

"I am," he said. His wicked grin reappeared, and steel gray came into his conversational colors. "I've been waiting a long time for this domino to fall. Once it does, it'll start to take others with it. Tomorrow's the beginning of a certain someone's cascade failure."

"Yeah," she replied. "But on a personal level? I'm not looking forward to tomorrow."

"Oh," he said. His colors turned in on themselves as the vivid greens of OACET gave way for his own cerulean blue core to shine through. "Me neither."

He rolled over on his back. "It'll be worth it, though. More press conferences, more public scrutiny… It's nothing we aren't used to by now."

"I'm not used to my friends thinking I've kept things from them," she said, thinking of Zockinski. Hill probably already knew; Zockinski wouldn't be happy at being the last one within their small group to learn what had happened to the Agents.

Mulcahy rolled over to look at her. "I wish things could be different," he said, his colors taking on her Southwestern turquoise. "It'd be easier if we didn't have to prioritize the endgame."

He started to spin a digital barrier around the fountain so they could talk freely. Mulcahy's version of a shield was made from rigid slabs of frequencies, banged into place. Rachel waited to see if he had improved his skills before she reached out and took the slabs from him. Then, she spun them out as fine as she could, and wove them into a dome around them: she despised shoddy craftsmanship.

He watched her shield go up around them, thinner than molecules and stronger than steel. "Very nice."

"Thanks." She sent her scans up, past the new barrier and into the open sky above them. The black of tree branches and new leaves came back, and she realized she missed having stars overhead.

Even if I still had my eyes, I couldn't see them. Not here. This isn't Texas. In Texas, the sky spread for a million years...

"I should call my family," he said. "I know I should—I just don't know if I can."

"Uh-huh." Rachel had had the same thought. She hadn't told her parents what had happened during those five years. She had vanished from their lives except for the obligatory phone calls on birthdays and holidays, and then reappeared five years later as a semi-stranger in their daughter's body. A morning talk show was a bad way to learn the truth.

I should go home, she told herself. *Make the time to put things right, maybe try to see the stars...*

"He's getting desperate," Mulcahy said.

"Who?" she asked, before catching the woody browns of Hanlon's core within Mulcahy's colors. "Oh. Sorry. I was drifting. Why do you say that?"

"He has to be. He wouldn't have made a play at that fragment of the Mechanism if he wasn't."

"What?!" Rachel sat up in shock, and Mulcahy gave her shoulder a little tap, just hard enough to knock her off-balance and tip her into the fountain.

"*Sonofa—!*" She came up sputtering, then grabbed Mulcahy's ankle and hauled. He was purple with laughter, his humor racing through her; she didn't have the mass to move him, and he tapped her with his other foot to send her falling backwards into the water again.

This time, she came up splashing.

It was a quick water fight, Rachel winning through sheer determination and Mulcahy's insistence that they shouldn't wake his wife. They ended up back on the same granite slabs, Rachel complaining bitterly about giardia.

When she was finished coughing, she asked, "You were kidding, right?"

"No," he said, grinning. "The Hippos have been going through Hanlon's contacts. They stumbled over a reference to the broker who hired Jenna Noura. Seems like Hanlon was researching professional art thieves a few months before the robbery."

The thrill of a new lead fell apart as quickly as it had appeared. "Circumstantial, at best,"

"Yeah. Also, Hanlon didn't approach the broker himself. They're still trying to locate the intermediary who did it for him. They must have met in person, as there's no data trail to connect them."

"And you tell me this now?"

"Priorities," he said. "The Hippos gave me their report yesterday morning, but it came in right after I learned the news story was about to break. And…" A trace of green guilt appeared as he chose his next words.

"You're not sure what the Hippos gave you was obtained legally," she guessed.

"I've put Mare on it," he admitted. "She's checking their

sources. I made sure the Hippos had a warrant before I turned them loose on his records—if they followed due process, she'll give you what they found, and you can turn it over to either the MPD or the Secret Service."

"God," Rachel groaned. She belly-flopped onto the slab, her wet clothing sucking at the rough surface. "*So* close!"

She didn't ask him why he had set the Hippos on Hanlon if he knew they might not return anything viable in a court of law. Mulcahy wasn't using the Hippos to bring Hanlon to justice, he was using them to retrieve material for OACET's risk management strategies. The Hippos had been trained to get results under conditions in which law was a secondary consideration. They'd follow Mulcahy's orders as best they could, but the legal process was complex. For an Agent who had worked as a government-sanctioned killer, it would be easy to stumble over data without fully appreciating the steps through which they had found it.

Hell, Mulcahy was probably glad they hadn't outright shot Hanlon in the head and claimed it was an accident.

"It might still work out," he said. "There was a large cash withdrawal from one of Hanlon's offshore accounts around that time. It would have been enough to hire Noura."

"It won't work out." Rachel knew the words were fact as she spoke. "He's too good at this. Did the Hippos tell you why he wanted the piece of the Mechanism in the first place?"

Colors flashed across Mulcahy in wild combinations; within these was the same unforgettably vivid blue that Rachel saw when a life was snuffed out. "They didn't find any mention of the fragment," he said.

Rachel sat up and started at her boss. "Do *you* know why Hanlon wanted that fragment?"

"I can only guess that he needed the information in the inscription for a project." Mulcahy's comment was reasonable, his tone of voice perfectly measured. It was only by the voids in his surface colors that she knew he was hiding something from her.

"I learned how to recognize lies of omission the other day," she told him. "Just so you know."

A pop of color in a very distinctive brown came and went across his chest, the visual equivalent of someone saying, *Shit!*

Rachel covered her mouth to keep from laughing.

"It's okay," she assured him, and reached out to touch his bare shoulder. She made sure he understood—*belonging, acceptance*—before she pulled her hand away. "It drives me stark raving insane when you can't tell me everything, but that's okay. You've got a hard job. I don't want it."

They didn't speak for a few minutes. She watched his colors churn, weaving and weighing outcomes, that vivid blue moving around as if he was trying to decide where it fit within their conversation.

"I don't just want Hanlon to go to jail," he said, his colors snapping into place, steely with the grays of stone and iron and edged weapons. "I want him to ruin himself."

"Hmm?"

"It'd be one thing if he could look at us and blame us for his downfall. I don't want that. When he finally breaks, I want it to be because the choices he made to save himself pushed him towards that end.

"I want him to hurt. I want him to *burn*. I want him to know that he put himself in a hell of his own making.

"I want him to go to prison knowing that he ruined himself. I want him to sit there and rot, forever, wondering what might have happened if he had made one decision differently."

"Or braid the bedsheets into a noose," Rachel said, voicing one of her own private fantasies.

That vivid blue flared like lightning. "Oh, he won't kill himself," Mulcahy said. "He's too scared to die. He'll survive as long as he can, and he'll suffer the entire time."

"Little single-minded of you, Señor Dantès."

"Yeah." He knotted his hands behind his head as he looked skyward. "I just have to make sure that I'm not so single-minded that I put us at risk. The best way to do that is to take

OACET out of the equation entirely, so we set up scenarios that seem like good opportunities for Hanlon, but are designed to backfire on him."

She nodded. OACET's administrative meetings often turned into *If-Then* assessments, where *if* they allowed Hanlon to take certain steps, *then* these outcomes were most likely to occur...

They usually played with scenarios firmly rooted in reality; taxes and fees, political alliances, and so on. But sometimes they got bored and cruel, and on those days they played with possibilities that were only open to those whose minds could exist within cameras, or who could bend security systems to their will.

They'd never do any of those things: Mulcahy wouldn't let them. Allowing the Hippos to go on the hunt was as close as he would ever come to letting an Agent break the law. OACET needed to be trusted if it was to survive.

(Rachel knew this—she tried her best to *live* this! And yet she still always felt better after those meetings where they allowed themselves to take that mental deviation from the straight and narrow. Like revenge, catharsis was a dish best served cold, but for different reasons.)

"We give him choices," she agreed. "Tempt him with possible solutions to his problems. Did you set this one up? Is the fragment of the Mechanism a solution to his problems?"

"It might be a possible solution, but it's not a trap that we set for him," Mulcahy said. "He found the fragment on his own. I only learned about his involvement when the Hippos found his connection to Jenna Noura's broker."

"You think he killed Noura," she said.

"I think he had her killed, yes," he said. "Another large sum of cash was withdrawn from a different account right after Noura was arrested. Except the Hippos can't find evidence Hanlon hired the hit."

Rachel tilted her head up towards the stars again. There was a breeze, and now that she had shed the heat of their race through the woods, she was starting to feel the chill. "We won't be able to prove any of this," she said.

"No," he admitted. "But it's information. It might lead somewhere useful."

"For OACET, maybe," she said with a shrug. "It's fruit of the poisonous tree for me."

"Yeah. I don't know what tipped him off to the fragment's location in the White House's basement. I've asked Hope to go to Greece and see what she can find over there. She's not an Agent, or law enforcement, so she's got more flexibility than we do."

Rachel tossed her scans over to Mulcahy's wife, still asleep within the pile of clothing. "Um…"

"She'll be fine," he said, a strong streak of red pride moving into his conversational colors. "And she can go a lot of places that we can't. Until we're cleared to travel outside of the country, she's the best investigator we have."

"Why were the Hippos following me?"

"They weren't," he said. "Why do you think they were?"

"Hell of a coincidence, Ami and Ken in the same part of town when I needed them…"

"Oh, that." He grinned. "I don't think it was a coincidence at all. Hanlon's known the Hippos have been snooping around, but they're almost impossible to spot. He saw a way to take out Noura and get the Hippos to break cover at the same time."

"Hmm." Rachel mused. It would explain why the gunmen hadn't targeted her. If the gunmen kept Rachel in danger, that'd be more likely to draw out her hidden allies than if they had simply killed her. Dead was dead, but if her death could be prevented…

"Yes. Hanlon used you as bait," Mulcahy agreed. "There's nothing you could have done about that."

Pale green guilt came up within his colors. It was fresh, unprocessed: something was on his mind, and it had happened during the car chase. She peered up at him, picking stray thoughts out of the night air—*What if…? Who might…?*—as he pushed the events of the day around in his head.

"What did you do?" she asked.

Mulcahy's colors moved back and forth in a loose weave of browns, turquoise, and vivid greens and blues. "I used the car chase as an opportunity to set another trap for Hanlon," he finally said. "I set up something for him, something irresistible, and he took the bait."

"You do that all of the time," Rachel said. "Why's this one gnawing on you?"

"I know there's always a cost," he said. "Some of the traps I set will result in collateral damage. Not might—*will*. If Hanlon follows through with this particular trap, someone will be killed. I don't know who, I don't know when, but the scenario requires it to happen."

"Do you want to get into specifics?"

"No," he said, almost sadly. Mulcahy's emotions searched around the edges of a bright blue light which kept his cerulean blue core away from her Southwestern turquoise. She associated this hunt-and-peck motion with the conflicting needs of wanting to give someone information while also keeping a confidence.

Too many secrets, she thought.

"Are you forcing him to act?" she asked.

"No."

"Then it's not your fault." Rachel didn't even have to think about it. "It doesn't matter how the gun got in his hands. The man who pulls the trigger is sometimes responsible, but the one who gives the order is always responsible. The burden isn't yours."

"That's what I keep telling myself," he said. "But I was the one who gave Hanlon a loaded gun. I won't pretend I don't bear some responsibility for how he'll use it. And where he'll point it… I don't know."

"Is he going to come after us?"

Mulcahy chuckled. "Of all of the possibilities, that's the one that won't happen. In this instance, killing one of us would be counterproductive."

"Is there any way this'll backfire on us? Is what you did illegal?"

"No. It's…" he paused, unable to put what he wanted to tell her into words. Finally, he reached out a hand. "Here."

Rachel hesitated. She had never been invited into her boss's mind before. Even with the invitation, it seemed an invasion of privacy.

When she moved into his link, there was the usual blurring of boundaries, but…

She looked down and saw her hands. Below those, her shirt and slacks, and a familiar pair of shoes. *A body? That's new.*

She glanced around, taking in the landscape of his mind. Mulcahy didn't have walls, not in the way she usually experienced them. Stepping into his sense of self was akin to stepping into an iron channel. Rachel knew there was more to see and feel than what he showed her, but he was allowing her to access one path, to know a single thought: *OACET above all.*

A stray thought—*wonder how his wife feels about that?*—drifted away from her.

Humor rolled across the part of Rachel that existed in Mulcahy's mind, and she turned to see Hope Blackwell's wild blue-black core at the other end of the channel, holding the same weight and mass as Mulcahy's commitment to his people.

Ah, she thought. *A balancing act.*

Exactly so, came a thought that she didn't think was hers.

She turned away from his devotion to his wife, and examined the channel. Scans didn't work, not here, not unless Mulcahy let them, and she got the impression that Mulcahy didn't approve of others snooping around in his head.

She moved towards the space he reserved for OACET.

A will-o-the-wisp of green with streaks of red bobbed across the iron channel; guilt, wreathed in shame. Deep within was that same vivid blue.

This? She held out a hand to the ball of colors, offering contact, and the sprite floated towards her.

Before she could touch it, she was back in her physical body.

"I'm sorry," he said. "I can't."

The shock of being thrown from his mind was minimal, but Rachel kept shaking her head to clear it.

Mulcahy didn't have any conversational colors.

(*Everyone had a conversational layer,* she reminded herself, flipping her implant off and on in a furious rush. *You just can't see it… Look over there, you can still see Hope's, so this is just an error left over from being in Mulcahy's head…*)

He stood, the stray thoughts whispering around him devoid of any emotion. "You're babysitting today," he told her. "Be at the mansion by seven tonight."

The request—the command—took her by surprise. "I'm not scheduled for another—"

"Public scrutiny is going to be high," he said. "Maybe higher than when we first came out. I'm pulling anyone off of the duty roster who's not capable of managing any problem that might come up."

"I…" She rolled onto her feet, uncertain whether she should fight his sudden change in attitude, or salute.

"It'll be a three-hour shift," he told her, and then walked into the shallow water to rejoin his wife.

A few steps into the pool, and he stopped. The slightest flickers of red stress and mournful gray moved across his body as his emotions returned. "Thank you for the run, Penguin."

She watched him walk away. She knew she should be pissed.

More than anything else, she wanted to give him a hug and tell him everything would be okay.

Mulcahy had been the first to break free, and he had been there to guide them when the rest of OACET came out of their five-year fog. Until she had seen the near-alien landscape of his mind, Rachel had never stopped to appreciate how that meant he had gone through the transition alone.

Going through the motions as a brainwashed husk one day; the next, learning you had been turned into a living weapon for the digital age. And maybe the day after that was when you realized you were responsible for the welfare of the four hundred other survivors who had been sold the same bill of goods.

That *had* to mess you up.

She stood and began her long jog home.

SEVENTEEN

First District Station had begun its career in public service as an elementary school. When it was converted to a police station, the building had been retrofitted and resized for adults, but the front entrance would always belong to children. The original design of the schoolhouse hadn't included a grand entrance, and that hadn't changed during the remodel. There was a tiny alcove and a set of double doors, all of it painted a bright primary blue.

No matter how many times she faced those doors, Rachel knew she'd always feel like the young, tender outsider she had been in suburban Texas. The difference between her and her younger self was that she finally understood why she shouldn't solve her problems with her fists.

Shame, that.

"How bad is it?" Santino asked her.

She continued to move her scans around. "Bad."

There wasn't a person within her range who didn't hold OACET's neon green within their conversational colors. As she and Santino walked towards First District Station, pops of Southwestern turquoise started to catch and run within the green.

Front and center on everyone's mind, she thought. *What a day this'll be.*

Santino turned towards the side door, and she grabbed his elbow and yanked him back onto the main path. "If we're going to do this," she told him, "we're going to do it right."

Two stairs up, a short walk down a freshly poured sidewalk, and they were at the front doors.

Rachel took a breath, and yanked both of them open at once.

Today, she was glad she had worn those boots with the heels.

The moment she passed through the front doors, her own unique turquoise had exploded throughout the conversational colors of every person on the first floor of the building. She pounded down the hallway while Santino's feet made small *shuffs* behind her. Other than the noise of their shoes on the linoleum, the precinct was as silent as a public space could ever get: the white noise of machines and people unseen filtered through the air, but no one near enough to know that Rachel had entered the building was talking.

She had planned to keep her chin up and push through, but there was a tug in the aether as first one smartphone started recording, then another.

Smile, she thought. *You're on Candid Camera. Always and goddamned forever.*

Might as well go ahead and shoot the elephant in the room. If there absolutely had to be a giant animal stinking up the place, it was simply common sense to make sure it wouldn't also gore you to death.

She tapped Santino on his arm, and the two of them stopped in the middle of the hall. "Public announcement, guys," she said. She barely had to raise her voice; every person in earshot was listening. "It's true," she said. "We were brainwashed for five years.

"We didn't talk about it. Not because we were hiding, but because we didn't *want* to talk about it. It's been an open secret for months. Chief Sturtevant knows. At OACET's request, he had me vetted by multiple psychiatrists to make sure that I'm sane enough to work as a cop."

She paused to see if anybody would laugh. Nope. Nobody had a sense of humor any more.

"Since I'm part of a federal agency, my personal options for what I could do, and who I could tell, were limited. It was a need-to-know situation, and the press, apparently, has decided everybody needs to know.

"Keep your opinions of what I should have done to yourselves. Those were the worst years of my life. I won't talk about them."

With that, she turned and resumed her long stomp down the hallway, Santino covering her back.

Her little speech seemed to help. The two of them walked away in a cloud of wine-red sympathy.

Rachel hesitated a second time at the door to their office. The gauntlet downstairs had been bad. This part, she was dreading.

She pushed open the metal classroom door, and entered the jungle.

The office she shared with Santino had spent the last year in a near-constant state of change, the single defining feature being that it was always stuffed full of enough houseplants to qualify as a pocket rainforest. When Rachel had first been tapped as OACET's liaison to the MPD, she and Santino had been given an overly large south-facing office on a middle floor, a near-perfect location for a greenhouse. His desk had been secondhand but huge, and stationed in the center of the room. Hers had been a lap desk with a beanbag bottom, shoved beneath a rickety wooden chair off to the side. After they had started solving cases and the MPD's opinion of Rachel had changed, a second desk identical to Santino's had appeared, and they spent their workdays facing each other across a wide expanse of pockmarked metal.

Later, after Zockinski and Hill joined their team, the secondhand desks were removed and a set of new library cubicles were installed in their place. The four of them had arrived back at work after a long weekend to find their office had been turned into a miniature cubicle farm, and had immediately disassembled it. Santino had rebuilt the pieces as a set of standing desks by the windows, Rachel and Hill had chucked a couple of easy chairs into the empty space, and Zockinski had hung a whiteboard and wide-screen television on the far wall. There were the ubiquitous bookcases and filing cabinets found in all government offices, and these were rearranged along with the rest of the furniture, but the rest of it was a deep living green.

(Each time a new plant appeared, Rachel and Hill would

wonder aloud about the likelihood of jaguars. Santino laughed them off, but they had something planned for April Fool's Day that involved a motion detector, a hidden sound system, and a giant stuffed cat that Hill had picked up at a yard sale.)

This morning, Zockinski and Hill had arrived before them and had staked claim to the two easy chairs. The men were layered in uncertain yellows and oranges, her Southwestern turquoise wrapped tight within these. Beneath this lay a sympathetic wine red, and at the base of this tangle of colors she spotted the harder reds of rage. Neither of them said a word as she entered.

"Three questions," Rachel said as she walked into the office.

Hill's eyebrows arched up.

"Any three questions you ask, I'll answer," she said. "Doesn't matter what they are. No tricks, no wordplay."

Zockinski kept his eyes on his laptop as he pretended to type up a report. "Are you okay?"

"A year ago, no. I wasn't. I don't know about now—some days are worse than others. But there are more good days than bad."

"PTSD?" Hill's voice was strangely light, as if a third party were using him to introduce a topic he'd rather not discuss.

"That your second question?"

Hill nodded.

"Maybe? I don't think so."

"Follow-up to the second question," Santino said, as he entered the room behind her. "Would you know if you had PTSD?"

Hill's colors flashed and shifted from Rachel's turquoise to Santino's cobalt blue, as if to tell him, *Good one.*

"I honestly don't know," she replied. "I've gotten pretty good at beating psych tests. After the first couple dozen, you give them what they want to hear."

Zockinski and Hill fell silent, searching for a third question. Rachel took it as an opportunity to toss her new purse on her desk. A carved wooden owl, solid and all too real, glared at her from its permanent spot behind her computer screen.

"At least it's finally out in the open," Hill said.

"What?" Zockinski jumped, yellow surprise rushing into his conversational colors. "You knew? You didn't tell me?"

Hill reached over with his good arm and rapped his partner on his shoulder. "Today's not about you," he said.

Yellows and reds clashed against each other as Zockinski wrestled his emotions back into place. "Who told you?" he muttered at Hill.

"Mako?" Rachel guessed.

Hill nodded. "Few months ago. Said it was a secret. Sorry," he said, his last word aimed at Zockinski.

Zockinski ignored him. "I'll bet you knew, too," he said to Santino. "Did Zia tell you? Did I have to fuck an Agent to get an invite?"

"*Christ!* Zockinski, if I knew you were going to be a weeping child about this, I would have told you myself," Rachel snapped. "You weren't intentionally excluded, okay? I didn't tell you because it's not something I talk about. Ever. I told Santino—he needed to know because we spend every single waking moment together—"

"—hey!"

"—but the rest of the world found out at the same time you did."

She turned her back on Zockinski, secretly relieved. A snit fit over not being allowed in the clubhouse was better than pity, maybe even scorn...

Yeah. She'd take the snit fit.

"Third question," she said. "Or are we done here?"

Zockinski's colors twisted into spiteful reds, and she suddenly felt cold as she knew what would come next. He had been hinting at it for months, he had never let the rumors go, she had stared him down with her broken eyes—

—and then, like a balloon hit with a pin, his angry reds vanished into scraps, and all that was left was sympathy. "We're done," Zockinski said.

"No, we're not," she said as she turned to face him. "Go ahead.

You don't want any secrets? Ask."

Zockinski didn't hesitate. "Are you blind?"

It had the weight of words that had waited to be said, but Zockinski couldn't look at her.

She didn't need to answer him.

"Waste of a question," Hill said. "Rachel's the best marksman I've ever seen."

Rachel checked Hill's colors, disbelieving—*Eleven words? The man doth protest too much, methinks*—and then she smiled to herself. She couldn't help it. She loved Mako all that much more to learn that he had told his cousin the collective's secrets, but he hadn't told Hill hers.

Hill caught her smiling. Electric shock raced through his colors as he fit pieces from the last twelve months together. "Oh!" he said. Then, more quietly, "Oh."

"Yes." She almost wasn't aware she had said it.

"And you knew?" Zockinski asked Santino.

"I'm her roommate," Santino replied. "She never turns on the lights."

It was something of an evasion, as Santino had guessed not too long after they had started working together. But it helped; Zockinski was thoroughly sad grays and rich wines.

"You coulda told us," Zockinski said.

Rachel turned off emotions so she wouldn't have to see Zockinski's sympathy turn to guilt. "No, I couldn't," she said. "Not after those first six months I worked at the MPD."

She focused all of her attention on a spider plant dangling just above her head, and left the rest unsaid. Because even if your male coworkers saw you run down a murderer (in heels), or beat eight men unconscious with a scrap of rebar (while wearing a fancy dinner dress), you couldn't cry about how they had been mean to you, not while expecting to still be treated like their equal after the tears were done.

Instead, she went over to the door, and kicked it hard enough to dent the metal.

"You tell anybody, she's gone," Santino said, as she limped

back to her desk.

"Especially now that the trauma's public knowledge," Rachel added. "They learn I'm—" Her mind and tongue both tripped over the idea of speaking freely around Zockinski and Hill, and she had to steady herself before she pushed on. "If they learn I'm blind now, they'll throw me out of the MPD."

She gave them a moment to process that information, and then flipped on the emotional spectrum.

Damn, she thought, Rachel would have liked to have seen some denial in their colors. A hint of uncertainty, maybe. Anything other than Southwestern turquoise and the grays of sad resignation.

"So, that's where we are," she said. "If you aren't okay with keeping secrets, let's get Sturtevant up here. I won't hold it against you if you want to tell him now, but if you decide to roll on me later…"

She trailed off as she watched their colors. Hill's were steady and strong, confident reds buttressing up her turquoise. Zockinski's fluttered slightly, and Sturtevant's core of burnished gold was weighed against Southwestern turquoise, but she also caught the bronze of his wife and the rough pastels of his twin daughters within the mix. *He's got a family,* she reminded herself. *You're not his first priority.*

After an uncomfortable minute, Zockinski nodded. "If you get caught, I never knew," he said.

"I can live with that," she replied. Relief, cool and liberating, washed her headache away.

Hill pointed at his injured arm.

"Are you asking if how I perceive my environment will put you in danger?"

"Yes."

"That happened before I got behind the wheel," she reminded him. "And I told *everybody* that I shouldn't drive."

He chuckled. "True."

"Speaking of Sturtevant," she said, and tilted her head towards the door to their office.

It opened easily (Rachel was slightly miffed at that; based on the throbbing in her foot, she thought she had at least knocked it off of its alignment), and the Chief of Detectives walked in. Edward Sturtevant was somewhat like a tall fireplug—round, solid, and usually running red. Today, his conversational colors were no different, but at least his anger wasn't aimed at Rachel. "Don't talk to anyone," he told her. "No formal statements. I've got reporters crawling all over me."

"Should I go home?" she asked. She couldn't decide if she wanted to spend the rest of the day in hiding, or just power through until bedtime. Both options had their appeal.

"No. Do something useful."

Her heart began to sink. The last time Sturtevant had wanted them to "do something useful," it had been traffic duty. "Like what?" she asked.

"The White House robbery," he said. "Remember that?"

"Yes, but Alimoren hasn't—" Santino began, but Sturtevant had already slammed the door on them.

"You were saying?" Zockinski asked Santino.

"Just that the Secret Service seems to have cut us out." Santino said. "Has anyone heard from Alimoren since the car chase?"

Nobody had. "Toldja we should have taken the credit, Peng," Zockinski said. "The Secret Service doesn't need us anymore."

"Eh," she said with a shrug. "It might be me. He might have heard that the news about OACET was going to break, and wanted to sever ties before that happened."

"Does he know about the…" Zockinski didn't finish, choosing instead to wave a hand in the general direction of his eyes.

"Nope. I can count the number of people outside of OACET who know that I'm blind on one hand," she said, before realizing that was no longer true. "Well. Two hands, now. Even Becca doesn't know."

That got a pop of bright surprise from Zockinski and Hill. They liked Becca.

"Thanks, by the way," Rachel said, pointing towards the dented door. "I like it here."

A wave of rich, red belonging came from them, carrying her Southwestern turquoise within it. It lasted long enough that Zockinski felt obliged to cut the emotion in the room with a joke, which turned into a minor insult war. By the end of it, Rachel felt worlds lighter.

"If Alimoren has cut us out, it's because of the bad press," Santino said, once they had settled down enough to do some real work. "They came down on him hard. He's high enough in the Secret Service that he'll probably lose his job over this."

"Poor scapegoats," Rachel sighed.

"You sure he's a scapegoat?" Zockinski said. "You weren't there when Santino and I talked to him about the chance there's a mole in the Secret Service. He got real defensive, real fast."

"Wouldn't you?" Hill asked him.

"Wait," Rachel said, remembering the creeping suspicion that had come over her when Alimoren visited her in the hospital. "Let's chase that one," she said. "Say Alimoren is the information leak, and he's responsible for helping Noura break into the White House. It would explain why he let Noura out of the holding cell, and how the hitters knew where she'd be."

Santino fell into his usual role of devil's advocate. "Letting Noura out was a calculated risk," he argued.

"Yeah, but why would he agree to it that quickly?" Zockinski asked. "Seems like he should have gone in and pushed her a little more, see what else he could get from her in exchange for that package."

"It was a solid lead, and he wanted to move on it," Santino said. "He knew he had a limited amount of time before the story would break, and he wanted to get ahead of the news cycle. It'd look good for the Secret Service if they not only had the thief in custody, but were also making progress on who hired her."

Hill pointed at Santino.

"Would twenty minutes have made that much difference?" Rachel asked her partner.

"With someone like Noura? No, but only because Alimoren knew she wasn't going to crack. She had set her terms, and

Alimoren knew that trying to negotiate would just delay the inevitable."

"Damn," Zockinski muttered.

Round One goes to Santino. Rachel winked at her partner.

"How about the package?" Zockinski asked. "Anybody know what was in it? We were supposed to get an itemized list from the Secret Service."

"Never showed up," Hill said.

"I scanned the package when we took it in," Rachel said. "Except for the watch, there was nothing in that package but printouts."

"Printouts come from somewhere," Santino said. "We didn't find a set of keys or any personal information on her, but she had to be staying somewhere in town. Somewhere she stashed her phone and her computer."

"Did Alimoren put a dead-drop notice out to the local hotels?" Zockinski asked.

"Probably," Santino said. "But if Noura is in a do-not-clean suite and if she paid through the end of the month, it'll be weeks before they call him and tell him they found her stuff… I don't know. Seems as though a woman like Noura would have had a contingency plan in case something happened to her."

That thought slammed into both Rachel and Hill like rocks to their heads. They both launched to their feet. She craned her neck to look up at the tall man, and his brilliant white smile lit the air around him.

"*Them*," Rachel said, and Hill nodded.

"What?" Zockinski asked.

"Them!" Rachel nearly shouted. "Back at the mail drop, Noura said she packed *them* herself! The crazy thief shipped off more than one package!"

"You didn't think of this before now?" More orange caught within Zockinski as his irritation built within him.

"Things got busy," Hill said, running his good hand across his injured shoulder.

"How do we find it?" she asked the men, but mostly

Santino. "Noura didn't ship both packages to the same location, obviously. Alimoren's team searched that mail drop, and they would have found a second package by now."

"If we had the original package, we could track its source and see if she mailed out more than one during that same trip," Zockinski said.

Santino's colors lit up before he managed to temper them within orange-yellow doubt. "Wouldn't Alimoren have his team check the site where Noura mailed the packages?" Santino asked.

"It's a lead," Rachel said, and Zockinski agreed, both of them eager to pretend things were normal between them. "He's been busy with the fallout from the car chase and Noura's murder. I say we assume he didn't, until we learn he did."

Her partner gave a silent purple-gray sigh. "All right," he said. "Tell me you recorded the drop."

She had: she did her best to remember that she was her own police body camera, and she tried to maintain an active recording while interacting with suspects. Rachel called up the file and passed her new tablet to Santino so he could zoom around for a clear image of the package, but she had been flipping scans as usual and nothing was legible.

Zockinski watched the mess on the screen, shaking his head in perplexed yellows and oranges. "Why didn't you just tell us you were blind?" he said to Rachel. "It'd have explained these godawful videos of yours."

"Fuck you very much," Rachel said, and felt another wave of relief that he could turn her blindness into a throwaway comment. "Call Alimoren? I don't know where the Secret Service stores their evidence, but he can get us the information from the package."

Alimoren didn't answer. His office did, but they told the team from the MPD that Alimoren was in press conferences all day, and wouldn't be able to return their call until later in the week. When Zockinski said that all they wanted was a photograph of a packing number, he was told that someone would get back to him shortly.

"As in, never," Zockinski said as he snapped his phone off.

She shrugged. She had thought better of Alimoren. "Fine," she said. "The hard way, then."

She called Alimoren's office, introduced herself as the OACET Agent working the case with their boss, and said in her sweetest customer service voice that she appreciated how they were busy, so she would just go into their servers and look around until she found the files, and there *prob-a-bly* wouldn't be any issues but if the entire computer system went down like the last few times she did this, she'd come right over to help get them back up again…

A series of files began rolling into Zockinski's phone before she had finished her last sentence.

"I hate pulling rank," she muttered as she hung up.

"That's not pulling rank as much as it's social engineering," Santino said, flipping through the images until he found the packing number. "Here we are."

From there, it was a short hop to the postal center where Noura had mailed the original package. The center was another private company, so Zockinski and Hill bullied their way through the bureaucracy until they got the poor kid behind the counter to admit that, yes, there had been another package. The second tracking number put them in a federal post office across town, and there they ran into a wall of a woman who showed them a package nearly identical in size to the first, but insisted on a warrant before she would release it to them.

The woman slammed her window in Hill's face. Rachel was impressed: not too many people had the guts to stand up to the detectives when they were in full-on cop mode.

"Do you want to call Edwards?" Santino asked her.

Rachel winced. She had something of a quid-pro-quo agreement with the judge, where she'd move to the head of his warrant queue as long as she'd fill in as his golfing buddy whenever he needed a fourth. Edwards' golf game was…not very good. "Let's try Alimoren first," she said. "We shouldn't cut him out."

As Zockinski went red, she added, "I want to give him the benefit of the doubt, just in case he really is tied up with the press all day."

More bureaucracy: they let Santino make the call, and Rachel found a quiet spot near the front door where she could watch the crowd. Zockinski and Hill wandered over to join her, and the three of them sat without talking while Santino waited.

After a glacial age, Santino hung up. "Alimoren said he'll get a warrant on his way down."

"He's coming here?" Rachel hadn't expected that: she had assumed their team would bring the package to him.

"Yeah, he seemed really..." Santino was staring at his phone, his conversational colors churning slowly. "...I don't know. He left an interview to meet up with us."

"Huh," Zockinski said, his own colors beginning to match Santino's in a slow, thoughtful turnover. "Anybody ever see what was in that first package?"

"Bunch of papers," Rachel said. "Another wristwatch."

"Yeah, but did you see it with your own—" Zockinski stopped, green guilt flaring.

She blew a raspberry at him as she punched him in the knee.

Nobody wanted to be the first one to suggest that if the contents of the first package had been spirited out of the hands of the MPD, there was a very good chance that this second one would vanish just as quickly once Alimoren arrived.

"You know..." Santino said, turning towards the clerks' windows. "We *do* have a warrant. We just don't have it on us right this moment."

Rachel knew what he was implying. "It's almost impossible to read a stack of papers when they're lying on top of each other. I could maybe make out a photograph or an image. We wouldn't get much that was useful out of it."

"What if it isn't just papers?"

"Fine," she sighed, and sent her scans out.

Santino was right. The second package might have looked the

same as the first, but its contents were different. Rachel couldn't help but jump to her feet as she found the motel key card.

Bingo. I need to get over there, fast.

"What?" Hill asked.

"Want to do one better than tracking down this package?" Rachel asked. "There's still an outstanding warrant to search Noura's hotel room once we find it, right?"

Zockinski nodded, while Santino cracked a wide grin.

She smiled back at him. "Let's go remind Alimoren that he asked us to join him for a reason."

EIGHTEEN

"In or out?" Zockinski asked.

Rachel figured cheap motels grew like mushrooms, with underground colonies stretching for miles beneath airports and convention centers, occasionally shooting up a Ramada or DoubleTree for reproductive purposes. They were all identical to her, the same boxy hallways with rectangles of rooms on either side, cinderblock and firewalls throughout.

The extended-stay motel where Noura had booked her suite was no different. Rachel had fed the data from the magnetic strip through an app on Santino's phone, and they had abandoned the package in favor of the larger prize. Now, standing outside of what they presumed to be Noura's motel room, they were mired in legalities.

"It'd be nice to search the room before the crime scene techs trample over the evidence," Santino said. "For once."

"It's not procedure," Hill replied.

Zockinski backed up his partner. "What if the guys who shot her also came here to trash the place? We'd catch hell for going in first."

"Right," Rachel said. She leaned against the wall, and slid down to rest her head on her knees.

"Hey, um…" Santino made a move towards her purse to retrieve her tablet, but she waved him away.

"Not today, dear. I've still got a headache. Let me focus on one thing at a time."

"All right," he said, wearing a reluctant orange.

Her team had seen this often enough to leave her alone. They assumed she was out-of-body on the other side of the wall, walking the scene in her green skin. Usually, she sent the live feed to her tablet so they could search the room along with her avatar.

Not this time. Today, her first order of action was to find out how Jenna Noura had recognized her at the farmers' market.

The easiest answer was that Noura had recognized her from the very few press conferences she had given after the Glazer case, but Rachel had grown up in Texas. A stereotypically southern part of Texas. There had been one other Chinese girl in her high school, and despite being separated by two grades and different haircuts, Rachel couldn't remember a single week when the two of them hadn't been confused by everyone from students to teachers to cafeteria workers.

Rachel didn't give too many people the benefit of the doubt, and saw no reason to make an exception for Noura. If she was wrong, and Noura had had an exceptional memory, there'd be nothing to find.

If she was right, she wanted to get to the evidence before anyone else.

Then, she wanted to learn how Noura had been connected to Jonathan Glazer.

And, if there was any time left, Rachel planned to nuke any potentially incriminating evidence into digital dust.

She sent her scans through the wall. It was a pleasant enough room: she had expected Noura to have rented the motel's best suite, but instead she found a clean, practical layout. A small kitchenette, a large bathroom, and a workspace next to a double bed. A professional makeup kit was open in the bathroom, its contents spread out across the vanity. On the bathroom floor, a pile of pajamas and a towel.

Nothing was packed; empty bags were still tucked neatly in the nearby closet. Jenna Noura had expected to return to her hotel after a quick stop at Dupont Circle, and Rachel felt a small pang at plans forever interrupted.

She moved around the room, searching for anything paper or digital. The usual guide to local eateries was on the counter, and a paperback book with a broken spine lay on the bedstand. Rachel pored through these as best as she could, looking for photographs, scraps of loose text, anything that would suggest content had been added or changed…

Nothing. Noura had packed up everything on paper and mailed it to herself as insurance. Rachel figured she hadn't wanted everything in the same place, in case she were caught and needed a bargaining chip.

Rachel turned her attention to the only digital devices in the room: the cell phone on the small work desk and the portable printer beside it.

She reached out through her implant into the guts of the phone. It had an incredible amount of battery life left, and she poked around to find that it had been modded out to survive for full weeks on a single charge. She suppressed the command to activate the screen as she searched through its drive. There, tucked within a bunch of innocuous puzzle games, were a series of files.

One of them had her name on it.

She opened that file. A standard dossier, with nothing about her that wasn't already in the MPD's record. A fast text search for *Glazer* returned a single paragraph:

> *If caught, find a way to talk privately with Peng. Give her this message: "Glazer says hello." She will then work with you to help you escape. Agree to her requests.*

Rachel swore at herself, then returned to the text. She quickly changed it to:

> *If caught, your best chance of escape is to manipulate Peng. She is an idiot who is easily tricked.*

She exited the folder, and began to apply the skills she had made Jason teach her.

It was like layering a fresh coat of paint over a bumpy wall. Changes to code left traces deep within themselves, and anyone with the knowledge could look at the surface and see that something had been changed beneath. Jason had shown her that changes to code couldn't be superficial—she couldn't just alter a time stamp and call it done. Instead, she worked within layer after layer of code, making sure that rewriting that one small paragraph didn't leave marks.

When she was sure everything was as smooth as possible, she poked and prodded the contents of the other files, just to be sure. Nothing stood out as incriminating to her or OACET. She fixed the time stamps on these to hide when they were last accessed, and had nearly decided to call it good when her implant did its twitching thing.

Something deep within the data was calling to her.

More damned puppies, she thought to herself, and grinned.

Despite a couple hours' of intense practice, she still lacked Jason's skill at moving from point to point within a computer; the raw code was still meaningless to her. Maybe over time, she'd develop the ability to consciously recognize a significant chunk of data. As it was, she could do nothing but command— *Take me there*—and let go.

And then she was there.

Files layered within files, hidden under passwords and programs and…

All of it was about OACET.

Well, fuck, she thought to herself, as she felt cold dread claw its way into her stomach.

"Peng? Everything okay?"

It was Zockinski's voice, and she didn't have to move her scans to him to know he was getting annoyed. She usually walked a room in half the time.

"Yeah, I'm fine," she said, and muttered something about checking the contents of the cosmetics case for poison.

Rachel called Jason, briefed him as quickly as she could, and turned control of the phone over to him with the order to back the whole thing up on OACET's private server before he scrubbed it.

"Make sure it's perfect," she said. *"This is getting curiouser and*

curiouser—from what I've read, those files are pure bullshit. It makes it look as though we've worked with Jenna Noura on other crimes."

"How did you find this?" he asked her. *"It's buried really deep. Nobody would have found these files unless they had a reason to go into the phone's source code."*

"The puppies were barking," she said. *"I need to go. The boys are getting restless."*

"Gotcha. I'll let you know what I find."

"Thanks," she said, and stepped back into her own mind.

"What didja find?" asked Zockinski, as her head came up.

"Efficiency suite. She'd been here a while, and nothing is packed. There's a phone and a portable printer on the work desk, and no other documentation," she replied.

"Room tossed?" Hill asked.

"No, it's clean. Unless it was searched by pros, we're the first ones here since Noura locked it up. I took my time looking for poison, but it looks clean."

"What's on the phone?" Santino asked.

"It's password protected," she said, not exactly lying in case Hill caught it. "I'd like to wait until the warrant gets here."

And there's the slippery slope again, Rachel thought to herself, as they all headed downstairs towards the motel's public coffee maker. She could justify anything—up to and including murder—if it protected OACET. Letting Glazer escape had been for the good of OACET and to protect her friends at the MPD, both, but now…

Well. Except for that one small change, she had left that one file with her information in it intact. Nothing in that file had struck her as dangerous to either her or OACET. It had been enough information for Noura to pick her out of a crowd. And purging the phone of those rampant red herring files didn't bother her at all.

Rachel tossed those ideas around as they sat, mostly silent, waiting for Alimoren and his team to arrive so they could enter the room itself. She took out her new tablet and pretended to play a puzzle game, the others around her also busy on their phones.

It gave her time to think.

She didn't like how things were starting to play out. It didn't have the feel of a long con, not like the Glazer case, but there was just enough evidence to suggest that OACET was somehow involved. Whoever had hired Noura had given her enough information to recognize Rachel on sight, and had told their hit men to avoid shooting the Agent...

Why did Alimoren ask us to get involved? Sure, the four of them were getting a good reputation for handling weird cases, but they were a fairly new team. A more seasoned team from the MPD, or a federal agency, should have been brought in to handle an incident at the White House.

And who knew enough about the Glazer incident to make an educated guess about her involvement in his escape?

She was flailing in questions.

She couldn't help but think of Mulcahy, setting traps left and right. Most of those traps would never be tripped, but they were there all the same, waiting for someone to stagger into them, unknowingly putting themselves right where someone wanted them...

"Got your data backed up."

Rachel was strung too tight; she barely managed to keep from shouting aloud when Jason opened a new link. She took a deep breath to steady herself. *"Could you please remember to ping me before you barge in?"*

"Yeah. Just wanted you to know the phone is clean. I left the relevant case files, but I took out the hidden content. I did some overwrites, too, and dated them back to the last restore a few months ago. If anyone goes that deep, they won't find anything."

"Did you..." She didn't know how to ask, not through a link. Private link or not, anyone within the collective might drift by, keeping a respectful distance from their walls but close enough to hear what they were talking about on the other side.

To her astonishment, Jason pushed Glazer's core color of

sandalwood towards her. *"Him?"*

"Yes!"

"There was some bullshit in there about the two of you," Jason admitted. *"Total bullshit, but it was good stuff. Anybody who had access to a timeline could put a plausible scenario together."* He paused, then added, *"That information doesn't exist anymore."*

She showed him the distinctive green of OACET's projections, with the yellow she associated with curiosity.

"I know what the green means. I don't get the yellow," he said.

"It's a question."

"Oh. No. Not on..." the OACET green was turned from his mind back to hers. *"...that server, either. It's gone. Gone-gone."*

She took another breath, and thought of a lovely blue.

"Uh...relief?"

"Yes! And, Jason..."

"At this point, I'm in this hole as deep as you are," he said, a little harshly, but then added, *"You're welcome."*

She sent him the feeling of a friendly hug as he broke their link.

Rachel got up for another cup of the motel's awful coffee, and by the time she returned her seat, Alimoren and two of his agents were walking through the glass double doors of the hotel lobby.

Let the games begin, she thought.

Alimoren got as far as the front desk before he caught sight of them in the lobby. There was a muffled moment as he asked the other agents with him to work with the desk clerk and find the room on the passkey, and then he turned towards the group from the MPD in a sickly orange-gray resignation.

The four of them stared up at Alimoren with their best cop faces.

"I wondered why you left the post office," he said.

"Matilda the Hun knew her job," Rachel said. "It was in safe hands until you got there."

Alimoren nodded. "So..."

"Room 228," Hill said.

"Hasn't been opened," Zockinski said.

"I performed a remote digital search," Rachel said. "Her belongings appear untouched."

Alimoren stared at her.

"Hill and I are fine, by the way," Rachel added. "Except for his shoulder, of course. I'm sure you were wondering."

Alimoren's orange-gray resignation bloomed, green guilt within its center. It was an ugly combination. "Look, I'm sorry," he said. "After Noura's death, my supervisors decided you were a liability."

"Not even a phone call," Santino said with a sigh.

"You tore up half of downtown D.C. I said I'd take the blame for that, and I did. There were diplomats and members of Congress in some of those vehicles. It was a security nightmare."

"Found the murder weapon, found the suspect, caught the suspect…" Rachel began, ticking points off on her fingers.

"Noura is dead." Alimoren wasn't budging. "The hit team was hired through an intermediary. We don't have any further leads to who hired her, and she didn't die under *my* care, so she's a literal dead end."

Ouch. That one hurt. "You don't have any additional leads *yet*," Rachel said, pointing in the direction of Noura's room. "You better believe that if Noura sent herself a second package, she knew things could go pear-shaped. She left you enough crumbs to track down the person who hired her."

"Lucky you got here before someone else did," Santino said.

"Really lucky nobody bothered to call the press and give them a hot tip on where the White House Murderess was staying," Zockinski added.

"We would have gotten here," Alimoren said.

"Some people might actually say thank you," Zockinski said to Santino, who nodded as he put on a small scowl.

"We had one loose end," Alimoren said. "Thank you for tracking it down for us."

"We live to serve," Zockinski said.

"What do you want?"

"To be treated as though we've been of use to you," Rachel said. "One little car chase shouldn't erase that."

The Secret Service agent's colors began to smolder in slow red rage.

"One big car chase," she amended. "One big…career-ending car chase?"

Alimoren gave in, a small breeze of purple humor blowing away the red. "Not that bad," he admitted. "Just do me the courtesy of remembering that I *have* been protecting you," he said. It was a general *you*, but there was OACET green and Southwestern turquoise in there. "My superiors thought it'd be better if someone else took responsibility for the chase."

Ouch, again. "Thanks," she said to Alimoren.

"It wasn't your fault," he said with a shrug. "I'm the one who made the call, and I promised to protect you."

"Any progress?" Hill asked.

"No," Alimoren said. "Not really. The hit team who chased you are mercenaries. Foreign nationals who entered the country illegally, most of them. It's turned into a jurisdictional nightmare, and we haven't gotten any leads on who hired them, or why. They're willing to talk, but all they've said was they were supposed to eliminate Noura and recover the package, while not harming the Agent."

"Why bother to leave Peng alive?" asked Zockinski. She gave him a soul-withering look, and he quickly added, "Not that *we* mind, but for them, that's just an extra complication."

"I don't know," Alimoren said. "I imagine nobody wants three hundred and fifty Agents pissed at them."

"Three hundred and forty-nine," Rachel corrected him. "Y'know. If I were dead."

"Have you at least run facial recognition scans of the crowd at the farmers' market?" Santino asked. "Noura was there to meet someone."

"Of course." Alimoren's conversational colors were beginning to go red again; he didn't like Santino questioning his performance. "Not too many hits, and we followed up on those that popped. Nobody rated as a suspect."

"Mind if we take a second look at the tapes?" Santino asked. "The same digital specialist from OACET who helped identify Noura might be able to find something new."

That red anger shot up and over Alimoren, but he gave a mild, "Sure thing. I'll have the files sent to Agent Atran within the hour."

Alimoren's team had finished their own brush with bureaucracy at the front desk, and were walking towards the elevators, the motel manager in tow. The men from the MPD stood, ready to follow them so as not to be accidentally-on-purpose cut out of the investigation a second time.

Santino glanced towards Rachel. "Coming?"

"Reload," Rachel said, holding up the motel's flimsy paper cup. "Meet you in Noura's room."

Nobody else wanted a refill; the coffee had the taste and consistency of watered-down motor oil. Two cups had been all that Rachel could stomach. She planned to drop the third in a convenient trash can on the way upstairs.

What she needed was a moment to herself. Something Alimoren had said was rattling around in her brain. He had said that his superiors wanted someone to blame. A car chase, a hit team in hot pursuit, Jenna Noura dying in the back seat… If anybody else had been driving, it was unlikely that the blame would have been pinned on the driver. But she had been driving—an *Agent* had been driving—and she would have made a great scapegoat.

And nobody seemed to care.

Rachel had assumed that's what Mulcahy had meant when he had said he was doing damage control. She had thought he had knocked this one out of the park: yes, the news coverage did name "OACET Agent Rachel Peng" as the driver, but so far the blame seemed to fall on that mysterious someone who had hired the hit team.

It wasn't what she had expected. When she had gone to bed last night, she was sure she'd wake up to another round of alarmist headlines—*OACET AGENT HATES AMERICAN FLAG, GOES ON RAMPAGE AT HISTORIC HOSPITAL*—or some such. Sure, the news of what Hanlon had done to them broke this morning, but it only broke within one specific media body. The others were now playing catchup, but yesterday they had had plenty of time to explore this next chapter of the White House murder scandal.

What was going on here?

She felt sure she was on to something. Something about the media, and news cycles, and...

"Agent Peng?"

Her train of thought derailed straight into Alimoren's conversational colors, where he offered her the deep wine red of sympathy.

Oh, dammit.

Well, she should have expected this.

"I heard the news. Are you—"

"I've been thoroughly vetted, if that's what you're worried about," she said, as she went through the motions of making her new cup of coffee fit for consumption. "My involvement with your case won't hurt your chances in court."

"That's not what I was about to say." Alimoren's sympathy strengthened.

She nodded. *Sugar, sugar, more sugar...something that may, or may not, be cream...*

"I'm so sorry," he said. "I had no idea what you went through."

"Is this personal or professional?" she asked as she turned to face him.

"Personal. We don't know each other, but if you need anything—"

"Thank you," she said sharply. "I don't want to talk about it."

The wine red began to take on the reds of irritation and hurt feelings. "Agent Peng, I'd like to help. Is there anything I can do for you, or...or any of the other Agents?"

Lord, save me. Is this going to be my life from now on? "Thank you," she said again, and realized she had fallen into her old habit of standing at parade rest when dealing with topics that pushed her out of her comfort zone. She shook herself, and turned back to her coffee. "The best way you can help is to treat me as though you never found out. It won't affect my performance on the case."

Frustration was beginning to displace his sympathy. "Agent Peng—"

She took a breath. "What happened is extremely personal and private. I don't want to revisit those memories," she said, reminding herself to be mild and polite and to not crawl straight down poor Alimoren's throat. "Ever. *Especially* with someone I don't know."

"Oh." Sage green moved into his colors as he finally got it, and then this started to turn red with embarrassment. "Oh. Listen, I'm so sorry. I didn't… I guess I didn't think."

"It's fine," she said, and began to fix him a cup of coffee as a peace offering before remembering that serving him the motel's brand could be categorized as aggravated assault.

"Can I ask one question?"

She added an extra helping of that scary, scary cream to his cup. "Sure."

"Didn't you all go through it? How can it be private if it happened to five hundred of you?"

"It's a hivemind thing," she said. "Some days the boundaries aren't really there."

"That's—"

"Weird? Hell yes," she said, handing him the cup. "But this would be just as hard—and just as personal and private—if it happened to five of us, or five hundred of us, or five hundred million of us. Big numbers don't make what happened any more or less traumatic. They just mean I've always got someone to drive me to therapy."

"Because you don't drive."

"I *never* drive," she said.

Alimoren took a polite sip. She had expected him to cough and sputter, but he seemed to be one of those people who considered all coffee to be drinkable. "You should," he said. "What you did yesterday was amazing."

She grinned at him. "That was luck. If I had gotten anyone seriously hurt or killed…"

"You didn't," he said. "If you had…ah…"

"Yeah." She nodded. "Today would be different."

They started walking towards the elevators. Curious yellows moved a little higher within his conversational colors, along with Hanlon's core of water-darkened wood.

"Yes," she said.

"I didn't say anything."

She sighed. "Yes, Senator Hanlon knew what he was doing to us. His pet reporter put a positive spin on it before someone else could break the story."

Alimoren didn't like that. His colors folded in on themselves, a defensive origami, with Hanlon's brown pushed just outside their edges. "I know Hanlon," he said. "He's always played fair with me."

Rachel shrugged, and poked the button for the elevator. There was the light *ding, ding,* of floor changes, and this filled the silence better than anything she could have said.

"I would have voted for him," Alimoren said.

It was her turn to wonder what he meant. "Hmm?"

"If he ran for President," the Secret Service agent said. "I thought he'd be a good one."

She shuddered. "No, he wouldn't. He'd play the part, and in fifty years, we'd find out how hard he fucked us."

"Isn't that true of most Presidents?" Alimoren said, some purple humor emerging from his colors.

"Probably," she said. "But I'm generally suspicious of anyone who's over the age of eight and still wants to be President."

Alimoren laughed, bright purple and yellow moving through his conversational colors.

The doors opened, and the two of them stepped inside. Alimoren reached out to press the button for their floor, and she noticed that he was no longer holding his coffee. Her scans hit on his cup, hidden behind a plastic plant on a nearby console table, and she winked at him as the doors closed.

NINETEEN

Of course there was a hidden room.

If you knew where to look, there was a skull with a gold-plated front tooth. Deep in its left eye socket was a switch to activate a concealed door. Flip the switch, and a section of bones swung open.

The Agents had found it while they were cleaning the mansion. The basement had required a great deal of attention to make it useable, as the drug kingpin who had last owned the mansion had remodeled it to look like the ossuary under Paris. Plastic bones tended to collect dust and debris. Someone had been getting the dead bugs out of the skulls, and was socket-deep with a vacuum when she thought the wall was leaping out to attack her.

They were sure the DEA had missed the hidden room during the original raid: the two thousand kilos of cocaine attested to that. There was a fuzzy black mold over much of it, a sign that the kingpin had gotten cheap or lazy, and had cut the cocaine with something that could rot. The ones who had discovered the room donned protective suits and poked around. They learned it was one part panic room, one part climate-controlled storage unit, and guessed that the cocaine had gone bad during the years when the mansion's power was off.

When Patrick Mulcahy was told about the discovery, he had come downstairs, an old face mask pressed against his nose and mouth. He had stared into the hidden room for about five seconds, and then asked two questions: "What's the best way to dispose of cocaine gone bad?" and "Is this room on the blueprints?" When he was told that cocaine disposal was hazardous and the safest thing to do was to bring in the DEA or the FBI, he sighed.

When he was told that no, the room was not on the blueprints, he smiled.

Mulcahy had his team of OACET engineers carefully remove the parquet floor in the solarium, and build a hidey-hole under the foundation that was just large enough for two thousand kilos of cocaine. Then he had the mansion cleared so he and Mako and eight other weightlifters could spend a full day transporting the cocaine upstairs, slow and steady so as not to damage the crumbling cellophane wrappers. Once the cocaine was secure in its new bed, he had the engineers entomb it under a cunning hidden door which blended into the parquet tiles. They cleaned the mansion again with sterilizers and chemicals and vacuums outfitted with ridiculously powerful filters, and then threw what Josh called the Ultimate Raw Meat and Ground Coffee Party.

This time, they didn't clean up.

They opened the trap door in the solarium, and called the DEA.

As predicted, the DEA ran their dogs through the mansion, searching for any additional troves secreted throughout the building. The dogs came up empty. Confused, but empty.

They got some good press out of that one. Josh and Mulcahy, standing tall over the pile of ancient cocaine, the men from the DEA smiling and pretending their predecessors hadn't messed up a bust three decades before.

And then the DEA had left, and the Agents had turned the old panic room into their new insane asylum.

Rachel leaned over a stack of boxes, and groped around in the eye socket of the skull with the gold tooth until her fingers found the switch. With an almost-unheard *click*, the wall began to swing open. She moved to the side so as not to bump into the boxes rolling towards her on their unseen casters, and ducked around the stacks of cardboard camouflage they used as a double layer of concealment for the hidden door.

The panic room had been renovated into a bunkhouse. Two twin beds and an overflowing bookshelf took up half of the room, and a couch and media center took up the other half. More books flowed off of the coffee table and across the floor, on topics ranging from financial analysis to roly-poly puppies. The selection of video games was as eclectic, as were the contents of the fridge in the corner: the permanent occupants of the room couldn't remember what they liked.

The two men in question were lying on the floor, immersed in a Sudoku puzzle. Green light flickered between them as they passed numbers back and forth, their conversational colors a riot of anger, joy, pain, pleasure…

In the corner closest to the door, a third man was painting. Shawn's core of weak-tea gold was visible, his conversational colors focused in intent blues on the canvas in front of him.

Rachel was running emotions just to check on Shawn, and she shut them down when she saw her friend was still himself. Shawn insisted on spending time with Adrian and Sammy. Everyone else in the collective thought this was a bad idea, but Shawn couldn't be talked out of it. The panic room made him miserable—he had spent too much time stuck inside of it to not feel miserable—but he said he wouldn't abandon the others. Not when he knew there was a chance they could come back, too.

She came up behind him and ran a scan across the painting. It was a seascape; Shawn was painting the ocean. "Hey," she said softly.

"Give me a minute," he said in the same quiet tone. "The light's just right."

Rachel reached out to him through a gentle link. She had been wrong: Shawn wasn't entirely there. She traced his connection, and found part of his consciousness standing on the rocky cliffs of Maine.

Rachel sat down beside him, her back against the wall, and sent her mind north. Her bright green avatar appeared beside Shawn's, who was staring out across the sea. Beneath them, the surf pounded against black rocks.

"I swear I can smell the water," Shawn's avatar said to hers.

"It's disorienting."

Great. Now he wants to talk. Back in the mansion, Rachel clasped her hands across her ears and shut down all but the most basic visual scans. She hated going out-of-body.

"How do you do it?" she asked him. "Split yourself so you can focus on multiple things at once?"

His avatar shrugged. "I spent so much time out of my own mind, going out of my body is easy."

"Ouch."

Shawn gave her a wide green grin. "It's either we laugh at ourselves, or go crazy, right?"

She gave Shawn's avatar a fast once-over. His hair and clothes were tidy, and he looked as if he was finally getting some muscle tone back. Rachel reminded herself to check on Shawn's physical appearance when they stepped out of their avatars to see if his body was as healthy as his mental image of himself.

"How'd you find this place?" she asked him.

"Somebody's Flickr account," he said. "They posted a photo I liked, so I came here to check out the location."

"I love it," she said, as she watched the waves smash against the shore. She adored water. When she was in her own body, it was as good as poetry to her expanded senses. "It's wild."

"Yeah, I was getting tired of painting meadows and haystacks," he said. "I'm trying to come out here on sunny days. Harder to do than it sounds. This time of year, this place is always overcast... Okay, I'm done."

His avatar vanished, and Rachel heard, as if from a very far distance, Shawn call her name.

"Yeah, yeah," she muttered, giving the shoreline a last look. It was beautiful, complex... *Definitely a step up from haystacks.*

She stepped off of the cliff and hovered in midair for a moment, then let her avatar drop. Her blurry visuals gave her an image of a set of eyes, just inches from her own face, and she instinctively threw up a hand. There was a faint *papf!* as she accidentally smacked someone on the chest, followed by grunting and scrambling noises as that someone scurried away.

Rachel stumbled through her visual settings as quickly as she could until Shawn appeared in front of her.

"Shit," she said. "Did I hit you?"

Shawn shook his head, and pointed. Adrian and Sammy were peering around the side of the couch, like wild dogs unsure if they were about to receive food or a thrown rock.

Cold fear shot up her spine as she realized she could have touched their bare skin. It had been pure luck that they were both wearing clothes today. "Who did I hit?"

"Sammy," Shawn said, holding out his empty hands to the insane cyborgs. The two men glared at him before disappearing behind the couch. Shawn watched as they hid like wild animals in men's bodies, and his shoulders folded in on themselves in despair.

She turned emotions back on, and deep gray appeared over Shawn, rolling thick and fast like the worst of storms. She realized his avatar was a clean copy of his body. Shawn was nearly a year removed from the days when he had been a full-time resident of the panic room, and he had recovered much of his mental and physical strength. Now, though, he seemed the same gaunt savage who had attacked Santino with a straight-edge razor. He was staring at his hands as if he didn't recognize them, the beginnings of a panic attack moving across him as he began to tremble.

"Come on," she said, as she stood and tugged on Shawn's shirtsleeve. She took him over to the couch and settled him within a nest of throw pillows.

"*I don't like it here,*" he said.

"Out loud, Shawn," she reminded him. "You start to withdraw when you speak in the link, remember?"

He nodded. His conversational colors had started churning, showing emotions that weren't drawn from his own thoughts and personality. "I know. I know. Please don't make me mad."

"Okay," she said, as she curled up at the other end of the couch. She tried to ignore how the leather was sticky and filmed over, as if toddlers had painted it with a thousand different meals.

It took Shawn almost an hour to get himself under control. Rachel read a magazine until her head throbbed, and then turned off reading mode to let her mind drift around the room. She didn't trust herself to turn off visuals, not after hitting poor Sammy in the chest, so she sent her senses crawling through the hidden spaces of the panic room.

She had done this many times before. Babysitting duty wasn't fun. Sometimes, those on duty left things behind for the next shift, notes or books or…

Rachel's scans tripped over a new addition in the room. Hidden under one of the beds was a long box, bolted to the floor and padlocked in three places.

A disassembled sniper rifle waited within its metal shell.

Damn, Mulcahy's gotten fanatical about security, Rachel thought, before she remembered that if the rifle had anything to do with babysitting duty, he'd have told her about it. No, that gun had been left in the most secure site in OACET's headquarters for a different reason.

She flipped frequencies as she explored the gun, coming to rest on one frequency in particular which showed the rifle resonated with a vivid blue aura. Her scans flinched away from the rifle at that, at learning the weapon had taken so many lives that it held traces of that unmistakable deathly blue, and decided Mulcahy probably had very good reasons for locking such a gun away.

If Adrian and Sammy knew the lockbox was there, it didn't bother them. The men had come out from hiding, Rachel and Shawn forgotten, and had turned on the latest iteration of *Call of Duty.* They were exceptional at it, and like all men in their late twenties, their mastery of trash talk could put sailors to shame. The two crazy cyborgs verbally smacked each other around, the insults ranging from genitalia to scores on intelligence tests. As they played, their kaleidoscopes of conversational colors slowed and faded, with blues starting to show beneath the swarms of reds, blacks, and oranges.

"*This is good,*" Shawn whispered in a hushed mental voice.

Rachel was about to tell him again to speak out loud, when she realized that while Shawn was curled in on himself, hugging his own legs to his chest as he rocked back and forth, he was also intent on the two men playing their game.

"It helps to focus on something outside of your head," he said. *"They need to remember who they are.*

"It's the memories," he continued. *"They've got so many other peoples' memories in their heads, and those memories are all so real. They don't know what to do with them. They don't know if their thoughts are their own. But you don't need memories to play a video game."*

The two of them watched as Adrian shot Sammy in the head repeatedly, and was in turn blown to smithereens by a fortunate respawn. Adrian hurled a particularly poignant comment about Sammy's sister, and as Rachel watched, Sammy's small blues disappeared under a growing tempest of reds. He put down the controller and wandered away.

"Sammy's an only child. He doesn't have a sister," Shawn told her. *"Deep down, he knows he doesn't have a sister. But he remembers having one—he remembers having hundreds of sisters!—and he doesn't know what to do with that information."*

"Yeah," Rachel whispered back across their link. If it had been any other Agent, she would have sent them the memories of her childhood Christmases, which had taken place in more houses and in more bodies than she could identify. But it was Shawn, and she didn't want to pretend she had had it worse than him, and she definitely didn't want to say the wrong thing to tip him back down that dark hole he was trying so hard to climb out of.

"Rachel? I want..." Shawn's mental voice trailed off. Rachel saw his emotions swirl around an unmistakable cerulean blue. Then, his voice hardened as he blurted: *"You need to tell Mulcahy to take them home."*

"They are home—"

"No!" Shawn's head came up. *"Where they grew up! Their parents, their families... They should be somewhere they recognize, with people who can remind them who they used to be.*

"*That's how I came back*," he said. "*I was trying to kill Santino. It was… It wasn't me. I knew my mother wouldn't have raised someone who would do that, and then I remembered her, and then…*

"*I was crazy.*" He pushed on, needing her to understand. "*I was hallucinating! I saw angels everywhere, blue ones, and one of them put a razor in my hand, and told me a stranger was trying to kill Zia. They were so real—*

"*And then…and then I saw what I had done, and I knew I'd never do that. It was the first thought I had about myself in so long, and…*"

Rachel slid over to him and began to rub his back, keeping well away from his bare skin.

"*They can't stay here,*" he finished. "*Unless something changes, they'll stay like this. They need the chance to break through.*"

"*I'll talk to Mulcahy,*" she told him. It might be possible. Load Adrian and Sammy into a van, drive them out to their childhood homes in the dead of night…

"*No,*" Shawn insisted. She didn't think she had been broadcasting, but he had still managed to pick the thought out of her head. "*They need to be around their families. They need to remember where they come from, or they'll never find their way back to themselves.*"

Rachel's hand slipped into the pocket of her jeans, where the 3D-printed replica of the fragment from the Antikythera Mechanism lay against the curve of her leg. She wasn't quite sure why she kept transferring it from pocket to pocket when she changed pants, but it was starting to take on the familiarity of a talisman. *I wasn't lost but three seconds,* she thought to herself, *and I still needed help finding my way back.*

"*Exactly.*" Shawn had heard her again. "*Can you help them?*"

"*Shawn—*"

"*Please, Rachel.*" Shawn was pleading, his colors a pleasing mix of teal, wine red, and her Southwestern turquoise, all of them reaching out to her in a slowly twisting liquid wave. It was beautiful, and she didn't understand what it meant.

A knock at the door saved her from making a promise she couldn't keep, as an Agent arrived to relieve Rachel's shift. Rachel barely nodded to her replacement, focused instead on forcing Shawn to come with her, out of the panic room, to put some distance between himself and a near-infinite number of memories.

He didn't resist, not until the hidden door had swung shut. Then he froze in place, and looked up at the plastic ossuary with wide eyes. "Rachel," he said, "why are we fighting?"

"We're not," she said, finding her way down the narrow corridor the Agents had left as a walkway between the cardboard boxes. "This is a tricky issue, and we're discussing it like rational adults. We're fine, Shawn."

Rachel felt his confusion, and she turned towards him to see him still staring up at the ceiling. She followed his attention, through the skulls and the walls... *Oh!*

Halfway across the mansion, someone was getting his nose broken.

Rachel grinned at Shawn. "C'mon," she laughed, and pulled him into a run.

Their path included two flights of stairs, and five long stretches of rooms and hallways, all of it layered in furniture and boxes and the occasional speedboat. Shawn struggled to keep up with her as she climbed and jumped, laughing the entire way.

Their race took them into the main entrance hall, and the two of them stopped and stared.

Rachel had never seen so many people in the mansion before. Never. Not even during their biggest parties, and OACET was renowned for events that would have been better suited to abandoned warehouses. It was a milling mess of people from the front doors of the mansion all the way down to the lawns and gardens. There were caterers and food trucks galore, with tents set up in the courtyard. She saw Santino's cobalt blue standing beside Zia's sweet violet, and the entwined greens of Hill's forests and Ami's spring meadows. There were others she recognized—hundreds of them!—and Rachel began to pick out the colors of those whom she had met through work. A kaleidoscope of colors from the MPD. Others she recognized from working crime scenes with the FBI... *Oh!* There, across the main room, was Alimoren's workaday denim blue.

Friends, maybe. Allies, definitely. OACET had surrounded themselves with a thousand witnesses.

She reached out to Mulcahy, and found him sitting on the landing of the great staircase in the entrance hall. *"You're a fucking genius,"* she told him.

He tilted his beer bottle downwards, to where Josh Glassman stood on stage, working the crowd. *"His idea,"* Mulcahy said.

"You could have told me to expect a party."

She felt him laugh. *"Puppeteering is our responsibility. I keep telling you—focus on alliances within law enforcement, and we'll handle the rest."*

"Are you expecting a raid?" Rachel asked, casting her scans towards the road that led to the mansion. She saw nothing but a steady stream of cars moving into whatever parking spaces they could find. She stretched her scans as far as they could reach without bringing on a headache, towards the woods and open fields around the mansion, searching for the professional blues of a SWAT team...

"No. We're good. Thanks to you, someone in the MPD or the FBI would have tipped us off if they were coming. But better safe than sorry. Besides," he said, nodding towards the crowd, *"we needed this."*

"Next!" Josh Glassman's voice thundered over the crowd.

Josh occupied the only clear space within the main hall, and stood four feet above the crowd as he strode across the portable boxing ring. The boxing ring was an old friend, one of the first items OACET had repurposed for their own use when they had moved into the mansion. Over the winter, it had been packed up and put away to make room for the holiday decorations. Rachel had missed it: the ring had been more sincere than a glittery tree. After the decorations had come down, the space had been left empty, yet another sign they were starting to venture out of the safety of their first home. Instead, the entrance hall had begun to fill up with clutter as it began its slow transformation into yet another storage area.

During those few hours she had spent in the panic room, the clutter had been cleared and the boxing ring had been returned to its old location. It was surrounded, ten deep, everybody shouting and cheering. The smell of fresh buttered popcorn was heavy in the air, and Rachel felt kernels crunch underfoot as she and Shawn pushed their way towards the ring.

"*Next!*" Josh was actually wearing a hat. An honest-to-God carnival barker's hat. His core, the unsaturated blue of fresh tattoos, was almost completely obscured by reds—*rich* reds, those of friendship, belonging, and more than a little lust—and the yellow-white energy that defined Josh whenever he was performing. "Come one, come all! Others say they have the greatest show on earth, but that's because they can't afford our rates!

"You've seen the rest," he said, and spun the hat from his head with a twirl of his wrist. "Now see the *best!*"

Rachel grabbed Shawn's arm again, the two of them giddy, as Hope Blackwell climbed up through the ropes and joined Josh on stage.

Mulcahy's wife was a hand shorter than Rachel, with dark, wild hair over her strange core of blue-black light. She was barefoot, and wearing an old blue Judo gi that looked as if it had been through the wash a couple thousand times. Hope danced around to limber up, shouting and waving as the crowd cheered her name.

Two Agents in martial arts whites, both of them men with eighty pounds on her, joined her in the ring. They bowed to her; she returned it.

Then, they rushed her.

Hope swept an arm low, and brought her fist up into the meat of the first man's thigh. He gasped in pain, and began to shift his weight to his good leg. This mistake took a fraction of a second, but it was enough for Hope: her leg shot out, her heel slamming into the tender skin on the arch of his foot. Off-balance, he began to fall, and Hope grabbed his belt and tossed him over her hip.

The name of the technique came to Rachel—*Obi-otoshi*, a belt throw—as the collective chattered about the fight.

Hope followed the first Agent down to the ground in a sacrifice fall. *Mistake*, Rachel thought, but Hope had already rolled to the side. The first man, struggling to recover, went after her with a low kick, and caught his teammate in the knee. Hope hit that same knee from the other side, and the second Agent crumpled into her range. Hope's legs wrapped around his head and neck in a scissor hold, and he found himself locked down tight. Caught, his free hand began tapping on the mat, and the match was over.

"What?!" Josh Glassman crossed to the edge of the boxing ring, one hand trailing against the top of the ropes as he worked the crowd. "That wasn't a *fight!* We're not here to watch a *demonstration!* We're not here to *learn!*"

The crowd responded with boos and catcalls, and the schoolyard chant of *Fight! Fight! Fight!* went up.

"Someone get up here and give this woman a fight!"

"Hey!" Hope Blackwell leaned over the ropes, Southwestern turquoise blazing in her conversational colors. "Peng! I heard you saw my ass last night!"

Rachel laughed, and shouted back: "Saw a lot more than that, Blackwell! Bring a bathrobe if you're gonna let Mulcahy tag you in public!"

High above them on the landing, Mulcahy maintained his poker face, but his colors flushed red in embarrassment.

"Up for some fun?" It was Josh, his presence in her head alive with good humor.

"Always!" she replied, as the adrenaline surged.

"Peng!" Josh shouted! "Get up here!"

"If I do, we're boxing!" Rachel shouted back. "None of that tricky Judo shit!"

"Deal!" Hope said, punching the air.

Rachel whooped, the sound lost within the uproar from the crowd.

She shed clothing as she ran towards the ring, until she was down to nothing but her tee-shirt and jeans. Phil took her gun before he taped up her hands, and patted her on her butt as she squirmed up and through the ropes. She bobbed and hopped in place to warm up, windmilling her arms until her heartrate found its fighting tempo.

"Rachel!" Santino's voice drew her scans to where her partner was clapping and shouting her name. "Kick her ass!"

She yelled back at him, a nonsense phrase thick with excitement, and let Josh slip a mouth guard between her lips before she moved into the center of the ring.

Hope Blackwell grinned at Rachel, her own colors high, and the two of them began to circle.

Rachel knew she didn't have a chance in hell of taking Hope in a fair fight. She had sparred with Hope in the past, and unless Hope held herself back, those bouts were always short and painful. The woman had been training in Judo since she was five years old, and once she had started traveling the world for competitions, she had picked up other martial arts along the way.

Boxing, however...

Martial arts was punches, kicks, and throws. Boxing was a straight-out slugfest. Rachel was counting on Hope's lifetime of training to work against her, to mentally exhaust her as she forced herself to keep both feet on the ground and concentrate on using boxing-legal techniques.

Rachel threw the first three punches, quick jabs to see what Hope would do. She expected Hope to be a counter puncher, watching for Rachel to make a mistake, and then closing on her in a quick rumble. Wrong. Hope lunged, pairing hooks and jabs to drive Rachel to the ropes, and Rachel realized she was a swarmer.

Damn! Should have expected it. Weird woman's all energy,

Rachel thought, catching the punches on her shoulders before coming in with an uppercut. It landed square against Hope's chest, and knocked her back. Rachel followed up on that first punch, bearing down hard to drive Hope backwards, until the ropes were all that kept Hope from falling four feet to the floor.

The first round was over faster than it should have been. Josh was there to pull her off of Hope, to send her to the corner where Phil was waiting with water and a dishtowel. "Good one," Phil said. "You got her mad."

"She should be mad. I wasn't pulling those punches," Rachel said. Her left hand was throbbing: she had injured it last October, and it was prone to acting up when she abused it.

"Keep her off of the ropes," Phil said. "It's a rope-a-dope. You keep her there, you're gonna wear yourself out while she's still fresh."

"Right," she said, nodding, and he stuck her mouth guard back in before he pushed her into the fight.

Hope came out low and hard, throwing jabs, looking for a way to drag Rachel into a legal clinch. Rachel kept some distance—if Hope managed to close, the round would be over—and landed two right hooks, split with a short left jab.

Hope saw her favoring her left hand, and her colors exploded in bright yellow-whites as she moved forward. Rachel tried to drive her back with another right hook, but Hope spotted this one before it could land. A fast parry, and she was in tight with Rachel.

Fuck! Rachel thought, as she felt Hope's shoulder press against the side of her windpipe. It wasn't illegal, but only because boxers didn't know how to maintain this kind of chokehold. *Worst place to be with a Judo master. Absolute worst.*

She began to drive her right fist into Hope's ribcage, hitting the same spot again and again. If she were fighting a big man, the move wouldn't have worked; the distance between him and her fist would have been too close to build up any real momentum. Against a woman, there was plenty of room for Rachel to maneuver. Six hard strikes, and Hope was forced to drop the clinch before Rachel broke her ribs.

They circled, then closed again, Hope listing slightly to protect her injured left side. Rachel noticed, just in time, that the pain red coming from that area was shallow, more of a patina than what she'd expect from an actual wound...

She barely got her hands up in time to block Hope's left haymaker. The crowd roared.

Hope recovered before Rachel could slide under her raised left arm, but it was an instinctive act. She dropped Rachel's forearm almost as quickly as she had grabbed it, walking away and raising her taped hands to show she recognized the foul. Too late: Josh had already called a halt to the second round, breaking up the action before Hope could turn the illegal arm lock into a throw.

They limped towards their corners. Phil had a folding chair waiting for her, and Rachel collapsed into it. "Ow ow ow ow ow..."

"Where'd she get you?"

"Nowhere," Rachel said, rubbing her right hand. "Woman's all muscle. It's like punching a brick wall."

"Rachel!"

She tossed her scans down, and saw Becca on the other side of the ropes. Rachel felt her face split in a wide grin. "Aaa-dri-aaaan!"

Becca laughed. "Kick her ass, Rocky!"

"One more round!" Josh called out. "These lovely ladies have work in the morning!"

The crowd booed his decision.

"Like this is the last fight of the night? No! Let's spread out the damage to our collective's brain cells, friends," he said, and gestured for Hope and Rachel to get on their feet. "Let's *go!*"

Rachel knew she was starting to flag, but she forced herself to bounce around like a tennis player before the last match. Hope just grinned at her, and then dipped to the left. Rachel turned right to block—*she's going left, she's building momentum for another haymaker*—and couldn't get her arms up in time to block Hope's sudden shift in weight and a lightning-fast right cross.

Stunned, Rachel vaguely realized Hope had followed the first punch up with a second, both of them solid hits across her jaw. Hope backed off a few steps to see if Rachel was done. Rachel shook her head to break out of the daze, and then charged.

Now it was a fight, both of them going all out. Rachel knew Hope could take a punch, so she laid into the other woman's head and torso with everything she had left. She went after Hope with power blows, trying to put her on the ground before the fight ended. No luck—there was no way to get through her defense. Hope blocked half of what Rachel threw, and turned the other half into openings for her own attacks.

Rachel stumbled. It was fast and next to nothing, and Hope still managed to follow it up with a powerhouse of a left hook.

"Time!" Josh shouted, and the crowd cheered.

Rachel fell against Hope in an exhausted embrace, both of them laughing. Josh stepped between them, and the crowd went silent as the scores came in. Then, Josh held up Hope's hand. "Winner!"

"Boo!" Becca shouted from Rachel's corner. "Recount! *Recount!*" Her colors were all high reds as she screamed for her girlfriend. The banker had caught a bad case of bloodlust, and Rachel realized she could probably spend the rest of her life with this woman.

She slumped against Josh, and he helped her towards her corner.

They were all waiting for her, Becca and Santino, Phil and Shawn and Jason and Hill and Bell and...*Oh! When did Zockinski get here?* She dropped into their arms, feeling strong. Feeling sane.

Feeling whole.

She reached out, across the room, to find Mulcahy within another cluster of Agents and their friends as they held his wife above their heads. *"I want you to talk to Shawn about Adrian and Sammy,"* she told him. *"He's got some good suggestions on how we can help them come back."*

She expected resistance. Stalling and delays, possibly some wordplay that would leave her reeling worse than Hope's left hook. Anything but his quick, decisive: *"Yes."*

TWENTY

The gentle knock on the door was hesitant, and mostly a politeness for Becca.

"One sec, Mare. She's asleep."

Rachel tossed blankets around until her legs were free. Every room in the mansion with a bed was currently occupied, so she and Becca had made do by piling spare comforters on a broken air hockey table in one of the basement storerooms. They hadn't been there very long; Becca's hair was longer than Rachel's, and was still damp from their shower.

She shuffled towards the door. The soreness from the boxing match was just starting to settle into her muscles. Tomorrow was going to hurt.

Rachel cracked the door and slipped into the hall as quickly as she could, trying to keep the roar of the party from waking her girlfriend. "You could have just called me upstairs if the pizza is here," she said. "I'm starving."

Mare blinked at her. "You're not running emotions?"

"What? No." Rachel made a point of shutting the emotional spectrum down when she and Becca were sharing a personal moment, physical or otherwise. At times like those, reading emotions seemed somehow dishonest. She flipped on scans to find her friend a mix of uncertain oranges. "What's wrong?"

Mare handed her a bright blue envelope. "This came for you via private courier."

"Whoa. Whose?"

"One of the cheap companies everybody uses. The kid said someone dropped it off this evening and paid in cash for late-night delivery."

Rachel slid a thumbnail under the fold, and sliced the envelope open. Inside was a small white card, the block lettering on its face crisp from a laser printer.

486-555-2128
0300J
MAD

"What the actual fuck," Rachel muttered, before handing the card to Mare.

Mare stared at the card, her colors a perplexed orange. "Why would someone send you this?"

"I don't know, but I'm military," she said, as she went to tell Becca she needed to do some work and she'd rejoin her when she could. "MAD is something you never want to hear."

They hurried towards Mulcahy's office. It was late; she had about twenty minutes before three in the morning. The party was still going strong, and she had to resort to shouting and elbows to get through some of the tighter places.

This is a major hazard, she thought to herself, suddenly worried that all of OACET's efforts might be swept away in the proverbial five-alarm fire.

Mare, her hand tight within Rachel's to keep from getting swept away, replied, *"The fire marshal is here. He didn't seem too worried."*

"The fire marshal has a weakness for brunettes, and I noticed Josh invited a whole bunch of his lingerie model friends."

They took the back way through the mansion. Rachel's scans had told her that it was the easiest way upstairs, but they still needed to crawl over partygoers in various stages of sobriety.

Santino met them at the top. "What?" He shook his phone at her. "What kind of emergency?"

A wave of yellow-orange surprise passed from Mare's hand into hers. *"It's Santino,"* Rachel assured her. *"He goes where I go."*

She handed the envelope to Santino, and the three of them hurried down the hall.

"Did you run the phone number?" her partner asked her.

"Legally? Of course not," Rachel replied. "But if someone

were to have crawled around in the registry, they probably would have found that this number was part of a block assigned to really cheap phones."

"Burners?"

"I'm guessing. The phone that number is assigned to is inactive."

"I bet its battery has been removed," Santino said. "Or it's been partly disassembled, depending on the model."

Rachel stepped on the urge to shoot her partner a Look. "You're probably right," she said. "Is there any other way to track it?"

"No," Santino replied. "Not until it's got power. If it can't receive or transmit data, there's no way to locate it."

"All right," she said, and the three of them entered Mulcahy's office.

Mare had briefed him during their mad sprint upstairs. Mulcahy was waiting in a beaten-down leather club chair, a pitcher of water on the coffee table in front of him; Hope was nowhere to be seen. He glanced towards Santino, then nodded.

"This is from Hanlon," Rachel said, tossing the card towards him.

Mulcahy snagged it out of the air. "What's your logic?" he asked, after giving the card a quick once-over. "The message is vague. It could be from anybody with a grudge against us."

"Unless you take into account how he used military time instead of standard," Rachel said. "In which case, he's not angry, he's offering a stalemate."

"How so?"

"MAD is military shorthand for *mutually assured destruction*."

Mulcahy placed the card on the coffee table and tented his fingers. "You think he wants to talk?"

"No. He knows we can go out-of-body in our avatars, right? A phone number is as good as an address to us, but these days, anyone—oh, say, the NSA—can record a phone conversation while it's happening. He wants to meet face-to-face, probably in a public place, where any witnesses wouldn't be able to see us and he'd be able to claim our recordings of the meeting are fakes."

"Think like a Senator who's in a battle to the death with three hundred and fifty pissed-off cyborgs," Santino said. He had picked up on Rachel's initial idea, and was fleshing out Hanlon's plan as he spoke. "He wants to meet with you, but he knows you have a technological advantage. Even if he makes sure you can't show up in person, you'll still record everything as evidence. How does he strip that advantage from you?"

"He creates doubt within the public theater," said Mulcahy. "The meeting will be under conditions in which recordings have reduced credibility. But Hanlon doesn't have an implant— he can hear us through a phone line, but how will he be able to see us?"

Horrified greens slowly pulled themselves into Santino's conversational colors. "I'm going to fucking *murder* Zockinski," he said.

"A couple of pairs of Santino's glasses have gone missing," Rachel explained, and watched as her boss began to turn red. "We didn't think it was worth mentioning."

"Ah," Mulcahy said. His reds began to subside, wrestled under control by professional blues, and he turned back to Santino. "What do we need to make this work?"

"Monitors," Santino said. "Recording equipment on multiple hard drives. Someone to go with Rachel to make sure that the conversation is recorded from different perspectives, to make it harder for Hanlon to argue it's been faked. And get some of those big-name law enforcement professionals who are drunk off their asses in your living room to get up here and serve as witnesses."

Mulcahy's colors rolled over on themselves, and forged themselves into armor. "I wish we could," he said quietly.

Santino looked towards Rachel, who shrugged. "Risk assessment," she said. "We don't know what Hanlon wants to talk about."

"*If* it's Hanlon," Mare added.

Rachel said nothing, but there wasn't much doubt in her mind about who was on the other end of that phone number. Not too many people knew about the Agents' out-of-body abilities, and nobody except Hanlon would call her out.

Within minutes, Mulcahy's office had been converted to a rough facsimile of a media center. Rachel had just enough time to take a few deep breaths, to try and locate her game face beneath the happy buzz from the party.

Fuck Hanlon, she thought. *We're all here, trying to recover from a shitty day—aw hell, that's why he wants to do this tonight—and he's figured out another way to come after us. I bet he would bomb this place to the ground if he thought he could get away with it… Could he get away with it? Would he try? Oh, that son of a bitch, I bet he's tried to buy a missile…*

Her version of a game face had sharp edges. When she was good and thoroughly angry, she glanced towards Mulcahy, and opened a private link. His own share of anger roared into hers, his cold blue fury steaming over her red-hot rage, and together they merged into steel.

"We are gonna feel really dumb if this isn't actually Hanlon," she admitted, and he smiled within her head.

The phone attached to the number activated.

Mulcahy noticed, too. "We're on," he said.

"Give me sixty seconds alone," she said, and managed to hide her fear that Hanlon might have found a way to murder them through their avatars.

She cast her mind into the aether and located the phone. It was nearby: she pinged it among the monuments at the southwest side of the Tidal Basin.

"Ready?" she asked.

Mulcahy agreed, and Rachel nodded at her partner before she put her head within the quiet nest of her arms. Santino flipped the power switch on the nearby monitor as she stepped from her body to her avatar.

Senator Hanlon was staring back at her.

Rachel stepped backwards before she could catch herself,

and found her avatar walking on water.

She took a quick look around to orient herself. Water cascaded down from massive granite blocks. Rough stone was everywhere; green and yellow light floated up from beneath the waterfalls and cast moving shadows against the walls.

Oh. This place again. Hanlon hadn't picked the Franklin Delano Roosevelt Memorial by accident. He was sitting on the flat rock where Hope Blackwell had been napping. It was as clear a message as he could send without erecting *YOU CAN KEEP NOTHING FROM ME* in giant letters across the Hollywood Hills.

She turned back towards Hanlon. In her avatar, her vision was nearly normal: she easily spotted the Bluetooth headset and the pair of glasses perched on his nose.

Rachel blinked as she recognized the glasses—one of Santino's more recent prototypes.

We owe Zockinski an apology, she thought, and hoped the faulty battery pack was burning the shit out of the Senator's ear.

"Not going to smile and ask if I want to sit down for a friendly conversation?" she asked.

Hanlon ignored her, and adjusted the glasses.

"Seems rude, to go to all of this trouble to speak to me, and not even a hello?" Rachel didn't like this at all. She pushed a burst of static into the Bluetooth receiver. It squawked loud enough to make Hanlon flinch.

"Sorry," she said, smiling. "I thought you couldn't hear me."

He glanced at his watch, and removed a small box from inside his jacket. The box was made of a sleek dark metal, about three times as thick as a smartphone and with a digital screen. It was almost too stylish to be useful, like a prop from a science fiction film whose only purpose was to impress the audience.

Rachel tried to ping it, and found the device couldn't reply. There was no substance to it, nothing other than a fancy screen powered by a battery. *This isn't good,* she thought to herself. *Not good at all.*

There was a pop, and Mulcahy's avatar stepped into the air

beside her.

"Senator," he said.

Hanlon ignored him, too.

"He's pretending he can't see us," Rachel said to Mulcahy. "I've already told him it's extremely rude."

Mulcahy's avatar began to walk around Hanlon's rock, like a wolf circling a treed animal. He leaned in, close enough to Hanlon to kiss…or bite.

Mulcahy's smile was sharp. "Interesting," he said.

Hanlon pretended to check his watch again, and then picked up his fancy hollow box. He stepped across the rocks to reach dry land, and began to head towards the Tidal Basin. Mulcahy walked in circles around Hanlon the entire time.

Rachel joined them on the granite pavers of the pavilion. The three of them went east, finally stopping in a secluded area just to the side of the Basin walkway.

She moved deeper into the tight, private link she was sharing with Mulcahy, and found nothing but sorrow and guilt.

"What?" she asked through their link.

"He's not here to talk to us," Mulcahy told her. His avatar's eyes never left Hanlon, but she got the impression he was frantically searching for something else, something not in plain sight. *"This is being staged for our benefit, and for anybody watching this recording."*

Then, Mulcahy's avatar turned to look towards the lights of the city. *"The distance isn't a problem, but there's thick tree cover… I couldn't make this shot."*

If Rachel's body hadn't already been sitting quietly on a couch in Mulcahy's office, her knees would have given way beneath her.

"I could," she said. She was surprised to find her mental voice was strong. *"Ami could."*

"Most very good snipers could," he agreed. *"But it'd be much easier for an Agent."*

Mulcahy's avatar turned towards Hanlon. "Stop this," he said. "I've got my people hunting. They'll find your man."

Hanlon tilted his head upwards, as if he wanted to gaze at the stars. Rachel could have screamed at his self-satisfied smirk.

It was a beautiful plan. If they had known the meeting spot in advance, Mulcahy could have had every combat-trained Agent stationed throughout the area. As it was, every Agent, combat-trained or not, within a mile's radius of the Tidal Basin had dropped what they were doing to search for Hanlon's sniper.

There weren't many of them. Those few Agents who weren't still at the mansion had gone home to their beds.

Barring a miracle, they'd never find the sniper in time.

"Should I call the police?" Rachel asked Mulcahy. She expected him to say no, that Hanlon's trap was crafted to catch OACET, that bringing in outsiders would leave them vulnerable to—

"Absolutely," he said, and turned towards the path to wait.

"I'll get Santino to make the call, but we need help now. There are always MPD and security guards around the Basin," Rachel said to Mulcahy. *"Let me do a sweep and find—"*

His avatar looked at hers, and she stilled her thoughts as she realized that there'd be no help coming. Hanlon had covered that angle, too.

"Can we shut him down through the Bluetooth? Distract him, maybe? Kill his glasses?" Rachel didn't know what else they could do. She reached out to learn what she could do about the glasses, but Mulcahy stopped her.

"Watch," he said.

A velociraptor—an honest-to-God *dinosaur!*—appeared in front of Hanlon. It was movie-sized, and the instant it took form in green light, it opened its mouth in a violent roar and lunged at the Senator's face.

Hanlon shivered, but said nothing, and smiled in Mulcahy's general direction as he stepped through the body of the snarling raptor.

"He knows our abilities," he said. *"He's ready for us. All we can do is collect information and bear witness."*

Her avatar moved to stand beside Mulcahy's, and they kept vigil as they waited for Hanlon's victim.

(The Rachel back at the mansion blurted everything she and Mulcahy had shared in their link to Santino, begging him to find help, to get someone down there, to stop this before it happened...)

Then, through her avatar's eyes, she saw Mitch Alimoren emerge from the bushes.

Oh, she thought. *I could've sworn it'd be Summerville.*

Miles away, Rachel yelled something to Santino, something about calling Alimoren and telling him to run, but she could already tell Alimoren wasn't wearing anything digital. Hanlon must have told him to leave anything that could be tracked by an Agent in his car.

"Don't do this," Mulcahy's avatar said to Hanlon. "You're digging your own grave."

Mulcahy's guilt surged again, and Rachel picked a thought out of his mind. The image of a sniper's rifle in a lockbox, two crazy men playing video games ten feet from it...

The force of the mystery crashed down on her as it all came together: the Hippos, drawn to the right place at the right time to save her; Ami's missing rifle, which wasn't missing, just locked away in the mansion's saferoom; Mulcahy's guilt at setting one particular trap...

I set something up for him, something irresistible, and he took the bait.

She wasn't sure if Mulcahy's voice in her mind was a memory or whether he was repeating himself—everything was taking on the thin, hazy quality of nightmares.

"Hanlon," Rachel said. "Mulcahy's telling the truth. The gun you took off of the roof? It can't be traced back to OACET."

Alimoren had come close enough for a proper greeting, and Hanlon walked the last few steps towards him.

Rachel's avatar swooped in front of Hanlon, blocking Alimoren from Hanlon's view. "You stupid *shit!*" she swore at Hanlon. "Mulcahy switched the rifles!"

"Agent Peng?" Mulcahy's avatar said. "There's no reason for him to believe us."

Hanlon winked at her avatar before he walked through it to reach Alimoren; Rachel didn't feel a thing, but she still gasped in impotent rage.

Her link with Mulcahy was uncomfortably tight. It felt as if they were holding each other as they waited for the unthinkable. Guilt and frustration moved between them: they had never hated Hanlon as much as they did that moment.

"Should we be meeting in public?" Alimoren said. His words were slightly slurred; he was a good ways down the road towards drunk. He must have come straight from the party at the mansion.

Hanlon held up his fancy stage prop. "I've had people working on this for months," he said. "It emits a frequency that prevents all electronic eavesdropping."

Alimoren glanced at it. "Agent Peng can do something similar."

"All Agents can," the Senator said. "And now we can, too. This device not only blocks standard surveillance equipment, but it can prevent Agents from observing or recording anything within a ten-meter radius."

You fucking liar, Rachel thought. *It's nothing but a beeping box of social engineering that'll put reasonable doubt in a juror's mind when they watch our recordings of Alimoren's murder.*

Alimoren, all unwitting, tried to help her. He glanced down at the device as he said, "Nice! Why haven't you put those into production?"

"It's a one-off," Hanlon answered smoothly. "Each machine has to be calibrated to the Agents. I was able to make this one before they caught on. It works, but I can't make more without their help, and they won't help me."

"You sure?" Alimoren said. "Agent Peng—"

"I'm sure," Hanlon cut him off. "I've asked. Many times."

"You might want to have someone else approach Agent Peng. She was extremely helpful with the White House break-in."

"I thought they would be," Hanlon said. "That's why I told you to bring Agent Peng and her team on board for the investigation."

Miles away, Rachel's heart missed a beat. She felt Santino's hand grab hers as they both tried to keep themselves from screaming.

Hanlon pretended to read something in Alimoren's face. "You don't believe what they're saying about me, that I developed the conditioning technologies?"

"Sir? I don't want to—"

"Alimoren, listen," Hanlon insisted. "I've always known that those with the implant would be useful. OACET… Well, I think OACET is a failed experiment, myself. I think they should be disbanded, and the Agents distributed among different organizations, instead of this closed hivemind they've cloistered away in that mansion of theirs. But at the time the implant was developed, I was running a multinational company while campaigning as a Congressman. There're not enough hours in the day to be *that* evil."

"Of course, Senator," the Secret Service agent said, adding a half-hearted chuckle. Rachel wished she could read his colors; she imagined the confused look on his face would go well with an uncertain yellow-orange.

Hanlon shook his head, the picture of long-suffering endurance. "You too, Alimoren?"

"It's not my place—"

"It *is* your place," Hanlon said. "Yours, and every other American's. It's all about public image, isn't it? Mine, yours, the Secret Service's reputation… We can't do our jobs if the country is second-guessing us."

Alimoren nodded. "You said you could help?"

"Not exactly." Hanlon's voice took on a note of iron. "Was this the first time?"

"Sir?"

"The first time you helped a thief break in."

Alimoren's eyes widened, and he stepped away from Hanlon. "Sir, I—"

"It's not going to take them long to put it together," the

Senator cut in. "If I could, the Secret Service and the MPD will be able to, as well. Someone with access to the White House had to tell Jenna Noura how to break in. Will the MPD find a copy of the employees' schedules on your laptop, Alimoren? Will they find the archivists' files of the fragment?"

Ten feet and ten miles away, Rachel closed her eyes as she heard her own suspicions bounced back at her. Poor Alimoren. Whether or not he had been involved in the break-in, Hanlon had found a way to ensure that all of the blame would be placed on a dead man.

She didn't catch the expression on Alimoren's face, but the sudden anger in his voice caused her avatar's eyes to snap open. Alimoren was furious. Drunk or not, innocent or not, he wasn't about to let Hanlon paint him as an accomplice to theft and murder. "No. No, sir, they won't. There's nothing to find."

"Are you sure?" Hanlon asked.

Alimoren's eyes widened. "What are you doing?"

"Don't lose your temper," Hanlon said. "I'm just here to talk. I didn't realize you were involved when I asked you to bring Agent Peng into the investigation."

"I'm *not* involved—"

"In case you're getting ideas about...ending...our conversation," Hanlon said as he held up his useless device, "I lied about this. It blocks everything but these glasses. I've been using them to record our conversation."

"Good!" Alimoren shouted. "I want this on record! I had nothing to do with the break-in. What evidence do you have that I did?!"

"Enough," Hanlon said, his cruel smile beginning to crack through his concerned façade.

"Prove it." Alimoren took a step towards Hanlon, enraged. "*Prove* it! You can't, can you? You called this meeting to get me to incriminate myself!"

Hanlon backed away from Alimoren, touching Zockinski's old glasses as if to remind the Secret Service agent that he was on camera. "Easy, Alimoren," the Senator said. "I can help you."

"I don't need your help!"

"Yes, you do," Hanlon said soothingly. "It's all about perception. If I'm wrong—if you're innocent—then you need me to help you deal with the media."

"I don't need your help," Alimoren said again. "I'll go to the press, tell them you're trying to set me up…" He trailed off, realizing he had no proof.

"They'll believe me," the Secret Service agent said. It sounded weak, even to Rachel. "After the OACET story, they'll believe me."

"No, they won't," Hanlon said. "How a story is framed in the media is only half of the problem—the other half is that the public already knows what they'll think about that story before they even hear about it. You could broadcast this meeting of ours to four hundred million people, and half of them would think it's a fake, and the other half would only be interested because they'd spot something in it which reaffirms their personal worldview.

"I'm sorry, Alimoren. Nobody will believe you. It's too convenient to think you're responsible."

"But I'm *not!*"

Alimoren took an aggressive step towards Hanlon, probably to do more shouting and waving. Rachel would never know.

She didn't hear the shot.

Part of Rachel knew what would happen even before Hanlon made a curious gesture with his arm, and spun to the side. She ran straight at Alimoren, trying to knock him out of the way, even as she knew that this version of her body wasn't made of anything more than photons, even as the top of his head dissolved into red and white and gray before her eyes.

"Oh," Hanlon said, as if he hadn't known it was coming. "Oh no."

Rachel heard him, heard Santino, heard Mare, all of them marking Alimoren's death in their own ways. The only two who were silent were her and Mulcahy, and she stayed silent because she was too stunned to speak.

Her avatar knelt beside Alimoren's body, trying to hold his brains in his skull with her useless fake hands. *Too late, too late, too late...*

"Agent Peng," Mulcahy said, and the rock-hard solidity of her boss's presence in her mind brought her back to herself.

She pulled her avatar from Alimoren to stand by Mulcahy's side.

A normal person who witnessed a shooting at close range would scramble for cover. Hanlon was doing this, perhaps a little more slowly than he should, but he needed to make sure his useless gizmo slipped from his hands and was accidentally kicked into pieces as he ran. It was only when he had reached the cover of the trees that he took out his phone and dialed 911.

He then did what no normal person would do: he crouched on the ground in a tiny ball, making himself as small a target as possible.

"It'd be more realistic if you ran," Mulcahy said, walking towards him in giant ground-eating strides. "It'd be more realistic if you shouted for help. In times like this, people without combat experience turn to the comfort of their community."

"He doesn't have one." Rachel didn't recognize her own voice. "He thinks he's above everybody else. That he doesn't need anybody else," she added, and steeled herself from turning to look at Alimoren on the ground behind her.

Shouts came from the direction of the Memorial, and flashlights began to cut through the trees.

"That's a mistake," Rachel said. At her feet, Hanlon was starting to uncurl as he called out to the police for help. "Nobody can make it on their own."

The first officer had reached Hanlon. The Senator was pure grace and gratitude, pointing in the direction of the shot, at Alimoren's body...

"You've made many mistakes over the last few years," Mulcahy said to the Senator. "We'll make sure this is the one that brings you down."

TWENTY-ONE

Santino was making coffee.

It had taken Rachel a long time to realize that her partner thrived on complications. It certainly wasn't true of his social life—the man detested high-maintenance people like slugs on his summer produce—but he thrived within structured tasks. The more effort that went into a chore, the more he enjoyed it. It was a way of thinking so antithetical to her own that she had problems processing it. Why bother to make coffee in something that looked like a meth lab when the end result tasted exactly the same as a standard drip coffeemaker?

He put the first cup on the table in front of her. *Okay,* she admitted to herself as the smell floated towards her. *It might be better than coffeemaker coffee.*

Santino took the chair beside her, abandoning his customary spot on their kitchen counter. It was a long, long time before he finally said, "I don't know what to do."

"I know," she replied. "Me neither."

"Did… Could we have…"

"No." Rachel shut him down. "Don't second-guess this. You and me? We did *nothing* to contribute to this clusterfuck. Alimoren was…"

She didn't know where to go from there. Alimoren was what? Involved? Innocent? Just a convenient target for a point Hanlon wanted to make?

"There were a lot of reasons Hanlon could have wanted him dead," she eventually said. "We start by finding the right ones. Once we do that, we'll have a better idea of Hanlon's motivation. Then we can end this."

Their kitchen smelled like good coffee and fresh bread. Once Mulcahy had decided there was nothing they could do about

Alimoren's murder, Becca had driven them home, and then gone out to an all-night grocery to stock their kitchen for them. Rachel guessed it was the only thing Becca felt she could do, as Rachel and Santino had gone into mourning, and she didn't entirely understand why. After an awkward hour of standing around and waiting for them to talk to her, she had kissed Rachel lightly on the cheek, and then run upstairs to hide in bed.

Rachel and Santino had left the groceries out. Rachel knew she should get up and put them away, but her legs didn't want to work.

"Tell me why you were shouting about the gun," Santino said.

She slumped over to rest her head on the table, and gasped as her chin pressed against her arm.

Santino reached over and turned her face towards the light. "You're starting to swell up," he said, and went to go put together an ice pack.

"The gun's...complicated," she said, exploring her face with her fingers. She had forgotten about the boxing match. Everything felt raw.

"Uh-huh," her partner said. He spread out an almost-clean dishtowel on the counter, and began to empty an ice tray into it. "I figured. You and Mulcahy knew what was about to happen."

"We didn't know it would be Alimoren," she said. Her excuse sounded evil and weak, even to her, and she was thankful she had the emotional spectrum turned off.

"But you did know it'd be somebody."

She flipped off her implant. The dark was almost a comfort. "Hanlon knew the Hippos were following him. We think that Noura's murder served two purposes—it removed her as a possible informant, and forced the Hippos to break cover. Sniper rifles are huge things, Santino. They're not what you see in the movies. It took Ami a few minutes to get into position after the car chase started, and when she needed to get to the hospital to help me, she had to leave it. She thought Ken would recover it for her. He was busy on the ground, and it...it didn't work out that way."

"Why did Ami have her rifle with her?"

Rachel didn't understand the question. She flipped her implant on to see her partner in curious yellows. "She was working. Why wouldn't she have her gun?"

"Because it's a… Forget it. Different cultures. Why would Hanlon want Ami's rifle?"

"Ballistics." This part of the story was solid ground for Rachel. "Ami used to be a government sniper. She's had her rifle for her entire career—its ballistic microstamp has got to be in some top-secret database you and I have never heard of. The only reason he'd want Ami's rifle is to frame her—and through her, OACET—for murder."

"But the gun Hanlon recovered wasn't Ami's rifle."

"No, but he thought it was. Mulcahy managed to swap Ami's gun out for an identical model."

"How?"

"I don't know," Rachel said, and the ground beneath her started to give way. "Just… Mulcahy used to be a spy, all right? He made Jason Bourne look like a kindergarten teacher. If anybody could pull it off, it's him. All I know is that Ami's rifle was locked in a box in the mansion's panic room at the same time that Alimoren died."

He handed her the dishtowel. Rachel pressed it against her chin, and felt the ice inside shift to mold against the contours of her face. It stung; she pushed through the pain until it had reformed as a cold, hard shell around her.

"Where did the replacement rifle come from?" Santino asked.

Rachel laughed into the ice pack. "It's got a long ownership history, but its most recent purchase was in Tallahassee during the Congressional winter recess, to a buyer whose information somehow didn't make it into the registry. Guess where Hanlon spent Christmas?"

"I hear Florida is nice two weeks out of the year," he replied.

"Yup."

"How did Mulcahy know he needed a duplicate of Ami's

gun?"

She shrugged. "He says he bought copies of all of the Hippos' favorite weapons, just in case. He's got resources. It wasn't that big a deal for him."

"Except..." Santino paused, wrestling with his red anger. "He knew there was a chance Hanlon would *use* those guns."

"I know," she said.

"I feel like an accomplice to murder," he said.

"Don't!" She slammed her left hand down on the table; a flash of pain cut across her scans. "We didn't put the gun in his hands. We definitely didn't pull the trigger. Those were *his* choices. I will not have you and Mulcahy beat yourselves up while that goatdick of a human being doesn't regret a fucking thing!"

Rachel found herself standing over him, shouting, the ice pack broken apart where she had lost her grip on the towel. She sent her scans down to the foundation of their home, and seized on the stability of the concrete, tracing the rebar running through the pad, long basket weaves of black embedded within the gray... *Slow down, it's not Santino you're mad at, slow down...*

"I'm sorry," she said.

"It's okay."

She came back to the table, and began to round up the ice cubes with little taps of her fingers. Their mail was everywhere, the cheap ink on the credit card offers starting to run beneath tiny flecks of melting ice. The ice puddled faster than she could get to it, and she swept the whole mess onto the floor with a small sob of frustration.

Santino let her cry herself out, his own colors a miserable gray. Then, once Rachel had dragged herself back to her chair and some semblance of stability, he pushed his own damp grays aside. "Better?"

"No. Let's work." She removed the 3D-printed replica of the fragment from her pocket, and slid it into the middle of the table. It spun, throwing ice and water as it traveled. "We need to go back to the beginning," she said. "We find out why Hanlon wanted the fragment of the Mechanism, we learn why he killed Alimoren."

"You're carrying that with you?"

"I liked it," she said. "Now it's…"

Santino knew the correct phrase. "Now it's a *memento mori*."

He was right: it wasn't just metal anymore; somehow it had turned into a reminder of Alimoren's death, and Noura's, and Ceara's, and that poor makeup artist whose name always escaped her…

She scanned the fragment, as if she could find what was different about it. Nothing. It was the same, and yet its story had changed.

"Come on," she said, standing. "I need you to drive me somewhere."

Santino had insisted she call ahead: Rachel had insisted there was no need. She had won on both counts. It was barely seven in the morning, but she had known Oscar McCrindle would be in his shop. They found him cleaning, the wreckage from broken drywall and old cinderblock slowly making its way from the front of his store to a dumpster in the back alley. She knocked on the store's plate glass window to get his attention, and the older man rushed to the door.

"Agent Peng!" McCrindle made a flapping motion, as if he wanted to hug her but didn't want to overstep. Instead, he ushered them into the Trout and Badger. "I… The news about… I'm so very sorry."

Rachel needed to bump his sympathetic wine reds around— *But he didn't even know Alimoren!*—before she spotted a familiar digitized green, and realized he was referring to Dunstan's news story of OACET's lost five years. "Oh," she said. "Right. Thank you."

"Agent…" McCrindle seemed unable to get past his sympathy for Rachel. It clung to him, smothering his thoughts, and his Australian accent was thicker than usual. "I'm so very sorry. What happened to you was terrible."

She took a deep breath, and found the pungent stench of ripe raccoons was gone. "The crime scene cleanup crew came by?"

"Yes. Yes! Thank you so much!" This, McCrindle could focus on. He flushed red, and showed her the hole where a buffalo's head used to be. "My lawyer's office received a court order to remove the bodies. I didn't even see a bill."

"They left a mess," she said. "If you want, I can—"

"No," McCrindle protested. "I asked them to leave it open. I want to put it back together myself. A labor of love, you understand?"

Santino smiled.

Lord, save me from kindred spirits, Rachel thought. Then, before Santino committed them to grief therapy via plaster repair, she asked McCrindle if he had been following the White House murder case.

"Yes, of course! It's the only story out there—well, it was, until it got swept away when the news of what happened to you broke. It's fascinating. Did you really recover a piece of the Antikythera Mechanism?"

"Yes," she replied. "You were right. The fragment had an inscription on it, and we now think the theft was done to recover that inscription. We were wondering if you could help us understand why it might be important."

"I'm not a specialist in ancient Greek translations," McCrindle said. "You should be consulting with a scholar, not an antiques dealer."

"Meet the scholar," she said, pointing to her partner. "Officer Raul Santino, and we only call him an officer because the MPD can't figure out what title to give a cop with multiple doctorates in a truly obscene number of disciplines. We've also consulted with a translator at the Smithsonian, and an expert mathematician in case the Mechanism could be applied to modern-day high-level mathematics. What we need is someone who can put it all in a general historical context."

"She says you tell good stories," Santino said. "And she says she needs a story, not another lecture, to put all of this into perspective."

"Oh," McCrindle gazed wistfully towards the hole in his store, a purple-gray sigh blowing over him. "Well, I'll do what I can. Coffee?"

"Please," Rachel said. The sun was up, and the sleepless hours were dragging on her.

McCrindle took them to the comfortable nook at the back of his store. "What did the inscription say?" he asked, as he plugged a canister into his coffee maker. "You don't happen to have it on you, by chance?"

"No, it's on its way back to Greece," Santino said, and McCrindle's shoulders and colors both sank. "But we've scanned the fragment, and the inscription is being translated. What we've got thus far makes it sound as though the Mechanism could also be applied to astrology."

"Ah," McCrindle said. "That makes perfect sense. Astrology was a significant aspect of astronomy during that era."

"Astronomy?" Rachel asked. "I was told that astrology was religious, not scientific."

"In a way, but our definition of religion is somewhat different than the ancient Greeks. We think of it as a form of worship. The Greeks thought of it as a way of understanding their world. Zeus explained the thunder, Apollo's chariot explained the cycle of day and night, that sort of thing. Gods created a context through which natural phenomena made sense."

McCrindle gave her the first mug. The coffee had an unpleasant chemical undertone, no doubt something left over from the effort of removing the dead raccoons, but she pushed through it to find the caffeine.

"At the time the Mechanism was crafted," McCrindle continued, "astrology was most closely related to fortune-telling, but a good astrologer needed to understand how the planets worked. Both astrology and astronomy were derived from the study of celestial phenomena, and both were used to define our place within the universe. Greek astronomy was very rough, of course—I think they only knew of four planets in the solar system? Five?—but we all have to start somewhere.

"If I remember correctly, the Mechanism could be used to plot how the planets moved, and to predict eclipses and other celestial events? And it worked backwards, where it could be used to observe celestial alignments on the date of a person's birth?"

"Yes," Santino replied. He took the second mug from McCrindle, and grimaced at the taste.

McCrindle didn't notice, lost in his story. "Then the Mechanism would have been invaluable to astrologers. A skilled astrologer needed to have an accurate understanding of celestial events, so he could accurately interpret the forces that governed human lives. This made astrologers somewhat of a cross between a scientist and a magician, you understand? If the heavens were a divine language of past, present, and future, then astrologers interpreted the word of the gods for humankind. They were a bridge between the worlds.

"I suppose," McCrindle said with a chuckle, "if you think about it from that point of view, the Mechanism was just another form of communications technology."

Rachel blinked.

And then, as easily as squeezing a silver juice pouch, the angles on the problem changed.

Hanlon, spinning the science of the implant out of data that nobody else seemed to have.

Mako, his old classroom blackboards holding a handful of known facts, and a hundred times that in unknown questions.

Santino's insistence that mathematics was made of constants that were governed by rules, and that understanding those rules changed how and why those constants functioned...

And Mulcahy, who knew why Hanlon wanted the Mechanism, but was unable to tell her.

The Mechanism isn't the only out-of-place technology in this case, she thought to herself. *I'm carrying around the other one in my head.*

She stood, and said in a voice that didn't sound like hers: "I need to make a call."

Rachel ran out to the alley behind the shop, and pinged Mulcahy.

He hadn't slept either, but where she was starting to waver around her edges, Mulcahy was simply not allowing himself to feel exhaustion. His presence in her mind was the same familiar steel. *"Penguin?"*

"I need information," she said. *"I'm going to ask you a series of questions about a possible connection between our implants and the Mechanism."*

Shock cut through their link. *"Rachel—"*

"No!" she shouted. *"No hedging, no wordplay. I need answers."*

He didn't reply. She wondered if she'd overstepped, if he'd break their connection and ignore her pings for the rest of the day.

"I'm considering it," he finally said, his double meaning carrying the slightest suggestion of humor. *"Ask. I've promised to protect this information, so I'm limited in what I can tell you."*

"I can work with that," she said. *"I don't need to know exactly how Hanlon intended to use the inscription on the Mechanism. I just need to know why he wanted it."*

"All right."

"Is there a connection between our implants and the Mechanism?"

More silence, until he answered, *"Probably."*

I was right, she thought to herself. *Or Mako was right… Throw a couple of millennia between technologies, and it's dinosaurs all the way down.*

"Don't get ahead of yourself," he said. This time, his humor was easier to feel. *"We're not completely sure there's a connection between them yet, but that's what Hope is going to Greece to learn."*

"Is Hanlon sure there's a connection?"

"Sure enough to try to rob the White House."

"Do our implants and the Mechanism operate on the same frequencies?"

"*What?*" Mulcahy's confusion bubbled up at her question. "*No. The Mechanism was clockwork—What does that even mean?*"

"*Talk to Mako. Did Hanlon think the Mechanism could be used to help him understand how our implant works?*"

"*Yes.*"

They don't operate the same way, she thought. *They don't use the same information, or serve the same function. McCrindle was basically pulling that comparison about communication technologies out of his ass...*

And then she had it. "*Was it something about how the Mechanism was made?*"

Another long pause, and then, "*Yes.*"

"*Last question. It's a big one.*"

"*All right.*"

"*Do I need to actually understand any of this bullshit to solve this case?*"

She felt him grin. "*No.*"

"*Thank fuck-all goodness for that small blessing. Never drop a case like this on me again. Bye.*"

"*Happy hunting, Penguin.*"

She waved her arms frantically through the window, then rapped on the glass, and then finally had to run back into the Trout and Badger to drag Santino away from the antiques dealer.

"I was too close to it," Rachel said, pulling her partner over to the dumpsters. "I thought Hanlon was trying to frame OACET for something—he's tried that before—but this isn't a frame job! This is his fucking exit strategy, and he's doing as much damage to us as he can on the way out!"

Rachel began to pace in circles, moving the pieces around in her head until the picture began to make sense to her.

"He wanted the Mechanism," she said. "That was his goal. That was why he hired Jenna Noura—she was the best thief-for-hire out there. He expected Noura to pull it off! If she did, none of the rest of this would have happened. But stealing an object from the White House is a long shot to begin with, so he put a backup plan into place in case Noura got caught."

"What did you say in Mulcahy's office?" she asked him, and kept going before he could reply. "Put yourself in Hanlon's position. He's *losing*. He knows he's losing his support with Congress, and Big Telecommunications is shifting their alliance to back us, not him. He knows there's a huge news story coming—the big one, the one that OACET's been waiting for, to drive the final nail in his coffin. When that news broke, it'd go badly for him, no matter what he did to try and get ahead of it.

"He's wealthy, famous, and politically connected. Which of those would you give up if you had to?"

"Politics," Santino said. He didn't need to think about his answer. "All you need to succeed in politics are the right connections. Fame and money will help you get those back, even if you burned yourself before."

"Exactly!" she said. "So, what do you do if you're rich, famous, and hold political office, and someone's about to yank all of that away from you?

"You make a sacrifice. Maybe you decide to give up the source of power you're least likely to miss. The easiest one to recover after the scandal blows over and the general public forgets the rumors about you. You start to set plans into motion that will allow you to bow out of politics.

"But do you say you want to spend more time with your family? No. That's what guilty people say. You want to make sure that there's so much confusion over what really happened that the media and the general public will never really know the conditions that caused you to leave. And you time it so the big career-ending revelation that OACET's been waiting for will break at the same time the public is focused on a murder in the White House. Because *White House!*"

Rachel realized that her circles had taken her over to the part of the alley where a single beam of sunlight managed to trickle down. She turned her head up to the sun and faced it. "And then," she said, "immediately after the news story that OACET's been waiting for hits the news cycle, the Secret Service agent who leads the investigation is murdered. Three major news stories—bang! bang! bang!—and the first and third are part of the same story. Oh gosh, a murder at the White House! Oh gosh, look at what Senator Hanlon did to those poor kids! Oh gosh, the Secret Service agent in charge of the White House murder investigation was assassinated!

"Now, given the limited space in the news cycle, and the abysmal attention span of the average American, which of those stories do you think the media would drop first?"

"I'll do you one better," Santino said. "What if the gun used to kill the Secret Service agent was the personal weapon of an OACET assassin?"

She froze as another piece of the puzzle clicked into place. "Jason's theory," she breathed. "Where it'd only take one big mistake to cause Congress and the public to turn on us, forever."

Santino nodded. "If Ami's gun were used in the murder, and the news of the brainwashing is still so fresh in everybody's minds, they'll assume Ami snapped."

"Not only that, but they'll assume OACET was involved in the break-in," Rachel said. "Those files on Noura's phone would incriminate—"

"What files?"

She knew the words were a mistake as soon as she had said them. Her partner's conversational colors froze, and then began to change into a furious red sunset against an icy winter sky.

"You went snooping around Noura's phone?" he asked. "You told me—"

He turned towards his car and left her standing in the alley.

Rachel flipped off her implant and counted to fifty in the dark, then went back into the Trout and Badger to retrieve her purse and to bid goodbye to McCrindle. A few minutes later, she tapped on the window of Santino's car before she let herself in.

"Did you tamper with the evidence?"

"Yes. Can we talk about this later? It isn't the time—"

"No!" He slammed a fist into the steering wheel so hard that Rachel thought the air bag might deploy on him. "It's *always* the time! That's the problem! These issues don't just stop when it's convenient!"

Rachel quickly slapped a heavy-duty shield around the car.

"Why the hell would you go and tamper with evidence?" he asked. "You and the rest of OACET walk around shouting that the law is this great shining object to be worshiped like a god, but it's... What? A selective god? An opt-in god?

"Shut the fuck up," she snapped. They both knew they were too tired to have this conversation. "You're as bad as I am. Five hours ago, I'm running an illegal search for the information for Hanlon's unlisted burner phone, and you have zero problems with it."

"There's a huge difference between retrieving information and tampering with evidence—"

"Not when both will get your case thrown out in court," she said.

"Yes, there *is* a difference!" Santino shouted. "Don't you think the general public would be more okay with a peek at a secure database instead of wiping information?"

Would you rather have someone prying into your emotions or spying on your naked body... Rachel shook herself to get rid of that thought.

"No!" she said. She ran her fingers through her short hair, feeling the bumps and bruises on her skin from the night before. "No, I don't! I think the general public'll be willing to believe the worst of us no matter what we get caught doing! Which is *why* I wiped those files, Santino! I'm trying my fuck-all hardest to make sure we're trusted, and those files would have ruined us! And they were all *lies!* I'm not going to feel like shit for erasing false information!"

He took a deep breath, then another, and he wrestled his reds down beneath professional blues. "Tell me what happened," he said, in a more normal tone of voice.

Rachel sighed, and gave him the version that wouldn't turn

the morning into a full-on confessional. "I found her phone, and wanted to know why she recognized me at the farmers' market. I poked around and did a brief search for my name. I found my name in one file, and when I went deeper, I found a whole bunch of data buried within the code. It was false information designed to make OACET look complicit in the White House robbery, and—"

"You *wiped code?*" Yellow-white panic erupted within his surface colors, and the professional blues bubbled away. "You can't just erase a file—"

"I know!" she shouted back. "I know! Jason taught me the basics, and I turned it over to him when I knew I was out of my depth. He's the one who wiped the false files, not me."

Relief moved up within him, choking out his panic.

"It's okay," she assured him. "I'm a terrible cyborg. I leave all of the tech stuff to the good ones."

"Jesus," he said. "Give me a heart attack, why don't you?"

"I know my limits," she said, and fought the urge to pout.

"Huh," he said, staring out the window. "Where was the first file stored?"

"It was hidden. Noura put it in her games applications."

"That's not hidden," Santino said. "That's just a superficial layer of camouflage. There's something I don't like about that, like…"

"Like what?"

"Let me play with that idea a little," he said. "Did you make a copy? I'd like to look at it."

"Jason backed up what he could to the OACET servers."

"What he could?"

"Some of it's gone," she said. "Permanently erased."

He glared at her, his anger sharpening to a point. "What aren't you telling me?"

"What I *can't!*" She was shouting again, eight inches from his face, and livid. "I wish you were part of the collective so I could tell you this shit! I really do! I wish I didn't have to use Jason as a runaround and I could just work with you! But I *can't*, so we both have to deal with that, okay?!"

He pounded the steering wheel again.

Then they just sat there.

"You running emotions?" Santino finally asked.

"Yeah."

"Turn them off," he said. And added, after a moment, "Please."

She did, and he went from furious reds to a man sitting in a too-small vehicle, his head propped on his hand as he rested his arms on the window ledge. It was about as far away as he could get from her while still remaining in the car, and she realized her own posture was mirroring his. She took her arm off of the ledge, and slumped down in her seat.

"What would you have done?" she asked. "If you found a bunch of lies that would have done serious damage to you and your…uh…"

"My community?"

"That works, I guess. I'd also go with 'family.'"

"I don't know," he said. "I do know if this gets out, your reputation is ruined. Not OACET's—yours."

"OACET's too, probably," she said. "Jason's one big thing, the excuse they need to pull us all down."

"Yeah," Santino said. He started the car, and pulled into the morning traffic.

"I'm sorry I told you to shut up," she said, as she dropped her shield.

"You do that all the time." He made a meaningless gesture with one hand. "Sorry I jumped to conclusions."

They went a few miles down the road without speaking. Santino found a drive-thru. They got coffee and doughnuts, and sat in the parking lot as they ate. The caffeine and calories brought them back to their senses, and they both felt the last five hours settle in their stomachs. Rachel wrapped up her third doughnut and dropped it back in the paper sack.

"I'm not okay with you wiping evidence," Santino said.

"I'm not okay with it either," she replied. "But when you see it, you'll understand why I did it."

"I understand *now*," he sighed. "That's the problem."

"Yeah," she said. "I don't know if it helps, but it was buried deep. So deep, anyone searching the phone might not have found it."

"That's not how it works. The FBI would have hooked it up to a data processor…" he started to say, and she gave him a mild glare.

He laughed. A little. But it was enough.

"We need to have another conversation about the slippery slope," Rachel said. "If we don't, you won't stop wondering what's going on behind the scenes with me."

Santino shrugged. "I don't think I'll ever stop wondering," he said. "That's part of the problem, too."

"Yeah," she said again.

"Ever since last October…"

He trailed off, and she took a chance by reaching over and poking him in his short ribs. "Ever since October, what?"

"You said something that didn't sit right with me. You implied…"

She had wondered when this would finally come up. "I implied I would have let the bombers get away with it," she said. "*If* if had benefited OACET. It didn't, so it wasn't an issue."

He didn't reply, and she was now glad she wasn't running emotions. "Santino, if you haven't guessed by now, I'll do anything I have to if it'll protect OACET. They're my family. You protect your family. Tooth and claw, if necessary."

"I know," he said. "I get that. On one level, I understand all of this, but on another level…"

She nodded, and wished she could crack the window; the longer they aired these things out, the smaller the car became, but it was the breakfast hour and the parking lot was packed. "Which is why we need to start talking about this again. We used to talk about this—we used to spend *hours* talking about the law."

"Would it make a difference? Will talking about the law change how you look at your job?"

She thought about that. "I don't know. I'd like to say yes, but I'd need a really good reason to prioritize the law above OACET."

Santino huffed, and she felt the car get a little smaller as his anger came back.

"Hey, I'm being honest," she said. "I try not to lie to you."

"You *try?*"

"Like I said," she sighed. "I wish you were part of the collective."

There was silence between them again. Not an uncomfortable silence like before; this one was sad, and more than a little lonely.

"Where were we?" Rachel finally asked.

"Stuck," he said, willing to return to the case to take his mind off of possibilities. "Do we have any proof at all that Hanlon was involved in the theft, or in…"

He stopped himself, unable to revisit Alimoren's murder.

"No," Rachel said, charging ahead. "We know that Hanlon and Alimoren were on speaking terms, and Summerville hinted that Alimoren helped him learn the schedules of people in the White House, so it's very possible he might have passed Hanlon some information. But we know that he wasn't Noura's contact."

"Do we?"

She thought back over last night's meeting, where Hanlon tried to entrap Alimoren into making a confession. "Yeah," Rachel said. "What was it that Hanlon said? It's too convenient to believe Alimoren was responsible? I think that's true."

"We need to go back to the farmers' market," Santino said. "Not, you know, physically, but that was where Noura was supposed to hand off the fragment to its buyer. It's too much to hope that Hanlon would be there to pick it up personally, right?"

She snorted into her coffee.

"That's what I thought," he said. "But we've been to her motel room. It had one of those dinky safes in it. The fragment is fragile, and Noura wouldn't have taken it out of her room if she didn't have a reason, so…"

"Yeah," Rachel agreed, as she dabbed at the coffee she had blown all over her shirt. She gave up when her scans hit on some blood left over from her boxing match with Hope. No wonder poor McCrindle hadn't known what to say to her: she was eight kinds of a mess. "Noura didn't go to that famers' market by accident. There was a handoff planned. We find the other person on the end of the handoff, we're one step closer."

"Alimoren was already there," Santino said, without a moment's pause. Then, he ran the timeline through his head. "Wait, no. That doesn't work. Alimoren never planned to be at the market. We brought him there."

"Maybe he *had* planned to be there," Rachel admitted. "The hotel was close enough to the market so he could sneak out, pick up the fragment, and come right back."

"True."

Her stomach grumbled, and she found herself fishing her uneaten doughnut out of the bag. "Maybe we should assume it was Alimoren," she said. "We all know Noura was going to the market to meet someone, but that's turned into a dead end. The Secret Service has already done all they can to find any possible suspects who were there."

"We haven't," Santino said. "Maybe we should check Hanlon's known associates and see if anyone was there to do him a favor."

"That's not a bad idea," she said, and reached into the back seat to get her purse. "Let's make a call and find out."

"Call who?"

"More of a what," she muttered, as she passed her tablet to Santino so he could be part of the conversation.

She sent her mind out, across the city, to Jason's office. *"Lulu."*

The computer's almost-feminine voice was politely curious, but it didn't have the capacity to sound surprised. Still, that was the impression Rachel got when she opened their connection.

YES, AGENT PENG?

"Lulu, did the Secret Service send over the videos from the Dupont Circle Farmers' Market?"

YES, AGENT PENG.

"Have you completed the facial imaging scans from that day?"

YES, AGENT PENG.

"Was anybody at the farmers' market involved in the Jenna Noura case?"

PLEASE REPHRASE, AGENT PENG.

"Oh hell," she muttered aloud, and grasped around for a query a computer would understand.

Santino jumped in. "Lulu, we're looking for a connection between anyone who was at the farmers' market and Senator Hanlon. Can you cross-reference all persons who were at the market with known associates of Hanlon?"

YES, OFFICER SANTINO. Lulu's disembodied voice came from the tablet.

Santino glanced at Rachel, and she shrugged to let him know she hadn't instructed Lulu to switch its operational status and talk directly to him. "Smart computer," she whispered.

THANK YOU, AGENT PENG. OFFICER SANTINO?

"Yes, Lulu?"

NO PERSONS AT THE MARKET FIT THAT PROFILE.

Santino wasn't ready to quit. "What database did you use?"

OACET'S ROSTER OF HANLON'S KNOWN ASSOCIATES, Lulu said.

Santino sighed and let himself fall back in his seat. "Thank you, Lulu."

YOU'RE WELCOME, AGENT PENG.

"Will you update us if you find a connection between people at the market and…Hanlon's…things?" Rachel asked.

There was a brief pause during which Rachel could have sworn Lulu was judging her. YES, AGENT PENG. WILL THAT BE ALL?

"Yes. Thank you, Lulu."

GOODBYE, AGENT PENG.

Santino went to flip the cover on her tablet closed, but she stopped him.

"Hang on," Rachel said. "I'm sure we're on to something.

What if…"

"What if what?"

"What if Lulu used the wrong database?" She reached out to the computer again, speaking aloud for Santino's benefit this time. "Lulu? Follow-up query."

YES, AGENT PENG? came the computer's voice from the tablet.

"Are there any…uh…are there connections between any person or persons who were at the farmers' market, and any person or persons who have been profiled as possible threats by OACET?"

"Include both past and present threats," Santino added.

Rachel had expected Lulu to need some time to process her query, but the computer's reply was immediate. YES, AGENT PENG.

Her fingers knit within the fabric of her tee-shirt. "Display name, please."

"Summerville…" Santino's soft gasp came before she could read the name. "Is this the guy who came to our *house?*"

"Yes," she replied. In her mind, the links between Summerville and Alimoren began to fill themselves in.

"It's not enough," Santino said. "This is the textbook definition of circumstantial. We need actual hard evidence to put him at the scene, like DNA or—"

"It might be enough to get a warrant ," she said. "OACET's a federal organization. We conduct threat assessments just like the CIA or the NSA. This would be setting a precedent for our files, though."

"No judge is going to give you a warrant based on nothing but a general facial recognition hit from a crowd during a busy day," Santino said. "Not even Edwards."

"Well, we might not be able to get a warrant," she said. "But we can still get what we need."

TWENTY-TWO

Over her brief tenure in OACET, she had visited more mansions than her eight-year-old self would have thought possible—hell, she had been to a party at the White House just this past week—but she had never seen a room like this one. Teak and brass chased each other in thick stripes through the floor and into the ornate wainscoting. The walls were plastered in that one dark maroon that could only be put to proper use by the super-rich, and the paintings were by artists whose names she actually recognized.

It screamed wealth and privilege, and she felt woefully out of place.

The receptionist was in the middle of her early morning chores when Rachel and Hill barged through the last set of doors. Rachel was wearing her best suit, the one she wore when she knew there would be at least one press conference at the end of the day, but it was still far below the pay grade of those who usually came this far into Summerville's inner sanctum. She thought her suit was the reason the receptionist was gaping at her, until she remembered her face looked like a half-made sausage.

"Agent Peng?" Randy Summerville, going over the day's tasks with his receptionist, was bright yellow in surprise at finding her in his office. He took in her face, Hill's arm in its sling… The yellow surprise turned into red concern. "What happened to you? This wasn't from the car chase, was it? I saw you right after that happened!"

"Detective Hill's injuries were from the chase. Mine were received in an unrelated incident," she said, as she managed the twinned thoughts that Summerville's information network needed an overhaul, and also that '*A Series of Unrelated*

Incidents' might be an excellent name for Hope Blackwell's fists. "May we talk in private?"

"Yes, of course," he said. "Danielle, we'll take coffee on the patio."

Patio? We're four stories up, how could there be a...

But Summerville's office had a wall made of windows and a set of ornate French doors, and these opened onto a patio with a glorious view of the monuments. There were enough container plants to make Santino weep in envy, and a set of furniture made from the same rich teak as was found in Summerville's office.

There was even a rug. Not one of those tacky indoor-outdoor affairs, but an authentic Persian antique carpet. Rachel's heart went out to the poor maintenance man whose job it was to roll it up every night, and wondered what Summerville did when it started to rain.

Her scans hit on Jordan Summerville puttering about the patio, grooming the ground around the plants for dead leaves before today's schedule began, and realized the kid's job probably included carpet duties. His uncle tried to chase him off, but Rachel stopped him—Jordan needed to hear what she had to say.

"This isn't a personal call," she said, taking a seat on a nearby couch. "It's related to the White House break-in."

Both uncle and nephew went a little red at that. "What do you mean?" Randy Summerville asked.

She had dreaded this meeting. One misstep, and the possibility of an alliance between OACET and the telecommunication industry might vanish.

And, God help her, she actually liked Randy Summerville.

"As you know, OACET is a federal agency," she began. "We conduct our own threat assessments, as do the NSA, the FBI, the CIA, and numerous other agencies. One of our analysts checked for possible connections between OACET and the White House murder." Technically true: she supposed Lulu qualified as an OACET analyst, even though the computer itself had been bought and paid for by the MPD. "We took the security footage from the Dupont Circle Farmers' Market, and we ran it through our own threat models. We were surprised when facial recognition got a hit."

Yup. There's the flash of red.

"Why are you here, Agent Peng?" Summerville asked, his conversational colors beginning to shutter themselves.

"I'd like to state for the record that we don't have a warrant," she said. "Your compliance is completely voluntary—"

"*My* compliance?"

"Sorry," Rachel said, holding up her hands for peace. "I didn't mean to be vague. That wasn't directed towards you… We're here for your nephew."

Summerville's colors locked themselves down. Behind him, Jordan's panicked red flared, fire-bright.

Hill touched Rachel's shoulder in warning; whatever he had spotted in Jordan was as accurate as watching his conversational colors was for her.

"As I said, we don't have a warrant," Rachel said. "We're merely eliminating potential suspects. We've recovered DNA from a victim. It's saliva trace—it looks like she hit her assailant in the mouth before he killed her."

Jordan's hand twitched, as if he was keeping himself from touching a half-remembered injury. Rachel remembered the first time she had seen him, during the reception at the White House, when his colors showed he had taken a solid punch to the face.

"We're collecting samples." She reached into her jacket pocket, and took out a laboratory-grade mouth swab in its sealed container. "This is only to eliminate possible—"

"No!" Rachel thought this was the first time she had ever heard Jordan speak. His voice was deeper than she had expected, and hoarse from stress. "*Hell* no!"

His uncle's colors fell to grays.

"Maybe you should call your family's lawyer," Rachel told him.

The lobbyist nodded. "Please leave, Agent Peng. If you're able to get a warrant, feel free to contact us."

"Right," Rachel said. "Thank you for your time."

Beside her, Hill took out his phone and hit a single button. There was a pause, and then he said, "Lawyered up. Go ahead and process it."

"We'll see you in a few hours," Rachel said to Jordan. "It'll take about that long to run the other sample."

"What sample?" The kid's panicked yellows started to whip around him. "I didn't give you permission to take a sample!"

"Officer Santino followed you to work this morning. You threw your Starbucks cup in the gutter. He's got the cup in evidence, so—"

Jordan Summerville took off.

Rachel knew from those whipping yellows that Jordan had been looking for an escape route. She had expected him to cut around her and Hill towards the French doors, and then run straight into Zockinski who was standing guard by the receptionist's desk. Or, if Jordan was clever, he'd find Santino waiting for him in the side stairwell.

She didn't think he'd jump over the edge of the patio.

"Fuck!" Hill shouted.

"It's okay!" she said, as she spotted Jordan on the fire escape six feet below. "It's not a suicide! C'mon!"

Rachel threw off her suit coat, and scouted around for a place to store her gun before she noticed Hill. The big man was still seated on his chair by the doors, statue-still.

He pointed at his injured shoulder.

"Aw!" Rachel groaned, and handed her gun to Hill. His colors changed to curious yellows.

"There's no way in hell I'm going to chase down this kid when armed," she said, looking at Summerville as she spoke.

"It's policy," Hill said.

"MPD policy, maybe," she said. "I'll bring him back unharmed," she promised Summerville.

The lobbyist didn't reply, his colors angry reds and mournful grays, and she couldn't help but wonder if a possible future had gone up in smoke.

And then she was gone.

A clean jump over the side of the balcony, and six feet down to where her feet clanged on the top landing of the fire escape. She had decided to be good to her much-abused body today, and was wearing her most comfortable work shoes, the ones where the sides and the soles were made from the same buttery-soft leather. These were perfect for her controlled fall down the side of the building, letting her grip each stair and every rung of the ladder as she descended from floor to floor. By the time she reached the ground, she had nearly caught up to Jordan.

As soon as she began running, she realized they were the worst shoes she could have worn. The alley was covered in broken glass and pieces of metal, and she felt each of these press through the thin soles. She slowed her pace and picked her way across the mouth of the alley, and spotted Jordan as he raced across the busy street.

"I am *not* doing this again," she muttered, and hailed a passing cab.

The cabdriver was a good sport. For twenty bucks and a story about a lover's quarrel, he was happy to follow Jordan at a discreet distance. It gave Rachel plenty of time to send the signal on Jordan's phone to Santino, and she watched in relative comfort as the kid's colors began to ease from fiery panic to the ruddy grays of stress. She watched as Jordan ducked into a coffee shop, and told the cabdriver to let her off at the next block.

Rachel looped around to the rear entrance of the coffee house, her implant firmly fixed on the signal from Jordan's phone. She flashed her badge to the startled barista, a finger pressed against her lips while she pointed towards the busy main room of the café.

He's not here… she thought, scanning the crowd for Jordan's core of sun-drenched purple velvet. But the signal from his phone was bright and strong, and she chased it down to where it lay beneath a nearby table: Jordan had ditched it so he couldn't be tracked.

"Fuckin' perfect," she muttered, as she sent her scans out in all directions.

She chased core colors up and down the nearby streets, as far as she could push herself without bringing on a headache, and when that didn't hit on Jordan, she expanded her range. So many people within these four city blocks, not just running wild on the ground, but all stacked on top of one another in rooms within rooms within buildings, or down along the highway a few streets away, an anthill of color, and so many of them were purple…

There.

She sent a brief apology to her feet, and began to run.

This time, her race through the streets wasn't even close to her relentless pursuit of Noura. She kept herself one street over from Jordan, and was able to jog towards him at a sensible pace. There was no traffic to dodge, no pedestrians to run over. Jordan thought he was safe, and while his conversational colors kept a trace of her Southwestern turquoise, he was mostly focused on the professional blues of the police. Rachel had no problem cutting down one street to run parallel to him, and then taking the next turn to bump into him at the corner.

"You're lucky I like your uncle," she said, as she clicked the cuffs on his left hand.

He hit her.

She saw it coming, and tracked the movement of his right fist as it came straight at her. But getting the cuffs on him had brought her in too close: it was either take it and keep her hold on the cuffs, or drop them and get out of his way, and she made the mistake of thinking, *Hey, what's one more fist to the face, anyhow?*

It wasn't nearly as powerful as one of Hope's insane haymakers, but her face was a step removed from ground beef and the new pain shooting through the old was *astonishing.* Rachel couldn't help but sputter, and she yanked Jordan towards her by the handcuffs.

Another mistake: he followed up by hitting her straight in the throat.

She was sure it had been a lucky shot. Jordan had all of the fighting finesse of a kid on the playground. And she still went down, gasping for air.

He kicked her in the face.

Broken noses were a force unto themselves. Rachel curled up in a ball on the sidewalk, and tried to breathe around the blood. Her scans took on a fuzzy halo, and her brain got the message that if she wanted to pass out for a while, her body would be totally okay with that.

She found her feet, and took off after Jordan.

Rachel knew she was a *sight*. There were fewer pedestrians out this way, and more cars, and the sight of a bloodied, battered Chinese woman running like hell on fire was literally stopping traffic. Jordan had managed to put some distance between them, but he had nowhere to go and he knew it. One block south, he was standing on the edge of the road, searching for something—a taxi, a bus, *anything*!—to take him away from the Agent.

Rachel kept going.

She knew she didn't have much left in the tank. Agent or not, she still needed air, and between her broken nose and the punch to her throat, she was doing an excellent impersonation of Darth Vader on the last lap of a four-minute mile.

Just another block, she promised herself.

Jordan looked over his shoulder and saw Rachel charging straight at him down the middle of the sidewalk. His colors went white in shock, then bloomed bright yellow in fear, and he picked up speed.

He was trapped: the street had turned into a four-lane straight shot, an overpass above the interstate entering the tunnel just below them, and Jordan wasn't fast enough to get to the other side before she caught up.

Rachel knew she had him.

Except the panicky kid decided his best option was to hop the low concrete barrier.

"Oh come *on!*" Rachel shouted.

She stopped running the instant Jordan became his own hostage situation, the kid dangling himself above a highway full of traffic, his footing barely there on a tiny ledge, his arms wrapped around the thick metal handrail running along the top.

"Jordan?" she shouted, as she sent a text to Santino's phone that said something along the lines of *Backup, now!* and *Where the fuck are you?*

"Stay away!" the kid shouted back at her. He was searching frantically for a way out, not realizing until too late that there wasn't one.

"I am," Rachel assured him. "I don't want anything to happen to you. Let's get you out of this."

"Leave! I'll come back up once you're gone!"

"I can't do that," she said. "I can't just walk away from a possible jumper. Regulations, you understand. What if your arms get tired? I have to be close enough to help you.

"You've got all of the power here," she assured him. She was inching closer to him, slow and steady. "All I can do is make sure I give you what you need. What do you need, Jordan?"

The look the kid gave her was almost hot enough to sear her bruised skin. Rachel shrugged. "Listen, I *have* to try," she said. "Give me something. We'll make it work."

Her mind was split between her senses. Sirens, growing louder by the moment; Jordan's colors, tripping between fear and panic; the pain of her broken nose, her face, her feet where she had run straight through the thin soles of her shoes...

Jordan saw the truck coming before she did. She had her scans fixed on him, not on the traffic beneath him, and it was only when she saw the complex colors of hope well up within him did she stop to look around.

"Oh my God," she gasped. "Jordan, *don't!*"

Fuck Hollywood, she thought. *Fuck those movies where the hero leaps from the bridge onto the speeding semi...*

Jordan readied himself to jump.

She almost didn't make it. She wouldn't have, if Jordan hadn't decided at the very last moment that he was about to do something irrecoverably, unsurvivably stupid, and hesitated.

It was just enough time for Rachel to grab the back of his shirt.

She *hauled*, throwing all of her weight and muscle into keeping him on the ledge. Fabric tore, but you get what you pay for: Jordan's expensive dress shirt held together long enough for Rachel to wrap both arms around his waist.

She couldn't lift him over the barrier, and Jordan was too heavy to hold up on her own. The kid spun in her arms to grab the handrail, and Rachel seized the cuff dangling from his left hand. The handrail was too thick around to accept the cuff—her own wrist wasn't. She jammed her right arm through the gap between the concrete barrier and the handrail, and ratcheted the cuff shut. Short of a key or an amputation, neither of them was going anywhere.

She heard the sounds of sirens dying, of Santino shouting, and her heart lifted to find her partner running towards her. In another minute, ninety seconds at the most, none of this would be her responsibility anymore.

Rachel turned her full cyborg stare on Jordan. His colors, already yellow and trembling, blanched as the bloodied woman with the cold, unmoving eyes glared at him.

"You are *so* fucking lucky I like your uncle."

TWENTY-THREE

He was the picture-perfect image of a broken man forced to pack up his office. If he hadn't been wearing Santino's glasses and a Bluetooth headset, Rachel might have actually believed that ex-Senator Richard Hanlon hadn't meant to reactivate the burner phone.

"What!" she snapped, as her avatar stepped into the open air beside him.

He would never go to prison.

If Rachel had had any lingering doubts about whether the justice system could hold Hanlon accountable, the last seventy-two hours had dispelled those forever. Jordan Summerville's full confession that Hanlon had masterminded the entire scheme wasn't supported by the physical evidence. Nobody actually believed that a Secret Service agent and a twenty-five-year-old kid could hire a master thief, let alone an elite team of hit men, but there were emails on Jordan's home computer showing that he and Alimoren were responsible for the White House break-in and its aftermath.

However, according to Hanlon, the damage was done.

Hanlon had put on a brave face, and had marched to his last press conference as a sitting Senator. He said that he was unable to serve as an effective political representative, not when the news cycles continued to churn out misinformation about his role in Recent Unsavory Events. He had been involved, yes, but on the periphery! Someone at his company had officially sanctioned the mental conditioning of those poor young people who had grown up to become OACET Agents, but not *him*. Nor was he responsible for Mitch Alimoren's murder. His heart went out to poor Alimoren's family, but those files on Alimoren's laptop proved he was involved—oh, and don't forget that Jordan

Summerville's DNA was on Joanna Reed's body, so pretending Jordan was an innocent child was ludicrous—but Hanlon's own involvement in these horrific events was circumstantial. In spite of this, he felt he could not remain a public figure. Not when such problematic news stories continued to pop up. This…*gossip*…distracted from his obligations as a Senator. He could not, in good conscience, remain in office when he was so frequently singled out within the media.

It was a lovely speech, short and to the point: Hanlon had decided to resign.

Everyone in OACET had watched it live.

Nobody had cheered.

"Why doesn't this feel like a victory?" she had asked Mulcahy, standing cold and silent beside her.

"Because if Hanlon's not responsible, the only other group that's been involved in each event is OACET," he replied. *"He's implied everything that's been said about him is slander, and he's stepping down because we'll never stop coming after him."*

"He's let us turn him into a martyr," she realized.

"It was his best option," Mulcahy said.

And that had put her mental hamster back on its wheel.

Rachel had paced, and thought, and had written it all down in a brand-new notepad, and reviewed those notes again, and had finally brought her theory to Santino. As he listened, her partner took on a halo of bright red rage, and she knew she was right.

Hanlon had waited two whole days after the press conference to slide the battery back into the burner phone.

Rachel and Santino had anticipated the call. After all, why carry out an elaborate master plan if you can't delight in the details? If Rachel had had her way, she'd have surged that battery and turned the phone into a hollow plastic wafer, but she rarely had her own way anymore. *(Hiveminds. What an unwieldy bitch of a thing.)* So when Hanlon called, she stepped into her avatar, and then into the open air of his office.

"Agent Peng? What a—"

"No, it's *not* a surprise. Go ahead. Gloat. I'm recording this for Agents Mulcahy, Glassman, and Murphy. They couldn't make it. They're busy with Senate hearings. You know how it is.

"Oh, sorry," she said, with a little sigh. "My bad. You *knew* how it *was*."

Hanlon's eyes narrowed.

"Yeah," she said. "We got you on that point. You can tell yourself you swept the awards, if it makes you feel better, but you're still going back to California thanks to us."

"I don't know what you—"

"Shut up." Rachel cut him off again. "I love how you're able to see me now, by the way. What's your excuse? You heard about Santino's prototype, and finally managed to get your own pair of glasses to work?"

"Of course," he said, settling himself on a corner of his desk.

"Right. Whatever. Listen, I'll make this short. We both know you're not going to incriminate yourself, so I'll do the talking. You can...I don't know, cough three times or something if I get it wrong, okay?"

She began to pace the length of Hanlon's office. It was nowhere as nice as Summerville's, but that was simply a matter of scale. Normal people would still find it overly opulent, with its old wood and marble, and far too many framed awards. Its large arched window had a view of a grassy park. She wondered who had used Hanlon's office before him, and who would come after.

The system kept turning.

"Let's just recognize I'm outraged by this entire case," Rachel said. She felt Santino's hands on her own, back in their kitchen, as he shoved paper towels in her fists to keep her from ripping open her own palms with her fingernails. "So when I say that I'm pissed that you tried to manipulate me into taking down OACET, that's me cranking it up to eleven.

There was the slightest twitch at the corner of Hanlon's mouth. She couldn't tell if it was the beginnings of a smile, or irritation that she had figured it out.

"This past year must have been really hard on you," she said. "Knowing that we were sitting on the brainwashing scandal. You must have been doing the same thing we were—watching reporters close in on the information, see how close they were getting to the truth... The cover story that someone else in your organization made a command decision would work for a little while, but there're too many documents out there with your signature on them, too many of your former employees who have gone missing... Most are probably dead, but I bet one or two of them went into hiding once they realized what you were capable of. It'd be really inconvenient for them to turn up and bust your lies.

"And while this was happening, you were also starting to lose your supporters. Your alliance with the telecommunications industry was beginning to fail, because you'd made promises you couldn't keep. Some of them were starting to look at OACET as a solution instead of a problem. Randy Summerville? Must have hurt when he stopped returning your calls. He was spending time with Judge Edwards—Remember him? He used to be on your team, too—and toying around with different strategies that could resolve the OACET crisis. You probably *freaked* when you realized none of these strategies included you.

"I bet that's when you decided to recruit Jordan," Rachel said. "Wouldn't have been hard. Kid went everywhere with his uncle. He was also rabidly anti-OACET; fifteen minutes on Google could have told you that. He must have looked like a gift from God.

"So you snatched him up. Told him to delete all of his online history that was anti-OACET—you and I know you can't get pee out of the public swimming pool, but he probably didn't—and he started feeding you information from inside Summerville's office."

She took a breath. She knew she was rushing ahead, tripping over her words, and prayed Hanlon would think she was simply furious.

Not terrified. *Of course* she wasn't terrified. Not of this man who had nearly managed to ruin her life a second time...

She took another breath.

"You knew Mulcahy stuck the Hippos on you," she said, once she had found her equilibrium. "They've been watching you for months, but you couldn't do anything about them without tipping your hand. All you could do was convince some poor kid to hire a thief for the greater good.

"What did you tell him? That the Mechanism would solve all of your problems? That it contained knowledge from an ancient civilization that would save the world? Damn, you got lucky you found someone so young and stupid, didn't you?"

Hanlon did a funny thing with an eye as he turned away to begin packing another box. It might have been a wink; she couldn't be sure.

"So, we get it," she said. "We get that you wanted the fragment of the Mechanism, and that when Noura screwed the pooch, you put your backup plan into action. We get that you were playing the news cycle to bow out with your reputation intact.

"And..." Rachel paused. Her avatar glanced around Hanlon's office, looking for the nearest concrete, before she laughed aloud at her mistake. It was an odd, grating laugh, and she had the impression that Hanlon's colors moved slightly towards an uncertain orange. "...we get that I'm the reason you told Alimoren to bring my team into the case. We didn't need to work the White House robbery—we *shouldn't* have been there! But I've been kicking you since the Glazer incident, and you decided that as long as you were leaving, you'd try and take me down on the way out.

"If it had worked, you'd have struck a serious blow to OACET, and probably removed me from the battlefield. Incriminated me, and put me in jail, or worse. And you would have bought yourself some more time."

"Oh?" Hanlon cocked his head, feigning interest. "How so?"

Rachel wanted to rant, wanted to get it out of her system, wanted to tell Hanlon that she *knew!*

She couldn't.

Hanlon wasn't the only one who had to worry about self-incrimination. Mulcahy, Josh, Mare…everyone in OACET's Administration would watch this confrontation with Hanlon. And since she was out-of-body, she couldn't easily throw up a shield to block anything that might have been recording from Hanlon's end. She didn't detect any equipment within his office, but that didn't mean it wasn't there. She knew she wasn't a very good cyborg.

Hanlon knew that, too. In fact, he had counted on it.

Jordan Summerville had admitted that he was Noura's contact. He had been the one to meet the cat burglar when she came to town. Noura had insisted that she manage her own security, so Jordan never saw her except at predetermined meeting places. The Dupont Circle Farmers' Market had been one of these, where they had planned for Noura to deliver the fragment of the Mechanism.

Jordan had also said that while he had been the one who gave Noura the phone with the details of the White House and other necessary information, the phone had originally come to him from Hanlon.

Rachel had been rather proud of herself when she found the first layer of files on that phone. She was notoriously bad with technology, right? But there it was, a hidden file, with a little piece of text that would incriminate her, and she had been the one to find it.

If Rachel had never found that phone, the Secret Service would have run it through their data processors and turned up a digital ton of misinformation about OACET. This would have caused problems, sure, but they had handled misinformation before.

On the other hand…

If Rachel managed to find the phone, and *if* she found that one file with her information in it, Hanlon had assumed she would erase that one line which implied she would help Noura escape. Once the Secret Service got their hands on the phone and ran it through their data processors, they'd find evidence of tampering. They would recover the deleted information, and then dig deeper to find the red herring files he had buried.

It would be easier to believe the information in those files if it could be proven that an Agent already had something to hide.

It was a series of *might-have-happeneds* that would have come from a single moment of panic, and not knowing how data storage and retrieval worked. If she had stumbled into Hanlon's trap, she could have undone a year's worth of work to prove that OACET could be trusted. At best, she'd have been asked to leave the MPD; at worst, the public's fears about OACET would have been confirmed.

It had been a very near miss, and she had already taken Jason out to dinner to thank him for being a very good teacher. It hadn't been his fault that she had sprung Hanlon's trap, but he was the reason she had escaped it without having to gnaw off a leg.

"Agent Peng?" Hanlon was waiting, a tiny grin twisting the edges of his mouth. "There was something you wanted to say?"

"Yup," she said. "You tried to get Jordan Summerville to kill himself, and to blame me for that before he went."

She spun out the story about Hill's interrogation, in which Jordan had said Hanlon had warned him that he should never allow Agent Rachel Peng to put her hands on him. "Worse than death" had been the phrase of the hour. There was a suicide note already mocked up on his computer, just in case. Unfortunately for Hanlon, the kid wasn't on board with that idea.

(Really, learning the toxicity of the poison that Hanlon had dripped in the kid's ear had infuriated Rachel. Nowhere near as much as nearly getting caught in Hanlon's technology trap, but still. Trying to frame her for driving a kid to suicide… New low.)

Hanlon gave a little sigh as he realized that whether she knew what he had done or not, she wouldn't spill it on tape.

"It's hard," she said consolingly. "You were *so* close. I don't know who would have believed that I was responsible for the kid's death, but if someone had filmed it happening…

"Oh wait!" she said. "They *did!* Not his death, though. More like me *saving his life.* Did you see that one video that's got a close-up on my hand, and it's sort of turning blue because I chained myself to Jordan to make sure he couldn't fall and get smushed into goo on the interstate?"

He didn't reply, but a few books hit the bottom of an empty box with a loud *bang!*

"Well, we can't always predict which stories will play on the news," she said. "I can't, anyhow. You must have been furious when you learned I was the driver in that car chase. You had the news cycles so tightly mapped out, you couldn't have taken advantage of that without shifting your schedule."

She took a breath, and moved her avatar to the office's single window. Outside, the spring rain was drenching the city in a sheet of sodden gray. The weather was too on the nose, so she turned back to Hanlon.

He was watching her, his head cocked. It reminded her of a big cat that hadn't decided whether to pounce or to play. "Did you have a point?" he asked.

"I know, I know," she said. "You're a busy man—oh! Sorry. You *were* a busy man."

"That's getting old."

"Not for me. How am I doing?"

The former Senator crossed the room to stand beside her at the window. He saw her shy away, and he began to smile. With each step he took towards her, his tiger's smile grew, that same smile he had worn when he first offered her the opportunity to join OACET…

Rachel felt goosebumps crawl over her skin as he approached. *You're not here, woman. Keep it together!* shouted her own voice. It was empty and echoed over a great distance as the monster from her nightmares came close enough to kiss her.

She shoved her arm straight into his chest.

He flinched. He couldn't not flinch. Her arm looked so *real.*

"Interesting, isn't it?" she said, swirling her arm around the general vicinity of his heart and lungs. She fixed her eyes on his. Her avatar's eyes didn't carry the same chilling effect of her real ones, and his fear came from somewhere more visceral. "Now, I know the Program was supposed to last our lifetimes, so I'm sure your scientists gave some thought to the long-term health implications of the implant."

She kept moving her arm in slow circles. Hanlon was a statue, unable to move, unable to take a single step backwards and pull himself away.

"We spend a lot of time trying to understand what we are. What we're made of. Whether these frequencies we've found just allow us to put on a pretty light show, or if they could have other side effects… One of the smartest guys I know is worried that we might cause cancer—"

Hanlon stumbled and fell as he tried to yank her green arm out of his chest. Rachel gave a wicked cackle, and stood over the former Senator like an avenging warrior.

"Not your day, is it?" Rachel said, and then retreated a few paces, her own heart pounding.

"Is this why you're here?" he asked, as he tried to recover his composure. "You want to kick an old man while he's down?"

"You're forty-seven, and a billionaire," Rachel said. "I think you'll be okay."

"Perhaps," Hanlon said. He grabbed the side of his desk and used it to haul himself up. His knee gave an arthritic pop; Rachel thought that was the most honest thing she'd ever hear from him. "Perhaps not."

"You poor thing," she said, as she glanced around for the best place to sit. She'd have loved to have taken over Hanlon's own chair, but it was shoved tight beneath his desk and she had no way to maneuver it. She decided her second-best option was to settle her avatar in the same spot on Hanlon's desk where he had been sitting. It put Hanlon at something of an angle to her, but that was acceptable: the sound of his bad knee would sing her to sleep for months to come.

"One question before I leave," she said. "All of this hinged on

Jenna Noura making a mistake. But we checked her background. Noura was one of the best, and incredibly expensive. There were easier ways for you to set up this domino effect than to hire her to break into the White House and hope that she failed.

"You wanted her to succeed," Rachel continued, watching Hanlon's face out of the corner of her eye for small changes. "But since you also wanted to get out of Dodge, I'm guessing that means breaking into the White House isn't the only scheme you've been running."

Nothing. The man's poker face rivaled Mulcahy's. She was tempted to shove her fist through his head, just to wipe that bemused half-grin from it.

She pushed on. "Jonathan Dunstan could have launched his story at any time, as long as he put it out before Kathleen Patterson's. This gave you…what? About three weeks where you could commit batshit-crazy crimes all over Washington?"

"Serious charges, Agent Peng. Do you have any evidence?"

"Of course not," she said. "Like with Noura and her theft—if she had pulled it off, we'd have never known it had happened. But I'll be cleaning up after you for the next five years, won't I?"

Hanlon resumed packing boxes.

"Nothing?" Rachel asked. When he didn't reply, she stood and pretended to straighten her pants. "All right, then. I'll guess I'll see you in Hell."

"The Mechanism, Agent Peng," Hanlon said. He hadn't stopped packing, but there was an odd set to his shoulders, as if he was preparing to strike. "If I did all of these terrible things, the fragment from the Mechanism must have been important to me. Have you learned why it would hold such value?"

"Nah," she said.

He put the stack of books in his hands down, and leaned towards her, as if he could read her avatar like he could her real face. His tiger's smile came out again. "Mulcahy's told you nothing."

"He told me enough to send your ass packing."

The smile slipped around the edges.

"Nice try, thinking you can drive a wedge between us as you leave, but I don't think you understand what you made. You didn't just create new technology—you created a community that happens to use that tech. OACET's been a real learning experience. We all figured out pretty damn quick that nobody has to be good at everything, or know everything, to still contribute. We're our own puzzle: the pieces might overlap sometimes, and there might be gaps in what we know, but we still manage to fit together.

"I don't think you've *ever* quite understood that," she said. "I don't know if someone like you is *capable* of understanding that together, you're more than you were separately. It's like, oh, I don't know…all of fucking *human civilization.*"

"No, I understand," Hanlon said. "All too well, believe me. I think most people in positions of power recognize that OACET is not only a failed experiment, but a serious threat. A small insular group with its own agenda is incredibly dangerous."

He left that thought unfinished, the idea that Congress still considered them a threat, maybe now more than ever as they kept proving themselves to be not only useful, but a *functioning* federal organization…

Rachel shivered.

"What you claim I did to you was clumsy," he continued, as he reached for a little statuette of a horse. He started to wrap this in tissue paper, carefully winding it between each leg. "The next generation of mind control would have to be much more subtle. They're learning wonderful things about parasites these days," he sighed. "Have you heard of *Toxoplasma gondii*? Mice infected by this parasite will fail to see a cat as a threat. The implications…"

He trailed off, as if thinking about possibilities.

"Well," he finally said, as he slipped the statuette into a box. "Thanks to you, I'll have a lot more time to work on new projects."

He left that idea hanging between them. She felt the shape of it. It was round and ripe, and Hanlon had been waiting to sink his teeth into it for a long, long time.

Rachel couldn't help but laugh. "You moron," she said, knowing somewhere miles away, her fingernails had shredded the paper towels and were cutting into the skin on her palms. "If I didn't hate you, I'd pity you."

Anyone else would have reacted to that comment. A gasp, maybe, or at least a little frown. Hanlon stared at her, utterly impassive.

She ran her avatar's finger across one of the framed photographs on Hanlon's desk, recently removed from the wall and waiting for its turn to be wrapped and packed. A much younger Hanlon, an arm draped around Bill Clinton, grinned back at her with that familiar tiger's smile. She lifted her finger from the frame and pretended to check it for dust.

"You already blew the best opportunity you'll ever have," she continued. "You develop this amazing, world-changing technology, and what do you do with it? You decide to uphold the status quo. Instead of using it to shake up the system, you try to make yourself richer, more powerful… That's pathetic."

"I suppose that would depend on your point of view," Hanlon replied.

"Fair enough," she said. "To me, money and power seem like lifetime achievement awards. You can't really do much with them once you're dead. Me? I like poetry."

"Good," Hanlon said. "With your salary, you can afford poetry."

"Ooh, poetry zing! And spoken by someone who doesn't understand it. See, money never really belongs to one person, and power disappears once you're dead. But poetry? That's humanity's permanent record. There're poems out there that're older than entire civilizations."

Hanlon reached across her and snatched the photograph of Clinton off the desk. She was sure the edge of the frame cut through her neck, but whatever. She had heard Hanlon's clunky knee fail on him.

He was *mortal.*

"You know what gets written into poems?" she continued. "Heroes. Epic deeds. The occasional monster, but those always get beheaded. Admittedly, we don't have that many heroes running around these days, but you could have been one of them."

That got his attention. For the first time since she had plunged her fist into his chest, that half-amused smirk vanished, and he turned to face her with empty hands.

"I don't know if you realize this," she said, "but the implant? With that technology, you could have changed the entire fucking world. Forever. All you had to do was work out the bugs and make it available to everybody, and you could have been a *legend*. Leonardo da Vinci? Thomas Edison? What did they ever do to unite the entire planet? You had the chance to redefine—and let me reiterate here—*all of fucking civilization*. And you would've been its architect."

She leaned in, inches away from his face, and this time she was the one to grin. "You could have been an Achilles-level, capital-L *Legend!*"

His face fell, as if realization had struck like a bolt of lightning. She didn't mind at all.

"But no," she said, waving her fingertips in idle circles. "You decided to throw that away and focus on money and power.

"And you left OACET in charge," she said. "And *we*, at least, are aware that we could either royally ruin everything, or try and leave a legacy our kids will be proud of. So we're trying to do the latter. Thanks for giving us that opportunity."

He stared at her, silent and motionless. Rachel wished she could read his colors. She had a brief, fleeting impulse to hop back to her body and throw her scans out as far as they could possibly go, to maybe catch the reds and oranges of distress...

"That's what *I* came here to say," she said. She pointed to the burner phone, and overloaded its battery. "Never call me again."

With that, she crisped the circuits in Santino's stolen prototype, and left Hanlon standing in his office, blinking at the empty air.

TWENTY-FOUR

The cherry blossom festival was something of a misnomer. The trees were blooming, yes, but mostly it was an excuse for tourists and locals alike to lounge around in the sun and drink excellent strawberry lemonade.

Everything is flowers again, Rachel thought, as she slurped up the fruit slurry at the bottom of her plastic cup. Avery, squirreled up in her lap, giggled at the sound before she squirmed free and waddled off to where her parents were sitting.

They had the park to themselves, at least for a little while. Not many people visited the Floral Library before the tulips were up. There were plenty of flowers, though: the old women who maintained this miniature park on the east side of the Tidal Basin had trucked in pansies, and a bed full of miniature purple and yellow faces bobbed in the breeze.

They were all here, Becca and Santino, Jason and Phil and Bell, Mako and his family... Even Hill and Ami were blissfully entwined on a nearby picnic blanket. Zockinski, busy coaching his twin daughters' first Little League game of the season, had said he'd drop by afterward. It was a party, of sorts. It was one year to the day from when Mulcahy had told the world there were cyborgs among them.

Rachel stood to stretch her legs. Avery was growing up to be her father's daughter, and was already big enough to have cut off all circulation to Rachel's lower body. She excused herself, and staggered across a parking lot and down to the water's edge.

Nobody was around, which was fine by her. Hill had reset her nose and it was healing straight, but the rest of her face had turned into one of McCrindle's long-dead bloated raccoons. Every time a stranger caught sight of her, they flashed a bright alarm-red, and she had been staying out of public places after an especially loud fellow made comments about women who needed rescuing from their abusers. He had been trying to be kind, and she was glad she had made it to the bathroom before she broke down laughing.

She kept her scans close, seeing the fish begging her for crumbs and not much else. She spotted a goldfish mixed in with the perch: someone's pet, dropped into the Basin when it outgrew its bowl.

"It's a myth," Santino said from behind her. "The one where goldfish only grow to fit the size of their tanks."

Rachel nodded. Her maternal grandmother raised goldfish, big ones that put this foot-long baby to shame. She watched as her partner flicked a handful of crackers into the water, turning it into a mess of mouths and churning fins.

She ran her scans through the concrete wall beneath her feet, and forced herself to look across the water.

Directly across the Basin was the Franklin Delano Roosevelt Memorial.

"Yeah," Santino said.

They didn't speak for a very long while. Their fight in the alley behind the Trout and Badger had sprained things between them. Their friendship wasn't broken, but it hadn't been comfortable for almost a week, and neither of them had wanted to put any weight on it in fear that they might make it worse.

"I wonder if we can get him on the beetle-frogs," Rachel finally said. She had taken the 3D-printed replica of the fragment from the Mechanism out of her pocket, and was turning it over in her hands as she spoke.

"Hmm?"

"Those weird beetle-frogs," she said, as she started to spin her EM barrier around them so they could talk privately. "The ones that Jenna Noura used as her murder weapon. We never did figure out where the poison came from. Maybe Hanlon imported a bunch of beetle-frogs."

"Okay, first, those are two different animals. Beetles *and* frogs," Santino said. "The beetles generate the poison, and they pass this to the frogs when they're eaten. Second, both the beetles and frogs are really common, so we'd have to start the search at the genetic level—"

He realized she was grinning at him, and punched her lightly in her arm.

"Do you think Alimoren was involved?" he asked.

"I don't know," she said. "I don't think we'll ever really know. If he was innocent, he was the perfect pawn—Hanlon chose him well. Throw a couple of files on his laptop, and everyone would think the worst."

"I'd like to clear his name, if he was."

"Me, too," Rachel said, thinking of a coffee cup hidden behind a plastic plant. "The FBI is working on it. They might be able to piece together what happened, what his role was in all of this. But even if we do clear his name..."

Santino nodded to show he understood. Alimoren's memory already bore an indelible brand. Alimoren had been killed by an unknown professional, in much the same way as Noura had been killed by professional hit men, and the public had already decided he had been a conspirator. Efforts to clear his name might just feed the rumors about government cover-ups.

She turned the metal replica over, and ran her thumb along the curve on its back.

"Let me see," he said. She dropped it into his palm, and he flipped it over to look at where the etchings would be on the original piece. "Did I tell you the final translation came in?"

"No."

"Most of it is operating instructions, but it also includes an invocation to the gods. '*O heavens! Speak! So we might answer.*'"

"Ah," she said.

"Thought you might like that," he said, as he returned the replica.

"Still not worth all of this," she said.

"Yeah," he said, and sat down on the concrete lip of the manmade Basin. "I know."

So small, she thought, turning the piece of metal over in

her hands. *There's almost nothing to it. It's not even a whole of anything—it's a small piece of something bigger. And it's caused so much grief—*

She chuckled aloud at that.

Maybe, a couple thousand years ago, someone had stared at this wondrous, almost magical piece of technology and thought: *Wouldn't it be easier if I just made sure this fucking thing got lost at sea?*

She pulled her arm back, ready to snap her wrist and send the replica skipping across the Basin.

"Don't," Santino said. "You'll want it someday. Put it next to Madeline."

She closed her fingers around the metal fragment. "I'll have Jason print me out another."

"It wouldn't be the same," he said.

"Good," she said, but the urge to throw it into the water had passed.

She settled down beside Santino.

"I still want to know why Hanlon thought stealing it was worth breaking into the White House," he said.

"There's a reason," she said. "Mulcahy knows."

"I *want* to know," he said. "There's something larger at work here. Can't you feel it?"

She could. She was no longer dreaming of the sea. Instead, her dreams were nothing but colors, some of which didn't have names but mostly blues and greens, stretching across time and space...

"I want to know what's really going on," he said, as he tossed another handful of crackers to the fish. A bright flash of gold came and went across the top of the water. "We're leaving things unanswered. That's bad policy."

"That's life."

"You can live with that? With not knowing why Hanlon wanted the Mechanism?"

She shrugged. "I'm a soldier, Santino. If my commanding officer doesn't know more than I do, I get really nervous."

He made a noise somewhere between agreement and anger, and she realized she wasn't running emotions. She settled her shoulder against his, and he sighed.

"I love you guys, you know that," he said.

"Yeah."

"I just need you to be…consistent. Do what you say you want to do. You're trying so hard to convince the entire world you can be trusted, but… You're going to get caught one day, and then it'll be over. For you, for OACET…for me, too, and everyone who's stood beside you."

She stole some crackers, and leaned over the concrete lip to coax the goldfish towards her. "I've been thinking about Cardinal Richelieu."

"Hmm?"

"*Give me six lines written by the most honest man in the world, and I will find enough in them to hang him,*" she quoted, wiggling a finger against the surface of the water. The goldfish came closer, and snapped at a nearby perch. "We talk about Richelieu in OACET meetings. A lot. Him and Orwell. About how it's not what you do—it's what you're perceived to do. As long as I keep representing OACET in a positive light, does it matter what I really do?"

"Yes." Santino's voice was sharp. "Yes, I think it does."

"Me, too," she said, as she slowly lowered her hand into the water, and did her best to ignore the matter of fish poop and viruses and all sorts of nasty microscopic swimming things. "I've also been thinking about Hanlon, and Glazer, and that case last October, and how we've all turned into these puzzle masters. We've given up direct attacks, and we're using what exists to destroy each other instead."

"Using the system as a weapon."

"Yeah. It's nothing new," she said, thinking of peace offerings in the form of wooden horses. The goldfish, now treating her hand as something which belonged in the water, swam around it as it hunted for food. "But if the system is the weapon, then the law's got to be the shield against it. What would have happened if I had left that phone alone?"

"The Secret Service would have found the hidden files. And then... I don't know. An inquiry, probably. You would have been asked to leave the MPD until it was sorted out."

"Yeah," she said, nodding. The goldfish was close enough to tickle its belly, and she managed to bump the sweet spot right below its gills with her index finger. The fish darted off, then decided that bump wasn't so bad, and came back for another belly rub. "We could have handled an inquiry. We've been handling inquiries for months. But I panicked. I'd psyched myself up, told myself there was something out there that could hurt me, or hurt OACET, and when I found it, I panicked. If I had just stopped and thought about what I had found..."

"I still don't know what I should have done," she continued. "It wasn't what I did, that's for damned sure."

"I don't know, either," Santino replied.

"I also know that I'm not the kind of person who should be trusted with an implant," she said. "I can pretty much rationalize anything, as long as it's done to protect those I care about. *Not* for the greater good," she added quickly. "The greater good can go fuck itself. The people I love matter more to me than any abstract ideal. And that's...dangerous, considering."

The goldfish nestled lower, snuggling against her palms, and she thought about how she let a murderer go free for OACET. How she nearly let the entire country *burn* for OACET. How she needed to get off of this road as quickly as possible, because if the scenery was this ugly, this soon into the trip, she didn't want to see what waited at her final destination.

"So," she said, as she netted her fingers beneath the very happy goldfish, "I've decided this is how it should be—I've got this metric fuckton of power in my head, and I need to keep remembering that the world isn't simple, and that the stupidest, smallest mistake could ruin it for everyone. So, from now on, you and I talk about this shit. All the time, like when we first met. And if we find ourselves running out of ammunition, then we start talking with Zockinski, or Sturtevant, or anyone who'll stand still long enough to listen. Somebody outside of OACET, to keep reminding me that the law's perfectly imperfect and *completely* necessary."

He grinned, a warm smile moving across what she could see of his face. "So, what you're saying is that you're Captain America now? Champion of law and order?"

"*Hell* no! I'm saying I was raised Catholic—we do penance for our sins. Here, have a fish."

She lobbed the goldfish at him, nice and slow, and in an arc that would return it safely to the water. Santino yelped and scrambled backwards.

Rachel collapsed on the bank, rolling around and laughing, as Santino threw the rest of his crackers at her.

"Fish water in m' mouth," he muttered, scraping his tongue against the sleeve of his shirt.

She came to rest on her back, staring up at the bright noonday sky. "What I'm saying is, the law needs to be a better shield." She sighed, and added, "Or maybe we need to recognize that a shield is also a weapon in its own right... I don't know. I'm getting my metaphors crossed.

"Just know..." she said, as she turned her face towards his before continuing, "Just know that part of doing penance for your sins is that you also pray for the wisdom to avoid them in the future, okay?"

He was quiet for a few moments, before saying, "I can live with that."

"You're going to have to," she said, as she stood and brushed the dead winter grass off of her jeans. "'cause that's the best I can do."

Santino stood and gave her a fast hug. He was warm and earthy, and smelled of the sun and green, growing things. "Thanks," he said.

"Back at you."

He let her go, and turned towards the Floral Library. He was already ten paces towards the park before he realized she wasn't following him. "Everything okay?"

"I want to check on the fish," she said. "Make sure I didn't hurt it."

He smiled at her before he resumed walking.

Rachel sent her scans into the Basin and searched until she found the goldfish, unharmed and swimming towards deeper waters. Then, she reached into her pocket.

The replica of the fragment shone as brightly as always, and she ran her thumb along its now-familiar shape. It fit within her palm, tight and flat, the perfect skipping stone, and she thought of workaday denim and poppy-seed gray.

She shoved it back into her pocket, and went to rejoin the others.

Acknowledgements and Apologies

To my husband, Brown, who's always there with a kind word, a strong shoulder, and a gentle headlock for the dogs.

Thanks to the second readers who were so very generous with their time. Gary, Tiff, Joris, Jean, Greg, Kevin, Dow, and Zach, I appreciate (and needed) the feedback. Danny, as always, thank you for the copy edits and for doubling down on those STETs that needed fixing.

Rose Loughran of *Red Moon Rising* is responsible for the beautiful cover art. The Franklin Delano Roosevelt Memorial has never looked better.

And my heartfelt thanks goes to everyone who's supported me over this past year. It's my first year of being a full-time writer and artist, and I couldn't have done it without you.

About the Author

K.B. Spangler lives in North Carolina with her husband, and as many dogs she can sneak into the house without him noticing. She is the author and artist of *A Girl and Her Fed*, where Patrick Mulcahy, Hope Blackwell, and the Agents of OACET are alive and well. Additional information about these and other projects can be found at kbspangler.com.

Made in the USA
Columbia, SC
24 July 2019